BOOKS BY WILLIAM O'ROURKE

The Harrisburg 7 and the New Catholic Left

The Meekness of Isaac

the Job: Fiction About Work by Contemporary American Writers
(Editor)

Idle Hands

Criminal Tendencies

CRIMINAL TENDENC

On

WILLIAM O'ROURKE

CRIMINAL TENDENCIES

E. P. DUTTON NEW YORK

Author's Note: I want to acknowledge gratefully a National Endowment for the Arts Fellowship I received—as well as a residency I had at the Thurber House, in Columbus, Ohio—during the course of writing this novel.

—W. O.

Published in the United States by E. P. Dutton, a division of NAL Penguin Inc., 2 Park Avenue, New York, N.Y. 10016.

Published simultaneously in Canada by Fitzhenry and Whiteside, Limited, Toronto.

Library of Congress Cataloging-in-Publication Data
O'Rourke, William.
Criminal tendencies.
I. Title.
PS3565.R65C75   1987   813'.54 · 87-481

ISBN: 0-525-24542-1

COBE

Designed by Steven N. Stathakis

1 3 5 7 9 10 8 6 4 2

First Edition

For Teresa

Reader, look at the plate in which are represented three individuals of this beautiful species,—rogues though they be, and thieves, as I would call them, were it fit for me to pass judgment on their actions. See how each is enjoying the fruits of his knavery, sucking the egg which he has pilfered from the nest of some innocent dove or harmless partridge! Who could imagine that a form so graceful, arrayed by nature in a garb so resplendent, should harbour so much mischief;—that selfishness, duplicity, and malice should form the moral accompaniments of so much physical perfection! Yet so it is, and how like beings of a much higher order, are these gay deceivers! Aye, I could write you a whole chapter on this subject, were not my task of a different nature.

—JOHN JAMES AUDUBON
Ornithological Biography, 1831,
discussing the Blue Jay, Havell CII,
The Birds of America

I cannot help thinking Mr. Audubon a dishonest man.
—JOHN KEATS
in a letter to his brother George,
September 1819

I

One

Kenner watched the Air Florida jet lazily approach the nearby airport, quicken its descent and slip behind the long, three-storied north wing of Cayo Hueso Condominiums that bordered the runway. All he could see of the plane now was its tail. The vertical stabilizer was bright chartreuse, a lime sherbet color. Kenner, pleased to be distracted from his work, watched it slide slowly along the condominium complex's roofline. He thought the aircraft's tail resembled a shark's dorsal fin slicing water: a lime sherbet fish and a red tile sea.

Kenner recalled a similar sight on Cape Cod. He had been interviewing a man who spent his professional life studying survivors. Kenner was interested; it seemed a timely specialty. The historian used the phrase "psychic numbing," before the condition it described turned into the national pastime. He thought such a state was unfortunate. Kenner wasn't so sure. The historian was seated in an Eames chair, and through the glass wall behind him Kenner stared at a sweep of Truro dunes and a straight gray line of Atlantic. He lost track of what the historian was saying; Kenner's attention had been caught by the black conning tower of a Polaris submarine cutting the ocean's surface: black wet skin and gray smooth water.

It was how Kenner thought of the North and South: one black and white, the other in color. He worked mornings on the condominium's balcony, a cramped coffin-sized flap of concrete, with room enough for a round glass table and two ice cream–parlor chairs. A withered potted palmetto tree crouched in the corner.

Kenner was freeloading, something he found himself doing more and more. Friends up north owned the condominium, and they had offered it to Kenner free for four months, except for the utility bills. Key West was much too hot for most folks this time of the year, but Kenner was game. He had a little quiet work to do and could do it here. He would be finished in another week and then he could relax; though, he had to admit, he was already quite relaxed.

The balcony was in the shade till noon: then Kenner usually stopped working and went down to the pool. While he worked he cooled his bare feet by rubbing them into the Astroturf that carpeted the balcony. The Astroturf's petrochemicals made the carpet feel alive, springy with resistance. Every time Kenner pressed his foot down, he felt like he was squishing something.

Kenner had come to blazing Key West for the usual, clichéd reasons: to get free, to air things out, to run away, to take stock. He had reached his mid-thirties. His career—and only with some derision and amazement did Kenner begin to view what he did as a career—was becalmed. Though what troubled him most acutely was that the deaths of strangers had begun to interfere with his life. He had been forced to spend five weeks trying to redeem his cowboy boots. The cobbler he patronized in New York City was a conspicuously large black man—so large Kenner found himself wondering: How much strength did it take to repair shoes? He pictured the man ripping shoes apart with his bare hands. Kenner had left an old pair of cowboy boots to be resoled and heeled.

The shoemaker had held the boots delicately—a diagnostician's touch; his large fingers where shiny with polish. Kenner had once interviewed a black oncologist with the same hands; his fingertips and nails were marred, made raw by repeated, ferocious washings.

The shoemaker also shined the shoes Kenner had been wearing. Kenner's legs were spread, one foot each perched on a steel mount, the fossil of a shoe's bottom, while he entertained

4

thoughts of obstetrics, looking down at the black man's gleaming bald head. He always felt slightly vulnerable in that position.

That was the last memory Kenner had of the man, bent over buffing Kenner's loafers. He paid, pocketed the ticket for the boots, and left. When he returned ten days later, a piece of shirt cardboard on the door stated in crayon letters CLOSED ON AC-COUNT OF DEATH.

For a month communication went on through cardboard signs. One finally announced that customers who had shoes within were to show up between four and five the following Saturday. Kenner arrived with his ticket.

Two white men were inside, one tall, the other short. Both had the rumpled yet secure air of civil servants. One chomped on a cigar that reminded Kenner of the cobbler's fingers.

Kenner learned from a few laconic remarks that after the shop had remained shut for a few days someone had complained. The police arrived and the shoemaker was found, dead. Kenner figured that his own residue of racism would have made the cobbler look younger to him than he actually was. Heart failure? Kenner didn't ask. The city buried him, and the city was impounding his property, until, or if, relatives could be located.

From what sorry annex to the coroner's office or nepotistic nook of City Hall these two fellows sprang, Kenner contemplated only for a moment. Rich pickings here there were not. The men seemed unhappy with what they found. Kenner's boots weren't in any of the sealed paper bags. Stapled shut and stacked in cubbyholes, they seemed, so many sad grammar-school lunches. What wild luck would it have been had the boots been fixed before the cobbler died? An omen? Something that might have changed his life? Kenner wondered. The short man wanted to show him the door, but Kenner insisted: "My boots have to be here, somewhere!"

"Let him come back!" boomed out from the rear. Kenner pushed aside the dusty gray cloth and stepped into what had been the shoemaker's living quarters.

The air was thick. Kenner felt his heart leap at what he saw. He knew himself to be a sentimental man: Kenner was always moved by sights such as a restaurant without customers. And by the tableau in front of him: the cobbler's single bed; a stripped, stained, gray mattress; an old refrigerator; the chipped enamel kitchen table.

The tall functionary pointed to a mound of shoes, a real Auschwitz bundle. Kenner was fond of his cowboy boots, another thing he did not like about himself; he knew that he had always admired people who seemed oblivious to possessions. Did Kenner like his boots well enough to go on with this search? He fell to his knees and began to look. His neighbors' shoes. Kenner felt as if he were rifling a hundred closets.

A small red high-heeled sandal stayed in his hand a bit too long, and the short man, with a bureaucrat's eye for every corruption, said testily, "Just find yours and get out."

Kenner admired both men's sternness. They were guarding the dead from desecration, even this pile of orphaned shoes. Kenner found one boot; its shaved, worn heel yet to be replaced. He continued to paw through an astounding variety of footwear. The dead shoemaker was popular; his was the only shop around. He found the other boot. Kenner departed, clutching his boots, feeling something of a grave robber. The short man slammed the door shut, locked it, pulled down a tattered green shade. There was no cardboard sign remaining. Had he been the only one who wanted to reclaim his shoes?

Kenner sat on the condo's balcony watching the plane, its chartreuse tail fin sliding slowly by the roofline, and considered why the boots had seemed like the last straw. Not long before their resurrection Kenner had read a small obituary in a shoppers' weekly that used news as fillers. An old man had died in a Village nursing home. Old men die all the time in nursing homes, Kenner knew, but this was Sidney Franklin, the bullfighter. And no one, it seemed, had taken much notice.

Kenner was surprised that Franklin had still been alive; his fame had departed him so thoroughly that he was deposited unnoticed on Hudson Street. Sidney Franklin, the Brooklyn matador, the marvel and miracle, the man whose life story was better than a picaresque novel, according to the sources Kenner checked. Well, the picaroon ended his days in a single room overlooking the *plaza de toros* of Abingdon Square. The only swordplay there was with miniature banderillas, hypodermic needles. Did the small park ring with "Olés!" when Franklin sat on its benches?

Kenner had found only one other obituary, nothing else, and thought about doing a story: seeing if there were any relatives, finding where the matador had been buried, taking a look at his room. Perhaps there would be mementos: a suit of lights rotting in a footlocker. It would make a good article; but the idea of it had covered Kenner only with fatigue. Writing such an article, like reclaiming his boots, was grave-robbing of a sort. Kenner had found himself being overwhelmed by the misfortunes of

6

strangers, knowing at the same time that it was his own life that was overwhelming him.

Kenner resumed his work on the balcony, the editing of a book. Its subject was a basketball player who, except for his marvelous hand and eye coordination, would have been a seven-foot sideshow geek. Five hundred pages of running up and down ninety-four feet of hardwood, written in flatfooted prose. It was, though, the easiest two thousand dollars Kenner had ever earned. The money would allow him to linger in the Keys for the entire summer, if he wished.

Kenner had risen only so far in journalism—then he plateaued out. He knew the reasons. NASA supplied him with his explanation: certain orbits are possible only at critical times. There is a keyhole in space, one that the trajectory passes through, and if the launch doesn't take place then, you need to wait, or readjust your entire flight plan.

Kenner had waffled, hesitated; he had turned down a few things and people who offer, despite other testimony, are not charmed by displays of reticence. They are not offering you a job so much as they are admitting you to an exclusive club; and so they take rejection not just as rejection, but as the realization that they have actually misjudged you; and all offers are withdrawn.

Kenner knew he lacked the sort of talent that was required in his line of work: you needed to see where things were going a few months before others. It was a race, a perception marathon, and someone would get there before everybody else. He knew he had been dead last about a few important things, but the only mistake he joked about was insignificant: waterbeds. He was flabbergasted that they were still being sold. Kenner had really begun to question his understanding: how could he have been so wrong about waterbeds? What else could he have been so wrong about?

But he could not bring himself to write about the death of Sidney Franklin.

The condo Kenner occupied had originally been owned by an émigré Cuban who had arrived in Key West shortly after Batista fell. Kenner once heard a famous violinist reply, after being asked why so many Jews had taken up the violin: You can run with it. And the Cuban had come with diamonds. His joke had been: You can swim with them!

Kenner's friends who bought the condo from the Cuban were shopkeepers. The Cuban, too, was a merchant who had moved on to Key Biscayne; but, in may ways, he had left himself behind. Kenner's friends had purchased the condo furnished, so the Cuban's legacy remained in the decor. The living room, which opened onto the balcony where Kenner worked, was mirrored; the walls reflected each other in a barbershop effect. Kenner found himself contemplating infinity whenever he sat on the sofa. The carpeting was a hot fluffy yellow. Glass and chrome tables and overstuffed chairs and a couch, upholstered with a floral design, some fey jungle pattern: pastel leaves and vines.

The balcony's sliding glass doors were covered by a gauzy curtain, a ragged net, which the slightest breeze would billow inward. The decorating, Kenner discovered, was not unusual; many of the other apartments had similar *ambiente*. Kenner thought it a retiree's vision of heaven: mirrors, reflections, chromes, white curtain wings blowing. A literal picture of a pensioner's paradise.

The master bedroom also had its wall of mirrors, but they were segmented, accordioned, since the mirrors masked a large closet. The bed was on a platform, illuminated around the rim with fluorescent lights. After seeing its effect—levitation, floating in space—Kenner had looked underneath to see how it was done.

The wall behind the bed was quilted fabric, which, the Cuban had explained to Kenner's friends, depicted Cuba's history. Kenner found it a disturbing sight: large birds, loosely stitched in the soft plump fabric, with predatory beaks; large women, with pillows for breasts; sugarcane made to look like spears rattled by demon figures, twisted imps wearing vests that Kenner saw were decorated with stars and stripes. The room's curtains and bedspread were made out of the same material, using the same colors: there was so much yellow everything seemed to be washed in a hot haze of pollen.

Positioned at the foot of the bed was a projection television with a six-foot screen. It was the first one Kenner had actually watched, though it was an older model: the room needed to be kept dark in order to see the projected images clearly. The bedroom was sealed from daylight by thick curtains. An air conditioner hummed. The TV screen was a dull silver, almost pewter, and was sensitive to any impression: there were a variety of fingerprints around its rim.

Kenner enjoyed the accommodations. At night he watched the six-foot TV, which was hooked into a cable system. The set received Atlanta, New York, Chicago, Miami; he would watch those cities' local news programs, and, after a while, in the sealed,

8

air-conditioned, padded bedroom, he would not know where he was. It was space station living, Kenner thought, everywhere and nowhere.

About the time Kenner would be finishing his work for the day, an old man would appear on the adjacent balcony. A woman Kenner took for a maid or a nurse would lead the man out of the sliding glass doors and put him on his exercycle. The ancient gentleman's legs would pump up and down; the woman would emerge a half hour later and lead him back into the apartment. The old man, though, had not appeared for nearly a week. Kenner had become slightly irritated at the break in his routine.

Kenner thought of making inquiries, but hadn't. The condominium complex created an odd sort of privacy for its residents. Each apartment's front door opened onto an outside walkway. The overall effect was the same as a motel's. Motels served two gods: anonymity and the car. Each doorway led straight out to an avenue of direct escape, affording as much privacy as there could be. And so the condominium complex was not so much a version of an apartment house where people live off a closed hallway, in some forced neighborliness, but the soul of a motel grown large, where you could come and go relatively undetected. Kenner found something slightly illicit about this sort of architectural egress: exposed but, paradoxically, the most private.

Kenner, touching up one of the many redundant anecdotes of the skyscraper's championship year, and attempting to unclot the description of another tedious play-off game, his ears full of the continuous *squeak, squeak, squeak* of giant sneakers, was about to lay down his pencil when the doors of the balcony next to his slid open. Kenner, expecting to see the frail old man and his nurse at his elbow, was taken aback. He was looking at someone entirely different. And, even more startling, Kenner realized he was looking at someone he knew but hadn't laid eyes on for at least at decade.

"Hey, Winston!" Kenner called out.

He was surprised he had immediately recognized Winston; not that Winston had altered that much, or grown new plumage, but he had changed, Kenner saw, when Winston turned to see who was yelling at him. But he had been recognizable, in the same way, Kenner thought, old friends were on the streets of New York, walking toward you. Something about the gait, the entire shape, as if, seen from a distance, you took in all of a person and it was that accumulation of detail that made you re-

9

alize somebody was familiar. At times, you were mistaken, but
that you only noticed when you were just about to call out. Kenner also thought there was another reason he remembered Winston. Being in a new place, a person almost irrationally looks for
people he or she might know—so even though Key West was not
the Sudan, Kenner looked attentively, thinking he might turn up
a familiar face.

"Hey, Winston!" Kenner called out once more, moving to
the edge of his balcony. Winston fully turned his head, then looked
straight at Kenner. Winston's expression registered what looked,
to Kenner, like damage assessment.

"It's me—Kenner," he said, "from Kansas City. Kenwood
Street. Lucinda's friend."

Winston, his suspicious expression unchanged, said, "I don't
think I know you."

Kenner was used to not being remembered. Especially by
Winston. The college slights came back. It was lucky Kenner had
gotten used to not being remembered, because he discovered it
was part of being a journalist. He recalled each small encounter,
since everyone was in some way necessary to him, whereas he
seemed not at all necessary to those he briefly met. In that way,
Kenner thought, journalists were similar to con men. He had
always assumed con men were successful because they took a
genuine interest in the people they were conning; people are
always touched by attention, since most people care so little.

Winston was not the last person he expected to turn up in
Key West, but he would have been hovering somewhere near the
bottom of the list. Winston, he realized, was something of a comet,
on an elongated elliptical orbit, spinning into view roughly every
ten years. Weren't comets thought to be portents, Kenner considered, bodies that foretold something about to happen? Calam-
ities?

Kenner continued to throw Winston crumbs of recollection,
memory bait, just nouns, phrases. He finally tossed him the one
he bit.

"Your London saxophone gig."

A flush appeared under Winston's tan, and, in addition,
Kenner detected a flutter of concern.

"If you're got some time, let's get together."

"How about down at the pool?" Winston said, and, at the
same moment, a woman stepped out onto the balcony. She was
wearing some sort of ensemble. A short, transparent jacket over
a corset. Nylons gripped by garters. She showed a lot of very

pale flesh. Her hair was curly and red, almost burgundy. She saw Kenner, turned and retreated into the apartment. Kenner tried not to register his noticing.

"In about an hour, say?"

"Sure. Sure. Good," Kenner said. Winston turned and followed the lady in, sliding behind him the glass door, covered with mirrored film, leaving behind just its square of silver reflection.

2

Two days a week Bridget had to open the store, Tanka Crafts. Usually, she didn't have to come in till noon, but on Tuesdays and Thursdays she had to be there at nine. She tried to leave Monday and Wednesday nights free, or she would feel wrecked in the morning. All the same, last night she had gone to play bingo. Something was likely to turn up there, but she had hoped nothing would. It had: Robin, the manager of the Beauty Box, had introduced her to a fellow and Bridget had let her evening be taken up. Bridget was weak on her pins this morning and would have told anyone who asked her just that, and if no one asked, there were at least two people she intended to tell anyway.

Front Street was empty when she got to the door of the shop. The Conch Train hadn't yet pulled up. There never was any business for the first hour of the morning; but before the customers started to come, she was expected to clean the cases, vacuum the floor, tidy up. Except on days when she felt as she did today, she enjoyed the hour alone; though, at its edge, she began to feel anxious for people to arrive. She left the overhead lights off for the first half hour she dusted; that way the store seemed to be something like a richly furnished home, the morning light filtering through.

There was always a smell in the store that disappeared as soon as people began to walk through: a trace of food, though they had a sign asking people not to bring any in; and cigarette smoke, and other scents. Warm caramel corn. The smell was rubbed into the carpet she vacuumed; the ashtrays were left heaped with butts and ashes overnight. Retail incense, offerings to the cash register deities, Winston had said. The thought of Winston made her body stand upright, her stomach knotted, her skin itched, and the vacuum she had been pushing forward went backward.

Winston was a strange boy, and though Key West had a collection of them, Winston still managed to stand out, she thought. Bridget had slept with lots of men young enough to be sons, though she had never had a boy. But they came and went, she liked to say, laughing at her joke. Winston stuck. He made her flush; she thought she had gone beyond that. And Winston came by the store to say a few words during the day. He was tall, and blond, and seemed to Bridget dapper, a prince in exile, and he had money to spend and money yet to get, the inheritance that he was waiting for. His first name was Jay, but he preferred to be called Winston; Bridget was glad, because Jay reminded her too much of Ray Pine, old Ray, the father of her child, the only man she ever really loved. Ray had looked so healthy, been in the navy, served in the Pacific, been one of the first to set foot in Hiroshima after the Japanese surrendered; and who would suppose a man of forty-one would die of cancer? But she didn't want to think of Ray now. She had once seen Winston's driver's license or she wouldn't have known his first name was Jay. Bridget didn't let herself think too much beyond what she knew for certain, but she was sure she was beginning to have some hold over him. She had cured Winston of one problem and no woman had pleased him as much, he had told her.

It was like a movie-house lobby, Bridget said to herself, turning the vacuum off, letting both Ray and Winston recede. The shop was a lobby; hundreds of people passed through it each day, thousands every week, until the end of April. It smelled the same way lobbies smell, except the shop didn't sell anything to eat, just pottery, jewelry and gifts.

Winston didn't mind her other work, except when it made her unavailable to him, though she had watched out for that. Winston enjoyed her stories of her clients and what she would do for them. Her dominatrixing seemed okay to Winston, she being English and all. He called it Edwardian, but Bridget did not know what he meant. She had started it in England, she told him, and it was the safest sort of work a woman could do if she did this sort of work at all. You didn't do the client's bidding, they did yours, or so it seemed to Bridget, though there had been times when it seemed to be getting out of hand.

Once out of her mouth, anything she said began to sound true to Bridget. Telling anyone her real life was unthinkable to her, but what she concocted came easy, spun off a spool inside of her she never knew could be so large. It was better, she knew, to be a dominatrix than a woman well over forty who fucked old men for money.

She didn't do it much here, only when Kristina was little; she had stopped, more or less, until Kristina had run off. Without Kristina at home and her money coming in, she began once more. Bridget had rules; none of the men were to be younger than sixty and, though that cut down the work, it made her confident she could handle them. Winston didn't mind. They seldom wanted to fuck her; or she told him that, since it was easy to make such tales convincing: a person would believe most any sex story you told them.

Bridget started working at the store after she met the manager, Candi Swift, playing bingo; after working a few months she was even able to tell her about her moonlighting, and she didn't seem to mind. Bingo attracted an older crowd and Bridget discovered it served as a good place to rendezvous; she had worried that it would get about, but some of it did need to get about, and even though the bingo was played in a church basement, so far no one had created any fuss. The crowd in the basement looked about the same as the one that actually attended the church on Sundays, except they dressed differently than the congregation: bright colors and patterns, crazy hats. The man who ran the wheel looked like a foreign missionary before natives, most of whom he hadn't begun to convert.

Bridget's work—her hobby, as she sometimes thought of it—didn't bring in a lot of money, between twenty and fifty dollars a night, except for the rare geezer she found who seemed to measure the experience by what he paid for it. Such men were usually transients, carpet and furniture salesmen, who had heard from other salesmen of Bridget. But now that Kristina had called and told her she was returning with a surprise, and because Winston wanted almost all her time now, she was going to have to lay herself off again.

Bridget sat on the stool behind the cash register and opened her pillbox, one she had got from the store. When she had offered to pay, Candi had made it a present. She took out two of the light and dark green capsules from the collection; there were small round apricot-color pills, larger smooth orange tablets, three red-and-pink capsules, tiny blue estrogen pills. They were new. The Librium would help till the part-time girl arrived at two.

The Conch Train had pulled up. A cartoon locomotive bolted over a jeep, painted in what seemed to Bridget African jungle colors, yellow and black stripes. Four trolley cars were hitched behind. But Bridget didn't see anything junglelike about Key West. Nothing at all.

13

TWO

Winston knew he should make only a single visit to the Audubon House himself. Once a tourist, twice a suspect. He would have to send the others one by one to double-check. The Audubon House had conveniently provided a brochure illustrated with pictures of the rooms, including the room that contained the double elephant folios.

The alarm system was the same sort that protected the gift shop where Bridget worked: tape on glass, window and door alarm, wired to the police station. It only needed to be turned off. There was a switch, operated by a key, high along the jamb of the back door. The switch was actually a lock and took a key that resembled a small old-fashioned skate key, with one tooth.

The Audubon House was not entirely a fraud. Winston was amused at how strenuously its literature implied that Audubon actually painted within its walls. Winston knew the evidence showed that Audubon, at best, had only entered the house socially, if at all. Deceit on the George-Washington-Slept-Here scale: a tiny front room was outfitted with an artist's paraphernalia. Audubon had met the house's original owner, a ship's captain, trying to curry what favor he could, as Audubon always did, the habit and inclination of a practical man.

Winston was surprised at the effect seeing the folios had upon him, spread out as they were in the cases. There was something birdlike about the opened bound volumes themselves, their thick paper curving, flaring out away from the spine like wings outstretched in flight. One volume was opened to the very first plate. Audubon had positioned the bird to highlight as much as possible the animal's long phallic neck. He had painted the head twisted nearly backward so the neck would tighten and elongate even further, supply tension, and, consequently, make more prominent the small horn on the bird's head, above the beak: a little pyramid, hairs protruding like radiance, looking like nothing so much as the pyramid on the back of a one-dollar bill: The Great Seal, Novus Ordo Seclorum: THE GREAT AMERICAN COCK (MALE). Winston had searched a reproduction once with a magnifying glass, hoping to see an eye at the pyramid's tip, but there seemed to be none, though he did feel the wings of the occult hovering over Audubon.

Winston realized he had been holding his breath, staring down into the glass case. Winston thought the wild look in the cock's eye staring out was prescient. He had seen the predator.

In Key West a few houses were open to tour, and the idea of strangers moving through corridors, the homes furnished to seem lived in, reversed reality: to Winston the tourists were the ghosts, the dead visitors, keeping quiet so as not to disturb the spectral occupants.

Winston had a number of problems. He did not see the apparition of Kenner as one of them. He barely recalled him. A fellow who had mooned around an old girlfriend of his. He did recollect telling him the London tale. He had told it too often. He had returned to the Midwest for a year. He had been shedding skins. That's how he looked at it, thinking of the papery cocoons he came across after they had moved to Arizona, all the dried husks he had seen left on the desert floor.

Winston imagined his own envelope of skin, what it would look like if someone stumbled upon it. Silvery, some construction made out of rice paper, a huge locust's shell.

He had told one of his doctors that, during one of the sessions he had after he had discovered his father's body.

Winston had come back for vacation from his first term at prep school; returning to Arizona after four months east was less surprising than he thought it would be. The Massachusetts landscape had seemed orderly to Winston, tamer, not at all feral like the desert. The house had been unaccustomedly peaceful since he returned. His father wasn't around. When he asked his mother where he was, she shouted, "He's in Tucson, living in the apartment he's been renting for his whore!" But that day, though, he was expected home. They were not going to open presents until he arrived.

Winston had walked through the kitchen, the flagstones chilling his bare feet, out the door and down to the pool. The water's surface was bright. The pool was diamond-shaped and its surface undulated, sparkled with sunspots.

Winston often tried to remember if he should have noticed anything out of the ordinary, something that would have lessened the shock, made him suspicious. He could only think of one thing: a hose trailed out of the pool and the water was as high as it could go, draining into the underlip of the pool's tiled edge. He had stood there, preening, looking down. A lizard flashed across the bottom of the pool.

He dove in; the cold radiated through his body. Diving in the pool, in the desert, always made Winston think he was diving into the center of the world. No other houses could be seen from theirs; his home was the center of the world and the pool was its soft core.

Winston scraped his chest against the pool's bottom; the tiles felt like glass, and that made him shiver even more than the cold water. He swam a few laps, hoisted himself up and sat on the pool's edge. He got up and walked over to the sauna, a redwood building that took up the corner of the deck on the desert side of the pool area. There was a dressing room and a bathhouse and a sauna; latticework ran in front of the separate doors. He did not go into the dressing room, but just stepped out of his trunks in front of the sauna's door.

He noticed that it was nearly three hundred degrees in the sauna. That startled him and he turned down the thermostat. There was a thick pane of clear plastic in the sauna's door, and across the sauna's back wall there was another two-inch-wide pane that ran the sauna's entire length, which let in some of the desert's light, a burning red bar. Winston pushed the sauna's door open; he waited for it to cool down. He looked in to see if there was anything wrong with the squat heating unit, its rocks guarded by a thick grate. The dry air of the desert was often scented, but the dry air of the sauna usually wasn't, unless his father brought in piñon boughs. Just before Winston turned his head he caught a different odor; and, as the question What is it? formed in his mind, he looked to his left and saw.

Slumped in a corner, hands resting open on top of his thighs as if he had just let go of something, legs outstretched, chin dropped against his chest, was his father. Winston walked in quietly, as if the sauna were a hospital room, and reached out to touch him on the shoulder, to stir him awake. Winston's fingers slipped into the flesh and slid across the clavicle, pushing a curl of skin before them.

He returned to Mount Hermon after the funeral. He told the other boys gruesome stories. *Boiled chicken. Flesh falling away from bones.* He threw ink bottles at the ceiling of his room and announced: That's me! He took to sobbing in class and then they put him in a hospital.

McLean was not that much different from the boarding school. In some ways it was more permissive. He had begun to enjoy it, after a fashion. He began to forget the gruesome sight. As the years went on, he recalled the day only spottily. Images would sometimes jump out on the periphery of his vision.

Winston was about to begin college in Boston when his mother returned to the Midwest and married again; he was summoned to meet the man. Max, his father, had been tall, handsome; even the thread of scar, a hook, from the plastic surgery to repair a harelip had not detracted from his good looks. He was athletic, hard. His mother's new husband was short and stout, encased in a Chesterfield coat; he was smoking a large, expensive cigar. "Hello, young man," he said, and shook Winston's hand. His nails were manicured, the fingers soft.

He was a real estate developer named Lordi and seemed to be even wealthier than Winston's father, who had left money from his family's mine holdings in the Southwest. Winston didn't leave the airport where the meeting took place. He told his mother he had a job waiting and flew right back to Boston.

Winston went to Cape Cod for the summer and worked in Woods Hole as a short-order cook. He began school and kept in touch with the friends he had made on the Cape. One of them had a lot of marijuana to sell, and Winston began to deal it in Cambridge. He was arrested, but not prosecuted.

He was ordered back to the Midwest, part of the agreement that would allow him not to be prosecuted, and enrolled in the local university. He transferred to the art institute, displeasing his stepfather. There were more drugs available in town than he had expected, even though the city had a reputation for being a regional center of organized crime. He began to skin-pop heroin. He told the London story, among others, to explain away some of his recent history. It was around then that he had last seen Kenner.

When Winston saw Kenner down at the pool, Winston felt he had to tell him something, some dotted outline, some star map of possible truth.

"You know, Kenner," he had said, "I didn't get along with my stepfather, so I left town without finishing my degree at the art institute. I finished up at Yale and worked for the Fogg for a while . . ."

The story was as plausible as any. He had had a rancorous falling out with his stepfather; Winston couldn't persuade his mother to part with any of the money she had inherited from his father's family. He was to come into the possession of a trust, but his mother, encouraged by her new husband, had blocked that, because of his hospitalization and the drug bust. Now she could hold onto it till she died. She did send some money each month, only enough to get by on; he had twice talked her into bankrolling a business venture.

Winston still had a few blank years that were hard to fill in. He had worked in a museum, but not the Fogg as he had told Kenner. He knew the Fogg well enough, which made it seem nearly true.

The museum he had worked in was a small one in Province-town. He had been hired as a night guard at a glass museum. There had been no regular checks from his mother then, just irregular ones. He had few duties at the glass museum. He was there for insurance purposes. If a guard wasn't present twenty-four hours a day, he had been told, the museum's rates would be substantially higher.

Winston sat during his 5 P.M. to 1 A.M. shift behind a Louis XIV desk and read by the light of a large Tiffany lamp. Drag-onflies, two feet long, their heads blue droplets, their glass wings parchment-yellow, wrapped around the circumference of the glass shade.

The owner of the museum, its namesake, showed up one evening; he had never met the man. He appeared to Winston to be something of an effendi, some potentate, a tropical man, overweight and sweaty; the flesh of his face consumed its func-tional parts. Eyes, nose, mouth, were overtaken with fat. The owner looked angry and was an old fruit, Winston had heard. Winston was not yet sure how he was going to make his way in the world, but he had, even with the experiences at the sanitarium and his three nights in jail for the drug bust, decided it would not be as a catamite.

The museum owner reminded him of his stepfather, who Winston wished was a pederast, but wasn't, it seemed. The owner sat down at the desk with him and conducted an interview of sorts, though Winston had been on the job for three weeks. He seemed pleased with the doctored pedigree Winston supplied.

The owner launched into an attack on "Negras, welfare cheats, and Communists" and told Winston an elaborate tale of visiting relatives in a foreign capital when he was a little boy. His relative was a member of the royal family of some Balkan state and the museum owner and his aunt had been in a coach—he looked over sixty and Winston concluded this must have been before World War I—and an anarchist, a Communist anarchist, the owner said, threw a bomb into their carriage, and his life was spared only because a footman within threw it back out.

The bomb was the cartoon variety, Winston imagined: it looked like a bowling ball with a tampon stuck into it for a fuse. The museum owner's small eyes glinted with indignation and rage while he told the tale. Winston wondered if this man's story was anything like the stories he himself told. He felt the owner was quite mad, especially when he concluded, "Let that be a lesson to you!"

Of what? Winston wondered. The owner then took it upon himself to dust the cases—not the cases, so much as the art within. Winston had only been instructed to dust the outsides. The owner went to a broom closet and emerged with a key and opened a case. Winston had not been told of, or shown, any keys, except to the front door.

The owner reached into one case and, withdrawing his bulky arm, he sent a red vase flying. Winston watched the vase's precise arc. It hit the floor, shattering into pieces as thin as a light bulb's shell. Winston was prepared to display some shock at this event, but the owner did not look in the least perturbed. He didn't even stop dusting.

"I'm leaving now," the owner, a bit later, said. He instructed Winston to sweep up the shattered vase and throw the remains away. The owner had removed the pup tent card that had sat before the vase telling its age and maker. Winston swept up the glass and marveled at the delicacy of the fragments. They looked far too fragile to be glued back together, though Winston did give this some thought. The wastepaper basket was kept in the closet; he had emptied it earlier in the evening. He now deposited into it the glass he had swept up, not much more than what a Christmas ornament would have left. He noticed for the first time, high up, a gray box, something like an electrical fuse box; its door, which had a silver lock, was not completely shut.

Inside Winston found twelve keys, for the twelve locked cases in the museum.

When he had seen the vase so easily shattered and so nonchalantly dealt with a notion had popped into his head: the owner didn't know what he had. There was no complete inventory; or, if there was, it was hardly ever consulted. No catalogue was handed out to tourists, just a brochure that listed some major pieces.

Winston went to a case, opened it, and removed a tapered flower vase, a vase that would not be the first one you would notice on the shelf. As the owner had done, he picked up the identifying card, but instead of throwing it out, Winston stuck it in the vase and put both in the paper bag that had carried in his take-out coffee.

Winston felt the weight of the tender object increase as he held it. Everything seemed to coalesce; the vase became the center of the world; he felt sucked into it.

Winston decided not to remove the vase from the building, but to see if its disappearance would be noticed. He left it in the closet, buried deep in a box full of brochures; if it was noticed absent, it could turn up. He could say the owner had left it out; an excuse could be found. Winston was oddly sure that the owner was not going to tell the woman curator that he had broken a vase. Winston emptied the wastebasket in the cans behind the museum ten minutes before his replacement arrived at one o'clock.

"Anything happen?" the young man inquired.

"No. Just the same old thing. Nothing," Winston reported.

Winston sold the vase eight months later. It surprised him how easy it was. He placed it with an auction house in New York City. It went for sixteen hundred dollars.

He couldn't unlock his trust from his mother's control, but he decided to release some art from the homes he had been in on the Cape. In Provincetown there was just the sort of early work he wanted. Modest-sized paintings, sometimes given to their owners by the painters themselves, others bought from the artists at the beginnings of illustrious careers and now heavily appreciated. They hung on the walls of summer homes. Often the art was not in the style that had made the particular painter famous; that made it easier, actually, to dispose of it. Hans Hofmanns, Jackson Pollocks, Ben Shahns, Edward Hoppers. The owners did not see themselves as collectors, but as friends of the artist, or, better yet, as artists themselves. They did not look upon the paintings as investments, but as work they liked or were sentimental about. Unlike dedicated collectors, they had not girded their homes with electronic devices.

Winston had attended parties in these homes or had just dropped in with other friends. He blended in nicely; he thought of his looks as nondescript, that is, hard to describe. He knew he was handsome enough, but not so much that he would be immediately singled out. He had the sort of face, he felt, that would be appropriate in many places and therefore not noticed. His face had the same effect as a suit in a big city: it made him anonymous, almost invisible.

Winston had picked a sunny day to tour the Audubon House, interrupted only by a poolside chat with his new neighbor, Kenner. Winston was not expecting many other visitors to be traipsing around the Audubon House. The place was kept in a state of high polish; a couple of rooms were roped off. But most were accessible. He toured the downstairs first, walking past the old fairy who was the guard for the day, who had the look of a pensioner pleased to be surrounded by tasteful decor. Winston began to appreciate the logic of his work at the glass museum in Provincetown years ago: the presence of a twenty-four-hour guard would discourage theft—except the guard's.

If there were twenty-four-hour guards it would be another sort of heist all together, for then you had someone to subdue. Winston's instinct was to avoid such occasions. What could round-the-clock guards cost? He had been paid, ten years before, the minimum wage. There must be plenty of people willing to work down here, even at minimum wage. Bridget didn't receive much more than that. She took home something like a hundred and thirty dollars a week. Two additional shifts of guards would be roughly a thousand more a month, twelve thousand a year. Maybe it was just too much trouble, though it would have kept him from planning to steal their double elephant folio. He wondered what the folio was insured for. But it was the simple alarm system, besides the fact it had never been robbed before, that attracted him to the Audubon House.

In the can Winston had discovered what made a place appeal to most burglars was that it had been knocked over many times before. If it was done before, it can be done again. And so the same gas stations and 7-Eleven stores would be hit over and over. Finally the robbers would be nabbed in the act, or shot attempting to flee. Winston thought that most thieves lacked either the most elementary kinds of imaginations, or were the most cynical appraisers of what mankind could learn from experience.

Winston liked to contemplate the unrobbed and the unsuspecting. Not that any place equipped with burglar alarms was unsuspecting; but no one can really imagine anything fully, he held, till he experiences it himself. The unmolested were Platonists; Winston would make them empiricists.

Three

1

There was enough of a resemblance, initially, to the boy Kenner had known to identify Winston: he was tall, a bit over six feet, and had blond hair that lay across his forehead with the uninterrupted sweep of a wing, hair that appeared white at the roots and the tips. But there was enough eerie difference to make Kenner believe that an imposter had taken possession. Winston had a broad, open face, though his eyes often became suspicious. Years ago his expression had seemed to Kenner slightly moronic, going, as it did, from naïve acceptance to hostile suspicion. Winston had to be considered handsome, but in the manner, Kenner had noticed later in his life, that successful yes men are: there is nothing unattractive about them, no oddity or imperfection that ages badly or stands out. Not much character, either, but people liked that look. Kenner realized Winston had grown up to resemble John Dean, or any number of Nixon's men.

Winston had worn glasses, he remembered; they had made him look more intelligent, though in a negative way. When he removed them his face seemed more vapid than before. There was something about this sort of face that Kenner, over the years,

grew to associate with low-grade fanaticism: the same blankness
that Kenner observed in Winston he had seen again and again
during his years as a journalist. Jesus freaks, economic zealots
with get-rich schemes, Mormons.

Simplicity would hover in these faces, cover them with a soft
confusion like a swarm of gnats, and then momentarily cloud,
become downright nasty. First innocence, then irrationality.

Kenner had known Winston for two periods in his life. Winston had lived conspicuously on the same block for two years at
the time Kenner reached puberty. Winston's family, the Crosses,
then moved out west. Years later Winston had turned up for a
short while at the same midwestern trolley-car university Kenner
attended. He remembered Winston's architect father had died.
Winston had attended schools in the east; his mother had remar-
ried a man who developed the first mall in Kenner's part of the
Midwest. And though Kenner and he were friendly enough when
they were boys, Winston had made it clear that he didn't wish to
carry their familiarity into adulthood.

Kenner's sharpest recollection of Winston from the college
period was a story Winston had told him. Kenner always considered it one of the saddest he had ever heard. It seemed to
him that Winston told the story often; a well-used confession, a
tale that offered intimacy and solicited it in return. Kenner was
hooked. Winston told the story without any irony, as if he didn't
understand the point he was making.

Kenner had been surprised to discover that there were quite
a few stories floating around Winston during that time; one
strange one was that he was actually the son of someone noto-
rious, but not acknowledged. And that Winston had found his
architect-father's body after he had killed himself. Winston, in a
number of ways to Kenner, seemed deserted, so hollow, empty,
that these sorts of stories grew up around him like weeds around
an abandoned building.

Kenner at nineteen thought it a mystery how someone who
appeared to him so bland could attract so much interest. People
seemed to rush to provide color for Winston, just as someone
rubs a cold hand to bring it some warmth. His stories were like
some makeup kit that traveled with him; there would be no face
there, until all the stories began to paint one on right before
your eyes.

But it was the one story he was told by Winston himself that
Kenner most clearly recalled. He had run into Winston at a party
given by someone connected to the art institute to which Win-

ston had transferred after dropping out of the college Kenner attended. Winston was sitting alone in the house's library; it was full of art books, large volumes, eccentric bindings; Winston had one of them opened on his lap.

Kenner sat down, across from where Winston was swallowed by a black canvas butterfly chair; he looked to Kenner like an insect caught within a carnivorous flower. Kenner had consumed a number of Purple Passions at the party, drinks made of gin and grape juice, a popular concoction of the time. Soon Winston began to look like a sinister moth.

Winston had no particular reason to confide in Kenner; their loose bonds of childhood had slipped off long before. In fact, Kenner felt like an audience of one, the only person to have purchased a ticket to this show. A record was playing. Music came from speakers built in bookcases. Gerry Mulligan.

"You may not remember this," Winston said, "but I play the saxophone."

That "remember" Kenner took at the closest thing to an apology he was going to get from Winston about the denial of their boyhood acquaintanceship.

"Oh," Kenner said. It was later when he began working as a reporter that Kenner realized that small "Oh" was all one needed to lubricate conversation. Kenner couldn't picture a saxophone among Winston's treasures of boyhood.

"Yes. Quite well, actually. I could have made a living at it."

Kenner looked around the room, hoping to see a saxophone so some proof of Winston's assertion could immediately be demonstrated.

"After I dropped out of school back east, I went to England, but I ran into some problems."

"Oh?"

"I worked for a year selling clothes in New Haven," and Kenner immediately wondered why Winston had needed the money, "and saved up. I booked passage," though Kenner knew he couldn't have meant on a ship, "and told all my friends," and Kenner wondered what sort of crowd that would have been, "and the night before I left they threw a large party for me, a bon voyage party. I had let my apartment go, burned my bridges. I arrived the next morning at the airport with one suitcase and my sax. A redcap took my bag and, looking at the instrument case, asked if I was a musician. I told him I was and he asked if I was flying off to some gig, and I told him yes, that I was going to London to play. He whistled appreciatively and he got my bag

25

checked through—right away. I had planned to live in London for a year and pay for my keep by playing in clubs. On the plane I had a few drinks, and when we arrived in Heathrow I was checked through customs and asked what I intended to do in London. And, instead of saying be a tourist, I said, quite openly and truthfully to them, that I was a jazz musician and I intended to get work in some of the small clubs in Picadilly and stay for a year or more. The customs official looked at me strangely and went off. Another gentleman appeared and asked me to come with him. They put me in a room; I was searched, and then asked more questions. Then I was told I was to be denied admittance to the country and would be sent back to the States on the next available flight.

"From what I could gather there seemed to be some problem with admitting foreign laborers—Pakistanis, or some such—and they weren't letting anyone in with plans like mine."

Kenner didn't know how much of this to believe, though there was something credible about the way Winston was telling it; he seemed fascinated by the humiliation involved. Winston went on to describe how he had been handcuffed, taken through the airport, escorted to a bathroom. He asked for, and was allowed to have, a drink at an airport lounge, since there were three hours to the next flight. This stop held the further embarrassment of trying to pay for a drink with hands still cuffed. Another patron put down the right amount of change for him.

It was a detailed account. Kenner felt in the library the air-conditioning of the dark bar off the brightly lit concourse; he could see the tufted stools Winston described, share the sight of the liquor in the glass, the heft of the cuffs around Winston's wrists. At last Winston was put on a plane, his passport stamped DENIED ENTRY, or something equally officious, and then he landed in more or less the same place from which he had departed. Winston's whole adventure, after a year's planning and preparation, took about twenty-four hours.

He arrived back in town with no place to return to and he didn't want to contact any of his friends after all the months he had been boasting of his plans.

There was something horrible about returning, like coming back after you had died, Winston said. It spoiled the texture of people's grief. There was only one bright spot to the whole sorry tale, he said.

As he was leaving the airport, with his bag and saxophone case, he saw, passing in the other direction, the same redcap who had helped with his luggage the day before. He waved appreciatively at Winston, some sign of salute and honor. The man looked truly impressed. What the redcap saw was someone tired, but supremely successful, having just flown to London and back to play a one-night stand.

Kenner expected Winston to supply the moral: that you could be, whatever the circumstances, a hero to somebody. But he didn't; it was just another detail he seized upon. The shame he had felt had slowly been elevated to indignation, and he launched into a description of how he had tried to extract revenge. Letters to congressmen and senators, to the British embassy. He amassed a file, but did not receive any relief. When he finished, he said, his passport was still stamped DENIED ENTRY.

What came into Kenner's mind at that moment was too simple so he did not suggest it: apply for another passport, saying his was lost, or wait until his had expired—which it may have already—and get another, one without the offending stamp. Who would know? Did they keep a list at hand?

But Winston seemed quite satisfied to be sealed within his bubble of persecution. He didn't want a way out. He saw it as a turning point, a bit of bad luck that had changed his life irrevocably; he was somehow less responsible now for what would occur. He had been denied entry into England, but he had been released from another country altogether. Kenner had been ready to disbelieve the whole story, but the business about the redcap, the signal of salute, that made him believe the entire episode had indeed taken place.

During the years before Kenner saw Winston on the condo balcony, Kenner had seen himself and his fellow writers molt a number of times; the seventies had been good and bad years for journalists. By the end of the decade, Kenner and his associates had shed plumage of a diverse kind: the first feathers to go were all browns and grays, serious and wintry, since most of them had begun as political reporters.

The feathers they now sported were gaudy and bright. His good friend Saperstein did a type of journalism that Kenner tried, for the most part, not to do. What Saperstein did, Kenner called Walter Mitty work. Fantasy stuff of a physical nature. Saperstein had stranded himself on a desert island with a small group of paying survivalists and lived on a diet of many-legged bugs for a week; he abandoned his identity for a month to see how difficult it would be to establish a new one. Saperstein was getting paid for what most people wanted to avoid but wouldn't mind reading about in a glossy periodical. Often Saperstein alone provided the socially redeeming material set down in between the blinding labia sunrises and sunsets of pudenda in men's magazines.

In the past, Saperstein and Kenner had covered events that thickened their freedom of information-obtained files. But, by 1977, they had been left with the Hardy Boys. Seeing Winston again reminded Kenner of the Hardy Boys. He had grown up with the Hardy Boys. Those small beige volumes, smaller than adult books, their shape proportioned to fit a child's hand, had been Kenner's first reading outside of school. The Hardy Boys. Suburban middle-class paranoia. Crime everywhere.

Kenner's parents had neither the money nor the inclination to hand him over to the Hardy Boys; but Winston, when he lived on Kenner's block, had a complete set. To Kenner, Winston's dad, Mr. Cross, appeared to be an outdoorsman, but of a classier type than Kenner's neighborhood typically boasted. He seemed to Kenner to be the educated sport, a fly-fisher, a hunter of odd birds. Winston's father had bought a typical midwestern bungalow and modernized it. All ramps and vertical lines and gray stain. The house looked like a ragged moth that had been turned back into a sleek cocoon.

The Crosses always seemed out of place, wealthier than everyone else in the neighborhood. No one was surprised when they moved. All Kenner heard was that Winston's father was going to work with a famous architect in the Southwest.

Kenner had seen for the first time what he thought was caviar in Winston's basement. Winston and his father were cleaning their weekend catch. Orange eggs spilled from a fish's gut. Winston's dad, named Max, Kenner recalled, had the remnants of a harelip; his face was marred by a scar that tugged at his upper lip. Max lifted up a tidy pile of the roe on the tip of his skinning knife. They were the size of BBs. Kenner looked from the knife blade to Max's harelip scar and made a connection that was unwarranted; Winston had told Kenner that Max had gotten the scar in a fight. A knife fight. No thank you, he said, to Max's offer to partake.

Winston was encouraged in a number of educated pleasures by his father. His room had framed prints of the sort Kenner considered educational, scenes of hunting expeditions, pictures of artillery, drawings of birds. Winston had constructed a telescope that had much impressed the ten-year-old Kenner. Twelve-inch glass, nearly two inches thick, that Winston polished laboriously. Winston, as a kid, Kenner recalled, had a host of didactic impulses: he had instructed all the neighborhood boys how to masturbate, since he was a few years older. Though he showed the boys how to do it, it didn't seem to have much effect on Winston himself. His penis wouldn't grow any longer than his fist: a turtle's head never poking out of its shell. He claimed to have a Miracle Whip jar full of his sperm, though he never showed it.

Winston kept his set of Hardy Boys on a shelf beneath his filled gun rack: a shotgun, a twenty-two, an air rifle. It took Kenner a month of displayed interest and a pledge to inform Winston of just what hour Kenner's teenage sister might be crossing a hallway window undressed to pry one of the books loose. Its unbroken spine was stiff, so Kenner supposed Winston had not read it. That seemed to be a more profound reason for Winston's stinginess: he seemed to be proprietary not with what he had, but with what he had not yet experienced. He didn't want them touched till he had mauled them, though that day might never come.

Kenner had begun to think of Winston as one of the Hardy Boys. Winston, like Frank and Joe, certainly had a generous father and an equal amount of equipment of all sorts. The Hardy Boys hadn't seemed so much rich as unrestricted. Kenner had a bat and ball; Winston had his rifles, his fly tackle, his model trains, his twelve-inch telescope, and even a cannon a foot and a half long, an eighteenth-century model, which Winston would often set off at twilight. Kenner would be enlisted as the loading soldier, Winston the cannoneer officer. His cannon covered their quiet block of homes with sulfur's sinister odor.

Those boyhood twilights would always be evocative for Kenner, since it was always at that odd hour, the time one should be going home for dinner, that the Hardy Boys would be sneaking off into a darkness not yet substantial; not dangerous, but seductive, since they were defying their supervisors, going into a world full of the deep plush of dusk, the spell-inducing shade of gray found, Kenner thought now, in limousine upholstery, certain kinds of leather boots long-legged women wore.

And it was just around that spell-inducing hour that Kenner and Saperstein had pulled up in front of the offices of the Stratemeyer Syndicate, ready to scout it, to soak up some good old atmosphere for the beginning of an article Saperstein was writing.

The Hardy Boys had lived, Kenner recollected, in a world that was eternally autumnal, whatever the season. And the corner of Maplewood, New Jersey, where the syndicate's offices stood was the same: large trees, solid homes, the air redolent with dark and richly scented green. It was a plain two-story building. Saperstein's interview with the woman who ran the syndicate had been quickly canceled when she saw a copy of the publication for which Saperstein was doing the article. But he still needed some color for the piece.

They parked in front of the building on a Saturday when the offices were closed. An old black man was raking leaves. In the world of the Hardy Boys, the old man would most likely have addressed the intrepid brothers as "Massa," just as the train porter in *The Twisted Claw* did, and generally shuffle around in an Uncle Tom routine. The syndicate, Saperstein had discovered, would update the old books, removing for subsequent editions what would be wrongly interpreted by the present generation. The man stopped raking when Kenner and Saperstein got out of the car.

"No one here today," he said.

Kenner feigned shock, took a step back, and, the picture of discouragement, said, "You mean, we're not going to be able to see it!?" Kenner was not sure the man had anything to do with the Hardy Boys, but there had been something paternal about his remark. *No one here today.*

"Oh, my, oh, my," Kenner went on, and to his ear he sounded like the worst racist parody, as if he had said, "Oh, Lawd." "And to think we came all this way for nothin'!"

Before Kenner had reached his boohoos, Saperstein gave him a look of reproach. The old leaf-raker gazed at Kenner sympathetically, though, and asked, "Are you an admirer?"

Kenner replied, knowing they must be talking about the same thing, "Why, yes, and we have driven all the way," and he glanced at Saperstein's New York license plates, "from . . . Buffalo, just to see."

Saperstein looked embarrassed. Saperstein always looked like a Jewish Ichabod Crane to Kenner, but just then he looked like he wanted Kenner's head to come off. The old man, who Kenner guessed was the building's custodian, took Saperstein's expression for dismay and said, "Well, maybe I can give you boys a look."

He put his rake up against the wall, neglecting the small pile of leaves he had collected, which began to drift off in the breeze. Since Kenner had not yet identified what they admired, and no signs were on the building, other than the smallest nameplate, there was some chance that they might have been in for a real surprise, but Kenner was sure that the fact no names had yet been used made their intentions seem even more sincere. Reverence for the unspoken had taken over.

The man produced a large ring of keys and selected one that opened the glass front door emblazoned STRATEMEYER SYNDICATE and led Kenner and Saperstein up the stairs.

"Now, I'll only let you boys stay a minute, just to look."

Kenner thanked him a bit too profusely, and Saperstein continued to mutter misgivings, since it was he, and not Kenner, who was going to be linked in print to this place.

Their guide opened an inner office door and turned on the lights. Before them was a wall of books. All the editions of the Hardy Boys, the Nancy Drews. Original watercolor illustrations from the stories covered the walls: trees blowing in the wind, the boys' collars turned up against the cold, furtive looks cast behind.

It did produce a small thrill for Kenner. At the time he thought of Winston's books, though not of Winston.

It was another small example of what journalism had done for Kenner; he got to see once again the backstage of his dreams. It had been that way when he first lived in New York City, first began to meet and interview the people who had played roles he had watched for so long, first talked to people who engineered events. It was as if his childhood was some sort of hallucination and now he got to wake up, to come out of it, to be told: See, it wasn't real.

The layout of the place was U-shaped and Kenner went one way with the old man; Saperstein dropped behind and went the other way. Kenner knew Saperstein would be looking for the office of the woman who had canceled his interview, but he didn't think he would be leafing through her files, which is what in fact he was doing when Kenner turned a corner and looked into the room.

"Hey, Frank, it's me, Joe," he called out.

"You boys better be going now. You've had your look," the custodian said. His tone made clear he smelled a ruse, that they were not just devoted fans, wanting to bask at the site, but something else again: folks with motives.

They thanked him for his time, looking about as they did, taking in every detail they could absorb, a looting they now both did by habit, since Kenner wasn't even going to write about it.

"Well, the boys couldn't have done better themselves. And that's just how it would happen: the fortuitous coincidence, the handyman deus ex machina," Kenner said later, in the car. Saperstein pulled away from the curb and his face took on a debit expression, one that showed a due bill would be arriving some day.

"It's a long way from checking out vandalized five hundred–pound bomb casings at a defense plant," Saperstein said. Kenner recalled the midnight inspection of boxcars at the AMF plant. The boxcar full of bomb casings could have passed for a biblical tomb just unearthed; inside, left untouched for centuries, tall earthen jars stacked side by side.

They both let a silence stand in Saperstein's car, acknowledging that the trivial had once again triumphed over the terrible.

Kenner recalled looking back and noticing that the man and rake had disappeared from the sidewalk in front of the building. The street was empty. And the trees, beginning to shed their autumn leaves, stirred heavily in the wind.

2

The first lawyer Winston, himself, had hired had given him both good and bad counsel. He had been convicted, which was proof enough of the bad, but only on one reduced charge, which had been the good. He was sentenced to one-to-three and served fourteen months. But the thefts that had remained unprosecuted, and the ones that remained undetected, had made that fourteen months profitable. Over ten thousand a month, Winston figured, for his time. He had taken over a hundred and fifty thousand dollars worth of art; and the paintings from the burglaries he couldn't be connected to were still in his possession and were appreciating.

His lawyer had mentioned what Winston took to be an old lawyer's saw: no attorney was supposed to be emotionally involved with his clients. Winston thought the man had been too cool to him, and, though Winston had tried to charm him, he never became friendly. He had asked and the lawyer had quoted the remark to him. Winston wondered if it was true for a thief, too: one should never become too emotionally attached to what he intends to steal.

Among the gifts his father had left him that Christmas he had died, in addition to the shotgun from Purdy's, were two books. A biography of Audubon and a volume of *The Birds of America*. His father had inscribed the picture book to him: *To my son. Kill-*

ing is not the most brutal thing men do to their fellow creatures. Your loving father, Max, Xmas, 1957.

In the hospital Winston was sent to from prep school, he had pored over the books. He read that Audubon had killed most of the birds, lashed them to boards, traced their outlines. None of that turned up in the paintings, except for what Winston saw as hidden messages, lessons of morbidity, death signs: images of destruction and decay throughout. The bald eagle with his claws in the white underbelly of a catfish, its gills rendered almost genitally, Winston had thought, comparing it to the beaver shots in the smuggled magazines the boys had. The whiskers of the fish were pink and serpentine; another fish's head with a ribbon of entrails lying nearby, the eagle's other claw placed on not so much a boulder but a tablet, some symbol of laws.

Audubon, Winston thought, was sending him private messages and, at the same time, seemed to be rubbing everyone's face in another lesson: the beauty of his birds, and the depiction of guts and shit he would scatter around the portraits. You want to look at beauty, he was saying to young Winston, well look, too, at beauty's fouled nest. That's what he liked about Audubon. As he got older he read more. Audubon, a dandy at nineteen, a bankrupt at thirty-four; wastrel, con man, and, now, a saint of sorts.

When Audubon's assistants painted the settings, the taint of the grave disappeared, but then the birds themselves would tell the tale. The white-crowned pigeon, from Cuba, shot down on the wing, painted while Audubon was in the Keys. His assistant, Winston had discovered, gave the print the flowering geiger-tree limb, but Audubon put one bird's beak into the other's, the horned beaks poised, opposed, menacing. The house wren was about to thrust a fat spider into an offspring's open mouth, the nest made from an old felt hat, the side of the hat dripping with bird shit, so fresh it looked creamy to Winston.

Audubon was able to insult those who praised him with what they praised. He got back at them for the indignities they had heaped upon his early life. His attack went virtually undetected in his bird prints, works that proclaimed virture, but which Winston saw as only framed vices, pictures as sour and damning, he thought, as Hogarth's etchings.

Winston had read only one puzzled commentary on this aspect of Audubon's work. In Audubon's depiction of the yellow-billed cuckoo, one bird had bitten down on a butterfly, a tiger swallowtail, and a writer had remarked, somewhat abashed, that since the bird ate only caterpillars, Audubon must have made its meal a butterfly, "for some reason—possibly a decorative touch." Winston laughed when he read that. A decorative touch.

The first print had been Winston's early favorite: *The Great American Cock (Male)*. He discovered that almost all the collections had removed Audubon's own handwritten caption, as if the name was objectionable, and renamed it *The Wild Turkey*. Winston liked Audubon's own description of it: "The great size and beauty of the Wild Turkey, its value as a delicate and highly prized article of Food, the circumstance of its being the origin of the domestic race now generally dispersed over both continents, render it one of the most interesting birds indigenous to the United States of America."

Winston liked "its value as a delicate and highly prized article of Food," for he thought that captured something he saw in the people around him: nice to look at, but better to eat. Winston thought that Americans liked to believe, whether or not it was true, in the existence of cannibals.

The Great American Cock, as Audubon protrayed him, was deliberately obscene, Winston thought. Audubon was, to Winston, more demon than saint. As a youngster he had been amazed at all the birds Audubon had depicted piercing other creatures' eyes: the black vulture, of course, among others—but also the golden eagle.

Over the years since his father's death, Winston had examined closely the copy of *The Birds of America* his father had left him as a legacy; he began to see all birds, all creatures, as birds of prey, scavengers. Audubon, Winston concluded, had the ability to make you think the opposite of the truth: he used his exaggerated lifelike settings to make you believe the bird were painted from nature, rather than from hunted specimens killed and mounted by a man who had spent a melancholy year learning the trade of a taxidermist.

II

Four

There must not be air-conditioning or it didn't work, Kristina thought. The air that blew through the overhead plastic nipple was hot and stale.

Both Kristina and Curt had flown down from Newark for less than two hundred dollars. Kristina had held Elijah on her lap, even though there were empty seats. But the tickets from just Miami to Key West cost nearly the same as the longer flight. Curt told her they should have taken the bus. The Douglas C-47 sat in line for a half hour behind the big jets waiting to take off. The sun came through the window with such ferocity that she had to change seats with Curt, even though she liked to look out the window whenever she flew to Key West. She liked to look down at the water, so blue and green, with the green sometimes almost white, as if someone had thrown milky green paint in the blue water. All she had to look out on while waiting, on their side of the plane, were old planes, some half eaten away, some that looked like parts had been amputated; others were just burnt-out shells. Curt had told her they were going to be sold to South American countries and would fly dope back here for their government officials, but Kristina didn't believe every last one of Curt's stories.

Like how he'd been married when he was seventeen and had a kid himself, a boy he hadn't seen since the child was Eli's age. How the last time he saw his wife was when she came to visit him when he lived in Maryland after he had joined the navy and she just stayed one night, just long enough to find out his social security number so she could report it to welfare back in Vermont. Curt said his wife blamed him for the boy's physical problems.

Curt was staring at the burnt-out hulks with true fascination. He seemed always to be interested in dead things: the body of a dog they had found rotting under the crawlway of the apartment complex. He had poked at it with a stick for what seemed ten minutes. On the highway he would always turn his head and slow down when they drove by any sort of road kill.

"Look at that!" Curt said to her as the plane began to lift off the ground and Kristina didn't want to open her eyes, but she did. Out the window, across Curt's lap, she saw the engine surrounded by dark gray smoke, like it was trailing a skirt made of heavy, wooly, oily cotton. It was more than she'd ever seen all the times she had flown from Miami to Key West, much more alarming than the usual rivets and bolts that were always jumping loose from their sockets in the engine's cowling.

"It's not supposed to be like that?" she said to Curt, who looked at her more angry than scared.

"No shit," Curt said. He stared at the smoke for almost five minutes and then yelled into the aisle, "Hey! Stewardess!" And before he said anything else a calm country voice came over the speaker: "Well, folks, we've developed a slight mechanical problem and we will be returning to Miami International Airport shortly. There is no cause for alarm."

Curt had turned back to the window; the smoke was now almost black and came thick from under the lip of the cowling. The prop was still turning.

Curt's face had gone red, though not as red as a picnic table, which Kristina had seen happen at least once. He had not been drinking for two weeks and had stayed on his medication. Kristina remembered one of the first things he had said to her, which she had thought was a joke: "I always wanted to take up with a nurse."

Kristina didn't explain to him that she wasn't exactly a nurse. She was familiar with his drugs, though; he had been prescribed a number from being treated by a variety of doctors and clinics:

Thorazine, Prolixin, Haldol. The last doctor had put him on lith-
ium. He took one or another, depending on how he felt.

"God, I wish I was flying this crate," Curt said. Kristina didn't
know he was a pilot. She had been surprised, as she got to know
Curt, at how many things he was, or had been. Eli was still asleep,
sweat-bound to her, plastered against her breasts, which were
still just a tiny bit sore from the implant surgery. Eli wore a small
pair of silver cowboy boots and a red satin jump suit. His red
cowboy hat, the rim trimmed with white plastic lacing, was between her feet.

The plane began to descend at an angle she hadn't experienced before; it was like the drop on a roller coaster, but not
quite straight down. The plane seemed to be leveling off, but
she still didn't want to open her eyes. She forced herself to look
and saw they were near the ground, but she didn't recognize
anything below her. They crossed over a highway, a wire fence,
and weeds; then she saw the end of a runway. She wondered if
this was where they brought all the crashing planes. Below she
saw a lemon-lime-colored fire engine and three other vehicles
racing along the edge of the concrete runway. The plane landed
with a bump and both engines immediately shut off. The pro-
pellers quit rotating before the plane came to a full stop. The
smoke from the engine died down, but men wearing tinfoil suits
surrounded the wing with hoses. They didn't spray anything on
the plane, though. Eli began to stir, starting to kick against her
stomach, and she unbuckled the seat belt and shifted him around.

Curt jumped up: *"I want off this plane!"* The stewardess walked
up to him from the rear and told him, "Sir, you should remain
seated. We will all be deplane-ing shortly."

Curt snatched up Eli from Kristina's lap, causing him to wail,
and yelled in the stewardess's face: "I WANT MY CHILD OFF
THIS PLANE, THIS MOMENT, FOR HIS SAFETY!" The
stewardess, who, Kristina thought, looked like a girl she had seen
at the Green Parrot, said firmly, "Sir, you have to follow procedures."

"Procedures!" Curt snapped and pushed Eli back at Kristina,
who, as Curt tried to climb past her, saw that he intended to
knock the stewardess out of the way.

A burst of light filled the back of the plane's cabin and the
stewardess turned around. The rear door had been opened. A
voice called out and passengers started to file off the back stairway. The cockpit door swung open and the pilots walked down

the aisle, brushing Curt aside, one saying to the other, "They didn't need to bring out all that equipment. The assholes just wanted to log some distress time."

Kristina picked up Eli and followed Curt, lugging the carry-ons they had brought. She stopped, realizing she had forgotten Eli's cowboy hat; the line behind her buckled. She squeezed through them, bent to get his hat, and knocked Eli's head on the armrest. He wailed loudly. Finally, they were out on the runway, in the blazing sun. The commotion had made her forget how hot it was. She couldn't see the terminal; she couldn't see any buildings. The runway had spindly weeds growing through cracks.

The stewardess, whose name Kristina was still trying to re-member, said a bus would be out soon to pick them up. Curt had moved off away from the rest of the passengers and stood alone, glaring at the plane and the people inspecting it.

After a bus brought them back to the terminal, they were told there would be at least an hour's delay before another plane could be readied to fly them to Key West. Curt complained loudly and threatened to sue. A man appeared who was supposed to be the manager of the company and told them, though they could not refund the tickets immediately, they would rent a car for Curt to drive to Key West if he wished.

"That's more like it," Curt said, pleased. "But you'll still be hearing from my lawyer."

Kristina was happy to get into the car, which was equipped with air-conditioning. Since the airline was paying, Curt had asked for the best car they had. It was a Chrysler LeBaron. It was big enough and Kristina stretched Eli out on the back seat so he could fall to sleep.

"They ain't getting this baby back," Curt said, getting behind the wheel, "till they ask 'pretty please.' "

Kristina wasn't quite sure how to get to U.S. 1 from the air-port, since she didn't have a map, but Curt said, looking satisfied behind the wheel, not to worry, that they would just look for signs.

"Where the hell are we?" Curt asked. Kristina could see he was upset. Curt's face was tight; hollows had appeared in his cheeks. The air-conditioning wasn't working that well, and Kris-tina wanted to roll down a window, but Curt looked as if he'd yell at her again if she did. It had taken them longer to get a map than she had thought it would—after she finally had per-suaded Curt to stop and get one.

They had gone into three gas stations before they found one that would give them a free map. The second had them for sale, but Curt said that they should be for nothing, that gas stations should give them away. Kristina now wished they had bought the one for sale; the map they were given didn't seem to have all the roads. They were in Coral Gables and finally found U.S. 1; but then they discovered they weren't really on U.S. 1. They were on something called West Dixie Highway. Curt had hastily turned off, and now Kristina didn't know where they were going.

"It doesn't look as simple as it does on the map, Curt. Why don't you stop and we'll figure it out?" Kristina asked. She knew once Curt was rolling he hated to pull over and stop. It irritated her that he was so stubborn, that stopping the car meant some kind of defeat. In the past Kristina had seen him go left and go right and go left again in a frantic search, rather than just stop and look at a map. You'd have thought he'd have gotten used to maps in Vietnam, but Kristina couldn't remember him ever talking about that part. Though he'd sometimes say "two kliks down the road," which sounded like map talk to her.

"Curt, these streets are confusing me. The have the same numbers, but some are avenues, some are streets, and I can't tell right off which are which. I think we're on One hundred and twenty-fifth Street, but it might be," and Kristina turned the map sideways, "Miami Avenue. Let's stop, please, and ask somebody." Curt just tightened up; his face got that mottled pink look.

They were heading down a large road, three lanes in one direction, with some grass in between and another three lanes going the other way. It was nearing dusk, and it looked like it might rain. The air-conditioning was overwhelmed. Kristina's clothes stuck to her, and she saw sweat running down the gully along the front of Curt's ear.

She began to see only black people out the car window, filling up the corners of the street, as if they were waiting to cross, but no one was. Mostly men and boys on bicycles who swerved around the bunches of men, doing wheelies on their stunted banana-seat bikes.

Kristina didn't know if it was just the way the air gets before a storm or her feeling bad that she had gotten them lost, but she was nervous and she wanted to take one of the Demerols she had saved from the operation. The neighborhood looked strange to her: all the people black, only the buildings white, chalky. The sky was gray, like a roll of cloudy cellophane tape, the kind that becomes transparent only after it's been pressed down.

"This ain't good," Curt said. "We must be going inland. I feel it. We've gone too far."

Kristina looked back at her son lying down on the rear seat; she was happy that Eli was still asleep. She looked back out the side window.

"You know, Curt, it looks like all those folks are just staring at us."

"It must be the car."

She hadn't thought of what they would look like from the outside. A new car, tinted windows, shiny and expensive. She began to notice the other cars around her; suddenly it seemed to her that there wasn't another car like theirs in the vicinity.

A traffic light turned red and Curt yelled, *"Jesus Christ!"*

Kristina couldn't remember if she had been startled by Curt's yelling or by the sound, a muffled thud that had come at the same time. The glass of the window by Curt's head had become opaque, splintered; Curt's head in the middle of rays, like a halo, a corona. Someone must have thrown a rock, she thought.

There were three cars ahead of them that had stopped at the light. People had run up to the first car; one man started pounding in the door; another threw himself against the car, turning around backward, so the blow came like a horse's backward kick. Kristina watched the balletic movements wide-eyed. Other men pulled open the driver's door and dragged a man out. A boy on a banana bike banged into the back fender.

That was all she saw, because she then thought to turn around and see to Eli. Kristina was slammed against the door. Curt had jumped the car over the road's curbing and the car was bouncing atop the grass median strip. The car's rear end fishtailed in the dirt and then crashed its bottom onto the roadway.

"Curt, oh, Curt," she screamed, "what's happening?!"

Curt leaned on the horn and Kristina saw people on the sidewalks begin to flow toward the street, as if an earthen dam had been breached: it wasn't all the people stepping forward, but as if a hole opened up and numbers rushed through it.

"Go go go," Curt was chanting, *"Move move move . . ."*

Eli began to wail in the backseat, but Kristina, for a moment, couldn't take her eyes away from the traffic they hurtled through. Curt was going the wrong way on the one-way street. Cars swerved, tries screeched.

"STOP, STOP!" Kristina yelled, and, as if in response, Curt turned right, quit blowing the horn, then turned left, going the opposite direction from which they had started. It was a quiet street; no people were around. She climbed over the front seat and lifted Eli up from the space between the seats where he had fallen. Kristina got him into her lap and brought his cries down to a whimper, whispering, repeating over and over, "Don't cry honey, don't cry, your mommy's got you now."

Five

After living next door to Winston for a few weeks, Kenner began to believe anyone could gather a group of apostles around him—if you weren't too concerned about the ragtag bunch you would end up with.

Kenner had trouble collecting people. *Come follow me* was not among the first invitations Kenner bestowed.

Winston also seemed to have the quality of getting along with little apparent effort and no employment; that, too, stung Kenner. Even though Kenner had now arranged for himself nearly three months of semi-leisure, there was that darkness at the periphery: having to think of what was to come. Guys like Winston, he thought, never seemed to have any difficulty with the future: some hidden source of money, usually family money, made the future a country road, shot through with sunlight. Winston hadn't seemed too pleased to see him.

Winston appeared to be the center of something. The piano keys of parking slots running along the perimeter of the condo complex would be filled with cars that were driven by Winston's callers. They would not go down to the pool, not the men, anyway. The women occasionally would. The men who showed up

at Winston's would have seemed a bit strange rimming the condos' turquoise pool.

The condos' inner courtyard was something of a backwoods
Shangri-La. there were only a few gays about, and they were not
young but rather were men who had closeted themselves for most
of their lives, and even though the closet door was now flung
open they still behaved with antebellum decorum. Beyond the
walls of the condo was Key West, and its definition of decorum
was the absence of consensual sex acts in public places during
daylight. Little else was frowned upon, except panhandling.

Most of the gentlemen of the condos' population seemed to
be middle-class retirees, former military men, lapsed engineer-
ing consultants, generally the foot soldiers the military-industrial
complex put out to tropical pasture. The few younger men, those
in their forties, seemed to be speculators: real estate, commodi-
ties, deal makers. They wore expensive jewelry: gold chains, tax-
shelter time pieces, Sunbelt wampum.

Kenner found it a rather disconcerting crowd; but, for him,
the price was right, and, with his judgments faltering, his politics
in mild disarray, he felt he could adjust. If you were looking for
sacrifice, altruism, serious people, Kenner knew you would not
necessarily take yourself to Key West in the off-season.

The phone rang. For a minute Kenner thought it was an
alarm clock. It was Saperstein. Saperstein was attempting to do
him a favor.

"The rag that did my history of rock 'n' roll piece is looking
for something you might be able to supply."

Kenner recalled his visit with Saperstein to the magazine's
offices, the talk with the young man whose father's fortune back-
rolled the publication as a tax loss.

"They want to get a bit away from so much youth-oriented
crap."

Kenner saw the staff in his mind: their dress was slightly
exaggerated and expensive. Suspenders, bright socks, funny ties.

"I had lunch with my main man there. I tried to interest
him in you once again. We tossed around some story ideas. First,
there's those Cubans. You're right in the middle of it."

"There's not a lot to see, Sap," Kenner said. Kenner had
first learned of the Cubans' arrival a month earlier by watching
the local news of a Chicago station on cable TV; Key West had
no local TV station.

"It looks like the Blessing of the Fleet, Sap, lots of zealots

45

hanging on to the rigging of shrimp boats. They're hustled off to the navy base, processed, and shipped to Miami aboard buses."

"Well, to speak the truth, they're not too interested in that anyway. They don't want to get too far away from youth. But, if you could get on a boat and bring them back the old blow by blow."

"Sap, the last time I was on a boat down here I was sicker than a dog—first time I ever thought of suicide."

Kenner was reviewing his aborted snorkeling trip. Never got in the water. "This Cuban thing is strictly TV. The immigrants arrive, kiss the ground, and are hustled off to Trumbo Annex. It's more *gusanos* who want to get in the South Florida condo business. I'll check it out, but as of now it's strictly TV."

"Yeah, all right—who cares about Cubans?" Saperstein said, "It'll just take up some time and give us a break from watching all those becrazed Iranians. But something they seem to be interested in is a profile/interview of a writer who lives down there. Our boy wonder, editor-publisher, it seems, read the guy's first novel when he was sixteen and has loved him ever since."

Kenner had an inkling who it was before Saperstein said his name. Daniel MacNaughton. "My man wants a rediscovery job, complete with an excerpt of whatever lame shit he's working on. Twelve hundred bucks and a two-hundred-dollar kill fee. You'll have to pitch the Cuban thing to him yourself, but you've got the green light on MacNaughton."

"Sap," Kenner said, feeling exhausted at the thought of pitching anything to a magazine editor, "how did we ever get to this sorry pass?"

"It's the rebound, a viral echo, a bounce-back effect."

Kenner remembered Saperstein had been doing medical stories lately.

"All this stuff has been in remission the last ten years or so. And now it's come back with a vengeance. Like some medicine that masks the symptoms of a disease and when you stop taking it the disease comes back twice as strong . . . Anyway, people are tired of the natural habitat bit. They don't want to be out there mingling with the chimps anymore. They want their old-fashioned zoos back. They want the fauna behind bars so they can stare safely again."

"What are you doing now, Sap?"

"Teenage sex. A fat tome of sociology and prurience. I have to interview two hundred teens and write it up. The money is good. You should hear some of the preliminary interviews."

"I don't want to hear."

"Well, it ain't like the old days. These kids fuck a lot and the only thing that gets in the way seems to be early burnout. What do you do after tying up your date after the prom? Anyway, give *Centipede* a call. Look up MacNaughton. What else do you want to do?"

"Nothing," Kenner said, looking out the closed sliding glass doors at the palm tree swaying in the wind; through the silver film on the doors, which had the effect of a two-way mirror, the fronds looked blue.

"That's no way for a former overachiever to talk—the eighties will be the fifties again, only more lethal. Give *Centipede* a call. You need the work."

Kenner realized there was a trace of criticism, along with sympathy, in Saperstein's concluding remark.

Kenner had begun to decide that being a freelance writer was a mistake; the designation itself, *freelance*, was so ugly, Kenner always presumed it had been coined by a person with a permanent job.

Kenner had always been amused, the few times he had been on assignment for powerful publications, by the magic of the corporate name. At those times he would be draped with a corona of influence, radiant with institutional success. Kenner might come and go but the multinationals would endure.

Friends of Kenner's were doing much better; Saperstein's star was in the ascendant. Kenner took some comfort in the success of his friends. He knew the color on the brush he was being painted with: an unwholesome shade of not-making-it, a dingy gray.

Kenner had called the sixties, in print, "the dematerialized zone." Money. Power. Influence. Who cared? The communal spirit—not that Kenner had ever belonged to a commune—seemed to prevail everywhere: recycled clothes, scorn for the haves. That was the only thing he was nostalgic for: *Jail the rich, free the poor!*

But then it had ended; or, Kenner realized, it had never truly been. He had misjudged it, as he had waterbeds. Kenner began to hear strange conversational addendas: who people were related to, background reasserting itself, conspicuous consumption again in a lather, advertising being praised rather than damned.

All of Kenner's story ideas, he was told, were too glum. Kenner realized what it meant was that the have-nots were being given the bum's rush.

By the late seventies, Kenner saw, a nightmare of his had been realized. The social world had again become high school. High school! What crowd you hung around with, who was most popular, best-looking, and so on. He knew that it was what, in part, he was escaping when he left New York City and came to Key West, the city different.

Kenner pulled back the door and stepped out onto the balcony. He saw the top of Winston's bright head of hair, shiny as a yellow marble, walking toward the pool. Speaking of reliving high school! Kenner thought. He decided to join him.

By the time Kenner arrived, he found Winston reclining on a chaise longue with a stack of dog-racing sheets at his side. He pecked at a hand-sized calculator with one finger.

"Hi there, Winston," Kenner said. Winston continued punching his calculator.

Kenner wondered if it was part of Winston's style, his method of captivating, that he never seemed to interrupt what he was doing when a person talked to him: it made his time seem important; any attention he showed you was made costly, since it took him from what he really wanted to do.

Kenner flipped through the newspapers he had brought along; he had some catching up to do. An all-white jury had been deliberating the case of four white Miami police officers charged in the death of a black businessman who didn't seem sufficiently businesslike on his Harley-Davidson. Kenner figured the odds for conviction were not good. The hottest news the last week had been the failed rescue attempt of the Embassy hostages. There was some confusion about how the mission was scrubbed, but what remained uncontested were the burnt remains of the C-130 transport and three helicopters and a few charred American corpses. The news of the Cubans arriving was beginning to die down. Kenner at first thought that the town was going to be swamped, not by the Cubans arriving from Mariel, but by all the Cubans arriving from Miami who had come down in order to embark. Kenner began to think of U.S. 1 as the anti-Fidelista Trail. Conchs had gotten into the act; shrimpers were going. The stomach-churning notion of easy money had taken hold in town; they were getting a thousand dollars a head per refugee, it was said. A lot of acid and bile was produced. Key West, it seemed to Kenner, had slipped into its prehurricane mode—wary, but slightly hysterical. The skies, though, remained sun-shot and blue.

Kenner grew restive with his page-turning and finally asked Winston what he was doing.

"I'm perfecting a system," Winston replied.

Kenner knew a bit about dog racing, but it now looked like Winston might know more. This bothered Kenner. He suffered a slight disappointment whenever he had acquired some hard-won knowledge about a subject and then someone came along who knew more. It was a petty disappointment, only momentary, the sort, Kenner supposed, an attractive woman who has been the center of silent attention on a bus might feel when a prettier woman gets on. Winston looked at his calculator, made notes on the sheet next to each dog's history. Kenner realized he would have to ask direct questions.

Pointing to the device, he asked, "What's the calculator for?"

"It's not a calculator," Winston said, without looking up, "or, rather, it's a calculator with a biorhythm function."

Winston turned it toward Kenner; he saw what looked like sine curves on a silver plate at the bottom.

"This will figure biorhythms, for any day of the year. All you need to do is punch in the date of birth and today's date and it will tell you whether you're high, low, or critical in three categories: physical, emotional, and intellectual. I check the dogs' biorhythms."

"That sheet only gives you the month and year, not the day of birth," Kenner said, fingering one of the blue programs.

"I know," Winston said, wearily, "I've factored that in. This is an approximation. The curve is regular. There has to be some risk, you know. Takes the fun out."

"Any luck?" Kenner asked, seeing that he had finally broken through Winston's shell.

"I've just started this particular system. The airlines use biorhythms on their pilots. They don't let them fly when they are in a triple critical."

Kenner looked doubtful.

"Japan Airlines," Winston said, and Kenner dropped his eyebrow.

"Do you use it on yourself?" Kenner asked.

"Yes," Winston replied. "I've double-checked it on historical events. It always makes sense. I did Kennedy's biorhythm for the day he was shot in Dallas. He was emotionally high, physically high, and intellectually critical. You see," he said, addressing Kenner directly for the first time, "that's why, against the best

49

advice, he chose to go the parade route in an open car. He felt great, but had impaired judgment."

Kenner was surprised at the number of thoughts and images that flowed into his head at the mention of the JFK assassination.

"How about Marilyn Monroe?" Kenner asked.

"I'll loan it to you sometime," Winston said, settling back onto the chaise longue, "and you can play with it."

Six

Kenner ate alone at the Lum's on North Roosevelt. If he had been a photographer, he thought, he would be able to sell a series of pictures of American fast-food joints that had spectacular views. The McDonald's down the road had one: golden arches overlooking white coral, opalescent water, limitless horizon. The contrast between tackiness and splendor was the sort of thing that appealed to slick magazines. The you-had-your-cake-and-could-eat-it-too school. But he had passed up McDonald's tonight for Lum's and Lum's didn't have a striking vista. Across the road was a one-story motel, an insurance business, a vacant lot, and three stumpy palmettoes.

Kenner, because of living alone, had begun to develop a number of disconcerting habits. He found himself eating in the kitchen standing at the counter near the sink, in the style of solitary old men. And he found himself indulging in other lonely pleasures, such as going to dog tracks.

The setting sun sliced into the restaurant, and even though Kenner had pulled down the cloth and bamboo shade, the light was piercing. Kenner had left the shade high enough so he could watch the traffic. A van sped by, one that he had seen before, parked outside the condo. The van was hard to miss. It had been hand-painted to resemble what Kenner knew as a novelty drink, one that had been popular a few years before: a Tequila Sunrise. The van was painted the same strata of vivid colors, a hot spectrum starting at the front with purple and then streaming back in evermore fiery shades of reds, oranges, and yellows. Its rear doors were white. Kenner had noticed Massachusetts plates on it, and that had interested him in a sentimental way.

Sunsets in Key West were different: you could see through the colors. They were not a flamboyant backdrop like the sunsets Kenner was used to in the Northeast, those one-dimensional Holy Card sunsets; here it was clear; the eye tired of looking for a place to stop. The night was appreciated because it provided a respite.

Kenner would, he knew, contemplate anything while waiting to be served; it was a dodge on loneliness, though he felt that his was somewhat under control. He turned to tonight's race sheet to see if he recognized any of the dogs that were running.

Large red neon letters stood out atop the track's grandstand burning into the black sky. KE WE KENNEL CLU . The moon was full and low, and the coral parking lot and stand's white façade were luminous with reflected light. Kenner could make out the dead characters of the sign; blackened wire, like spent Fourth of July sparklers. Behind the track was a harbor; shrimp boats' rigging spiked the sky.

Kenner saw the Sunrise van parked two rows ahead of him. He was staring at it and had to jump when a pickup truck equipped with a trailer cap containing yelping greyhounds turned in front of him. He hoped those were tomorrow's greyhounds, since Kenner liked to suppose these races were run on the up and up. Tonight's dogs should have been in holding pens since the afternoon.

Admittance was by a half-dollar inserted in a turnstile slot; Kennedy half-dollars: he rarely encountered them elsewhere these days. Kenner hurried past the man from the Salvation Army extending his cigar box.

Kenner once frequented a track outside of Boston in the deep of winter. The track's running surface was heated, so no snow accumulated on it; but there was the pond in the middle of the oval track that was iced over. Steam rose from the sandy running surface. All the patrons huddled beneath the grand-stand seats, in the betting corridors, near concession stands. They all wore the thick padding of the season and were clutching the racing sheets in gloved hands, stamping their feet to keep warm; the atmosphere resembled a holding pen's: all braying and shuf-fling, steam flowing out of the mouths of the bettors, their faces tilted up at the TV monitors that showed the races. The dogs raced through clouds of steam around the hellish track.

The conditions made for crazy odds, and Kenner had won a good deal of money on the first race—a good deal for him at least, over four hundred dollars. But he had stayed for the whole night and left fifty dollars behind. "You can beat the race, but you can't beat the card," he kept repeating to himself on the cold ride back home.

The Key West track, Kenner knew, was the second smallest in the country. Kenner viewed the patrons as three distinct groups: welfare entrepreneurs, trying to parlay their meager federal re-mittance into a living wage; the tourists, a diverse lot, but rec-ognizable from their slightly displaced air, the look of someone passing through; the last, a core of regular gamblers. A certain steadfastness singled the gamblers out. Kenner couldn't tell for sure if they were consistent winners; but some of them seemed to make enough unreported income to finance home beauty par-lors, knickknack shops, a medley of other cottage industries.

Kenner had reserved a table—a two-dollar luxury. The table area was partitioned with railings, two tables within each square, more animal auction space. Kenner would sit alone, bent over his sheet; his stubby pencil would mark it sporadically, like a fork picking at the remains of a meal. He saw Winston at a nearby table, sitting with two women and another man. One of the women he had seen before: the fleshy redhead on Winston's balcony. The other two people he hadn't seen, though he guessed they were connected to the Sunrise van with Massachusetts plates.

Kenner was not much for socializing at the track; betting had become such a solitary habit for him any chitchat seemed intrusive. But he had gone long enough without talking to any-one that conversation would not be unwelcomed. Given Win-ston's laconic replies, he didn't think he had to be worried about being too bothered.

"Hi, there," Kenner said, sitting down, catching Winston's eye. Winston had been punching his small calculator, making no-tations on a pad.

"Hello, ah, Kenner," Winston said, and returned to his figuring.

The track announcer had just set a tone arm down on a scratchy forty-five; a raspy voice warbled: *"Key West welcomes you-u-u-u."*

He had discovered the redhead worked in a shop near his friends' store in the old-town section. The two strangers had their backs to Kenner. They were oddly symmetrical; both had the same thin, long, muscular backs. The man had short, curly black hair; the woman long, thick, wirey hair, dark mahogany in color. The grating voice sang on.

At tables the seating was usually governed by who was going to bet. Kenner didn't have that problem since no one else was at his table. The redhead was going to do Winston's running around, it was clear; she and the curly-haired fellow occupied outside chairs. He didn't look as if he was going to do anyone's errands. Kenner had the impression that only Winston would actually be betting. He could see the other women only in profile. He heard her say, "I'd like to see Bruce Jenner run a race with a tiny model of a Cadillac out ahead of him about twenty-five feet."

Kenner laughed out loud, but no one at Winston's table did. Perhaps they heard too many funny remarks, he thought. The fellow next to the woman who had spoken continued to stare intently at his race sheet.

"Hey, Winston," Kenner said, "what do you like in the first race?"

Kenner confounded himself by making such a remark. It was not the sort of thing he would normally do. He knew what he wanted was to be introduced. Winston looked up and said, "Like to help you out, Kenner, but it would change the odds."

The thick-haired woman turned around and said, "Number one has possibilities."

Though Kenner was startled that he had gotten what he wanted, Winston stepped in, as if some protocol had been breached.

"Rea, this is an old acquaintance. Kenner, I do believe I've forgotten your first name."

"That's okay, Winston, it doesn't get used much these days." Even when he was twelve, people called him Kenner; he considered he might have always seemed too serious. He didn't expect that Winston would remember Kenner's mother calling him Joey. Joseph Patrick.

"Yes, well, Kenner, Rea. Rea, Kenner."

"Rea Kramer," she said. Kenner clasped her offered hand.

"And Duane and Bridget," Winston said, and he slumped back in his seat, coming out from under his spell of good host. Duane turned only enough to allow his peripheral vision to gain some sight of Kenner.

"What do you like about dog racing?" Rea asked. "I've been trying to convince these jokers it's a mug's sport."

Kenner was struck by the fact that she seemed actually to want an answer. Usually such questions are sent aloft on a gust of politeness and they quickly tumble back to the ground before they reach you.

"I like the fact no humans are involved," Kenner said, and, realizing that might not be an ingratiating remark, he added, "I don't like jockeys, I mean."

"You're right about that," she said, smiling. "It's hard to hold in high esteem anything we can't control—like dogs. Even a magnificent animal like Secretariat has to have a man on his back—or so we like to think."

Rea was, Kenner noted, the first person he had met in some time who immediately launched ideas at a high velocity of interest into the fragrant night air of Key West.

"Dogs have always gotten a bad rap. The Dog Star was always credited with causing great heat," she continued, "pestilence, and the like. How could dog races ever be thought to be anything but inferior? Dogs supposedly guard the mouth of Hell."

Kenner was sure a classical education lurked somewhere in this Rea's past. He said, "Yeah, you're right. A dog is about the smallest animal that can race without being ridiculous." Since Kenner was rather short himself, he realized he might be revealing too much about himself. "Big is best in our culture. Horses have always been the largest animals that can be raced effectively."

"Camel races!" Rea said, eyes glinting. "Elephant meets!"

Kenner smiled, and Rea turned back to the racing form she had been studying earlier.

Kenner was surprised that she had started up open full bore, with no apparent warm-up. Kenner could be smitten by a voice and Rea's had the smoky allure of intelligence in it. Duane had not taken much interest in their conversation. He didn't seem to mind Rea's promiscuous display; he did emit some unacknowledged claim, just as Winston seemed to have possession over the large expanse of the redhead's flesh spilling out of her dress. Bridget's breasts were spilling over; Rea's ideas were spilling over.

Kenner was habitually attracted by both sorts of excess. The redhead's body, though aging, still held the appeal anything that once had great power retains. First there is wild idolatry, then respectful honor. Ten years ago she must have been breathtaking, Kenner thought. He could make out, beneath the sheen of tan and oil, marbling stretch marks.

"Did you know Al Capone was last sent to jail because of dog racing?" Kenner asked Rea, regaining her attention. He noticed Duane's head incline a bit.

"Capone used a man named O'Hare as a front—boasted of it around town. But O'Hare, by this time, had enough money and was lusting after respectability—the airport in Chicago is named after his son—and he turned Capone in. That was the tax conviction that jailed him. A week before Capone was to be released O'Hare was gunned down on a street."

Kenner was surprised to notice Winston staring at him.

It was time to bet and Kenner excused himself. The redhead, Bridget, had preceded him; Kenner chose another line.

Kenner was easily seduced by the sucker bets: daily doubles, quinellas, and the like. And he always bet too much money on the first race.

The pari-mutuel clerks reminded Kenner of journalists, since their facial expressions were not supposed to reveal what they thought of the information that was being imparted to them. They did not smirk with disbelief at the bets that were made, or laugh wildly out loud, register profound amazement, or even nod conspiratorially.

No one had taught Kenner to assemble a poker face when he talked to people on a story, even though he had often felt astonishment at what he was hearing. He was certain that if he displayed surprise the fellow would instantly realize he was saying something he shouldn't be saying. It often would be something innocuous, but still be the piece of the puzzle Kenner was looking for. Kenner thought this ability had served him well in other parts of life: a beneficent blandness to show the variety of idiocies or outright perjuries daily life provided.

Kenner returned to the table with his tickets. He saw an animated discussion at Winston's table cease when his approach was noticed.

Duane and Rea did not look like a typical couple to Kenner, though it appeared they could argue like one. They both had thin faces, but Kenner was always struck by what fine instruments were needed to measure the slight differences that made one face look smart and another only cunning. He had often thought about the difference. Duane looked like a handsome fox, like the kind of boy who was good with cars. Rea certainly seemed to have advanced education, and would have looked upper middle class to Kenner, except he had never before met an upper middle class American woman with less than perfect teeth.

Kenner would have guessed Duane came from the type of family who would lose one boy to a war, another to jail, and another to the local interstate.

Kenner bet the number three dog, Chappaquidick Flash. Kenner had felt a tug, based upon both the rational and the irrational, to bet the number one dog. The irrational was its name: Rights of Man. The rational was that he was the class dog, a good breaker in the one box. *Class on the inside* was a prudent rule. But, nonetheless, he had gone with the three, a closer.

The Key West track had never been modernized, updated, Kenner assumed. The lure the dogs followed appeared to be part trolley car, part fake rabbit. The contraption ran on an electrified oval track, making a loud racket, spitting out blue sparks. The fake rabbit jutted midway over the sandy track on a pole.

"Here comes Swifty!" the announcer called; the lure began to rattle around the track.

The number one dog beat the box. The starting box's front wall was pulled up to begin the race, and the one dog seemed to pass through the wall before it was entirely raised. Kenner knew the reasons for this phenomenon: dogs rock back and forth in the separate chambers, and, if a dog is a good breaker and is rocking forward just as the barrier is brought up, he is out a length ahead of every other dog. Like the one dog.

He was three lengths ahead at the first turn. Kenner's Chappaquidick Flash was running second. His bet was not yet totally lost. He could still win the quinella. The one dog looked uncatchable. But, down the stretch, the seven dog, on the outside, began to come up and beat Kenner's dog for second by a nose.

Kenner saw nothing but the dogs during the thirty seconds the race consumed. When the dogs crossed the finish line, he slammed his hand down on the table, yelling, "Goddamn it!"

He had forgotten all about Rea and Duane and Winston and the redhead. Which is why Kenner went to the track: he would forget, forget about everything else. "Class on the inside," he ruefully repeated to himself.

"You didn't bet the one?" Rea asked, hearing him mutter.

He shook his head and, for the first time, noticed that on her racing sheet the one was heavily circled.

"His biorhythm showed him a triple high," Winston said. The buxom redhead was squealing with delight as she went down to cash Winston's tickets when the prices appeared on the tote board.

Kenner had a hundred dollars with him to bet. A few years ago that would have been more than a month's rent. His old slum apartment between avenues B and C, not the new slum apartment on Charles Street he was thinking of giving up, had been seventy-five dollars a month. Kenner had worked too many years for so-many-dollars per hour: that, he knew, was the most dreary of calculations, and the one that persists. How many hours did you have to work to buy it?

Kenner owned nothing except a battered sixty-eight Plymouth Sport Fury that he had bought for two-hundred-and-fifty dollars, a junk-dealer's price. It amazed him by getting all the way to Key West, burning a quart of oil every two hundred miles; only the muffler fell off enroute, and Kenner had been able to jerry-rig it.

Kenner could not afford to lose gracefully the hundred dollars. BET WITH YOUR HEAD, NOT OVER IT, he recalled from the small type of OTB advertisements in New York. The same sort of halfhearted injunction the Surgeon General supplies on the side of cigarette packs.

Kenner considered betting an acceptable way of taking risks; it was less dangerous to society, he thought, than reckless driving: better someone should test his nerve this way than the way some jerk in a Trans Am does before he creams a set of grandparents in the old sedan coming up over the hill.

What Kenner liked about gambling was what everyone liked: getting something for nothing. Something for nothing was the sweetest equation, he thought, since it was the simplest. There was always the aura of magic around even the most beat-up of tracks; that is what Kenner liked. They all had the atmosphere of a medieval fair: the milling crowds, the refreshment stands, the pious attention given to the event. The race. And then the trick, the magic. Two will get you four; four will get you ten; ten will get you one hundred.

Kenner won the second race, recouping most of his loss on the first, but lost the third. He won a small amount back on the fourth. But the fifth race was the sort Kenner longed for. He had fifty dollars left. Kenner had always thought that inner-city and suburban schools should substitute a race sheet for the Stanford-Binet tests and watch the inner-city scores go up and the suburban schools' decline.

You need to plot the whole race in your head, what each dog is likely to do, based on the dogs' past performances, since it is consistency that is the hallmark of dog racing. It was celestial navigation; the inside of Kenner's head for the moments he was figuring the race resembled the display boards at NORAD that track all the junk orbiting the earth.

Kenner saw the fifth race's orbits clearly; he felt that strange confidence that comes when you are sure of something that is always uncertain. The number two dog, he thought, the number two dog would win.

Rea, Kenner noticed, had made no bets, though she was figuring each race. She showed amusement at the combinations Kenner chose. "You bet like tarot card readers, crazy ladies, Ouija Board devotees," she told him, laughing and shaking her head. Kenner realized that she would only bet win, place, and show. He always hoped for long shots, a duffer's hope.

Kenner was delighted to see that the track handicapper had not selected the two dog. Kenner decided he would try to bet smart, play to win—along with wheeling the two dog on the quinella, betting it once with every other dog on the track. He spent all the money he had left, except for his change.

The two dog, National Fury, Kenner was overjoyed to see, went off at six-to-one odds. The stuffed rabbit lure came sputtering around the oval, sounding to Kenner like the Canarsie line leaving the Fourteenth Street subway station sending off celebratory bursts of blue sparks. The stuffed white bunny bounced up and down suspended at the end of the pole.

The two dog, National Fury, broke on top, just as Kenner expected he would, and took the rail. The sheet's information revealed that the two dog loved the rail. He was in the lead by four lengths heading for the first turn. A dog on the inside of the pack behind went wide, bumped another dog, causing two other dogs to stumble and collide.

Clearing the pileup on the turn was the race's longest shot, a ninety-nine-to-one dog, Claim to Fame. Kenner saw the odds on the tote board and realized with great glee that if that dog came in with his, the quinella alone would pay over two hundred dollars. National Fury, on the back stretch, was eight lengths ahead; no one would catch him. And the ninety-nine-to-one dog was far ahead of the rest of the trailing pack.

Kenner's heart was beating rapidly, and his attention was fixed on the dogs running around the sandy oval. Their positions stayed the same as National Fury made the final turn. Then, down the stretch, a hole of silence was bored through the screaming from the stands. The sparking, rumbling lure had become silent.

National Fury flew into the air, turned a spiraling cartwheel, and landed on his side. Before Kenner could completely comprehend what was happening, the next dog, the long shot, Claim to Fame, made things clear: he had been able to stop and was in the middle of the track jumping on the fake rabbit, biting at it through his muzzle. The lure had stopped, gone dead.

Kenner couldn't believe it. The lure had suddenly quit; and, before National Fury could react, the dog had struck the pole that held the fake rabbit. All the other dogs had caught up to the lure; they were yelping, hurling themselves at it, biting, snapping. The attendants who had paraded the dogs before the race ran out onto the track and began dragging them away from the tattered lure. One young man stooped, picked up National Fury where the hound lay motionless on the sand, and walked off.

In a voice laced with nonchalance, the track announcer said, "Hold all tickets. The judge has ruled a No Race. A No Race. Ticket refunds will be available at all betting windows."

"Refunds!" Kenner wailed, "Refunds! I don't want any refunds. I want my winnings. I had that race won! I can't believe it. The goddamn rabbit quit!"

Kenner knew he wasn't displaying the proper sort of insouciance. He did manage to notice, through his discontent, that Winston's party was leaving. He saw Rea wave good-bye. The others did not look back.

Kenner tried to smile and wave back, but he knew a ridiculous expression must be stamped on his face. Rea had looked at him in a manner that Kenner interpreted as fond.

The dogs had been cleared from the track, and two men were kneeling down by the mechanism that moved the lure. The track announcer intoned, "Folks, there will be a short delay before the start of the sixth race."

2

Kristina stared out the front window. The road ahead looked like a dark throat; it opened wide at the end: a reddish mouth, a way out of the cave, the last flicker of sunset. Then it closed again, became black. Finally she could see stars, and, every now and then along the road, the silver water pipe glowing like phosphorous. The air was itchy with night sounds. She turned on the radio, searching for her favorite music, and Curt grabbed her hand when she reached a news broadcast. "That must be it," he said. "Did you hear that? They killed some people." Curt seemed cheered by the news report.

"They weren't after us. They were after anyone."

Kristina looked over at Curt and was grateful. He did save them, she thought, though his actions had terrified her.

They stopped just beyond Key Largo and ate at the International House of Pancakes. Eli played with the six-pack of syrups on the table. He smeared one side of his face with strawberry flavor and the other with mint.

"Why isn't he the cute one," the waitress said, putting down plates. "He looks like a Christmas tree ornament, one of them balls."

Curt looked to Kristina as if he has just swallowed some nasty crack about the waitress's size. She was enormous.

"And he's so quiet," the woman continued. "I'd rather a kid make a mess instead of a racket, anytime."

Curt finally couldn't keep his insult down. "Why do they hire those tubs of lard? Anyone would lose their appetite," he said, watching her walk back to the kitchen.

Curt began to finish Kristina's pancakes while describing to her what it would have been like if he had had his M-16 in the car. She stared at the cut-up pieces of pancake floating in cherry syrup.

It was after midnight when they reached Bridget's trailer court on Stock Island. Pair o' Dice Park. She had tried to prepare Curt for what it would be, but his expression, as they turned into the park's driveway, worried her that she hadn't told him enough. Curt had liked the idea of going down to Key West when she had first proposed it, but now he didn't look so sure.

"It's all nicer in the daylight," she said.

When they crossed the Seven Mile Bridge, he had expressed some pleasure at the sight, what they could see, though the roadway was so narrow Curt had to look straight ahead into the oncoming traffic. He couldn't see out his shattered window, and he didn't want to lower it, fearing that it would all crumble and fall in on him.

All the trailer park's spaces had been occupied for years, and the mobile homes were long settled into their spots. Some of them had semipermanent attachments and add-ons. Vegetation had grown over and around the metal shells: flowering poinciana trees, hibiscus, lots of bougainvillea. It was kind of pretty during the day, Kristina thought; all the trailers looked, amid the flowers and vines, both out of place and familiar, like a bottle thrown in a grassy ditch alongside a road.

They parked the LeBaron by Bridget's trailer. There were no lights on within, except for a rosy glow in the rear. Bridget's Toyota was there. Kristina had a key and let them in, after knocking and calling out; no one stirred, until she pushed open the louvered door.

"Who is that?" a voice called out from the rear of the trailer.

"It's me, Mom. Krissy." The folding door beyond the kitchen galley was hastily pulled shut.

"Oh, Krissy, could you please wait outside. How about coming back in a half hour?"

"Mom," Kristina yelled back, "I've got Eli and he needs to be put to bed." Eli continued to squirm in her grip, as slippery as an armful of magazines.

"All right, all right, just wait outside for a few minutes and I'll be out."

Kristina backed out the door, saw Curt leaning against the car, his cigarette glowing bright then dull. A harbor light.

"She's there, but she's not alone, I guess."

"You guessed right," Curt said. The trailer door had opened and an old man stumbled out. One pant leg was clasped by the elastic of his sock. Pleats of hair that should have been lying down across a bald spot stood up stiff on one side, like the crown of a bird, quail's feathers. He limped off down the gravel walk, and Kristina pushed open the door again, carrying Eli cradled in one arm, his head hanging back over her shoulder. Curt followed.

"Well, hi, Mom," she said to Bridget, who was standing in the kitchen in a Chinese robe, "this is my friend Curt."

"Hello, ma'am," Curt said. Kristina saw him look at her mother with an expression she recognized. His eyes dropped down to her feet and stayed there and Kristina looked too. Her mother had four-inch high-heeled black shoes on and black hose. Her robe stopped at the edge of her ass.

"Nice to meet ya," Curt drawled.

"Kris, why didn't you call me, honey, tell me you'd be get-

62

ting here tonight?" She reached out for Eli and Kristina was glad to hand him over.

"I sent you a card, Mom. Oh, Mom, it doesn't matter. We were almost killed, Mom! First the plane caught on fire and then we were in a riot. Haven't you been watching TV? I bet it's on television right now."

Kristina's voice was full of pride; the day seemed full of accomplishments.

"Tell me in the morning, Krissy. Just let us find a place for you all to sleep. I've been very busy tonight," she said. Eli began to cry, and she gave him back to Kristina. Bridget began to lift the orange plush cushions off the hide-a-bed couch.

"Aw, Mom," Kristina said. Curt stared at Bridget's bent-over behind, as if he had never seen black panties and garters like hers on a living person before. Eli continued to whimper on Kristina's shoulder, and, while rubbing his back gently, Kristina went to look for something she could put Eli in for the night.

Seven

On Rea Kramer's first day of work after she had returned to New England from the West Coast, a horse was put down. The stable's owners had been constructing a new corral, but hadn't yet put a fence around an embankment they had created. There was a steep incline there and the horses stayed away, except for a fresh arrival who had been chased by an older stud over its edge. The two-year-old had run down the incline and at the bottom, not able to stop, stepped in a hole, snapped its right front leg below the knee, and plummeted headlong into the creek that ran behind the stables. The creek, a stream at this point, fed the campus's two lakes.

Rea arrived just as the sheriff's car did, and she followed the young officer and the stable manager across the corral, now emptied of horses, down the same steep path the horse took, the embankment made of freshly bulldozed soil and rock and sand. They went through a thicket and reached the stream where the horse lay, his body more than half submerged. He raised his head, just his nose, out of the water in order to breathe, though he made no effort to rise. The cannon bones beneath the knee

64

were broken in two, but skin still joined the limb to the rest of the body. Hoof and bone floated, independently, in the direction of the current.

Rea had stopped when she saw the horse; the two men walked down to it. The stable manager said a few words to the officer and walked off alongside the stream, back to the stables. He was dressed half-English, half-Western, divided at the waist. Jodhpurs and high boots, and a gingham shirt with pearl buttons, pocket flaps cut in the shape of a W, like the simplest pencil drawing of a flying bird.

The officer took out his revolver. One shot, to the side of the horse's ear. The horse didn't move. Rea reached the edge of the creek and gazed down at the horse: now completely submerged, the horse looked, to her, like a prehistoric fish.

Blood seeped from the break, the bones white and splintered. The horse's eye was staring, but was somehow extinguished: it was as dull as a cap on a jar. The horse's lips were pulled back, doubtless in pain, she thought. The teeth looked petrified, wooden, yellow, scored. They were clamped together.

There was no blood coming from the gunshot wound; in fact, it was hard to locate: it appeared a small drain, water flowing into it, a new eddy in the creek. The hair around the rim of the wound was slick: it had become another sort of primitive ear. Blood flowed from beneath the head. The wound must be larger there, she knew. It was a large gun, a long barrel, blue-gray, its cylinder as blunt as a turbine's.

The officer was stroking the horse's face, which was as hard and narrow as a walnut banister. Rea said, "I'm sorry for you," seeing he was not pleased with what he had done.

"Is this the first time you have had to do this?"

"I had to shoot a cow, once," he said, softly. "Dogs."

It seemed as if he intended to remain a long time. Rea walked back up the embankment to report to work.

She didn't last long at the job. Rea didn't warm to the young women. They were too familiar, too spoiled, and so she moved on. Rea found that jobs tended to flow into one another, if you stayed within the same system. If you really want to change, you have to pluck yourself out of the river and trek across the mountains. Rea let herself drift along the animal tributaries, and one stable led to another, except that there was more life in the next. She found work as general help at a breeding stable.

Rea saw her first colt born shortly after she started: it slid out, hooves first, as if it had been leaping in a dream, leaping, its head tucked in the furrow its front legs made. She helped take it out of its bluish sack. The colt was on its feet sooner than she ever imagined a newborn could be. The woman who ran the stable had already begun to predict the colt's future, reading his fate by the size and conformation of his parts.

Most of Rea's time, other than feeding and mucking stalls, was spent helping to inseminate the mares. There was a stud of some winning history and lineage. A few mares were boarded at the farm until they were pregnant; some until they foaled.

The stud was kept outside in his own corral; then he would be brought into the barn to tease the mares. He would be put in a stall, and one by one the mares would be brought into the stall next to his. They would excite the stud and, at the same time, reveal just how deeply they were in heat.

The collection of mares ran the gamut of sexual interest. Some fastened themselves in disdain to the opposite side of the stall; others, though not truly in heat, would sidle up to the stud and whinny; others stayed quiet. One seemed determinedly direct, touching the stud's nose in a friendly fashion with her own; another was a violent mixture of fear and desire.

Individual mares would display heat more than others, and the manifestations would vary. Tails would raise, unveiling sexual parts. The owner called it *winking*. Rea thought *winking* a nickname till she saw that the word described the action perfectly. Some mares would do it slightly, the lips of the vagina parting once, twice, a gesture that throughout nature is taken for invitation; a movement mirrored even by someone's hands when beckoning, a cupping gesture. Just as an open door entices, there is little resisting such shapes and motions.

Some of the mares would open wide, frantically, pulsate, showing the hidden spectrum of their organs, reds and purples. The hides of their rumps looked to Rea as smooth and strong as moss-covered rocks; they were all cleft with this soft division: the opening of the genital was pendant-shaped, and it had the length and grace of long cut-glass hangings of ballroom chandeliers. At its lower end, a seemingly perfect point, one mare secreted a clear stream.

The stud would be milked once a day; at times he would appear less interested than the owner wished. His organ would emerge, but then droop, in a curve of disappointment. Rea wondered if that downward path always represented depression.

66

There were a couple of mares the stud obviously preferred, and, pathetically, some of those who were most interested in him he seemed particularly to ignore. Rea tried to discover his criteria, what flaw one mare showed, what bit of charm another possessed, but she couldn't find it. After six mares, one by one, had been taken into the stall to tease the stud, two things were clear to Rea and her boss: which mares excited him the most and which of the six mares were ready themselves to be inseminated. They were not necessarily the same.

Rea had been shown how to do the procedures: readying the artificial vagina, "or 'AV,' as we call it," her boss said, adding her own wink. The AV had something of the inner tuber about it; it was rubber, a rose color, between orange and brown, and held water. There was a spout.

"Warm water," her boss said, and the temperature needed to be right, neither too hot nor too cold.

"Certainly not tepid," her boss instructed. "But you don't want to fry him either."

The shape of the uninflated AV was that of a soft rifle case, a bit over three feet long. It tapered to one end, where a removable receptacle was attached, similar to a condom, Rea noted, but much tougher. The collected sperm could be refrigerated and used later, but they usually did the whole job, collect and inseminate, as quickly as possible. Retrieve and insert.

Rea's boss lathered the inside of the AV with KY jelly, which she purchased by the case at a drugstore in the local mall; the manager had been amazed at the quantities she ordered until she told him why she needed it. It was cheaper than ordering through a veterinarian supply.

The woman had been pleased to hire Rea, though she still had male hands assisting her, working the farm. Rea wondered about the woman; she was only around ten years older than herself. But the male hands were all farm boys from birth, so this pullulating business probably did not arouse them especially. Though when she and Rea worked together, both women's expressions turned wry.

Her boss had taken a course in artificial insemination one summer at the nearby state "ag" college; she was now quite expert at it. At first the farm had seemed a wealthy couple's hobby, but her boss had made it into a going concern. Her husband already owned one: a glass company.

Rea thought there was something incongruous about the look

of the medical supplies, the discarded pipettes, syringes, gloves, strewn about the barn floor, as if battles were taking place elsewhere and the barn had been commandeered as a field hospital.

When the AV was ready and the other instruments prepared, they brought the mare that excited the stud the most back into the teasing stall once again. The mare hadn't shown much interest, but the stud quickly began to kick, to whinny, to show his teeth. The mare finally did turn her haunches toward him and raise her tail. It was an elegant gesture, Rea thought: the tail made a waterfall turned upside down. Her jobs had already provided her with a number of animal poems; she thought she would soon have enough for a small volume of them.

"Now we can begin," her boss said. "Lead her out."

Rea took the mare and walked by the stud's stall and through a doorway and into another stall that was closed and out of sight. Her boss led the stud through the same doorway, but out through another door into part of the barn where a false mare had been built.

The false mare was a solid piece of construction. It jutted out from a wall, was about ten feet long, and was covered with old mattresses. Only its shape resembled anything like a mare. The black stallion was wild-eyed from the teasing, and Rea's boss led him in a semicircle to the false mare, which, much to Rea's surprise, he quickly mounted. The stud came down on it so hard that she feared for his safety, to say nothing of the mare's, if it had been a real horse.

The stud's penis was hanging to one side, long and black, faintly veined; its tip was rather unshaped, blunted, on a slant, like the end of a long ax handle. The tip was slightly puckered, resembling the bottom of an apple.

Rea was to have her first go at administering the AV, which she cradled in her arms. The surprising violence of the horse's mounting had startled her momentarily. She stood staring, until her boss yelled, "Now, now, before he loses it."

The AV was much easier to slide on than she thought it would be, but holding it on was another matter altogether. With both arms wrapped around it, she discovered that she actually was part of the AV itself. Without someone holding it, the AV would be a rather dismal device.

The stud lifted Rea up. She resisted and moved with him, till her face and shoulder were up against his side. His hide, sweat, and smell pressed around her like a membrane itself. She felt in him as much as he was in her. The odors were familiar from the farm, but now were more powerful, distilled: an extract.

She felt herself later to be a matador, between the horns with her sword, but now she was taken up by the force she was both confronting and exerting. This must be how it is to hold onto a firehose whipping with hundreds of pounds of pressure.

Under her armpit and throughout her arms and chest, she felt him release. His tension vanished and for a second she thought, pushing as she still was, she would hurt him; but he slumped, still on the mount, legs dangling, his energy now transformed into enormous weight. She felt it all around her. From where she was she felt sensations of claustrophobia, as if, half beneath him, she was in a tunnel and was now worried about its collapsing on her.

"Take it off. Take it off," her boss was yelling, breaking the spell. Rea did, but, as she retreated a few steps back, she did not realize how she was holding the AV.

"Hold it up, hold it upright!" her boss commanded.

The stud's penis was already retracting, but a goodly length still remained, glistening from the KY jelly and dripping. He then thrust himself up and off the false mare, looking more confused, Rea thought, than anything else. Her boss led the horse outside.

"Aren't you glad it's slam-bam-thank-you-ma'am?" her boss said, returning. "Think if he wanted to do it for fun. Think if he had read *The Joy of Sex!*"

The mares were simpler. They had been prepared at the other end of the barn. Their parts had been washed, and their tails tied up, braided with muslin so they would not get in the way if they switched. The tails now looked like baseball bats, handles crisscrossed with tape.

A pipette was attached to a large hypodermic syringe; the pipette, a catheter, would be filled with the stud's sperm and injected. The seminal fluid could have been human for the look of it, but the great gouts that had been collected would be more than sufficient for the four mares they were going to do. Rea's boss would do the inseminating; Rea needed to see it done, assist her a few times, before she could attempt it. The procedure with the stud was coarser, but difficult to get wrong; the female end was fraught with more potential problems.

The lower part of her boss's arm was about as long as the

69

stud's penis. Rea thought this was why many animals could be dominated by man, because man's limbs could double as animals' sexual parts. Man could intrude sexually on almost any species by now. First farm animals, then a single cell.

The mare's cervix would be dilated. It could be felt, a bit like a good-sized plum, toward the end of the mare's birth canal. Rea's own cervix, what she could feel, was more like the tip of a small thumb. The catheter would be inserted, though not deeply, through the os of the cervix.

"It would help, in the procedure, to be ambidextrous," her boss said, "but I've taught myself how to use my left hand with some agility." Cows, she told Rea, were easier to inseminate than horses. "You put these gloves on both hands, up past the elbows, and you stick one hand and arm through the cow's anus and the other into the vagina. They run parallel. You can reach down with the hand above and hold the cervix. That makes it relatively easy to insert."

With a horse, though, Rea saw, only a single intrusion was made; the manipulations were more delicate and difficult. If the mare was well in heat and the cervix completely open, then the insertion was done fairly easily. Each mare would be inseminated more than once, risking trouble, spontaneous abortion—except if the cervix was closed.

The mares stood with more patience than Rea could imagine. They didn't kick. Her boss's arm would disappear; both the mare's eyes and her boss's would drift into different sorts of concentration. Her right hand would depress the syringe's plunger and the sperm would be introduced. Her gloved arm would pull out, glistening.

One mare took longer to inseminate; her boss's left arm and hand adjusting within, turing back and forth slowly: safecracking. Done, she pulled out, and her arm was followed by a cataract of yellowish opaque fluid, a soup that splashed Rea's and her boss's feet.

She peeled the long slickened glove off her arm and hand.

"Don't tell me she wasn't enjoying that," her boss said and grinned.

2

Duane Rooks's father tried to teach him the value of a dollar, but he didn't bother to show him many ways to earn one. Duane

70

never asked his father much, though he did have a few questions. Once, when he was about six, he crept into his parents' bedroom and got into bed with them. His father stirred, and before Duane fell back to sleep he felt his father's hand fall upon him as if he was looking for something in the dark. He picked up Duane's small penis and moved it around, and Duane, for a moment frozen awake, didn't know what he was doing. The old man stopped, but Duane didn't sneak into their bedroom at night anymore, even when he really felt scared.

Duane at fourteen stole a pint of his father's rye and went to the house of a girl who lived alone with her mother. The girl's name was Cindy, but he couldn't remember the mother's name. But the mother was there and had some of the rye and suggested that he and Cindy dance. She put a record on, some dance music, as she called it, that Duane hadn't heard except in the movies. The mother rolled back the front room's rug and mixed his father's rye in ginger ale and gave them all paper cups full.

Duane danced with Cindy, who was about his height and had hard little breasts. The floor they danced on, Duane remembered, was warped. An amusement park roll, some ride. Cindy's mother was standing in the shadows (she had turned all the lights out except for one that sent a scallop of yellow up a rust-streaked wall); she came up and put her arms around both of them while they danced, and she whispered in Duane's ear, "Don't you get a thrill when you dance close? Doesn't a thrill just run up and down your spine?"

Duane hadn't known any other mothers like Cindy's mother, though some aunts had acted this way with him. Then she pushed Cindy away and danced with him alone. Her body pressing into Duane's was full and smelled not of the weak citrus odor of Cindy, but of a strange collection of smells, some sweet, some damp. She was larger than Cindy, and she seemed to blot out most of the weak light in the room. She managed to move his leg in between her own and squeeze her thighs, which excited Duane as much as it surprised him. He stiffened and knew his hard-on would be easily felt. She spun him around and then found his leg again and began to press up and down on it; Duane felt he was going to spray against himself any minute.

She abruptly backed off and, twirling around, said, "Isn't it thrilling?" Duane couldn't guess her age; she wore what he had heard his mother call a housedress. Cindy was standing in a corner, one hand up at her mouth.

71

Duane went over one night he knew Cindy's mom was out; and though Cindy wouldn't take him into the bedroom, she did lie down on the couch. Its cover was as stiff as a hairbrush. Duane got her blouse and skirt off and finally her brassiere; her breasts were small, tight as a fist, and one had an oddly shaped nipple, though he couldn't see too well in the dark room. Cindy had kept murmuring no, no, but she let him pull down her panties, though she wouldn't spread her legs. No, no, she'd say, but she really didn't try to stop him much, he thought; she just wasn't helping. He held her arms back by her thin wrists. For a second he had the funny thought holding her bony wrists that they were like his holding his own stiff prick. Cindy wasn't yelling, just saying no, no, softly, don't; and he hooked his knee above hers, into a soft place on her thigh, and worked it down, like you open an oyster shell with a knife, and when he got bone to bone, he was able to pry her open. He had taken off everything but his T-shirt. He forced himself into her; she was hardly wet, and inside her his prick felt like his finger did, rubbing the thin mist off a windowpane, drops on a rainslicker, but he forced his way in an inch or two. She had turned her head, he now saw; his attention had been fixed below, and her eyes were shut and tears rolled down her cheek. He came and it felt hot, too close to pain to be really pleasure; he slid down beside her and she did not complain, or say anything, so he didn't imagine he had done anything he wasn't meant to.

Even though there were a couple of neighborhood guys his own age, Duane found himself spending most of his time with older boys who had cars, liquor, and talked about women and would show him magazines full of beaver shots, women down on all fours. Duane was struck by the fact that the men in the pictures were hairy all over: he was not.

He kept a job for over a month that his old man had gotten him at an industrial supply house in Dorchester. He got fired for talking too much to a stock clerk named Ronnie. "After you're gone," the warehouse manager told Duane, "instead of having two fuck-offs, we'll have one guy who will get some work done." Ronnie had been there for fourteen years; he advised Duane to go to Hollywood to seek his fortune, become an actor.

Ronnie had been taking courses through the mail to learn how to become a piano tuner. He had already received one diploma, which he had taped into an oversized frame he had found broken behind the warehouse. The tuning equipment he had purchased from the school was spread out over his rented room: silver tuning forks, tiny hammers, a heavy case lined with purple velveteen. Ronnie had had moved in an upright piano he had gotten from a woman who moved out of an apartment on the same floor of the hotel. That had led to the tuning lessons. The piano was taken apart, exposed. The instruction book compared the piano a student worked on to a corpse medical students dissected, Duane saw, thumbing through the leaflet. Ronnie worked on the piano for weeks, though Duane never thought it sounded right.

"I lack a natural ear for the work," Ronnie said, "but the company said it wouldn't be a hindrance to my success."

Duane began hanging out with some other people, North End Italians, and Ronnie disappeared from his job and the hotel. Duane tried to find him. No one knew where he had gone. Ronnie was the one person of those years that Duane never thought of with resentment.

One of his North End friends was an artist named Roy D'Angelo. Roy painted three pictures at a time on masonite, then sawed them apart with a scroll saw and sold them to an art gallery on Boylston Street. Duane had to laugh when he found out in the can from Winston that it was the same gallery that had got Winston arrested. Roy also dealt dope and often did both the same day. He was a hard worker. He lived in a factory building. His place was smaller than Duane thought it would be, considering the size of the building. A rock band lived a floor below.

Bookshelves, two fish tanks, a bed in the corner. Above the bed were cut-out photographs, nudes, breasts, vaginas, black garters.

Duane helped Roy frame his paintings. Roy was painting rabbis then. He could never find his hammer and his nails. He found a wooden mallet, but threw it down. "Shit, this thing's no good," Roy yelled, exasperated spit on his lip. "Why can't I ever have the right tools?" Roy's paintings were stacked against the walls; three identical subjects on each panel. More rabbis. Bunches of flowers. All of them finished with a high gloss; Duane sometimes did that job, spraying them with a can of varnish. The frames were wide and fancy, HECHO EN MEXICO burnt into their backs.

They managed to get two pictures framed and Roy said, "Let's split." He shut off the light, leaving only the fish tanks glowing: seaweed, plaster castles, large goldfish circulating.

Roy had actually been to India, an unbelievable place to Duane; Roy had just up and gone. He now had somebody who would send him hashish straight through the mails.

"I only wanted to make back what I spent and pay for the trip. But I got so much I had to find somebody who could handle it. Louie told me about this dame and I gave it to her. But I haven't got any money yet. The last time I went over there she got hysterical, yelling, 'Take the kids, take the kids, hold one for ransom. You'll get your money.'"

They got to the top floor of a tenement in Roxbury. Duane thought it smelled like a chicken house as they waited under a skylight in the hallway.

A tiny voice asked, "Who is it?"

"Roy. Roy D'Angelo."

"Ma. It's Roy . . ."

"Let him in, David."

Duane was surprised to see the apartment's hallway deserted after the door cracked open. There were clothes all over the floor, pants, underwear, shirts. A mouse fur odor dropped around Duane. Where the hallway came to a point made by two doorways, he saw a pair of bare feet. Roy walked toward that room.

"Hello, Olivia."

Duane listened for a while to their conversation. The woman spoke in what sounded to Duane like a foreign accent. "Our men were killed by the local mafioso in Taxco . . ."

What Duane thought were stains on the walls he now saw were cockroaches; they started moving. A procession traveled across a molding high on the wall. They looked to Duane like the Zulus on a mountain ridge in a movie he had seen.

Duane looked into the room and saw the woman, Olivia, on a bed. She didn't look too old to him, but a pair of false teeth were in a Hires root beer mug on a chair next to the bed.

Duane's presence didn't interrupt her. "Now this bitch wants to try to take my kids away from me, but she's a speed freak and we can prove it. Our lawyer . . ."

Duane noticed a cat walking along the tops of books; one stack tumbled beneath it. The cat screeched and the woman shrieked: "Josephine, get this cat out of here!"

A door opened and a perfectly naked little girl, around six years old, entered. Duane stared. Red hair, her skin the color of new plaster, light orange freckles; her nipples were orange, too, Duane saw. She collected the cat, left the door open, and re-

74

turned to a room where other redheads sat before a television set, all on a small mattress, ribbons of a sheet entwined between them. The TV was a large, old console model. From where he stood Duane could see most of its back, broad and blank as the rear of a theater building.

"My connection took some concoction of his own making, the whole alphabet, and we haven't seen him since Tuesday."

Duane realized that what Olivia was lying on was two baby blue leatherette couches pushed together, covered with an old table cloth, one with a lacy pattern. A long purple coat was pulled up to her chin.

"I've had this damn cold for a week and it's left me helpless. Been taking this foul cough medicine. Of all the stuff I've swallowed, this stuff's the worst."

Olivia licked both sides of a spoon.

"David, get me some water!"

Duane felt agitated, itchy, but there was a lot to look at. Except for being male, David was the duplicate of his sister.

"The kids are doing well in school. They even like it, so the whore-cunt-mother-in-law can't get any authorities after me. She's the most hysterical bitch. She's crazy to think she can get custody. If the Law thinks this is bad they should see the outback where I grew up."

All the while the smallest girl child had been tying a string to the doorknob of the room in which her sisters and brothers looked at television. She pretended to be holding the door shut with the string. She smiled at Duane, making him an accomplice in her play entrapment of them. Duane continued to stare at her. She looked very clean. Her cunt was hairless, the flesh split like the nib of an old-fashioned pen.

"There's no good grass to be had these days. We still haven't reestablished contacts in Mexico. There's smack, pills, and hash like yours, but no good grass."

The door the young girl pretended to hold shut with the taut string opened, and she, a fish arching out of water on a line, lunged forward and hit her head on the doorknob. Duane reached out to grab her and she let out a wail, the first sound any of the children had made since Duane and Roy arrived. Duane was surprised by the feel of the child's shoulder under his hand: it felt like a warm loaf of bread. Quickly the other children surrounded her, summoned by her cry, four redheads, their hair tight coiled springs. They tended to her whimpering.

"What is she screaming for? Tell her to stop screaming. Stop your yelling."

Duane flushed, turned and screamed at Olivia, "You fucking bitch," and leapt onto the baby blue leatherette. One knee slid over the greasy surface of the leatherette and his whole weight landed on Olivia, knocking the air out of her.

Roy grabbed Duane around the neck and jerked him back. "What the fuck are you doing?!"

Duane didn't answer. He breathed heavily, and when both he and Roy stood upright Roy let him go. Olivia had one hand up on her throat and the other reached down between the bed and wall and came back up holding a gun.

"You bastards get out of here and don't ever fuckin' come back!"

"Easy, easy," Roy said, "It was a mistake, he's sorry . . . Say you're sorry, goddamn it, Duane. Take your time, Olivia. I'll wait for my money. Just take it easy."

Roy backed out of the room, pushing Duane without looking at him.

He followed Duane out the door after stopping to pick up the paintings he had left in the hallway. He yelled, going down the stairs, "What are you trying to do to me, man, get me killed? You dumb fuck, if you ever pull another stunt like that . . . What the fuck got into you? Man, that wasn't cool. Dumb dumb dumb."

Duane knew Roy wanted to hit him. He could feel the heat behind his back as he bounced down the steps. Roy wanted to, but Duane was sure he wouldn't.

"Don't ever mess up on me like that again, man."

3

Rea's return to university life had little of the prodigal daughter about it. Being part of a graduate writing program left her with the thinnest of attachments to the institution. Rea was on scholarship and received monthly computer-generated checks of grant-in-aid. Though it had been coincidental and unplanned, Rea's delay in entering graduate school, her five-year hiatus, let her come back at a ripe time: women were unbearably sweet and money flew to them. It was like the heyday of the civil rights era, Rea thought, when money had been thrown at black students. Women were now the favored minority. Here, catch. Rea caught.

She was used to getting along on very little, so the sums she attracted, though not excessive, were enough.

Rea was aware that she had always seemed to be given a way out. For some of the men she had been involved with there was only a dark cul-de-sac at the end of some foreshortened canal. A doctor who examined her once had referred to her vagina as a barrel. Rea had always thought of it as a tunnel, a pathway, leading somewhere; it caused her to travel. But when the gynecologist had said "barrel," she had had the fanciful idea that it well could be a barrel. There was something about the notion that pleased her.

After five years, more or less, on the road, even Rea admitted to herself that she was tired of the vagabond life. She applied to graduate schools and was speedily accepted. She quickly regained respectability—which she always had available to her, but, with some concentrated effort, had abandoned.

At the time she began thinking of returning to school she was living with a horse trainer. He had a wonderful name, even for a horse trainer, all of whom seemed to have names as colorful as the animals they raced. Jimmy Machine. He had left a mare for insemination and after a month she went away with him, took to the circuit of country fairs and two-week racing meets. She become more interested in them than him. He began acting strangely, heard voices, attacked passersby on the street. She had moved out when his delusions had become not so much dangerous as unnerving with possibilities. Then the barn burnt, the one horse he still owned dying; and at a restaurant a week later he assaulted other diners. He was hospitalized before Rea learned of it from his mother. His mother had praised Rea for keeping her son "normal" for so long. Jimmy had been hospitalized before, Rea learned, though he had never spoken of it.

Rea visited Jimmy before she left for Boston. He recited a strange vision: he was a twin; a brother had died in his mother's womb; he was in touch with wizards; he had to attack a man who wore one red and one green sock, since that was a sign of evil. Rea might have worried in the past about how shrinks glibly diagnosed schizophrenia, but they were dead right about Jimmy.

Rea stayed away from the university's campus life. She was older than most of the other writing students, but it wasn't her age that made her aloof. She worked on her book of animal poems. She played softball on a team from a local dyke bar, a fact that left her removal from the students' social scene somewhat misinterpreted but unchallenged. She became friendly with the children who lived on her block, became known to shopkeepers. She had always been attracted to the backside—of a track, of a town.

Rea took her time, got her degree, settled into the city's life. She applied for and received a grant from the state arts council. Some of the money was tied to civic service, and in order to receive that portion she gave writing workshops in the state prison. The arts council arranged it. They had a male writer doing it, but after two visits he declined to continue, not stating his reasons. Rea volunteered after looking over the list of other organizations she could tithe her time to: suburban writing groups, nursing homes, library societies. The prison job stood out.

Rea had some prison experience. She had been in jail, albeit for forty-eight hours. She had left another man in Los Angeles, where she had gone soon after she finished college, and, walking along a highway, ineffectually hitchhiking, she had been picked up by the highway patrol. She didn't have her purse or any identification on her, and she didn't want to return to the apartment she had just run out of. She was, though she wouldn't admit it at the time, a bit plastered. It was the weekend, and she was put into Sybil Brant on a vagrancy charge. Only in California would they name a women's prison after a sybil, she thought. Monday morning the judge, an image of her Uncle Sid, said what she expected: Why is a fine young woman like you standing in front of me? Tell it to the two cops who hauled me in, she wanted to say, but she responded to the judge in a way that confirmed good home, good education, good girl.

She felt prepared to teach writing in the prison. "The convicts who will be in the workshop have been well screened," she was assured by the young woman who worked at the arts council. Rea smiled, knowing perhaps better than the expertly made-up woman across from her what sort of Swiss cheese screening those cons would have passed through.

"Well, I'm certainly pleased with your gumption," the young woman said. "Six months of every-other-week workshops will earn you the eighteen hundred dollars due on your grant." Maybe you'll discover someone with real talent."

Rea was not too pleased with the young administrator across the desk, the woman's long red nails tapping on the Formica top, dripping with polish as if they had just been lifted out of the belly of a wildebeest. Rea usually didn't dislike pretty women, unless they were especially stupid or mean. "Well, you never know where real talent will turn up."

The workshop neither surprised Rea, nor was it what she had expected.

Eight men were signed up and six came regularly. The prison was visible from a well-traveled highway. It was the dark red brick of the last century's schools and asylums, turreted on the corners, built in a series of squares. The outer square was high chain-link fence, topped with barbed wire. There were a few un-attached buildings, the warden's home among them; the road to the prison from the highway was as old as the facility. It rose and fell in a pleasing way, unlike the new highway, which was straight as a guy wire.

The inside halls of the main building seemed coarsely hy-gienic. Heavy blocks of tile from floor to ceiling, smooth concrete floors, an entry foyer covered with linoleum. It looked as if they planned to wash the whole place down with a firehose; perhaps they did, Rea thought. There was something shiplike about the prison, a lot of metal: metal doors, fittings, bars, crude latches and hatches. Like the bowels of some merchant ships, the iron bars chipped by the locks, revealing successive generations of paint. The prisoners seemed to do the maintenance, and some were always at it in the halls. The hall floors were being constantly swabbed down with mops, the sort of mop that always reminded Rea of drowned hair. Ophelia under water.

There had been a few attempts at bringing the prison up to date; Rea's presence, for one, was part of that movement. She knew she was just another version of social-worker-in-disguise. But one cosmetic change that had taken place was startling. There had been complaints that the institutional greens and grays of the cell blocks deadened the mind, damaged eyesight, and re-forms had come, but Rea thought some ironist had been in charge of them.

One cell block she walked past had been painted orange, one purple. All the colors were loud poster board shades. How could they live with that? she wondered.

On her first visit, a state official met her at the gate. He was on the governor's staff, and he oversaw such projects as the one Rea participated in. No murderers, she was told, or at least no one with sentences longer than five years yet to serve would be allowed in her class. Rea amused herself thinking of sentences five years long. She thought lifers would profit more than most from developing the habit of writing.

Walking down a hall with the dapper official, she felt herself going deeper into the prison's interior, felt it thickening around her. She passed a small room. Three walls were hung with large rings from which dangled picturesque keys of various sizes. It had a strange effect on her: she thought of herself at seven when she had seen a picture of Lourdes in *Life* magazine, of crutches covering the shrine's walls, left there, the caption read, by cured believers. She had taken the magazine to her mother for an explanation.

The official took her through two sets of sliding barred doors, then handed her over to a guard, a correctional officer. The workshops were to be held in what served as a classroom building, adjacent to the dining halls.

Rea never got used to the guards' contempt for her and all civilian do-gooders. She seldom got the same escort twice, so she couldn't make friends. Some days she would take the bus out and then just have to return.

"They're in lockup."

"There's no one free to take you in."

Rea would complain, but she knew her complaints would only make future obstacles more likely. She was finite in this system. They only needed to bother her, harass her, eliminate her, and she would run out of time, be gone. They knew that, so when they would ruin one day for her, that would be a day forever ruined.

She only got to experience, she realized, a small fraction of the control games that were played daily in the can. It was one of the true noble clichés. Prison was its own world, cellular, microcosmic.

The first session the guard had left her off in an empty room. There was a beaverboard table that served as a desk. Folding chairs. Windows began high up on the tile walls, grated on the inside, barred on the outside. Working in that room was a bit like being underwater; the light always changed high above you.

Rea sat on the table in front of the empty chairs. A side door opened and men began to file in, like a jury coming back with its verdict, happy to be convicting someone. Rea watched them move to seats, mark out territories, react to her. Walking through the last corridor a chorus of Hey Mamas, and more direct salutations, had followed her: Suck it darlin'. The guard had worn his representation of a smile. Because her father was a lawyer, Rea felt, she always had a cozy familiarity with the law. As she would have had with lions if he had been a lion tamer.

The men who filed in had touches of individuality about their dress; more progressive improvements, she surmised, like the orange walls. A red western neckerchief twisted as a head-band around a shock of hair. Some sleeves rolled, some jean bottoms turned up, different styles of buttoning. Two blacks, one short and slight, the other beefy and bald. They all formed an odd seating pattern; she would have to try to gather them together, have them use the table. Some brought papers with them, some pads; she remembered she wasn't the first writer they had met.

There was one older man, much older than the rest. A narrow alcoholic face, crumpled inward. There was a tall young man, with patrician features, blond hair, who could have well been one of her graduate student classmates. She looked down the list the last writing teacher had provided of the men that were signed up for the workshop. His name should stand out, the way he did. This has to be it, she thought to herself, considering what little she had to consider. Jay Kennedy. Jay Winston Kennedy, at that.

Eight

"Well, you've seen me at my worst," Kenner said to Rea as she walked by. Rea paused and looked down at Kenner lying on the chaise longue.

"I doubt that," she said; then, as if she just recalled his name, she added, "Kenner."

He realized that though he had spoken with Rea at the dog track and seen her come and go at a distance, he still knew nothing about her, no facts. Rea was thin, about his height, which made him, not her, short. He guessed they were the same age. Rea wore a two-piece bathing suit and her lean body sported two mean scars: one at the shoulder joint, which looked deliberate, and an abdominal scar, some teenage crisis, since the scar was wide, spread, and looked unplanned. She appeared to Kenner like a hard piece of wood, a balustrade, that has been somewhat distressed.

Rea didn't seem to him like a woman who figured her looks were going to abet her life. He watched her jump into the pool and begin to swim laps. After ten Kenner stopped counting. He figured it was energy, doubtless a variety of kinds, that Rea had decided was to be her life's chariot.

Kenner listened to the portable radio he had brought down to the pool: he tried to find a news report and then settled for a while on the Cuban station, the only one in the radio's hundred-mile radius that broadcast classical music. The symphonies were played by Soviet-bloc orchestras. They sounded as if they had all been recorded in a huge, echoing airplane hangar with a single small microphone.

He turned the dial and ran through the familiar weird spectrum: revivalism and manic sales pitches, all sounding the same. He stopped at the sound of some music—not top forty, not disco, Kenner knew it had a name, but he did not know it—and read the *Miami Herald*.

The front page was covered with ash: riots in Miami, some neighborhood called Liberty City. Kenner thought of the race riots in his youth in Chicago. Whites driving through black neighborhoods and beating on blacks. Here it was the other way around. A volcano had blown in the Northwest. Ash and death in its wake. New photos had just been released of the bodies of the dead airmen in the Iranian desert: a pilot's helmet blackened but the shape unchanged, the body scattered twigs of ash.

Kenner looked up to see Rea still swimming laps. No one was storming this courtyard. He expected to smell smoke. None of the condos' geriatric cases seemed to be planning to set sail for Cuba. He continued to read the paper, thinking: we are being overwhelmed by events. He watched Rea swim, noting her professional form. He thought he should start trying to locate the novelist he was supposed to interview. MacNaughton.

Rea lifted herself out of the pool with a practiced gymnastic maneuver. She picked up the towel she had left at the side of the pool and pulled a chaise longue next to Kenner's.

"I meant last week at the dog track" he said. "I'm at my worst at the track . . . I noticed you didn't bet."

"I understood," Rea said, drying her hair. "I bet, but not until I feel I know something about what I'm betting on. That was my first time at a dog track."

"What do you bet?"

"The flats," she said, and continued, "horses," perceiving his lack of comprehension. "I used to work at racetracks. One night I finally bet big and won a bundle. Then I lost my wallet crawling under a fence. I don't bet often, because I know how badly I take it when I lose."

Kenner knew how badly he took it, but still he bet; he was

83

trying to curb his tongue, not ask the obvious questions: who-what-when-where-why stuff. He turned anecdotal.

"I knew a woman who was taken to the track and given money to bet; she became entranced with one of the nags, loved its legs. It was a spectacular long shot and she bet a thousand dollars on it; and the horse won, but then had to be destroyed after the race. It literally had run its heart out. And she gave all her winnings away, passing them out to people leaving the track. She got her picture in the papers, was considered a wild American eccentric. This happened in England. But she never bet after that."

"Not everyone is charmed by extravagant gestures," Rea said. "Though it seems you are. I don't even like sunsets."

"Well, she was young."

"And you were in love with her."

"Not really. It's just a story."

"There are plenty of those."

"What's yours?" he asked.

"Can't you guess?"

"I didn't think sunset-haters were supposed to be coy."

"Okay."

"Where did you meet Winston?" Kenner asked.

"Winston? Oh, you mean Jay. Jay Winston Kennedy."

"Kennedy? What's that, his stepfather's name? His mother must have married again. I always knew him as Cross, Winston Cross."

"I thought you were his friend."

"Boyhood. And I knew him for a bit in college. I haven't seen him in ten years."

"I wouldn't have thought you were a Yalie."

"I'm not," Kenner said, momentarily derailed. "At a college in the Midwest. It looks like Winston, I mean, old Jay, went to a lot of schools. Where did you meet him?"

"In Massachusetts. He was my student."

"Of what?"

"Creative writing."

"Oh," Kenner said, unable to suppress a laugh. "Was he any good?"

It looked to Kenner as if Rea was thinking seriously about the question, not willing to give him a flip answer.

"Well, he wrote one arresting story. About going to London to play the saxophone. It was an interesting story. But it came out rather flat on the page."

"Do you write yourself?"

"Poetry."

"I don't know much about contemporary poetry," Kenner said. "I couldn't begin to tell you who the best living poets are."

"Or the best dogs," Rea said, laughing.

Kenner shook his head, looked contrite.

"Do you think Winston's really the illegitimate son of JFK?"

"The what!?" Kenner said. Was *that* the story?

Rea grinned. "I don't believe it either, but that's what he tells people."

2

Duane stole five cars before he was caught the first time. He had taken a four-door, dark green Jaguar sedan from the alley behind a store where the owner parked it daily. Duane had the car for a day and a night. He had pulled over when the Jag became full of blue swirling light from the patrol car. He didn't try to run. He was thrown into a paddy wagon for a trip downtown. It had begun to rain. The raindrops on the paddy wagon sounded like cloth-covered hammers striking vibes. Duane's back was bent, sitting along a bench bolted to the wall of the vehicle. The inside was built so it forced you into that position, bent forward, some attitude of dejection, remorse. The paddy wagon stopped. The back doors were opened and a man was thrown in. He was about Duane's age. His pants were hitched up high, held by a thin silver belt, chewed at its end, turning around on itself like a dog biting fleas. He wore a crinkly see-through shirt, turquoise blue.

"I'm no criminal," he was saying. "They can't put me away."

He began to grab his head in his hands and pull at it, then let go, as if he were trying unsuccessfully to pick up something much too heavy.

"I'm no criminal." He started to sob.

Through the steel mesh covering the rear windows, Duane saw them pull into a cement garage, gray as a bad tooth. Duane and the other man were taken to an elevator; Duane had decided the guy with the silver belt was some sort of punk and he stepped closer to the cop. The elevator was split in two by a metal fence; Duane and the sobber were put behind it. Duane, in the bright light, could see a peach-stone-sized bump rise on the man's forehead.

The cops didn't take much notice of them. Duane figured they just weren't the kind of guys that interested cops. Duane

85

and his companion weren't exuding an air of menace; they were small-timers. Zeros.

The elevator opened and three young blacks and two cops were about to get in as they stepped off. The sobber stopped moaning and stepped back onto the elevator with the new load going down. The cop that rode up pulled him off. The boy began to moan again and fell to the floor.

"I'm no criminal . . . You can't arrest me. I didn't do anything."

"Now stand up there, buddy," the cop yelled, "or I'll really rock you to sleep."

Duane stood for a while watching the police joke with one another, through bars that separated the hallway elevator from the booking room. They put their guns in metal lockers attached to the wall. One cop held up a black can of Mace and threatened to spray it on another. There was a long buzz and the booking-room door swung open.

"Has this man been frisked?" Duane nodded yes, but he was frisked again. The room looked like what he imagined a bank in Russia would look like, Duane thought: teller windows, evil lighting, bruised desks, sick paint, a lot of glum people doing paperwork.

They filled out a yellow sheet and he was taken to be fingerprinted. A cop not that much older than Duane did the job. He inked a metal plate with a hard rubber roller. He pressed Duane's fingers onto a stiff white card after he had rolled each one individually on the plate. Duane did not like being handled so much. The cop did one of Duane's fingers twice. How could anyone be so stupid? he wondered. The officer noticed it when he came to the end of five squares and still had Duane's little finger yet to do.

"Damn you," the young cop said and twisted Duane's hand, trying to hurt it. Duane's hand jerked into a fist, and before he thought about it, he had hit the cop in the face, and then the light in the room went out as Duane crumpled under the pile of bodies that covered him.

3

Saperstein had been a little too optimistic about *Centipede's* rates; they would pay only eight hundred dollars. Kenner couldn't believe anyone would name a magazine *Centipede*. It smacked of the editor's rich-boy indulgence. Maybe, he thought, the young man wanted the name to stick in his daddy's craw. Eight hundred, and a hundred-dollar kill fee.

Well, Kenner hoped, he could get it done in a week; it wasn't a crime to earn some money while on vacation. MacNaughton had made a splash with his first novel when he was twenty-eight; his second, following quickly, was also well received. And then, a few years later, browsing on a remainder table, Kenner had come across a novel of MacNaughton's that he didn't even know had been published. The next one, too. A shooting star: what you see is not the rise, but its fall. MacNaughton seemed to have courted fame and obscurity with equal success. The rich-boy editor of *Centipede* wanted to resurrect him; MacNaughton's first novel, *Famine's Feast,* was set in the editor's hometown, and the plot made much use of a pet pony, yet another coincidence with the editor's own boyhood.

Most of this he had learned from Saperstein. Kenner now regretted not buying the remainder novels; but, he presumed, the local library must have copies.

MacNaughton was not quite ten years older than he was, but Kenner considered MacNaughton's an odd generation. Too young for Korea and over draft age for Vietnam. Its men reached their manhood in a gap of peace and it left them all a little violence starved. They took it out on the wildlife and each other. Some of their writing had been smelling a bit gamy the last few years, lying out there baking in the desert of the feminist revival, but it still held a powerful sway in some circles, especially with older male reviewers. Kenner recalled a boyishness in the jacket photos of MacNaughton's novels, the altar boy gone bad. The brashness. Oh, they love the brash.

But, somehow, MacNaughton had lost favor, melted the wax gripping his feathers, and had plummeted to the Florida Keys. No movies were made from his books, which caused them to drop completely from sight. No niche had opened up in the popular culture for MacNaughton. The answer probably lay in between the covers of those last two remaindered novels, and Kenner would have to look for it there.

MacNaughton lived on Cudjoe Key, about a half-hour drive from Key West. Kenner enjoyed the ride: everything blue and white. In the Keys, Kenner noticed, you tended to look straight out at the horizon, because you couldn't look up for long into the brightness of noon. Heat waves shimmered around structures; even three inches of asphalt kicked them up, pulses of heat, waves in motion, bathtub currents. Kenner, even with the windows of his Sport Fury down, felt as if he were transporting heat. Another load for the frozen Northwest. He thought of himself as an ice wagon in reverse, carting blocks of fire. Even the styrofoam jacket that surrounded his can of beer had softened; it showed the imprint of Kenner's fingers. If it was this hot the end of May, what terrible heat must lie ahead?

He drove past the white onion doppler radar domes of the Boca Chica naval air station. Kenner, glancing to his right, watched a jet come in; the navy practiced simulated carrier landings at Boca Chica. The jet seemed to vibrate, as if it wanted to turn into a hummingbird and hover, instead of touching down. The plane looked as if it were about to stall, shake apart, landing so short. A Cuban defector had piloted a Mig to a Florida base, causing both joy and consternation. It had flown in undetected, under coastal radar. Kenner had heard that since that time everyone on Key West was getting fried with microwaves since the radar beams had been lowered to the horizon. There were explanations abounding, Kenner thought, for the local citizens' behavior.

A school bus painted olive drab passed him, full of Marielitos, heading for the mainland, Miami. Carter had already juiced up the military down here, instituting a new Caribbean Command, and the military presence again flourished.

The school bus's windows were full of faces, mostly male. Very few farmers, Kenner had heard, mostly city folk, were leaving Bulgaria-on-the-Gulf for Sodom-on-the-Atlantic. They looked, staring wide-eyed out the windows, like a busload of fundamentalists on a church excursion.

The first boats had come in to Pier B festooned with humanity; there was a lot of ground-kissing; ABAJO CASTRO scrawled on a piece of cardboard. *Abajo:* down. Kenner had bought a dictionary and looked it up. Down, down, down. A few were carried off on stretchers. The Freedom Flotilla. Some phrase-making leftover from the Bicentennial.

Well, Kenner thought, at least they were used to the heat. Kenner had not yet fully adjusted. Most of May had been like a midwestern August, but now the sun felt different on his skin: it did feel like radar, searching between his layers of skin for low flying Migs.

The waterpipe from the mainland ran alongside the highway. It looked to Kenner a rather honest thing, painted silver, an indicator of limitations and vulnerabilities. *Water water everywhere*, and only what comes down the pipe to drink. The local desalinization plant was always breaking down. Kenner vaguely remembered once seeing a pamphlet from the Atoms for Peace era about experiments with an atomic-powered desalinization plant at the Guantánamo Bay base in Cuba.

There was dredging along both sides of the highway, cranes creating new real estate: ground-up coral, looking like dried oatmeal, but nasty, sharp. By the highway were crusts of businesses, all rather hard-bitten establishments, the sort that catered oasislike only to passersby.

At mile marker 21 Kenner, as instructed, turned right and went along a road through what seemed more bayou than coastline. It was flat, swampy; scrubby ten-foot pine trees were enough to obliterate the horizon. He came to an intersection, a dead end, the beach road, and turned left. He went by wooden fences, more windbreaks, and came to a sign he had been told to look for. A hangman's noose, encircling an oval of wood, on which *MacNAUGHTON* was painted. There was a high cement-stuccoed block wall. Wooden gates were swung open.

Kenner was on time, but no one appeared to be at home. The house was elevated atop cement pylons. Kenner thought of egrets, the long-legged birds that would stand in the shallow water of the pond near the condo. Plump and white on their thin reedy legs.

A cement stairway ran down one side of the house, ending at a driveway. A sports car was parked under the house in a breezeway. It looked the sort you bought as a kit, an ersatz Morgan. Kenner had seen them in airports. The house was well shaded in the back; frangipani, oleander, mandevilla, some periwinkle, all in bloom. There were tall Australian pine trees, an apple blossom cassia, the usual croton bushes, bougainvillea growing on the property's wall, hibiscus.

Kenner called out, "Hello, hello," but no one answered. Kenner was taken by tropical flowers, the reds, pinks, all the body's interior, secret colors. He walked up a cement stairway, to the front of the house. The sliding glass front doors were open, their screen door shut. He looked into the room, but it was hard to see. In front of the house was more pulverized coral; water began about forty feet from the front door. Kenner, squinting, could see what looked like a reef right below the surface some hundred yards out. A channel, about twenty-feet wide, had been cut not far from the house's sawed-off beach. The water was purple there, deep, and then became turquoise, the shallow white bottom visible. Viewed from the balcony the channel appeared to be a clean cut, a surgical trench.

Kenner walked back down the cement steps and went and sat on one of the beach chairs facing the sea. The sun was broiling; the crushed coral radiated heat. Kenner felt he was on a spit.

He put down the small tape recorder that he had brought along. He had never used one before, but he had found it among the stereo equipment at the condo. He bought one blank tape and decided he was going to make the interview no more work than it had to be. In the past he had always claimed to prefer to let himself edit the way he remembered. But since MacNaughton was an author, not a politician or an activist, folk who either gave set speeches or had little idea of what they were saying, Kenner figured he might be touchy about quotations.

Kenner was thinking of checking his car for a hat, when he saw someone walking along the shoreline. Kenner knew that most book-jacket photos were almost fraudulently flattering; he presumed it was MacNaughton coming this way. When the man finally got to the front of the house, Kenner would have guessed he was in advertising, a youngish executive who had just lost his biggest account. Poplin slacks, loafers without socks, a white shirt, a chunky chain-link gold bracelet.

"Looking for someone?" the fellow asked.

"Waiting for someone," Kenner replied.

"Who?"

"Daniel MacNaughton."

The man blinked: small eyes, a small nose, small mouth—but a rather broad and fleshy face. Straw-colored hair; orange-tinted tanned skin.

"That's me."

"I thought so."

"Well, what do you want?"

Kenner stood up, thinking that their exchanges had become a bit too much O.K. Corral-ish and extended his hand.

"I'm J. P. Kenner. I'm doing the piece on you for *Centipede*," he said, wincing a bit at the name. "I talked with someone here the other day to set this up. I thought it was you."

"It wasn't."

MacNaughton did look like he might know who it was. Kenner also let fly the thought that it had been MacNaughton on the phone and he was choosing not to recall.

"If you have an hour to spare," Kenner said, gesturing to the tape recorder stuck in the coral dust.

"Why do you want to interview me?"

Kenner swallowed his first answer: I don't want to interview you; *Centipede* wants you interviewed. But he saw his eight hundred dollars blowing out to sea and replied, "You're of interest. My editor admires you and he thinks his readership would too."

It was one of the things about this work Kenner hated: at least politicians wanted to talk to you. Intruding, trying to wedge yourself into someone else's life, unbeckoned, so displeased him that it had cost Kenner many assignments.

The man he had talked to on the phone sounded happy enough to be approached. Kenner tried to remember the conversation, sifted through it for traces of irony or imposture.

The distress that occupied MacNaughton's face had not entirely left. MacNaughton looked somewhere over Kenner's shoulder, up toward the house, and said, with an odd note of defeat, "All right. A little conversation. What can it hurt?"

MacNaughton marched across the crushed coral to the house and Kenner followed. Kenner had a list of unfortunate statements, bad remarks, ones that made him uneasy, and "What can it hurt?" was, unfortunately, high up on that list.

4

"You have to be a millionaire to be immune in this society . . ."

MacNaughton's voice filled every room of the condo. Kenner had slipped the cassette into the condo's stereo equipment, and MacNaughton's high-pitched monologue emerged from speakers everywhere. Such amplification gave a religious cast to his voice; it came, from all appearances, from the clouds.

Kenner was having difficulties transcribing the tape; he just played it over and over.

"Everyone in New York reveres success and most books fail and most authors are not successful. Publishers treat most authors like terminal patients. They're pushed off into small rooms and everyone hopes they will die quietly and quickly. Soon they won't take your calls. The few authors that make them money they listen to. It's the neurosis that you find all through the business, a crazy mixture of sycophancy and dismissiveness. The few they have to butter up, the many they just sneer at and erase from their minds. To do one, they need the other. They can't act as valets to some without being executioners to others."

Kenner recalled too well the look in MacNaughton's face as he ranted on: a spaceship had just landed on Cudjoe Key and MacNaughton was bringing Kenner the news.

Before MacNaughton had begun his diatribe, he had rustled up drinks, mainly for himself, but Kenner had one too. Bitter Lemon and Jack Daniel's. MacNaughton called the mixture "a fast-food mint julep."

Though born and bred in New England, MacNaughton had lived, he said, the last six years down south. The extra flesh that encased his once athletic body did give him the look of a certain type of Southerner: Jimmy Carter's brother. Something fetal in the look, an infant grown large, but still the aspect of an infant. MacNaughton's voice caught his attention again:

"It all has to do with my theory about money. It was in my last novel, *Top Dollar*, but not bluntly stated. You read it, I presume?"

Kenner recalled, not moving his head. A journalist has three key gestures: the first two are nodding yes and nodding no, semaphores used to shunt information, but sometimes you made a mistake and everything would end up on the wrong track. The third gesture is not to move your head at all, trusting the speaker to detect the movement he wants.

Kenner regretted that he had not bought the novel when he saw it for a dollar at the Marboro on Eighth Street. The local library's copy was missing. MacNaughton's earlier novels were almost all dialogue; but his last had no paragraphs, just solid blocks of print running down the page. Oy vey, what a headache.

"You're looked upon favorably in this world depending on how much money you make for other people, not yourself. It is some powerful form of atavistic patriarchy: you have to provide for the tribe, not just yourself. Making money just for yourself will leave you still a rogue, a bandit, a stick-up man. That's what happened to me, that's why I'm on everyone's shit list, why no one reviewed the last novel."

Kenner was going to suggest that it might have been the absence of paragraphs, but he didn't. When a subject is wound

92

up, you don't need to say much; it's only when you see him winding down that you need to turn the key again.

The sun had begun to fill the room by that time with red light; outside, Kenner observed the surface of the sea was colored, as if irradiated with strips of foil: gold, silver, metallic coppers. It was difficult to look into. It wasn't the face of God, so much as the guts of a reactor.

"I made money off the first two books. The publisher cleared a little, but he didn't do as well as he hoped. They ate a lot of the paperbacks. But I lived off of movie options, got all this . . ."

MacNaughton had gestured; his arm and hand shut out the red glare for a moment, put his face in shadow.

"But they never made any movies. They just put the dough out. Then the third novel did nothing. The fourth was a clandestine affair between me and the publisher. I didn't make enough money for enough people and that's what's resented. It's the only way you keep supporters. They had hopped on the bandwagon when it seemed to be rolling, but they hopped off just as quick."

Kenner, listening to the tape, realized he had lost, or never had, control of the interview. It had begun with MacNaughton's recent history, and Kenner had a hard time trying to push it back to MacNaughton's beginnings, the early times, the good times.

"Posterity no longer counts. You've got to occupy the present consciousness. You've got to burn into its brain and then you have to grab enough to last for the rest of your days."

MacNaughton had slowed down. His eyes had darkened. His talk was full of further guttural denunciations of various cabals, critics, his ex-wife.

Kenner needed to flip the tape over. Doing so, he knew he had a dead horse to kick. *Centipede*'s youth culture audience wasn't going to want to hear this shit. Even the infatuated editor probably wouldn't want to hear it. And even to link Kenner's own name to this sour tirade was going to be another pair of cement galoshes fastened onto his freelance career. Doesn't the dude fish? Kenner hadn't been able to get MacNaughton onto other subjects. He was shocked to hear his own voice on the tape intrude into MacNaughton's spiel. Kenner had been desperate. He asked MacNaughton about people he had been associated with. But this was no less dark. MacNaughton denounced his former "good buddies" of the "I-shoot-grouse school of letters," naming all the well-known writers who had hit it big in "literature and real estate" and lived in the Keys. They had all gone on to the lotus land milk and honey of screenplays and movie directing.

"Do you realize," Kenner heard MacNaughton's voice raise itself to a jet-engine screech, "what happens when those boys get that kind of money?!"

Kenner had pictured wine-women-and-song—or, rather, cocaine, tootsies, and rock 'n' roll.

"They begin to believe they deserve it! That it was their destiny! That they were goddamn fated to become culture heroes. Not one of them thinks it was a big joke . . . And they look down at you! From Montana tax shelters. They say Danny MacNaughton just ain't got it anymore."

Kenner hadn't been able to tell if it was the sun going down, or if MacNaughton's face was actually flaming from his own furnace's stokers. Then MacNaughton had begun to decompress; he let out a lot of air and grabbed his chest and said, "I've got to take a pill," and swallowed two capsules from one of the prescription bottles on the cocktail table. Then Kenner's tape ran out.

But MacNaughton had gone on, now somewhat off the record because Kenner hadn't brought along a notebook: his divorce, the alimony, troubles with his new book, his agent neglecting him. Afterglow flared at the edge of the sea.

MacNaughton was covered with a mist of sweat: Kenner couldn't shake the notion that MacNaughton's face looked like a hamburger bun covered with a fine spray of grease.

While throwing back another Bitter Lemon and Jack Daniel's, MacNaughton began to look at him with an expression that caused Kenner distress: he decided to close up shop when he saw it. Longing, the dude is looking at me with longing, Kenner had thought.

MacNaughton had tiny teeth, what is often described as an unwholesome mouth. That's why his smile in photographs always looked cocky. The lips were always shut, pressed together. Kenner didn't consider himself a classic homophobe, though he had a number of similar prejudices; but he had overstayed his own welcome and was saying good-bye when MacNaughton suggested, "Let's go take a swim. We can go skinny-dipping."

Kenner liked to think it was not so much the invitation as the euphemism he found distasteful. Kenner declined, and as he was packing up the recorder, the screen of the sliding glass doors opened and a young man stepped in, younger than Kenner.

"Am I early?" the young man said.

"No, I'm just leaving," Kenner said. MacNaughton remained silent.

"Hey," the young man said, "if you want to make it a scene, that's all right with me." The fellow must have lifted weights. He was short, shorter than Kenner. Wearing olive drab shorts and T-shirt and heavy polished black boots and thick white socks, he looked like a mascot commando.

"That's all right," Kenner said, realizing that the bloom might have vanished from MacNaughton's literary rose because his novels *were* actually fictions. Kenner thought MacNaughton might resurrect himself if he would cleave to his current material. MacNaughton had stood silently in the dusk-filled room; a violet haze had replaced all the furnace colors of the late afternoon. He did not look embarrassed, or even bemused, but slightly baffled, as if he didn't know where he was.

Kenner signaled good-bye and went out on the porch, down the cement steps: he noticed a bicycle leaning against the railing, the young man's silent conveyance. The bike's wire basket held a towel wound tight as a bed roll. It must be something that MacNaughton is still in the thick of, all forest, no trees, Kenner thought. He pictured MacNaughton's former world now as some sort of exploded asteroid belt, all the pieces spinning about, collecting into new orbits. Kenner also had realized, going down the steps, that *Centipede*'s eight hundred bucks was not going to be a cinch to earn.

Nine

1

Duane had been released a week before Rea's prison writing class had started. An older con named Jack who taught Duane a few things about life in the can had, after Jack had impressed Rea with his manner and ideas, suggested she look up Duane on the outside, take an interest in him, perhaps be a guide to the world of privilege—as he had put it—of credentials, of certifications. As a favor, but not without curiosity, since Jack had told some interesting stories about Duane, she said she would. What was funny, she recalled, was that Jack had said he would send approving word about her *to* him, that she needed a letter of recommendation. Duane had been informed, filled in, doubtless better than she had about him. All she knew from Jack was that Duane was a young thief with higher aspirations and a sense of humor.

When Rea looked back at the men in her life, she saw they all shared one quality: they invented lives different from their backgrounds. They flew over some gulf. They weren't successors. They weren't self-made men, either, for that would imply that they had clawed their way to the top, made their mark. Most of them had, actually, been barely able to pay their way; though some of them, now departed, were doing well enough. The men whom her parents might have approved of, the chosen, she never brought home to visit. When she and Duane drove down the East Coast to the Keys, they had passed through both towns where her parents, long divorced, now lived.

She thought of the qualities Duane possessed that her father and mother might, in their own way, admire, but which would need a long incubation time to be seen: his brand of loyalty, strength, directness. Even the qualities locked within his flesh that they might applaud would only trouble them since those were just the places *she* adhered to; Rea thought about them, those sticking places. To her parents he would always remain one of the fallen. With Duane's image in front of her, as seen by others, the words she would use to describe him seemed absurd: charming, boyish, daring, willing to act; all of that attracted her—but it was his desire, his . . . well, she had only been able to think of the feelings as an image: what she felt was the same powerful emotion you would have in the middle of railroad tracks with a locomotive heading straight at you. It was concentrated.

She would have extricated herself earlier, except—well, again, there were many reasons. One was that he was, and she still smiled at her susceptibility, fun. Fun. He could have a good time as long as a car was running. And, in the beginning, he didn't interfere with what she wanted to do. It was banal, but hard to find, such a simple thing. And she had felt responsible for entangling him. She had sought him out, coaxed him into her life. Rea had never caught a fish, but she knew how she had reeled Duane in, with what lure, what bait. "You don't want to be messin' with a guy like me." A note he had left her, early on. At the time, she took it as a simple statement; only later did she begin to hear it as a threat.

The prison reform movement, like most movements Rea had been involved with, had come and gone: they were tremors, social earthquakes: a violent eruption, then a period of putting the pieces back together. Some good and some bad came when the original order was upended, before a new sort of status quo returned.

Because they were judged to have so little respect for laws, Rea was always amazed by cons' sensitivities to codes, to elegant permutations that could be detected in their perpetuation of myths: the good con, the bad con, the lame, the chump, the stand-up guy. Cons had too much respect for laws, saw them too plainly, which was why they broke them so crudely.

The men in her prison class illustrated a system so refined that, after being exposed to it for almost five months, Rea still couldn't detect it. Once it was pointed out to her she could see it. Where the pulse originated, where it came rippling through, she could see the consequences. It was like the days before she could read music. She looked at a score, all silent spots and lines, and an older woman's finger pointed to the notes being played: all of a sudden she heard. The markings on the page made sense: she could follow along.

The prison world to her seemed Ptolemaic, whereas the outside was Copernican. Concentric rings within concentric rings; man-centered, fixed, and the world of prison didn't want to hear any heresy about individual orbits. They believed in, relied on, ancient systems, tradition, immutables, not eccentric orbits.

Rea was not afraid to admit things to herself. Duane had taken her breath away; in the beginning, it had seemed to her something of a dalliance. It was strange, in many senses of the word, and would appear so to anyone who looked—except it was the strangeness that was necessary. It took her from her own world, made her think less, not of herself, but stopped her thinking, always the lure, of other worlds. He was a challenge. *He doesn't think the way I do.*

Rea read books as if they were maps: all roads, places to see, vistas, horizons, cities to explore. She could live in them. Duane lived on the streets, was all exteriors; the street corner seemed to be the only promontory that inspired him.

Rea knew how such matches were viewed. The educated woman and the untutored brute. Beauty and the beast. Well, she laughed to herself, in her case the reasonably attractive and the beast. What did people usually think first about such couples? Sex? Yes—that was what was supposed: that the man was being used, a gigolo of sorts.

Why was that decried? It was the idea of slumming, of stooping, that the woman couldn't find someone of her own, ah, class, to serve the same purpose. There the defeat hung. In the typical matches of Rea's acquaintance, you would, or could, presume that the men in nine out of ten cases were deficient in all respects, but you wouldn't know that from the surface, the look of things. There was no ambiguity in Rea's hookup with Duane. The one element stood out. Noses were rubbed in it.

At times Rea did not try to understand herself too well because, when she did, she put herself out ahead of her own life, and that made her discontented and, sometimes, worse. Long ago she had begun to gain on herself and Duane.

Duane had confirmed her intuitions about her own desires. She did not shrink from possession, both by passion and by another, for she wanted to be overtaken, taken over. She could always make herself come, but she never could whip up the frenzy of possession; and she needed to take, and men had seemed surprised by this. Though not Duane. He wasn't surprised by her wanting, her singlemindedness, the fact that she was after something, her taking.

Duane had met it head on. He had said it was like fighting with his older sister. She had come at him with the same fury, the same pure intent, except at ten years of age it was to claw him, to attack him, and though it may have been sexual, it was foremost violent and passionate. He had lost skin to his sister, was cut by her nails, left with welts, claw tracks, red wires. He wouldn't smack her right off, but would hold her as she struggled against him, her whole body wanting to break free of his clutch, wanting to break free of itself. Often neighbors would yell when his sister's screams pierced the night; and once a relative had broken up their fight. Like cats and dogs, they'd be described, going after one another; but, even then, Duane hadn't made the connection between the heat of their encounters and fucking.

It was the energy involved, the forward motion; it was like getting at one's self, Rea admitted; it was like making love to a man. She liked to be held down, pinned, though she would resist, need to resist, because it was at the juncture of resistance and acceptance that she found release. Duane's world utterly lacked languor and that was good; she wanted active desire. She wanted sex to be unlike herself, though she recognized that she had found what she wanted in males who were apt to resemble their sexual selves when looked at straight on.

She also did not want to be hurt, or abused. Though she most hated being talked to dismissively, like a child, she did not want to be condescended to sexually, either. And she had been, early on, surprised, though not for long, by what she took to be most men's distaste for women, or sex, or both. And she thought it rare to discover anyone who truly wanted what she wanted; his life deposited him in Rea's bed and prepared him to be her lover.

What harsh, smoky foundry had manufactured his attitudes

she was to learn, but it had turned out a product that met her specifications. The rest of him needed to be invented. He was nearly ten years younger than she was, and she could see her influence on him, though now it seemed like a stain to her. A wild child not quite fit for civilization—not hers, that is, and, thanks to her, no longer ready to be sent back into his. But she knew better than to truly believe such symmetries; though, nonetheless, she felt she owed him something, even though he had begun to hit her, had become dangerous. Now he left marks, but she too had left marks. What she did truly believe was that the ones he left would disappear more easily than the ones she had inflicted.

She had set her own trap, made herself the bait: hanging out, testing the waters. She had noticed right off his thin arms, the way his pelvis cocked. She liked his body, enjoyed his posing, a cigarette dangling from pretty lips. She had always been attracted to mouths: lips, smooth-rolled skin, the body's own wreath. A judgment of sorts, one's mouth; like all portals, archways, it signified. And he had a large, eclectic vocabulary, which signaled to Rea that he was smarter than he realized.

But it was the way she was literally drawn to him, the way she slipped into his presence, as if he was the shadow she made; it felt that comfortable.

Duane had told her stories full of canny observations: he had described visiting the apartment of a woman who sold drugs, being surrounded by naked children; he described the hairless genitals of a little girl looking like the "nib of a pen." Jack was the same way, full of the oddities of the autodidact.

Their connection had started too frivolously; she saw how it changed. Beware of being too relaxed, of letting things happen, feeling safe. Working in prison had made the outside seem safe. Beware of letting things happen, for then they do: the guard is dropped and everything is replaced. One of the eerie moments of her youth was the first time she had gone into a movie in the afternoon and emerged after dark. It was a birthday treat, letting her go to a matinee alone. Coming out of the movie into the darkness was strange; the light had been snatched away from her; she hadn't seen it go dark. It had never gone dark unnoticed before.

Well, Rea thought, it had been light with Duane; then came the movie, and now it had grown dark. The movie had been interesting. The trip to Pennsylvania with Duane, where she had gone to school, lived off-campus, been considered a hippie a few years before the name was coined. For her pains at establishing her independence, she had been raped by a townie, who, along with boon companions, had come out to bother the strange girl living alone—though not always—in the formerly abandoned farmhouse on Starbright Road.

Rape had come up in conversation. Duane had made a remark about being no one's bunboy in the can. Had she implied it? He told her that he had started a fight, threw things in the cafeteria, got locked in the hole; but they were going to leave him alone henceforth. Crazy was sacred in the can; crazy was a mystic's aura and they wouldn't fuck with you. *That guy'll do anything.* In the joint it was best to be unstable.

"Didn't you have to watch your cute little ass?" Was that what she had said? She must have been drinking. Some compliment with a twist. He talked about guys being raped. She told him of being raped.

Four teenagers throwing beer cans at the windows, breaking in. She alone, in bed, wearing a nightgown, the usual victim's robes. Downstairs the boys rummaging about, breaking things. No phone. The oldest, nineteen or twenty, drunk and stupid enough to come up the stairs. He was wearing a gas station attendant's shirt, unbuttoned, JETHRO stitched in red thread above a pocket. She fought him, but he finally succeeded; she was so furious that she felt him almost everywhere but in her cunt. More a fist in the belly, till he slid in and it was as if she had found him, caught him; but he pushed in further, collapsed into climax. Earlier she had sunk her teeth into his upper arm, through his shirt.

"It looked like a horse bite," she told Duane, along with the other details. "That really was his name, Jethro. He pumped gas at the local filling station."

He was arrested and then let go, because the public prosecutor did not want to press the case. Rea lived alone. She had boyfriends. Plural.

The college she attended forced her to call her father; the woman dean put the phone in front of her and waited for her to dial. Rea wanted to go to court, but she would have to hire an attorney; her father, a lawyer, wouldn't loan her any money. Charges were dropped.

Jethro was released, though the cops promised to keep an eye on him. Rea graduated and left town. Duane listened to the story and said, "Let's pay ol' Jethro a visit."

Duane suggested the trip after he had moved in with Rea;

it was late spring and the writing program didn't make many demands on her time. Her higher education was proceeding without complications. Rea was willing to take a trip. Duane drove her car. He had plans: they'd find out where Jethro lived, if he still lived in town, where he worked, and then they would extract a pound of flesh.

Duane spun out his idea: to find Jethro walking along the street, preferably at night, preferably in a lonely spot. Rea could appear, Duane rhapsodized, at the end of the block, be some sort of apparition. It would make Jethro pause; from behind Duane would douse him with a bucketfull of gasoline. Duane kept devising different ways to ignite him. And then skedaddle. It would only take a little reconnoitering, but Duane thought it a workable plan. Rea was chilled, thinking of the empty three-pound can of Morning Cheer coffee they had filled with gas. It sloshed in the back well of the car beneath a Saran Wrap cover, held tight with a thick rubber band.

They had looked up Jethro in the phone book at a convenience store; he lived on Milton Street. On the way over to his house, Duane suggested they just ride by the gas station where he used to work, on the odd chance he would be there.

The gas station had greatly altered; it had become a self-service island and, driving by, Rea was startled to see Jethro in a glass booth, all alone, like a ticket seller at an old movie house. Closed in, air-conditioned, locked against theft, a small depressed dish open in front of him where the money was pushed through.

"That him?" Duane asked. Rea didn't have the good sense to say no.

The passing years hadn't done much for Jethro; he did look, to Rea, like some sort of specimen in his cage, a light shining down on him from above: RURAL RAPEIST, GAS STATION ATTENDANT VARIETY, late twentieth century.

"Ain't he a piece of work," Duane said. "It's like a subway booth. I can spill the gas in, torch it, and he'll never get out. We'll block the door with the car."

Rea watched Jethro take money and make change. There weren't many customers. Duane was gauging their frequency. Jethro once stood up, reaching for a carton of cigarettes that lined the inside of the booth, high up. Rea knew that had she had a gun that night at the farmhouse she would have shot him. There was something about summary execution that seemed just. By committing a crime you have agreed to shoulder certain risks.

You lost your ticket. Bam. But, sitting with Duane, she found the notion of execution beyond her. Perhaps if Jethro's life had changed, if he had done more, worse, become something, say, like mayor of Providence, Rhode Island.

"Let's not and say we did," Rea said.

Duane looked at her: his eyes had receded. Their pupils had locked into some tight, dark recess of consent. He was prepared to do it. Rea was, all of a sudden, afraid for Jethro. Duane *would* do it. His readiness leeched her anger, replaced it with alarm.

"No. Let's forget it."

Duane shrugged his shoulders. She couldn't read what emotion played on his face; but, she could barely describe her own feelings right then. Duane started the car, left the shadows where they were parked, headed off. Rea looked back at the self-service island and its glass cubicle. A bubble had burst within her. Hate metabolized into other substances. The present began to become unmoored from the past, and Rea felt herself beginning to float away.

Even now she began to wince, from the memory not of Jethro in his glass cage, but of Duane masturbating her during the ride back home. In the dark night, on the deserted old state highway, Duane had driven as fast as her little vehicle would go, and Rea had pushed the seat back so she could recline, her feet flat against the dashboard. Duane, with his eyes mostly on the road, touched her in ways he had become expert at, and, though he did not lose control of the car and run off the road, she felt herself bouncing in her seat, her legs pushing against the dashboard as if she were trying to push through to the other side of the world, the center of her body finally dissolving, turning as loose as her legs were taut.

The night wind whipped through the car's open windows, and, after a while, Rea began to smell the countryside, to recognize the odors, identical to her recollection of them from years ago: fecund furrowed fields and the offal of farm animals.

2

The six-foot projection television screen did not provide as sharp an image as the older console model in the den, but Kenner could not work up the energy to switch the sets from room to room. He reclined on the bed, eating Cheese Curls and watching rather watery but large figures flit across the concave screen. Perhaps that had something to do with it, he thought—the console's tube reflected the image on a convex screen, the tension flowing outward, like on the surface of a balloon. On the six-foot screen it was pulled into a depression, a softening, a slackening.

However it was caused, the fuzziness kept reminding Kenner of his father's home movies. The same size screen, the same lack of crisp outlines that he had watched growing up. Cinema verité in the fifties suburbs: Christmas, birthdays, all regular, all cyclical. Each Christmas film had the same opening sequence: down the hallway stairs, running to the tinsel-strung tree, Kenner's mother following last, her salmon-colored nightgown filling the screen. Kenner recalled his father's head, invisible, behind the bar of blinding floodlights.

Kenner had a plethora of channels and geographies to choose from, but a few stories turned up on all the channels: Atlanta, Chicago, New York, Miami. They had been showing scenes of flames in the night, people running in the streets, police barricades, spectral figures. One outburst in Washington, another in Miami. Mount St. Helens; Liberty City. The old one-two. The networks loved it: Fire in Miami, smoke in Washington—from sea to shining sea.

Kenner was enjoying himself. The air conditioning hummed, the beer was cold, the Cheese Curls satisfying. The screen, albeit slightly unfocused, was livid with startling images. He had mailed his profile of MacNaughton today to *Centipede,* calling it "Stowing Away in Margaritaville," though he didn't expect *Centipede* to use the title.

Watching TV convinced Kenner that the press functioned like Noah with his ark: all it could handle was two of each species. Any more was superfluous. Catastrophes had to be different enough, or they canceled each other out. The newsmen were getting a little breathless these days. Liberty City had totally replaced Key West for South Florida news. The crews filming refugees had packed up and flown to Miami. Liberty City was typical riot coverage: checkpoints, lots of police reports, fires at night, ruins during the day.

The cause of the disturbance, acquittal by the all-white jury of the four white police officers who had stomped the black insurance man for his biker proclivities, was quickly forgotten. Ah, Liberty City. Drivers yanked from cars and set upon, buses attacked, the usual reparations demanded, unequal justice under the law doled out with additional unequal justice on the unlucky passersby. More wrong-place-at-the-wrong-time retribution. The mob. Kenner thought of mobs, ate Cheese Curls, watched the twenty-four-hour news station, but soon its reports were duplications, the same loops of film.

There were still photographs of Mount St. Helens exploding. Kenner was impressed. That elemental violence was greeted with a response that Kenner thought chilling. Awe. Awe always coats the sphere of wonder with appreciation.

The peanut-farmer president, whenever lately photographed, looked distressed. Even Nature was opposing him: couldn't a volcano wait till after the election? Carter, a religious man, would not be cheered, Kenner supposed, by such omens, this writing on the wall. The Freedom Flotilla had been demoted to the more shabby "boatlift." Liberty City. Desert One.

Kenner remembered the charred soldiers stretched out on the Iranian desert, their helmets the only shape that retained their former size; everything else shrank, was reduced: legs, chests, arms, subtly deflated, but not the helmet. Carter stayed in his Rose Garden. And, Kenner was distressed to see, the press had stopped displaying Reagan as a complete nitwit. His fellow journalists had concluded that Reagan was going to win, and, for their own sakes, they all had agreed, for their own pride and sanity, to pretend he was somewhere this side of acceptable. President Reagan. Kenner, munching Cheese Curls, tried not to take too much satisfaction in the order of political events. He knew he was indulging in a weakness for easy extremes, wishing for all reversals to be pronounced.

Kenner, playing with his remote control device, switched to the religious network shows and watched the polyester snake-oil salesmen strut their stuff in front of banks of phones. The faithful tithed incomes, donated surplus capital, and pledged souls to a whole series of fat-cheeked, slightly bloated, but clean-shaven males. They all had the look of men, Kenner judged, who are revealed later to be convicted child molesters.

A name had been coined and Kenner knew it had struck home. The Moral Majority. Now someone deserves to make money with that sort of talent, he thought. All advertising was religious, an attempt to create both devotion and reverence. People have to buy the stuff and be loyal to it. They really didn't care what you bought, as long as you went out and made purchases. Had he ever seen ads for Cheese Curls?

The hucksters and the religion boys had been going around and around so often they were now Sambo and his tiger, both turned to butter. But the born-again sort were the bigger teasers, Kenner thought. Their sex was pure fervor; advertisers got their fervor from sex. He had decided that most advertising he saw, featuring a woman staring into a lens, broke down, at least for men like himself, into one unasked but always implicit question: Would you like this young lady to sit on your face?

3

It was Bridget's morning to open the store, and she had slept badly all night. Ever since Kristina had returned, she hadn't had a good night's sleep. One by one Bridget's fears were coming true. It looked to her as if Kristina had gone off with Winston. Kristina hadn't come home some nights, and not last night either. Curt was passed out on the trailer's hide-a-bed. And now Bridget had to get up and open the store.

They had been with her a week before Kristina confided to her that Curt didn't have much interest in her, that the drugs he took often made him impotent. Curt, Bridget agreed, was a strange boy, but he wasn't impotent. She stood in the kitchen galley, watching him deep in sleep, mouth open; his prick bowed out his underpants. Bridget, staring, felt like one of her veins had broken inside. She seemed to go wet, her body irrigating, and she felt like going over and bending back Curt's shorts and watching that hard-on spring out and just sucking on him till he came. And then what excuse would he use on poor Kristina?

Her impulse was followed by a fluttering feeling of weakness, and she sat down on the stool by the Formica counter. She worried about her heart and thought she was having palpitations. Curt took more medications than she did, and he drank, too. Bridget hardly drank at all. Eli was asleep in his playpen. It was different from the wooden one she had put Kristina in; Eli's was made out of some sort of plastic webbing. Curt would feed Eli, play with him, roughhouse. Eli would be awake soon. Bridget watched the kettle she had set on the range; she intended to pluck it off before it started to whistle. It was as quiet at this hour as the trailer park ever was. Too late for partying, too soon to get up.

The windows were turning violet, and soon they would become pale; then gray light would float into the trailer, and she could see beyond the circle of white light she had turned on in the kitchen. The pool of light sometimes bothered her: she could see Curt's open mouth and white stiffened shorts and the corner of Eli's playpen. It was so still it looked like a photograph. That bothered her.

Winston, she knew, always had some sort of interest in Krissy. There had always been a lot of grabbing and goosey-goosey, but it seemed to Bridget like Winston was playing daddy. But in the months Kristina had been gone, she had become, well, more sultry, Bridget supposed, less girlish. She had noticed Winston look at Kristina differently right off.

Bridget thought it was a bad mistake for Winston to have involved Krissy and Curt in his plans. There now seemed to be a whole crowd, and Bridget knew hardly any of them.

The excitement didn't make Bridget excited; it made her nauseous. She was sure she had stomach trouble, an ulcer. And Krissy was the only one who had to work—if you could call the job Kristina had found work. She had refused to go see Kristina perform. Topless dancing. Bridget never thought she'd be hired; she didn't believe Kristina had been a Playboy Bunny either, though Krissy had a Polaroid picture of herself in the Bunny costume. It did look real.

What Bridget had to do had seemed simple, but now it was getting more complicated. She had only to set off the store alarm a few times by mistake during the week before. She would call the police, say it was malfunctioning. The police would get used to hearing a false alarm from that part of Old Town. They would think it was just another snafu in the system, Winston had told her. It seemed to her to complicate matters, but that was what he wanted to do. It was a daylight robbery, anyway. Winston wasn't going to change any of his plans, even when the shop owners' association announced their COME BACK TO OLD KEY WEST parade for the same day. Winston said it would actually help. To Bridget, it seemed just like another one of her fears coming true. Winston was smart. She should trust him. But if he was sleeping with Kristina, that would be the worst sign of all.

She didn't know, sipping her tea, how many of the stories Kristina told about Curt were to be believed. She would have thought Winston would be bothered by some of them. That Curt wanted to be a policeman, had been in the service. It didn't ruffle Winston. He said it proved Curt was a born crook. Bridget didn't think Curt was really a Green Beret. Oh, he might have been in the military, but she didn't believe all the tales that Kristina had been gushing at her. Strung out on dope, she believed; and how he had been married in high school to a girl who had a kid and ran off with someone a few months later, she could see; how he'd been a draft dodger and had planned to go to Canada, but had enlisted at the last moment, maybe. How the

VA had mistreated him; how he had been turned down by various police departments. She spooned a glob of honey into her tea and turned off the overhead light—it was now gray enough to see in the trailer.

Curt's hard-on had begun to droop. He was a good-looking boy. He reminded her a bit of Ray. Ray, at first, was built like that, and was pretty. Ray's own history sounded like made-up stories, too, She thought of how proud she was when the pet store/jungle land did so well that Ray contacted the local TV station that had just started and proposed doing a show for them. Ray Pine's Jungle Land. He would take little kids and show them various animals. It was only fifteen minutes long, but it had stayed on for nearly half a year. Almost laughing out loud she recollected one show, the last. Ray was showing the kids snakes, and to scare them he took an old python they had out of the straw basket—make it look more like a snake charmer's act. She was watching her Motorola, and it was a couple of minutes before she realized that the python was dead.

Ray must have known immediately. But he was swinging his arms a lot and turning around and doing his best to make it look like the snake was still alive. The kids sat on the ground in front of him and stared up. Bridget didn't know why the look on Ray's face so touched her as he tried to make that snake look alive. It was funny to her that she remembered how he looked on black and white TV better than other ways.

Ray was kind. Curt didn't look kind. But he did play with Eli. Kristina told her some strange tribe he worked with in Vietnam—what had Krissy called them? the Mountain Yards?—had considered him a god. A god to them, maybe, a loser to Bridget. It was his drinking and temper Kris most complained about. He would cry, she had told Bridget, and the stories would become hateful and he would tell her all manner of horrible things he swore he had done. Bridget did not know what to believe.

Curt never seemed to boast about anything nice he might have done; Bridget wondered if he'd ever done anything nice. He was sweet enough to Eli, she considered. But what about his own, if he did have one? She became aware of herself looking at his prick, now folded over, but still fat, in the pale light that filled the trailer. His chest was hairless and tanned: his dark brown nipples stood out distinctly, like two metal snaps.

I had better get ready to go, she told herself, before I do something as foolish as my daughter.

108

Ten

1

Rea was the first woman Kenner had met whom he had actually seen changing her own oil. He had last talked to her when he had recognized her feet sticking out from beneath the Sunrise van. He had begun thinking about lube jobs, but saved her his crude remarks. And it had been nearly a week since he had last seen her jogging along a path that ran alongside South Roosevelt Boulevard. She had put her thick hair into two pickaninny braids sticking straight out from the side of her head. Both the day's heat and her exertion had been impressive. Kenner had waved, but had received no response. Kenner had been keeping his physical activity limited to dips in the pool. When he took showers, he could hear, through the open bathroom window, the *pock-pock-pock* of tennis players down on the court below.

Kenner was not in great shape. He would admit to being twenty pounds overweight. He meant to lose it, but was undecided on how to go about it. So he decided not to do anything. The weather would make him thinner. He was, anyway, leery of being too body conscious.

But Key West in May reveals a lot of flesh and a walk down Duval Street led Kenner to various kinds of speculation. In such places as Key West, where sexuality is overloaded, so upfront and in the marketplace, usual forms of courtship and display short-circuit quickly; and, in a town where so many men are interested in men, women seem scornful and perplexed. Nothing is certain. The ante has been raised, and to stay in the hand they have to reach down deep. Kenner liked that quality, but, at the same time, he knew reckless women had a shorter spectrum of sight than most—less visual purple—and what made them look your way was not necessarily the sort of sight Kenner provided. Thrills. Kenner realized he did not display a lot of thrill potential: danger, money, lethalness, power. Kenner had not come to Key West primarily to meet women; he had, in fact, resigned himself to jacking off; but, since he had met Rea, another sort of interest surfaced. He was beginning to feel himself attracted by her gravity. Still, the local fleshpots were getting to him; he could feel all his good sense puddling.

Below Angela Street, Kenner noticed that some small portion of federal funds that had escaped the whirlpool pockets of local officials had been spent on roadwork, widening the sidewalks, paving portions with bricks, placing some stumpy palm trees at intervals, trying to create the illusion of a promenade, past the buildings that had yet to be renovated. These structures were a scruffy lot and retained some of Key West's actual history, which the other new façades had erased. A haberdashery that would look right at home in Scranton, Pennsylvania; a narrow pawn shop, its barred and screened window displaying unransomed wares; a dirty movie theater, its billboards without posters, except for the crayoned announcements of the co-feature, underlined with XXXs, the Old West's sign for poison. A pirated print of *Deep Throat* ran every night.

In an effort to counter the image of Key West swarming with freedom-crazed Cubans, Kenner had heard that local merchants had decided to sponsor a Memorial Day weekend celebration with a parade, thinking that the attendant publicity would help restore the island's reputation as a tolerant and lazy resort.

But commerce was far from Kenner's mind by the time he reached the bottom of Duval Street; his flipflops were flapped out. Sunset was two hours away; he decided to wait for it at the Wharf House. The atmosphere there was the sort that made New Yorkers feel safe: exotic, yet familiar. Though the management

did not encourage it—at least not to the point of hiring shills—
the Wharf House's tiny beach area had become topless. It was
one of the seeming contradictions of gay resort culture. The
women who were attracted by all the sexual openness would bare
their breasts—in the spirit of equality with their preening male
friends who were not interested.

Nudity had spread, a sort of venereal dress code, and had
reached the Wharf House. Kenner often thought the popular
culture was passing him by, since he still found it hard not to be
thrown into reverie by female nakedness.

But, he realized, this was the same group that had passed
him by during the sixties in New York. Or, rather, it hadn't moved.
The interfaced world of art, fashion, money: never having gone
away, it was just now back out in front, since most everything
else had receded. But Kenner had not come to Key West to organize a tenants' strike at the condo, he kept reminding himself.

He wandered up to the patio bar and while waiting to order
a drink heard his name called out. He looked over to a large
round table, the occupants shaded by an overhead umbrella. He
recognized MacNaughton, wearing mirrored sunglasses.

To Kenner's surprise there were two other familiars: Howie
Cohen, an editor at *Parapet.* Beside Howie sat a young lady Kenner had known before she met Howie; but he had not known
her well enough for his liking. Danielle Perot had been a girlfriend of an older reporter, a fellow with whom Kenner shared
many things, though, unfortunately, not Danielle. Her person
always made Kenner ache—some erotic arthritis, an affliction that
affected Kenner when in the moist and chilly atmosphere of a
woman like Danielle.

What Danielle saw in Howie, Kenner could only guess; and
he guessed the most superficial things. He employed her at *Parapet,* a political journal financed by money hanging from an old
robber baron family tree; the cash now bloomed on its most junior sprig. He was useful, provided contacts, was more than solvent, and seemed extraordinarily neat. Kenner was actually fond
of Howie and realized that whatever frantic criticism leapt to his
mind did spring out of the old salmon run of sexual jealousy.

He wanted to be called Howard, and Kenner had always
annoyed him by calling him Howie. As Kenner walked over to
the table, he remembered their last meeting with some chagrin.
Parapet published his article on a minister-activist-diplomat and
paid him four hundred dollars. Thank the Lord for the petro-

dollars funding that leftish sheet, Kenner thought. He went by *Parapet*'s office to answer queries. For some reason, Danielle's presence, the freshly decorated rooms, the Ivy Leagueness of Howie, made Kenner notice, under the fluorescent lights, how shabby and threadbare his trench coat had become. So, though he needed the money for rent and food, he spent the four hundred on a new coat and wondered what had happened to him that he could be overtaken by such feelings of shame.

"Hi, Kenner," MacNaughton said, brushing smooth the ragged edges of their last encounter. "It seems you know some of these good folks."

Kenner could not decide if Howie had seen him and mentioned him to MacNaughton, or the other way around.

"Small world," Howie said, extending his hand.

"Yeah," Kenner said, "we all live on the head of a pin these days."

"Hello there, Kenner," Danielle said to him, in the lazy, full tones of a woman who had been courted and has declined. Kenner smiled and waved, not wanting to plunge his voice into the wake of mixed emotions her voice had just made.

There were a few faces Kenner didn't know around the table and a lot of camera equipment stacked by the chairs.

"This table is something of a media event itself," Kenner said, standing behind two unfamiliar backs.

"Sit down, sit down," MacNaughton said. "Kenner, as I told you, is doing an article about me for . . . what magazine?"

"Centipede."

"Which one is that?" Danielle asked. Howie answered, though Danielle had tossed her question at Kenner.

"It's that rock 'n' roll bimonthly."

Kenner's arrival had interrupted some story and it resumed; he found an empty chair and wedged himself into the seating arrangements. He looked toward the water, noticed a number of bare-breasted females. One had enormous breasts, though elsewhere her body was thin to the point of starvation. Kenner thought that must be some sort of genetic phenomenon. She was tall and stood thigh-deep in the water with a short, thick-haired fellow who was wearing a lot of gold chains. They both emerged and settled onto chaise longues; the hairy fellow then proceeded to oil the woman, slapping her breasts punching-bag fashion till the woman, laughing, pushed him away. It was vulgar, but Kenner didn't always mind vulgarity. He looked over at Danielle and saw she had been staring at him.

"I didn't come here to look at the mammaries," Danielle said. "I came here to look at those looking."

Howie smiled. Kenner felt he should say something. "Oh, I don't know—it's all a trendy mixture of *Vogue* and *National Geographic.*"

Kenner dropped his gaze, thinking he might be treated, at last, to a display of Danielle nude. If so, perhaps, he would be able to notice something that could dampen his idolatry. He cherished the myth of the dispossessed; or at least what the deprived were piously taught: that things weren't as wonderful as they appear, that perfection was an illusion. That life never exceeds one's dreams. But, alas, Kenner knew that was bunk. The wonderful usually turned out to be wonderful. The beautiful disrobed were, often as not, beautiful.

Danielle, he realized, was unlikely to bare any more of herself than need be, since what was bared was more than sufficient. It had been the unfortunate experience of Kenner to conclude that lovely women were more affected by their loveliness being belittled or denigrated—slap those tits!—than by having it extolled. They liked to believe men were moved not by it, but by them.

Kenner, absorbed in his thoughts, half-heard a name and asked: "Is Somoza still alive?"

"Yes. For now," a young man sitting near a stack of film equipment answered. "He's in Paraguay, a lovely place, spending his loot." Kenner realized they had all been talking about the Sandinistas in Nicaragua. "Old Tacho is helping to fund some counterrevolutionaries. *Contras.*"

Kenner deduced one of the men he didn't know was a documentary filmmaker; the other, a cable-news stringer; and the dark young man in a waiter's uniform was attached somehow to MacNaughton.

Danielle had turned her radiant attention to MacNaughton. Kenner wondered what sort of twisted attacks had already sprung from MacNaughton's side today; but he looked rather composed. Danielle asked him, "Have you ever thought about writing a commercial novel?"

MacNaughton looked at her with some alarm, Kenner detected, since MacNaughton, he knew, had considered all his novels commercial.

"Something that was bound to make money?" Danielle added, another little gust hoping to fill MacNaughton's sails. He finally moved.

"I wish I could," MacNaughton said. "But you have to believe what you are writing. They recognize insincerity. Though I
am thinking of writing something that might do the trick. Here,
you'd be interested in this." MacNaughton inclined his head in
the direction of a fellow who had been discussing the Sandinistas. MacNaughton's hair fell forward, fringing the tops of his
silver sunglasses.

"I'm thinking about writing a novel of thermonuclear espi-
onage. The main idea is that Israel is holding the world hostage.
Never Again—I'm using that for a title—is the code name of its
defense department's secret plan. They have planted some rather
cunning nuclear devices all around the globe, and they are set to
go off if Israel ever feels itself terminally threatened. How about
that?"

"Sounds like a moneymaker," Danielle replied.

"I hope so," MacNaughton replied. "I'd only do it for a mega
advance."

"Well, Kenner," Howie asked, "are you doing something on
the flotilla, too?" Kenner heard a trace of business behind the
question.

"Not me. Cuba sí, viva Fidel, el Jefe," he said; then, recon-
sidering, looking about, since Key West was thick with gusanos,
he went on: "This whole scene is one of the many nails in the
peanut farmer's coffin. Cuba, if you haven't yet noticed, is the
fifty-first state, and Castro has cast all its electoral votes for Reagan."

"Well," Howie said, "David," indicating the documentary
maker, "is hoping to get across, film it."

"Groovy," Kenner said, letting his eyes drift toward the beach
and the figure of a young woman, her breasts ripe to bursting,
some living incarnation of a WPA painting, nut and bolt nipples,
the people's realism at a hundred dollars a night at the Wharf
House. Why am I affected like this? Kenner wondered. He felt
some sympathy for drug addicts.

"They want a thousand dollars apiece for us," David said,
leaning toward the young woman next to him, "the same price
they'd get for a body coming back."

"Carter is cracking down, calling for controls. Soon the coast
guard will be stopping everyone," the cable stringer said. Kenner
thought a television had been turned on. The fellow had slipped
into an announcer's cadences.

"Yeah," David said, "that's another reason we haven't been

able to get any cooperation—too much evidence if everyone is on film."

"Tell them they'll be stars," Kenner said. "Stars have nothing to worry about." He looked at MacNaughton, since Kenner was restating one of MacNaughton's favorite notions: it had been covered in his interview.

MacNaughton smiled, but Kenner could not see the look in his eyes behind the mirrored surface of his glasses.

"Ah, yes, stars," MacNaughton said, tilting his face upward, "there's great safety in that firmament. But it's not without peril, the celebrity orbit."

"Going to Mariel ain't safe either," David said. "Even Manuel doesn't want to go back with us." He glanced toward the evenly tanned, silent young man sitting next to MacNaughton.

"Manuel doesn't even want his story told," Howie said.

Kenner found himself looking at the young man, "Manuel," with new vision: he originally had wiped his glance over him, thinking he was just another of MacNaughton's young hustlers. That still might be true, he considered, though Kenner did now look at him with considerably more interest. Did he understand English?

"I'm his sponsor," MacNaughton said.

"I have an uncle in Miami," Manuel said in a soft voice, "who is my sponsor."

"I'm a buddy of his uncle," MacNaughton said. "I'm employing him."

Can he type? Kenner wanted to ask.

"Manuel's already told us his story," Danielle remarked to Kenner, since she understood Kenner's silence to be a request for information. "He doesn't want to go through it again. He doesn't want to be news."

"Yeah," MacNaughton said, "the boy has enough experience with *pincheros* in old Havana. He doesn't want to be ripped off anymore."

MacNaughton struggled up from his beach chair, and Manuel gracefully floated up beside him.

"Well," MacNaughton said, "got to put the young man to work. Idle hands, you know. Viva Cuba Libre! you all." He waved and waddled off. MacNaughton was thickening at the hips. A kind of adipose softness. What Kenner would have called in his youth a lard ass.

"How long have you known MacNaughton?" Kenner asked Howie, after he had departed.

"Oh, didn't you know? Since college. I was at Harvard. He was at BC, wasn't it? We met at the Grolier one day."

"Be here long?"

"No," Howie said. "Just in and out. Danielle and I wanted to get away from the city for a weekend. David was coming down, so we decided to come."

"What is Manuel's story?" Kenner asked, hoping someone would answer.

Howie obliged, but looked first in David's direction, who said, "Go ahead. I'm not going to use much of it."

"Well, evidently, Manuel is not quite your typical Mariel emigrant," Howie said. "There seem to be two groups. The volunteers and the conscripts. Manuel was among the first thousand who were emptied out of the Peruvian embassy grounds. The ones who have been coming in lately are the ones Castro is sending out. They're a bit different. A substantial share of them are blacks and mulattoes."

"What's different about that?" Kenner asked, realizing the question betrayed a fundamental lack of knowledge, which he knew to be unwise. But he was curious. He thought he knew something about Cuba. It was one of the things Kenner took strange pride in, that he had almost been killed by some anti-Fidelistas himself. He had been visiting a woman who ran a Cuban center in New York, having become interested in her, though, so the story went, she had been one of Fidel's early amours. Kenner realized he was not in that league. Omega 7 had placed a bomb outside the door Kenner had exited, and it exploded at the same hour Kenner left; but Kenner had left three nights before it was placed, so he was unscathed. He knew this was a sort of dubious, and rather thin, proximity to danger to boast of, but Kenner did feel some residue of close-escape-ness.

"Well, Kenner, you may not know this, but whatever we or you consider Cubans, they consider themselves white, like all Spanish; and most of the Cuban refugees, from the fifties, sixties, and seventies, until now, have been, statistically, ninety percent white. As was the first group out of the embassy. But now there are a lot of blacks and mulattoes—and even though they are more representative of the Cuban population overall, they make for a different kind of refugee. That's why they get confused with the Haitians. It's one reason that the State Department is not happy. Traditionally, Cuban blacks, in the old days, would emigrate to Europe. They knew what race relations were like here. What's being complained about is not overtly racist, though I know David thinks differently. You know, our former congresswoman from New York was saying recently that just about every adult male she had talked to down here had admitted being in prison in Cuba."

Kenner felt he was learning something; though, at the same time, he wondered if his friend Howie had been doing his homework, or if he was actually in the CIA, as a number of acquaintances thought, since his information, though accurate, often seemed to have a bureaucratic tinge. But Kenner liked to hear what sounded like the truth, regardless of the source.

"Carter is up shit tributary, because immigration is a jobs issue. It was his bad luck to have Liberty City blow, for other reasons, but now you have a lot of unemployed blacks resenting black Cubans getting assistance."

"Right," Kenner said. "But what of the well-tanned Manuel?"

"Oh, Manuel doesn't add much to the picture," Howie said. "He's typical in some ways. He's young. He was born after, or just before, the glorious revolution. That was, what, nineteen, twenty years ago? He wasn't a joiner, not a member of the Communist Youth, Committee for the Defense of the Revolution. Making do, street smart, he wants to come here for a piece of the good ol' American dream. And most likely he is gay. Cuba is funny when it comes to that sort of liberation."

"They don't want him on the six o'clock news," the stringer said.

"A lot of the young people have bought the milk and honey line," Howie said. "They've come over expecting good jobs, the whole scene. Cars, condos, clothes. And they are not looking to be dishwashers, janitors, McDonald's counter people. Anyway, they are not the same as the earlier waves of upwardly mobile Cubans with family connections and money. At least, not the biggest percentage of them. I'm not sure how Manuel got tied up with old MacNaughton."

"Well," Danielle said, "he's had one part of the American dream. From sleeping on the Peruvians' front lawn to eating overpriced chow at the Wharf House." She pointed to a plate in front of Manuel's empty chair. The meal's remains looked like

Carmen Miranda's hat run over by a truck. "It's cracked, but it's a real version of it."

2

Rea saw Kenner as she walked around a large clump of croton heading for the Wharf House's pool. It surprised her that she recognized him immediately from the back—since it told her that she had become more attached to him than she realized. But Rea couldn't deny it. She had picked him out instantly: broad back, wispy hair, bald spot. She saw he was staring across the table toward a woman who was something of a dish.

On the beach below where Kenner and his party sat, bare-breasted women walked carefully across the meager strip of sand. Rea found an empty chair by the pool and sat down. The pool was the family zone. The beach was a meat rack, but to Rea it had the atmosphere of a produce section: turnips, cucumbers, and radishes, all beaded with water, piled up, and hosed off. But she wanted to swim and the beach was crowded and its water left you covered with a gritty film. She was supposed to return to the room soon. They should all be there within the half hour. The gang! She laughed. Since she had met Kenner, she had begun thinking of Jay as Winston. Jay always had sounded a little too sporty for a man with his boardroom pretensions. Winston had taken two adjoining rooms. He wanted to move the operation away from the condo. He didn't want any more coming and going to attract attention. The latest arrivals had crowded the apartment. It was odd, Rea thought, what Winston would choose to sacrifice, and what he wouldn't.

The motel was near the Audubon House, but she could see that Winston had selected it for its panache. Rea thought the cinder-block construction, dark halls, and clay tile floors, meandering walkways around inner courts, made it resemble an experimental college campus, one with progressive ideas about dorms. Most of the clientele looked like aging graduate students anyway; their eyes jumped around aggressively, as if they couldn't find the right classroom. They had signed up for the S&M seminar, but couldn't locate it. Then there were the student lounges, the cafeteria, the pool. Yes, UC Santa Cruz.

She adjusted her visored cap. She didn't want to get spots. She had always been appalled at how easily her body was marred. Her skin was a register for any distress. Touch it with anything

118

other than a tender grip and it would bruise. Insect bites raised welts; the sun developed spots. It wasn't typical cosmetic problems, rashes, pimples, but other more blunt reactions to the world around her. Ordinary things would cause her distress: she was sure some of it was psychosomatic, but part of it was just hyper-reaction to being in the world. Her running had stopped her periods—her body thought she was preparing for some natural disaster.

Rea knew she was obsessive; but she needed to be, to keep on top of things. Running, exercising, stretches. Who's in charge here?! she kept having to remind her body. But whenever a sore popped up on her ass, she knew that she wasn't in charge as much as she hoped.

Rea heard voices behind the door and instead of using her key, she knocked. The voices stopped.

"It's Rea," she called out and stuck the key in the lock and let herself in. There was one new face in the room. An older man, in his fifties, overweight. His complexion was heavily scarred: cheeks, nose and chin, with tiny perforations, ice-pick holes. It almost made a pattern. A man's wing-tip shoes.

"Vern, that's Rea," Winston said. "Rea, Vern."

Vern struggled a bit as if he were trying to stand up, an odd side-to-side dance in the overstuffed cushions of the room's wicker furniture.

"Don't Vern. Sit," Rea said, leaning over to shake the hand that was waving in front of his face. For a moment Rea thought he wanted to be pulled up.

"Jack Dawes told me about you," Vern said. "Glad to meet ya'."

Rea smiled at the familiar name, her prize pupil, her first link to Duane.

"Hey," Winston yelled, "you're turning hundreds of dollars of chicken soup into plaster!"

Rea looked down and saw that she was dripping onto the glass coffee table; a drop had hit a line he had prepared.

"It's birdshit now," Duane said.

"I'll go change. It'll dry," she said.

Vern must be the alarm man they had been waiting for, Rea thought, stripping off her suit. World's fastest shower taker, she loved water, but felt claustrophobic in an enclosed space.

She hadn't kept close track of Winston's plans. Thinking

119

lightly about it, she considered herself to be friends of actors, but not in their show. It was somewhat theatrical: a road show coming to town, one performance; rehearsals, schedules to meet, opening and closing night. Winston tried to manufacture an air of professionalism about it. Another reason he had taken the rooms. A trade show's hospitality suite. Only the two newcomers, Curt and Kristina, seemed babes in the woods. Rea knew it wouldn't be real to them.

"I gotta get something to eat," Curt said.

"We left one for you," Winston said, as she came out of the bathroom.

Treats for the troops, to ensure esprit d'corps, Rea thought.

"A toast to our endeavors," Winston said.

"Where there's property there's theft—how does that go?" Duane asked Rea. It was the first thing out of him that sounded vaguely friendly in a long time.

"Something like that," Rea said, and accepted the worn brass tube Winston offered her. She wondered about single use: was a short brass tube like this used for anything else?

The cocaine went off the glass top, up her nose. Rea used it so infrequently its effect was still a surprise: the world jumped out at her, as if the power of the lens of her eye had been turned up one notch, as you could a microscope's. And Rea felt newly benign about the people around her. But it did speed her up and she didn't require that.

Cocaine made everyone a raconteur. "I'd take 'em to a dump where a buddy worked," Duane was saying, evidently describing to Curt his car-thief prowess, "and we'd strip 'em of everything and then burn the shell. My buddy would run what was left over with a bulldozer. You can't easily recognize a new car that's been burned and run over by a bulldozer. Looked like one big penny."

Duane, she saw, then took his finger and wiped up the remaining chalky grains. He stuck his finger in his mouth, rubbing it along the side of his gums. She felt now as if she were watching Duane on film. She could get up and leave and Duane would remain there on the screen and not take any notice.

She looked toward the walled garden beyond the room's sliding glass doors. She saw a few people wandering through the elaborately planted grounds. The room was full of light, yet there were no slanting rays. It wouldn't be dark for another hour; there were gardenias and a Star of India tree, both near flowering. The air-conditioning was on high. She could smell the rind of refrigeration.

"What's the secret of life?" Winston asked. Rea turned. Winston had evidently been musing on that subject while Duane and Curt had been chatting about cars.

"Oh, I don't know," Curt said, eyes glinting, "You got to go to the place where they do the guillotining. You go to the guillotine guy and pick up the head right after it's been chopped off and ask it: 'What's the secret of life?' He'll tell you if anybody can."

"I want some ice cream," Kristina said. She reached out in Curt's direction, but he ignored her, lost in thought.

"Get on the road. You need a taste of it," Curt said. "That's the secret. Eat simple foods. Peanut butter, sardines, cans of tuna. Come on. Let's get some pizza.

"You better start working out with weights," Curt said to Winston, hitting him on the arm. Winston flashed a look of anger but let it soften to scorn. "Don't let the little gay guys chump you Winny-boy. That's the secret. It's a jungle out there."

"Come on. Let's get some pizza," Vern said.

"Ice cream," Kristina said, hopefully.

Winston jumped up and pointed out the sliding glass doors. He could see people getting ready to check in, taking luggage out of the trunks of cars.

"It is a jungle out there. Look at all them monkeys." Winston laughed. "It's a jungle. Get the monkey gun."

Rea wondered if she would go through with the outing she had agreed upon for tomorrow. Kenner had asked her to go fishing and she said yes. Everyone else would be busy.

Kenner had come by the pool and seemed surprised and pleased to see her. And he had asked. Rea liked men who asked.

Eleven

Kristina thought almost being killed in north Miami might have led her to being so fearless. She had never thought of herself as fearless before. Newly proud. Puffed up with pride. Maybe that was it: she *was* puffed up. She wasn't stoop-shouldered anymore, hanging back, unassertive, flat-chested. You are what you are, Curt was always saying. If it wasn't confidence she had gained, she didn't know what it was. The operation had helped her grow up in any number of ways.

She was still on the operating table, Kristina remembered, when she began to regain consciousness. A voice was saying, "She's coming out." She felt pressed down, caught in a huge hand, in the same way that she had held bugs in her fist when she was little. Her head was behind a green cloth, and two figures were bent in front of it. She felt as if she were lying under a television screen with just her chin sticking out in front of the tube.

"The left still seems a bit larger to me."

"Leave it. There should be a bit of asymmetry."

Kristina realized they were arguing about size, or, at least, she recalled later that that was what they were arguing about

122

when she awoke in the recovery room, her chest swaddled with bandages. The gauze wrappings were crisscrossed and made what appeared to be a huge clown-sized padded bra.

Kristina had wanted the implantation surgery—the doctors called it augmentation mammoplasty—for a long time. She had needed to wait a year after Eli was born, even though she hadn't breast-fed him. Kristina, years before, had gone to a doctor in Miami, but she did not like the way he touched her. She knew she couldn't come up then with the two thousand dollars he wanted, anyway. She left Key West a year later, went out west, and married Johnny. That didn't last a year, but after the divorce papers came through, she decided to visit her former in-laws in New Jersey instead of going back to Bridget and the trailer park and Key West. She bundled Eli up and, with some toys for him in hand, boarded the Greyhound for the trip east. Her in-laws loved Eli, though that led to further trouble for Kristina. She had only been at her in-laws for a week when Johnny, her ex and their son, arrived from Wyoming. Then she was asked to leave—or rather they wouldn't let her back in one night; she had to go to court in New Jersey to get Eli back.

The in-laws wanted to raise Eli. Bridget just yelled at her over a bad connection. Kristina finally had called her, standing at a payphone in front of a Mini-Mart, and Bridget was screaming at her that life was trouble and Kristina was more trouble than life itself.

Kristina had found a Legal Aid lawyer, a young woman who advised Kristina to quit her job and apply for AFDC, aid to families with dependent children, welfare, which would pay for her pleadings, make payments, and even please the judge, since the job she had would not—at least not the judge they were likely to get.

That woman with the frizzy red hair was the first human being ever to tell her to quit a job, and from that moment on Kristina trusted her. Johnny had never suggested such a thing to her, though he had suggested it to himself enough times. She had been happy to give up Bunny Life, after she had done it for a while. Kristina did think it was funny that she did so many things because of her breasts. She wasn't being led by her nose, but it did seem at times, she joked, her tits had her in tow. Bridget had snorted with disbelief when she had told her on the phone about the Bunny job. I never thought they'd hire me, she told her mother, and Bridget said, "I'll say." Though her breasts had been small, her legs were long, and the Bunny costume, she was told by the woman who hired her, could make mountains out of molehills. The other girls showed her how to stuff the bra cups with pantyhose. The locker room where they dressed always smelled of sweat and perfume. The combination was something like bug spray, Kristina thought. The men's locker rooms she had been in had smelled of sweat and rubber, or sweat and ammonia. But the locker-room odor at the resort came from absorbent stuff, it seemed to her, pads, nylons, and spray, satin polyester and spandex. All the girls' legs looked great because they wore support hose under their black tights.

She had only done food waitressing in the dining room, nothing prominent like receptionist or working the lounges. The couples never seemed too disappointed to have their shrimp salad served by someone whose breasts were small.

The locker room, with its mixture of weird and familiar smells, still troubled her. She had never seen quite so many naked women. Bridget was inordinately proud of her breasts and was always showing them off; ever since Kristina could remember men stared. She once walked a few steps behind Bridget when she was ten and was amazed to see all the men turn their heads, their eyes fastened on her mother's chest; she couldn't get over the variety of expressions—they didn't even *see* her walking behind.

Kristina was surprised that her tits hadn't gotten much bigger when she had Eli; she had hoped for that, though she didn't get pregnant just to have her breasts grow. She just got pregnant and wasn't about not to have it, despite her problems with Johnny.

But in the resort's locker room she saw women who had wonderful breasts. There was every sort and the Bunny suits, she saw, did to the women's bodies what their satin high heels did to their feet: made them all look the same, except fatter and thinner. The same fleshy incline: the odd toes hidden, their shape made uniform, pointed.

Kristina only worked three weeks before the redhead lawyer told her to quit. Kristina had worked longer as a candy striper, then a nurse's aid, at the Key West hospital before she met Johnny and cut out for the West, but she never discussed her desire for surgery with any of the people who worked at the hospital. Kristina had developed an understanding about the world, just as her brushes with hospitals had allowed her to do with medicine, which was a combination of expertise and ignorance. Kristina knew she could seem bright and competent, but only if she wasn't asked to do more than she could. Bridget had wanted her to go to college. Bridget had hoped she would meet men who suited her own dreams, for Bridget claimed for herself some fancy forebears. Bridget told people she was British, but since she had come to the States her relations had risen and now seemed to Kristina to lurk somewhere in the margins of *Burke's Peerage,* a copy of which, bought for ninety-seven cents at K Mart, rested on the shelf by Bridget's bed in the trailer.

Kristina Sue Pine had a jumble of tales to sort through. She thought she was part Irish (her mother's part) and part French (on her father's side). Her father, Bridget had assured her, had been in the navy during World War II, but she wasn't sure Bridget had ever really married him. He had died when she was little. He had opened a pet store in the middle of Florida after the war and had expanded it into a small jungle world, even before Walt Disney had such ideas. If he hadn't died, Bridget had always told her, they'd be rich. All Kristina could really remember was Bridget.

Kristina had never given these matters that much thought, but when Eli was born and forms had to be filled out, questions came up and she thought she needed to be able to tell Eli who his grandparents were. Everyone commented that Eli was a singular looking child, with the longest blond eyelashes ever seen, and Kristina hoped to be able to place him with a modeling agency and eventually in TV commercials. And she had planned to get started on that as soon as she got him away from her ex's parents; those grandparents he knew too well. But she hadn't done anything about that since they got back to Florida.

Curt had lived in the same apartment complex as her in-laws. They resented Kristina's taking up with him. Curt painted houses and did handyman jobs; he was originally hired as a security guard, but that position didn't amount to much, though he continued to wear the uniform while doing yardwork. She was not sure bringing him back with her to Key West had been a good idea. Curt had encouraged her to get her breasts operated on. He, like her ex, had seemed to take little interest in them; he would play with one for a minute and squeeze the other with a free hand, and then forget about them both. No man had ever made a fuss over her breasts.

It was what she told the doctor, one she had been referred to, a woman, a foreigner, a Scandinavian. Kristina could have the work done at Bellevue for only a hundred-dollar charge to herself. The doctor had to approve the surgery as therapeutic and Kristina had told her of the feelings of humiliation she had and the way men had treated her. Medicaid would pay. She did not tell the doctor she had worked as a Playboy Bunny. She sensed that did not fit, somehow.

The woman doctor was sympathetic and touched her the same way the doctor had in Miami, the same wire for her crotch to her nipples had electrified, but she did not resent it, since she felt that this woman wouldn't abuse her. Her mother had women friends, though Kristina felt no particular interest or distance. She certainly didn't feel scared of the woman doctor. Kristina's nipples always seemed to her to be too large, though she realized that was because her breasts were so small, and they quickly stiffened when the doctor caressed the underside of her breast, saying, "This is where the scar will run," as her finger trailed the path, "along the inferior submammary fold. It will hardly show. The thinnest scar—my insignia."

She didn't use silicone implants, but new saline implants; their size could be adjusted after they were inserted. It was a *prosthesis,* a word Kristina found hard to pronounce. The woman seemed genuinely helpful to her, wanting Kristina to feel better, to look better, to be happy. The doctor's own ample breasts, though not too large, left a question in the air Kristina did not venture to ask.

She was only in the hospital three days—actually only forty-eight hours; one afternoon and then a whole day and another morning. The first thing she had to do after being admitted was to change into a string-tied gown and take an elevator down into the basement of Bellevue. Her hospital room was in what looked to Kristina like a new building, though she had entered into an old building by a side door. The only thing that had been in the hallway was an old wheelchair, one with a high wooden back and large spoke wheels. BELLEVUE was stenciled on the back of the headrest, though Kristina thought no one's back could be so long, and no head held that high. She had finally found the reception desk, filled out forms, and was put in a room with five other patients. Then she descended to the basement.

The room she went into was a photography studio, or, at least, it had been turned into one. It was the same setup she had seen at Sears when she had taken Eli for pictures. Except there were no homey touches here; just a gray metal stool in front of a dull screen.

A young man, not much older than she was, walked in through a side door and asked, "Would you please remove your gown and sit on the stool?" He was wearing nothing that would connect him to the hospital, no jacket even of the sort orderlies wore. Kristina had not been bothered by any of the examinations and measurements that had been lately taken, but she found herself feeling embarrassed in front of this young man. Not that she was especially modest; but she took no pleasure in the way she looked naked. When she thought of herself being undressed, she always thought of her breasts being exposed, though Johnny had taken nude pictures of her and had them blown up to poster size. And not until Kristina saw them did she realize how much they showed. She was sitting with her legs up, but fallen apart, and one arm demurely across her breasts—so you couldn't see how small they were—and since they were covered she didn't realize her genitalia were the center of the picture. The photograph was taken at the house of a friend who had some fancy equipment, fancier than what was in this room, and the lighting made you look at some places more than others. She had never before seen herself quite the same way. Gee, I have a large cunt, she had thought, though she meant the amount of pubic hair that was visible.

But in the gray room the young man in his button-down shirt made her feel conspicuous, so she began to talk to him. "Say, do you do anything else but take these pictures here?" His expression altered just for a second. "Oh, yes. I'm really a painter. I just work here to pay the rent."

He was not trying to be charming, to flirt, but to be professional. Kristina thought that might be in the job description. He took a few pictures straight on, and then from both profiles, having her sit left and right. And from angles in between. Kristina thought this must be an odd job for a young man to have, but she had had any number of odd jobs herself.

"Are there going to be pictures taken afterward?" she asked.

"Not by me," he said. Kristina was not sure what he meant.

She had been groggy when she came back to her hospital room and high from the painkiller she had been given, but a black orderly did not act in the least surprised when she ordered him to measure how much urine she had left in the pan.

"One hundred and two ccs," he sang out, as if she were a physician and not a patient. When she worked in the Key West hospital, that had been one of her duties and it stuck in her mind as a necessity.

Some of the beds were no longer occupied; there were only two other women in the room. One was an old woman, who at first looked dead to Kristina. She was white as plaster and piebald, with splotches of purple and brown. But then she finally stirred herself and in a voice that was a shocking boom, as if whatever was left of her life had sunk into her vocal cords, she had roared: "Hello, young lady, how ya doing?"

The other was a large black woman who had had a breast removed and was weeping steadily. A doctor had yelled at her, telling her not to carry on so, that she was going to live, that that was what was important. But the woman continued to cry, and he had angrily pulled shut a curtain that ran in a track around the bed. Kristina had talked to her after the doctor left.

Kristina had been told not to jar herself, that things needed to remain in place until healing was under way and that that was why the bandages were so firm. She had been redrawn, her doctor said. They had advised her to wear a bra for at least six months, but she knew then she would not obey. She was sore, but excited, and found her hand touching herself, but the weeping in the bed across from her increased, and Kristina felt funny: this mixture of her excitement and the other woman's sorrow.

After she was back in Key West, for a while, Kristina thought Bridget didn't notice the difference. That her own mother didn't know her only daughter's flesh! Kristina had caught her mother giving her odd looks, and Bridget finally said, "Krissy, honey, you do look more mature now, older, but I can't put my finger on why."

Kristina told her it was a year's worth of exercise and good living. Even though her breasts were now firmer and larger, they still didn't hold a candle to her mother's. So, Kristina supposed, even though she had changed, the change was not enough to outdistance her mother. But it had affected Winston. He had noticed right away; or, at least, he seemed to notice in a way he never had before, Kristina thought. One year she was just Bridget's brat, and the next, well, something else.

Rummaging around the trailer, Kristina had found a diary she had kept in high school. It was practically empty, since she had left off making entries *(Dear Diary, Saw Rick look at me during civics. I know he's gonna ask me out)* almost as soon as she started, but she thought it would now be a good idea to start again. So much had changed. She decided just to make a list:

escaped death on May 17th (twice!)
got job a week later
slept with W!
chicken soup (cocaine)

joined the gang

And now she would have to add:

took mom to the hospital

Kristina had not been back at Pair o' Dice long when the phone rang. It was the shop on Front Street, saying that her mother had passed out at work and would she come and take her home. Curt was nowhere to be found; but the rent-a-car was still parked out front. Curt said it would be at least a month or more before the airline would even notice that it hadn't been returned. Curt figured the airline would have to pay anyway, since it was charged to them. The address on his license, the one he had given the rent-a-car company, was in Boston. He had a Vermont license, too. He scraped off the small identification decals from the car and didn't seem worried, so Kristina decided she wouldn't be worried either. Curt had finally rolled his shattered window down and it did crumble. Kristina was forever finding little chunks of glass, with odd edges, like they were pieces of rock instead of glass, and she was concerned that Eli would swallow one of them, but he hadn't. Lately, he was always putting things in his mouth.

Kristina had taken the dancing job reluctantly, but she had to admit she liked the idea of letting her new implants earn her some money. There was so much turnover of dancers that she pretty much was allowed to make her own schedule. She was paid in cash and still could collect AFDC, unless someone snitched on her.

Kristina looked after Eli during the day. She would take him along to Smathers Beach, buy him hot dogs, cotton candy from the roach coaches, then to Winston's pool at the condo. Bridget would watch him at night and feed him, sometimes. Curt would, if Bridget or she couldn't. Other times, she got a babysitter, usually Juniper, the daughter of Bridget's hairdresser. All in all, it was working out all right. Except she knew she had to get Curt out of the trailer, out of Key West, out of her life, and on his way. He'd been telling her that there was something wrong with Eli, that he didn't hear right. It didn't seem to Kristina that there was a lot going on between Curt and her to bust up, even though he had stood by her when she had gone to court to get Eli back. She had gotten custody and she didn't have to let Johnny's parents see him. She and Curt only slept together a few times in the beginning and then they just sort of stopped.

Winston needed them both. Bridget hadn't kept what Winston was up to a secret long. She might not have been able to tell that her daughter had bigger breasts, but her mom couldn't wait to tell her what Winston was planning. Two men were supposed to come down from Providence with Vern, but they had backed out.

Her own hesitations were calmed by the fact that Curt agreed right away. Ten thousand dollars for maybe two days work, Winston said. They had to tour the place tomorrow. Everyone would go in different directions after it was done. That appealed the most to her. Curt would be out of Kristina's world.

But she knew Winston was going to be unhappy with tonight's news. That her mother was in the hospital, stomach pumped, and talking in her sleep. The doctors had said it was just a reaction to the combination of drugs she had been taking. But what if they listened to what she was saying?

Kristina hadn't planned on taking her anywhere but home, but by the time she had found Juniper and gotten to the store, her mother was gone. She was told an ambulance had been called. Candi, the store's manager, was upset, because the shop had gone unsupervised for some time.

A customer had called the number for emergencies on the store's front door. Candi had run right over and found Bridget curled up behind a counter, hardly breathing. She didn't know how much had been stolen from the store, what with people just walking in and out. She was also, Kristina could tell, concerned about Bridget, who had begun to twitch. It was then she called the ambulance. Kristina was supposed to meet Winston at the Wharf House, but now she had to go to the hospital. She knew her news would make things unpleasant. Some part of her worried that Winston was going to blame her for Bridget's problems. Curt better be there, she thought, dialing the condo's number. He hadn't shown up back at the trailer, and Kristina had had to ask Juniper again to look after Eli while she did all this running around.

2

There had been for Kenner the smallest touch of luxury about coming down to Key West, leaving the city and a handful of women behind. He had lived there long enough, and with enough friction, to become just a worn part, spinning in place. He had given a good deal of useless thought to the sort of woman he attracted and had an image of the prototype: the vamp who wants to call it quits, settle down, hang up her spurs. Kenner had the air of a homesteader about him: the fellow who'd watch the crops come in, no longer the bounder ready to light out for the open range. He had even seen the same glimmer in Rea's eyes, that dim lantern held aloft in the storm, slicker on, torrents gushing down. A yellow glow, feeble, but there.

Kenner regretted leaving the Sport Fury at the condo. He waited for the local bus, another mass transit fund grab by the city fathers; the buses that were purchased were one step up from the Conch Train. They looked like something that would pull you around an amusement park. Their air-conditioning usually worked, though. Every day—and those to come—made the Sport Fury, absent of air-conditioning, more infernal. When he stepped on the bus, the chill of the inside air was exceptional. It seemed to be laced with so much Freon it smelled like formaldehyde. Kenner thought he had stepped onto a traveling morgue. Yet another magazine assignment that hadn't gone well, though it had left him quite rearranged. The oddest thing, he thought, settling into the bus seat's contours, was that the corpse he had seen, after the autopsy was well under way, had looked like a Salvador Dali painting. The body was carved up in straight lines, geometric cuts, by power tools, the top of the skull removed as if a drawer had been pulled out. That was what looked so strange: the body taken apart like a wooden Chinese puzzle.

Kenner decided to get off the bus at Sears Town and see what movies were playing. But Kenner had seen both movies: *Bronco Billy* and *The Shining*.

He could catch another bus back to Cayo Hueso condos, but he decided to walk along U.S. 1. Kenner thought of this part of the highway as an old horror movie, where the heroine's face had been hideously scarred, and she covered that side of her face with a chiffon scarf, a swag over the unsightly. On one side was the water: in the deepening dark as smooth as stainless steel, black, but still iridescent. And, on the other side, it was blotched and pitted with fast-food joints, motels, gas stations, all facing perfection: the deep, the Gulf, the night.

There was a bright white sign ahead that had attracted him. Black letters: NEED DANCERS GOOD PAY APPLY IN PERSON; and below: TOPLESS DANCERS XXX NO COVER. Under that, another message, with one letter fallen away: F I-NITE HAPPY HOUR 4–9.

It was Friday night, and Kenner was certainly tempted by the idea of a F I-NITE happy hour. Kenner thought that if he went to the bar there would be a fifty-fifty chance of his not calling any of the women in New York that he was intending to call, planning to offer an invitation and air-fare.

A little topless dancing might be just what he needed.

Kenner found the Florida practice of attaching liquor stores to saloons sensible, more sensible, it seemed to him, than the combination liquor-and-ammo store that was found in other states. That, though, was meeting madness head-on.

The interior of the lounge was brown: laminated, rec-room paneling, small round Formica tables, all dung-colored, slightly fecal, scatological, since the carpet, too, was brown. At the far end, a horseshoe-shaped bar; the only other color came from the candle globes on the tables: red, a sacristy hue, all sheathed in plastic mesh, the fishnet stockings of a fifties' pinup. There was a stage off to the right, next to it a jukebox. Two small baby spots were wired to the ceiling, pointing toward the stage, a raised dais, not much larger than a kettle drum.

The crowd fanned out from the stage in concentric ripples. Kenner found an empty table on the periphery. A young woman vacated a stool at the bar and detached a short jacket from around her shoulders, revealing a black string bikini bottom. She stood by the jukebox, dropped quarters in, and punched a series of numbers. Blue-gelled spotlights were turned on.

She looked very young to Kenner, hardly more than eighteen. She began to move with the beat of her selection, a song familiar to Kenner, but he could not name the singer. He had known he was getting older when the names of popular singing groups were unknown to him; just as when he realized he no longer could tell the model years of cars apart. Kenner thought of the power of dance and how dancers were erotic paragons for him. He would watch the chorus lines on TV variety shows in the fifties, transfixed by the notion that if he just stared hard enough he would see more than their outfits meant to reveal. And even though Kenner had had intercourse a variety of ways, it never could be called dance; even when the girl on stage pantomimed the motions of intercourse, Kenner knew they were not duplications. Dance seemed to him idealized motion, not so much abstracted as isolated, meant to be the conveyance of imagination, fitting it to what it could never hold.

Kenner looked away for a moment from her body and watched her face. He realized she wasn't a stranger. A sexual shunting took place; immediately he felt himself kick over onto another track, and the swampy appreciation he had been feeling became flooded with other concerns. His reflections lost their erotic edge. They didn't sour, but they certainly curdled, and since Kenner now recognized the young woman with the taut breasts as one of Winston's crowd, he drew himself up from his slouch, sat straight-backed on the bentwood chair and looked about, attentive. If he had missed something, he could have missed a number of other things.

Kenner once had been in attendance at a politician's wedding, a rather showy affair, full of the city's pushers and shakers; a tall, middle-aged man said to him, "I know you." Kenner looked at his mature, reflective face and, though he felt a shudder of familiarity, couldn't place him. He said, to be polite, "Yes, we must have met somewhere once, but I'm afraid I've forgotten your name."

For some reason the man looked pleased. Later Kenner thought this must have confirmed some sour judgment he had made long ago about Kenner. The fellow said, quite merrily, "How about selling you newspapers every morning for two years!"

That's who he was! Kenner realized. The owner of a candy store on Sixth Avenue that Kenner had patronized before he had moved to Charles Street. The man was a relative of the politician. Kenner had never thought that he canceled out certain sorts of people. He felt chastised, since he always thought he was a man of the people, except it was the people he had trouble remembering.

And how could he have forgotten this young woman's tits? They did not loll around her chest, cats in a sack, but jutted out, stood firm, her nipples in the air-conditioned chill tiered like an elaborate wedding cake with excitement. Kenner looked to the spot at the bar that she had vacated and there was a young man whom Kenner had also seen in Winston's company. The young man was staring at Kenner.

Kenner raised his hand in recognition and the young man slid off his stool and, navigating the crowd, came over to Kenner's table. He did not glance in the direction of the stage where his friend, the dancer, was bending over, each cheek of her ass clasped by one of her hands. He stood by Kenner's table, and said, in a peculiar combination of nervousness and aggression, "Say, I wanted to clear something up right away. A misunderstanding you might have. If Winston said anything to you about what I said, about wanting to knock the smirk off your face, I really didn't mean it—or have cause to say it—I just misinterpreted a look you had."

He did not loom over the table, since he was no more than Kenner's height. Kenner watched his hands while he talked. They were doing amazing things in front of his chest: a pantomime, their own Punch and Judy show. Kenner was caught off guard by the young man's speech. Not so much by the implied violence, but by the fact that he was, had been, discussed at all.

"Why don't you sit down?" Kenner said evenly, thinking that would defuse him.

Kenner could see the invitation cross his mind. It flitted behind his eyes, went from east to west like a cyclone. Kenner grew somewhat uneasy. He knew things were amiss when a person watched himself think. The fellow looked at the empty chair and then, as if high-stepping over a fence, vaulted it with one leg and sat down.

"You're . . ." Kenner let hang.

"Curt Wren," he said. "I've gotten a bad rap in the past by misunderstandings and I don't want it to keep happening."

"Aren't you a friend of . . ." and Kenner turned his head toward the stage, just as the young woman's head was disappearing behind the lower part of her body. She was forming a parabola; her pelvis was thrust forward, the top of the arch. The tendons and muscles in her legs became pronounced, rigid: guy wires straining toward the peak of her crotch.

"Kristina. Yeah, Kristina. She's a friend," Curt said, not looking in her direction, but waiting for Kenner to turn back to him.

Curt, Kenner quickly discovered, was the sort of Vietnam veteran who Kenner had heard all about, but never met. The slightly psychotic, temperamental, druggy vet with a lingering fondness for violence. Kenner had known a fair sampling of veterans and none was Curt's type, though his sort had received a lot of play. Kenner was sure they were out there somewhere, but he had always tried to make it a habit not to run into any kind of walking aberration, if he could help it.

Curt had the sort of male prettiness that Kenner had noticed before only in a couple of child actors he knew. It didn't age well. After they were out of their teens their looks became puffy. They usually stayed small, too; that was part of it. And Curt was small—not just his height—there was the quality of reduction all about him. Built not quite to scale.

Curt's fatigue jacket had gone out of style in the early seventies; so long ago that it was coming back in. It didn't look that

134

strange to Kenner. Curt had cut the sleeves off, so it was now a vest. He had the sort of up-front sincerity that troubled Kenner; it was usually the hallmark of a fanatic.

Curt hadn't really started to talk until they both had a couple drinks more. It allowed Curt to retreat into his own screening room, and when the picture came into focus he finally turned on the sound. He had been in the navy, and that made sense to Kenner. He didn't look like a grunt. He claimed to have been on the nuclear carrier, USS *Enterprise,* at the time its own planes had blown up on deck.

Kenner instinctively doubted anyone who claimed to have been present at a famous moment in history. And Curt didn't look quite that old—he'd have to be twenty-nine. But Curt's version of those events seemed incontestable. Someone, he had said, left the yellow gear too near a plane. Jargon acts as passwords. Yellow gear. Auxiliary power supplies. Tractors, Diesel-fueled electrical generators. The exhaust of a tug's jet turbine pointed toward an underwing. An officer, Curt said, actually saw the first rocket heat up, start to change color. Curt said he watched some guy run over to it, but it went off before he got there. Then it was hellacious, Curt said. July Fourth for adults; bombs away.

He laughed a strange laugh when Kenner supplied the fact that some twenty-seven people were killed. Curt said, "People get killed aboard the carrier all the time. One guy got cut in half by the catapult horseshoe. It really zips back at tremendous speeds. It came off and went right through the middle of a guy, sawed him in half.

"Some guys get sucked into jet exhausts just on small power and get cut up something fierce.

"One guy was playing around, sitting on the rail, and another, they were both cooks," he said, "playing around, threw a hundred-pound sack of potatoes at him, expecting him to catch it. But it knocked him off the rail and into the water and he was never found. But when we blew ourselves up, that was something different."

Curt certainly had been successful in taking Kenner's mind off of female flesh. Kristina had come over to their table, after putting her Chinese jacket back on. It did restore some modesty, though she wasn't allowed to sit long. Each dancer had to take a turn working the crowd, passing a plate for donations to feed the jukebox.

Curt went on about his time in the Pacific: Curt had been

impressed by Subic Bay. He said he was on shore patrol there. All the sailors crossed over a bridge to get into the wild part of town.

"Beneath the bridge," Curt said, happy with his recollections, "ran a river of shit. We would throw coins into it and young Filipino kids would jump in after them. It was my introduction to the truly fucked-up."

Kenner felt, in Curt's presence, that Kenner was on the verge of error. That was whenever he was likely to go against what he considered his common sense. But, these days, he began to think of his common sense multiplying at too fast a rate: he pictured it as yellow curd, thickening, leaving deposits in veins.

Kenner normally would have stood back from the likes of Curt—and even Winston. Winston, though, had kept his distance, so he had made it easy for Kenner to follow the dictates of his good sense. In the old days he would have gone the long way around the likes of Curt and Kristina. Rea was another matter. But, Kenner realized, times had changed. An hour of death and dismemberment stories hadn't been enough to keep him from accepting a ride back to the condo in a fancy car.

3

Winston arrived at the hospital feeling slightly sick himself. The coke had left him sensitized, and hospitals made him feel the onset of illness. The hospital was located at the elbow of a dredged arm of coral, stuck out into a blue lagoon. Even in the purple afterglow of sunset, night not entirely clamped shut on the horizon, the orange building seemed to glow. The color looked alarming to Winston, as did the cement disc, painted with cross hairs, by the front doors: a helicopter landing pad, for patients scooped out of the sea, or scraped off the highway.

The lobby was empty. Nothing was going on. He hadn't wanted to come, but Kristina's call made it necessary. Got to calm the bitch down.

Just talk to her, Kristina had said. He heard voices and saw what he took for a doctor and a nurse drinking coffee in a room off the reception area.

"Hello," Winston called out. "I'm looking for Bridget—" and he realized he didn't know which last name she was using. He guessed Kristina's. "Pine. She was admitted this afternoon."

A doctor looked his way. He could be from the navy base,

136

Winston thought: blond, short hair, thin. His stethoscope was draped around his neck like a feather boa. He remembered an acquaintance he had in Boston whose connection was a doctor at Mass General. A nurse walked out from behind him and answered, "I'll look."

"That'll be the barbiturate poisoning in room one twenty-eight," the young doctor said, looking at him. "Are you her husband?"

"No," Winston said, feeling himself prickle, "just a friend."

The doctor seemed to want to amend his mistake by giving information, or he had intended to give it to a relative and couldn't stop.

"She was mixing old and new prescriptions, it appears. She'll be okay. She's suffering from malnutrition, actually. There are a few things we need to look at, but nothing too serious."

Winston didn't care for the doctor looking at him so closely as he spoke. He began backing away.

"I'd like to see her," he said, retreating from the doctor's voice.

She was not alone. Bridget shared the room with another woman. Winston had not considered that; he had expected privacy. The woman was young, reading a magazine, one leg elevated, a foot bared, jutting free. It was painted with Mercurochrome. Bridget was asleep. She wore a plastic tubing chin strap, except it was not hooked under her chin, but under her nose. It supplied oxygen, he saw.

She was wearing a paper hospital gown and was hooked up to two bottles. Both were full of clear liquids. Winston would have had to walk around, get next to the other woman's bed in order to read what they were. He realized he hadn't ever before watched Bridget sleep. Maybe she wanted it that way. She was usually up before he was. Her face did not soften, but sagged. It was the mobility of her mouth and her darting eye that made her face expressive, he realized. Her eyes were shut, one false eyelash curled up half-detached, like the wing of a locust. Winston was moved to pull it all the way off, but didn't. Flat on her back, her breasts had fallen to her sides; they were so large they would slide over, as if gravity wanted all the flesh to be on the same level. They puddled, one on each side of her rib cage, making her chest weirdly flat.

Winston remembered she avoided ever placing herself in that position; usually she would be aside or astride him. Her breasts would hang down; she would drag them across his face, one way, then the other. He liked it, the flesh rolling over his features, the nipples' rubbery roughness.

Bridget thought it was her body, but it was what she said that he liked. He never once doubted the dirty sincerity in her voice; it excited him, would make him come. Other women couldn't keep the play-acting out of their voices, even the ones who tried. Or, they couldn't keep it up. He didn't believe them. What they said would lose its dark sting. Bridget was a natural. But now it was her voice that was giving him troubles. All that could spill out, make difficulties.

"She's been out for quite some time," the young woman in the other bed said. She put down her magazine. Winston looked at her: small, streaked blond hair, quite long, thick, and her flesh an odd bronze color. Man Tan.

"They sedated her. Knocked her right out," and she gestured to the IV bottles hanging next to Bridget's bed.

"She was conscious when her daughter was here, but babbling. The doc said she was coming out of a bad sleep and he was going to put her into a good one. Your name Winston?"

"Yes."

"Well, you must be something, from the way she talked about you."

The young woman's eyes drifted up and down over him.

"Couldn't make out most of it, but it sounded really trashy. I don't mean to laugh," she said, trying to stifle a giggle, "but it was first-class ravings. My name's Helen. I stepped on a sea urchin."

She wiggled her bare foot. Winston saw a circle of dark spots on its bottom, on her heel. Some gang's tattoo, buckshot.

"They told me they would work themselves out eventually, but they have a guy here who specializes in them and he will take them out in the morning."

"Tell her I was by, would you? And tell her I'll come back tomorrow, in the afternoon."

"Hey, stick around. You're obviously worth getting to know. She kept mixing you up with a bird. A swan, I think."

Winston saw her smile as he turned. It hung there in his mind, a Cheshire cat grin, all teeth above a limb.

Twelve

Rea hated running, but she forced herself to do it. If she ran in the morning before seven, the heat wasn't bad, but now the sun sliced down. Up to the airport and back; a little over three miles. Her father ran. She ran. It wouldn't please her father; but he would think less of her if she didn't. She wasn't in the father-currying-favors business, but she knew it was too late to erase his standards. Kenner should run. Kenner should do something. It was obvious to her, seeing him by the pool, that he was strong, but overweight. Not very appealing. Something had to be appealing, though, or else she wouldn't be going fishing. Winston was putting the troops through their paces this morning.

The speed bumps in the condo's driveway always interrupted her stride. She had to jump over them. She passed by the deserted tennis courts, a hedge of oleander ringing the high cyclone fence around them. She saw Kenner leaning against a car.

"You're early," she said. He was wearing a red T-shirt imprinted OZARK BAR-B-CUE. He looked like most overweight stocky men do in a T-shirt. Five months pregnant.

"Is that," she said, gesturing, "a testimonial to what fills it?"

Kenner looked down at the printing on his shirt.

"No, it just settles the natives down. This sends out I'm-one-of-you messages."

Rea could tell he thought himself something of a sport in his boat shoes and cutoffs and redneck T-shirt. A regular Eugene V. Debs of the beachcomber set.

"I'll be back down in a minute," she said, running up the condo's outside cement stairway.

Rea put on a red halter and white shorts. She was glad to get clear of the condo for the day. The apartment had begun to resemble a city slum. Each of the bedrooms had been turned into a separate domicile, as if different generations of immigrants had moved in on top of one another. Duane had been heating up cans of chili on a hot plate in their room and had burnt the dresser's top. No one picked up the communal living room. There they had spread diagrams and maps over the thick monkeypod wood table. Rea thought it had begun to resemble a scene from *The Golden Bough,* the men bent around that piece of jungle slab, some fallen, dead tree; and the women—Krissy at least—painting toenails, watching television. Yet another reason why Winston had rented the rooms at the Wharf House. For maid service.

Rea found herself susceptible occasionally to current theories of institutionalized personality. Some people just needed to be in prison and they committed crimes in order to be let in. When she started the prison workshop, her own homework had been reading some criminology. The books had seemed to miss the point. She realized that the condo's bedrooms had been turned into cells. That's why Duane had the hot plate and cooked in the room: he liked to be autonomous, control his space. Or was it just habits that had been impressed on his most vulnerable nerves? Or the knowledge that such a small space was all that he could control?

At times the graduate school lectures she attended overlapped with her outside interests. "Briefly," the professor had begun, "what Heidegger's deconstruction discloses is that the tradition, from Plato through Hegel to, say, Jeremy Bentham and the Age of Technology, assumes the world to be, in one way or another, fallen, a condition characterized by the dispersal of Eternity into time, Identity into difference, the One into the many, the Whole Picture into fragments." She had actually written it down. The classical tradition, seeing the world disintegrating—

no wonder Duane dropped out after three weeks. She had struggled and pulled strings to get him in. The prof had been enchanted by Foucault and his discussion of the Panopticon, a prison built in a circle, a prison modeled on Bentham's notions for the perfect system of incarceration. All seeing. Guards in a central tower are able to look into every cell at once. " 'They are like so many cages' " the professor had quoted, " 'so many small theatres, in which each actor is alone, perfectly individualized and instantly visible. . . . it reverses the principle of the dungeon. Rather of its three functions—to enclose, to deprive of light and to hide.' " Foucault had a better prose style than the professor and Rea had sat up during those portions of the lecture. " 'It preserves only the first and eliminates the other two. Visibility is a trap.' "

She wondered if the prof had ever been inside the can in Joliet that had been built on the Panopticon model. He kept stressing the psychological effect on the prisoners of being watched at all moments, how it impressed upon them their condition, how it turned them into convicts, taught them lessons of incarceration. They knew they were prisoners since they were watched.

Rea had laughed out loud in the large lecture hall at that remark. No one else had. Some students turned and stared at her. The prof didn't seem to have taken notice. He was lost in his own oratory. The prisoners knew they were prisoners from the moment they had been arrested. They did not need the Panopticon to tell them that. Rea was certain, though, that the psychological effects were much more potent to the builders of such prisons, to the bureaucratic minds that would *see* the supposed efficacy.

Nothing like a fancy idea that seems simple to sway the minds of the purse holders. The prisoners knew who they were. They had that straight all along. The professor's lecture had been billed as an attack on the idea of a classical curriculum. Oh well, Duane had attacked that, too.

It was odd how the joint gave order to the chaos of some prisoners' lives. Rea hated clutter. Duane hated clutter. She could be very disciplined, even though she admired spontaneity. Duane was capable of some discipline, of a sort—a counterpressure. The prison pressed a discipline upon him and he, in turn, created a discipline to press back. A diving bell. He could live well underwater.

As she came down the condo's steps, the flipflops she had

put on sent out their *slap slap slap* and caught Kenner's attention. She saw him looking up at her, smiling.

2

Kenner felt he had lost a certain kind of ignorance, the sort that was productive, akin to curiosity. He had had it as a teenager, when the world was full of possibility. The future might hold a terror or two lurking in its darkest corners, but Kenner had enjoyed being able to look ahead and to see: What? Who knew? That's what he had liked. Kenner had not attained any grand summit from which to squint ahead at all that lay before him; though it wasn't much more than a rise, some barely swollen embolism on which Kenner now stood, much to his regret, and saw: not his life ahead, but what the likely possibilities were.

Kenner assumed that this was merely something that came with age, something you got when you galloped past thirty. The land of promise, now realized. There was something terrible about the promised land.

He knew how some of his contemporaries arranged never to attain even the tiniest hillock: drugs helped, a neurosis faithfully watered, anything to help stay that peak, the other side of the incline: what lies ahead.

He was so certain of his foresight that he enjoyed being wrong, for then he could doubt all his certainties. Even small misapprehensions gave him comfort, he thought; then Kenner noticed the turnoff to the dog track on U.S. 1. He laughed at the coincidence: enjoy being wrong, my ass!

"What's funny?" Rea asked.

"I was just thinking I enjoy being wrong occasionally. Then I saw the turnoff to the dog track."

"It's easy to misjudge, especially dogs."

"I know," Kenner said. "Once, though, I was on a stalled train in Newark waiting to get into Manhattan. And something happened that made me happy I was wrong. I was reading a newspaper and a card with a trinket attached was slipped—no, it really just *appeared* under my thumb. The reverse motion of a master pickpocket.

"The card read: I AM DEAF. Then there was a pitch. Money for the trinket."

He looked over at Rea and her face was full of concentra-

142

tion and patient interest. At that moment she did look like a teacher.

"It was the PATH train. I was in the end car; the last car is treated like a parlor car. A lot of food is consumed, wine drunk, and marijuana smoked. You can get a contact high from just being there.

"Well, when I looked at the card I immediately thought: the guy is a fake. He's not deaf. I'm always wondering about that sort of thing: if the blind with their tin cups are really blind."

"It's a common enough skepticism," Rea said.

"Well, yeah," Kenner said, looking at the road and seeing the scene simultaneously. "The man passed out a card to every passenger and then took them back. One guy did give him some change for the trinket. It was a key chain, I think. I didn't give him anything when he took the card back from me.

"He walked away putting the change the other guy had given him into his pocket. One coin—a quarter—fell. I heard it hit the floor. He didn't. He continued walking away from the money. The guy couldn't hear a coin drop. Stone deaf.

"Another man on the train saw the coin. He looked like he needed the quarter himself, but he saw me looking and he bent down, picked up the quarter, and caught up with the man with the cards.

"He tapped him on the shoulder and gave him the quarter. The deaf man gave him a card with a trinket. The samaritan gave the card back to him, trying to explain in sign language what had happened."

Rea smiled as Kenner displayed some one-handed lunatic semaphore.

"At that point the deaf guy thought he had just then dropped some money. Finally he left the train and the car doors shut and we went into Manhattan."

"Did you ever consider that the guy just might have been a superior scam artist? That it was the old let-the-coin-drop ploy? Anyone playing deaf knows it." Rea laughed.

Kenner suffered a moment of deflation. He was cynical, but he was still surprised to discover he wasn't cynical enough. Rea seemed to be able to illustrate that in a number of ways.

"I didn't mean it," Rea said, after Kenner remained silent. "I think you were right. Maybe I need some of your gullibility."

"Those always intrigued me," Kenner said, restored to good humor, indicating a sign ahead, stenciled white on red: AIR. "I didn't know what it meant. I thought it was like an old EAT sign. I thought it was some sort of code."

He pulled off the highway, the car generating coral dust as it came to a stop. AIR BAIT TACKLE.

"You can figure," Rea said, "that if it's three letters long, it is for sale. GAS. FUN."

"SEX. LAW."

"FBI. CIA."

Kenner laughed. He was happy with the day's prospects. He had always meant to fish in the Keys. He had lived along a northeastern shoreline for two years without ever throwing a hook in the water. But he didn't intend to do the same here. The colors in the Keys seemed to demand action. They were startlingly active: primary colors, bright blues, a backdrop to throw yourself against. You were always outlined, he thought. The beach here, unlike the beaches of the Northeast, seemed a porch, and the sea beyond pasture. You looked at it as a farmer looks at his acres and acres of rolling fields. Islands, Kenner had come to think, did not look inward, but outward. Continents could be vortexes, swirling masses drawing things in, but islands were centrifugal; everything tended to fly off.

Rea had assured Kenner that she was no expert fisher. From his encounter with her at the dog track, he already knew she was a savvier handicapper. She knew, he had discovered, more about baseball than he did; names and batting averages poured out of her when he made a passing comment. All her exercising, he was sure, put her in better shape. Fishing, they should be about equal. He had some unclear memory of how to cast.

The inside of the bait shop was overgrown with equipment and supplies. Not just every species of fish but every individual within the species seemed to warrant its own hook and lure. The bait fish they purchased looked bigger than anything Kenner hoped to catch.

3

Every time Kristina went into a store, she felt like a shoplifter. She hadn't done any of that for a long time, since she went out west and had Eli. She wouldn't shoplift with Eli on her hip. He became the store's protector, its angel. In the past, shoplifting was often the day's activity. She planned it about as much as Winston planned robbing the Audubon House, Kristina thought.

Winston had told her that if you alter your circumstances you can make the world look different. He said that even though he had looked at the Audubon House a hundred times, as soon as he decided to take the prints it looked entirely different. He said his eyes became a drain, everything swirled into them. He spent part of almost every day sitting on the bench in the small arrowhead-shaped park on Whitehead Street, looking at the Audubon House and figuring things out.

She had only been caught shoplifting twice. Once at the Woolco when she had taken some cosmetics, Angel Face makeup. It cost more than the others; it was the only one over a dollar. She would hover around the counter, circle it a few times, locate the bottles and tubes she wanted, and then, without really looking, seeing, snatch them up.

She felt as if she were flying all the while, slightly off the ground, around and around. Maybe that was how Winston felt on the bench. She had come out of the Woolco, back into the blast of heat radiating from the asphalt. She felt safe, out of the zone of the store, and there was Mrs. Kruchnik, Wanda's mother.

"Kristina! What do you have in your bag?!"

Mrs. Kruchnik and Wanda lived in the apartment building she and her mom had lived in before they moved to Pair o' Dice. Kristina realized that she must work at Woolco. She didn't say anything, but felt her face grow hotter. She reached into her bag and handed Mrs. Kruchnik back the Angel Face. "I should have you arrested like everyone else," Mrs. Kruchnik was saying, "but I won't." Then she said, pressing down hard on every word: "Kristina, don't you ever do this again!"

She never did it again at Woolco. But she continued at the Sears Town shopping center. The last time she had exited Kresge's with her catch, seven dollars worth of lipstick and eyeliner and Flame-Glo nail polish, another woman appeared yelling at her, but not by name.

"Here, you, girl, come here!"

Kristina looked and saw a heavy woman in her fifties and had a simple thought: she can't catch me. Kristina turned and ran, her bony legs flying. She really was in the air.

Now she felt that the man taking her five dollars—she was paying for Curt, Eli was let in free—knew exactly what they were planning to do. Her thoughts could be read—she thought she could read his. But she just smiled and laughed, and the man looked at her quizzically and said, "Just walk around downstairs, or out in the garden. The next tour will begin in ten minutes. My, isn't he a cute little boy." He brushed Eli's cheek with the backs of his fingers, and Eli stirred, turned his head in the stroller as if it were a leaf in the wind, and fell back to sleep.

Winston sent them to see the inside of the house, what they were going to take. He kept changing his mind whether or not Curt was going in the house with Vern and Duane. Winston said that with Eli along she and Curt would be inconspicuous, just another family.

Bridget had never taken her to the Audubon House, and Kristina had never thought of going herself. Boyfriends of Bridget's would, every once in a while, take them all out: the beach, a couple of times to dinner, once on a boat. But Bridget never was much for excursions, as she called them. Kristina would come home from school, Bridget would be at work, or out drinking, and Kristina would put on her bathing suit, get on her bicycle, and go hang out.

Curt was looking around like he was a welfare investigator, and Kristina wanted to say something to him about it, but she decided you were supposed to look at everything here with special attention. She pushed the stroller out onto the back porch and Curt tapped her on the shoulder, lifted his head in the direction of the doorway they had just walked through.

A white box with louvers, the alarm. It was just like the one at Tanka Crafts. What's the use, she thought, of having a fancy alarm if it could be shut off with just a single key? Oh, well, this wasn't as dangerous as shoplifting. No one would be there watching. No Mrs. Kruchnik staring at her like an owl in a tree.

The backyard did look like a jungle. Lots of places to hide. She could barely see the chain-link fence at the edge of the property and the scrubby vacant lot where the van would be parked.

People began walking back up the porch steps and past them back into the house. She hadn't heard any announcement, but the tour must be about to start. Maybe it was just the time; someone looked at his watch and everyone followed. Curt was running his hand along the thick edge of the wide wooden door, polished and heavy, like a huge slab of butter brickle. There were only two locks on it: one that was turned with an old-fashioned skeleton key and the other a plain dead bolt that had been attached some time ago, just a regular apartment door lock, not something to fit a door so big.

Kristina left the stroller by the stairs, took Eli up in her arms, held him against her chest, and followed the last of the crowd as it ascended the staircase. She couldn't get her mind to hold on to what the tour guide was telling them. He seemed to love the house, love the people who restored it, who spent so much money making it look nice, finding all the antiques that filled it. They were wonderful people, the owners. Kristina couldn't picture anyone living in the house. Not herself, not Bridget. Everything would be broken.

She began to feel odd, like she was going to faint. She turned to find Curt, but she couldn't see him. She steadied herself and walked into the room, the gallery, where the books of bird pictures were. It was dark, like a funeral parlor, cold. She felt like she was going to see a corpse. Like her dad's funeral. She could only remember the smell, hibiscus and ice. She saw Curt standing in the far corner. He had gone in the other door.

There were four cases. She had never seen books like these. The size of the pull-down maps they had at school. Old maps in scrolls, places she was supposed to learn about. The Holy Roman Empire.

There were other large pictures of birds on the walls. Were they all that valuable? Stealing pictures. But they were only going to take the books. It was the books that were valuable. The pictures on the wall were easier to see. Wings, Kristina was struck by the wings. Above a case was a large print of two buzzards, one above the other on dead branches. One buzzard was in profile, just looking: Mrs. Kruchnik. The buzzard below had his wings extended, unfurled. The feathers were draped like Dracula's cape held out open, ready to surround you.

Kristina looked away, but she had started to think about birds. Did she like birds? They were always just there. Bridget and her dad had owned what she was told was a zoo. She remembered Bridget saying she liked ducks. Mallards. Her mother liked mallards, she recalled Bridget saying, because the males were so faithful. They just swam after the female, following right behind.

Eli started to whimper, grow heavier on her chest, and cry. She patted his back and then looked up. The tour guide had stopped talking. He had been telling everyone how valuable the books were, that they were "one of the world's great art treasures, the only set on continuous display in the country." He was just staring at her now, annoyed at the noise Eli was making.

The little man had caught Kristina's eye and she thought she had made a bad mistake. She turned and saw Curt glaring

147

at her, too. No one was supposed to take any notice of them, especially the person who worked here. She turned quickly, walked out of the gallery, down the steps, hushing Eli, but glad to be going, glad to get away from the rooms filled with so many old, dead things.

4

After two hours of water-gazing, Kenner was tempted to hallucinate. But he couldn't prompt any hallucinations. He realized that fishing on a first date might have been a mistake—unless they had been in a rowboat, which they weren't. Rea and Kenner cast and waited, reeled and cast, stood and sat. Waited. There was a boat-launching ramp and space for parked cars. There were two. Kenner's and an old Ford Fairlane. Down some distance from them—Kenner and Rea were twenty yards apart— was a lone woman, in a striped blouse. They had exchanged hellos when they had arrived. Then she had come to their aid when they had needed to cut up bait. Kenner's Swiss army knife had proved an inefficient tool for that task.

"It's good on Swiss fish," he had told Rea, struggling.

The woman let them use her long bait knife and showed Rea and Kenner how to prepare the hooks, work the reels. Rea had made a cast, swinging the rod stiffly; the line flew out, plunked into the calm surface, smooth and clear as Lucite. Almost immediately she yelled, "I've got something!"

The woman had raced to her side before Kenner got there and showed Rea how to release the drag. She slowly reeled in a foot-long fish.

"See what you got," the woman said. "A nice red snapper."

She bent over the wall and scooped up the fish out of the water with a net. It flipped in its reticule and Rea stared. The woman seized the snapper and extracted the hook. Kenner heard the fish's cartilage crack.

The woman then volunteered her ice bucket for the snapper's safekeeping, since that was one of the many things Kenner had not thought to bring. He had imagined, he supposed, a row of fish lying resplendent next to him; though he now realized the beating sun would have cooked them immediately.

But Rea's red snapper had been the only excitement for the last two hours. They cast, reeled in. Rea had placed herself at the tip of the boat-launching ramp, which jutted some twenty feet into the water. Kenner could see she was trying to perfect her casting. There was a bit of the softball player in her method, Kenner noted. Casting, she looked like she was continually going after bad pitches. She *had* caught something, he reminded himself. Kenner had only managed to lose his hook on a snag, and he had somewhat sheepishly borrowed one from the woman, who had a full tackle box with her. Kenner began to question his organizational skills; he hadn't even brought a hat, so he was thankful when the weather began to change. It had been bright with a few iridescent clouds and clear—so clear you could see under the clouds. The only other place the sky had seemed that stereoscopic to Kenner was the Southwest. The clouds glowed from within. Over Rea's shoulder, he could see a thin line of land, an inch of horizon, but that was the only thing that divided the sky above, the blue sea below. Rea's shorts were white as the clouds and her red top was a drop of blood in all the blue.

Kenner leaned his rod against the seawall, anchoring it with some slag, and walked over toward Rea. She was casting with so much concentration that she didn't hear him approach.

The older woman had left her rod and intercepted him ten yards from Rea. "They're not biting today," she said in a friendly manner. "It's still too early."

Some of Rea's earlier conversation, mimicking fishermen's stories, flooded his mind: *It's always too early, or too late; the water is too deep or it's too shallow; there are too many fish, there are too few; the tide is in, or the tide is out.*

"Well, this is our first time," he said to the woman.

"Around sunset is good here, but I have to work then," she said. Kenner let himself ask.

"Tanka Crafts, on Front Street," she said. "I'm the manager. Candi Swift." Kenner recalled being in the store. He started to think of Winston's redhead, Bridget.

"You must know my friends, the Baillys," he said, the friends who had loaned Kenner their condo. "They own the First Impressions shop."

"No," she said, "I've seen them, but I never met them. They have a nice store. I have seen her before," she said, raising her chin in Rea's direction. "She's come into the shop once or twice. She didn't buy anything."

Kenner took a nervous glance at his rod, hoping to see it being yanked out to sea.

"It's hard to smoke and fish at the same time," she said, by way of explanation for abandoning her rod. Candi looked like she had lived in Key West a long time. Weathered.

"Your girlfriend came in," she said, "with a guy who goes out with one of my clerks."

"Bridget," Kenner concluded.

"You know her?"

"Only by sight—we've never talked."

Kenner could feel the woman expand, some bellows of gossip, all puffed up, ready to be expelled. Some sort of fish, frog, bird—he couldn't remember which.

"Bridget's been in the hospital," Candi said, looking back toward her pole. Kenner glanced in Rea's direction. Still casting. Strike three, he wanted to yell.

"That woman is going to get herself killed," she said.

What woman? he wondered. Kenner's face must have grown serious enough to prompt her to elaborate. "If Bridget keeps on the way she does. Go, go, go. Work, work, work. And she's crazy the way she throws herself at that boy. She's old enough to be his mother."

Kenner considered she might want all this information to get back to Winston, or to Bridget, since he couldn't figure why she was so forthcoming. Unless she expected any friend of Rea's to be a friend to them all.

The woman's face darkened, became something more than shocked: angry, mad. "And he sleeps with her daughter. He takes advantage."

She and Bridget must be around the same age. Is this jealousy? Kenner wondered.

"I don't know that much about Winston's business," he said.

"Well, he's a bad apple," she said. "Rich as he's supposed to be, he never gives Bridget anything. She pays for him." Candi paused. "Bridget took a loan out on her trailer to give him money. She works two jobs. That's why she passed out. Just as if he had come and hit her on the head himself. I'm mad at him, still." She looked back at Kenner, away from her rod. "I don't mean to call him names to a friend of his."

"We're not that friendly," Kenner said.

"Is she?" Candi asked. "I thought she might have recognized me. That's why I came over."

"I don't know. I suppose. They have mutual friends."

"Bridget likes her. She said she doesn't have any airs. Winston, now he's got airs." She got up and threw down the stub of her cigarette, still burning. She didn't step on it. It smouldered in the crushed coral. Kenner stared at her feet, shod in flipflops. She had painted toenails, pink, horny, thick. Kenner thought it funny what parts of the body seemed to show age most accurately. Toenails: like the rings of a tree.

"Well, I'm still trying to catch my supper," she said, and walked back to her pole.

A thought flittered through Kenner while he watched Candi: she might have been—he found himself gingerly phrasing it—romantically interested in Bridget. She had talked like something more than a friend. A protector. For an old broad, Bridget seemed to be an advertisement for the power of allure, no matter how cheap.

Kenner opened a bottle of Tahitian Treat he had purchased at the bait store. He had been able to keep it cool, along with the snapper, in Candi's ice chest. He walked up to Rea; in between casts he offered her a swig. She looked suspiciously at the bottle and declined. She asked for one of the beers he had also bought.

"I'm getting the hang of it," she said, flipping her rod, when he returned with a beer.

Kenner went back to his rod and desultorily began to reel in his line. It held for a moment, and, thinking he had another snag, he tried to jerk it free. But it pulled back and shot off, taking line. Kenner was so surprised he almost let go of the rod. He put on the drag and reeled some line back in. Whatever it was wasn't putting up a lot of resistance. But it felt heavy. He didn't want to holler down to Rea or Candi, in case it turned out to be nothing at all. His rod tip was bent double, the filament taut.

The sky had changed: storm clouds had come up from behind while he and Candi had been talking and now the sun was totally obscured. There was a silver line at the bottom of the horizon, and gray clouds drifted into Kenner's vision, dangling tufts beneath, goat's chin hair. The water's surface lost its shine. The shoals ran out for a hundred yards in front of him, thick with green reeds, and he could see the path his line cut through them.

Rea was walking down the seawall toward him.

Kenner had no idea what he had caught. He had managed to raised its head for a moment out of the water: it was the ugliest thing he had ever seen, but he still didn't know what it was.

Could I have hooked a turtle? he wondered.

151

He got up on top of the wall and continued to reel in. If he had any notion of what he was doing it had come from memories of plucking bluegills from midwestern lakes. He wished he had gone fishing with Winston and his dad. He had forgotten that Candi's net would be useful. He expected just to pull whatever it was up to the tip of his rod.

Kenner's catch broke the surface, and he finally recognized it: an eel, a large eel. It looked more than half a foot wide, olive drab, greenish, a fleshy fin down the back. About the size of a large fire hose, flattened out, drained, still stretched along the street after a fire.

I'm going to catch a moray eel, Kenner thought to himself. He began to pull it from the water and when about three feet had emerged the eel did something so amazing that Kenner just stopped and stared. The eel leapt, it seemed, entirely out of the water and, at the same moment, began to twist itself around, to spool, not into a ball, but into the shape of a wheel. Dangling from the end of his rod was something that looked to Kenner like an olive-drab manhole cover, about seven inches thick. Kenner realized it resembled something else: the sort of magnet hanging from a crane in scrap-iron yards. In the second or two it took the eel to accomplish the maneuver, Kenner just did nothing, not even thinking to swing the rod over to the side, to complete the catch. He was broken from his fascination by another sudden event: the line snapped and the eel splashed back into the water and disappeared.

"Jesus, what was that?" he heard Rea ask.

"I think it was an eel, a moray eel," Kenner said.

"What a thing to pull out of the water."

"You're not supposed to eat them," the shopkeeper's voice said. Kenner saw that Candi was standing behind him.

"There's one that lives over by the rocks where you were casting," she said to Rea. "I feed it. But I don't think you could have caught that one. He's too cagey. You can't eat morays. They're poisonous."

Kenner stared at the limp filament that dangled from the end of the rod.

"I'm pretty sure it wasn't my eel—mine's a different color, light green. It saved you a lot of trouble by snapping the line. They bite bad. You would have had to kill it good before you could get the hook out."

Kenner began to picture the process: the eel flopping on the

152

crushed coral behind the seawall. Kenner with his hand in its mouth. Kenner jumping up and down on it. Kenner hitting it with a bat, except he didn't have a bat.

"Some things ought to stay where they are," Candi said.

"I'm getting cold," Rea said. "I never thought you could feel cold in Key West in the summer."

"It might rain soon," Candi said. "Time to pack up and go home."

"You can have my snapper, if you'd like," Rea said to her. "It's probably enough to feed one, but not two."

"Why thank you," Candi said. "It would make a meal."

She proceeded to clean it. She cut off its head, slit the fish quickly into butterfly sections. "I'll give the rest to my eel," she said. "Do you want to see him? I can usually get him to come out."

Kenner and Rea followed her along the seawall. Kenner looked down into the clear water, marveling at the number of sea urchins adhering to the rocky bottom: their prickly spines stood stiff, star bursts.

Rea and the shopkeeper crouched down near two large rocks. The woman dropped bits of the red snapper's flesh into the water.

"There he is, there he is," she said. Kenner saw a green eel appear, all sinewy undulations. Chartreuse green, yellowish, spotted. It looked to Kenner smaller than the one he had hooked.

"This one is too smart to get caught," the shopkeeper said, looking down into the water with a fond smile.

"Well," Rea said, "the other one wasn't too dumb to get away."

5

Bridget had to call a cab when the hospital released her. No one was at the phone numbers she tried. Not at the condo; not at the trailer. She had called the shop, but Candi wasn't in, just some temporary help she had found to replace her, and the girl didn't know anything. She suggested Bridget call a cab.

Bridget phoned the taxi company and waited in a wheel-chair—the nurse had put her in it and rolled her to the front door—for fifteen minutes until a cab pulled up. She was surprised, but not shocked, to see Curt behind the wheel.

He wore a yellow cap, something between a captain's hat and a policeman's cap. It was mustard yellow with a short black brim; he was wearing cutoffs, tennis shoes, and a rayon shirt, pink flowers on the back. If he hadn't been wearing the cap, she would have thought he had stolen the cab.

"Kris told me you were here, but I didn't think it would be you when I got the call," Curt said, getting out and holding the door open for her. He slammed the door shut, ran around to the other side, climbed in, settling behind the wheel with an agitated motion, as if he were trying to burrow, bury himself in the seat. "She and I went touring this morning."

Bridget looked at the back of Curt's head, his dirty blond hair curling up around the bottom of his cap like rat tails. Shiny and thick.

"When did this start?" she asked.

"Yesterday. Needed a job. Found a job."

"Doesn't Winston mind?" she asked.

"Nah, he thinks it's good cover. I can pick my shifts, more or less."

"I thought you had to know a city to drive a cab in it, have a license," she said.

Curt snorted. "Not a dime-sized burg like this—I got a map," he said, holding up a Chamber of Commerce brochure. "The company got me a license."

Bridget felt strange. She realized she was clutching her bag as if she thought someone was going to run by and steal it.

"Where do you want to go?" Curt asked. "Back to Pair o' Dice?"

Bridget watched the red digits on the meter change. The inside of the cab looked very old, but she remembered the outside was brand-new. The meter was a tiny thing the size of a radio. Red, electric lines that didn't meet entirely, but were clearly numbers. Was Curt going to make her pay for the ride? She guessed so.

"I want to go to Winston's warehouse. It's near the dog track. I'll direct you. I was working there on the store's float for the parade. It's not far from the trailer park."

They were waiting to turn onto the highway. Bridget continued to stare at Curt's curls. They were slick, oily, but they also looked like they were ready to be cut off and tied with a ribbon and placed in a Bible. Baby curls. She watched his head swivel rapidly and her vision followed.

"Wasn't that girl Rea?" she asked, seeing a car pass.

The light outside was funny, Bridget thought. Storm light; a whiteness surrounded by gray. Everything looked exposed, like under fluorescent lighting.

"Yeah. It looked like her, didn't it?" Curt said, turning onto the highway when the traffic breached. He followed Bridget's directions to the warehouse.

"I'll be able to walk home from here, anyhow," Bridget said, giving him a five-dollar bill. Curt counted out the change from coins and bills he kept in a cigar box at his side.

"I'll give you your tip some other time," she said, and could hear in her own voice a coquettishness. It sounded as if she were talking into a plastic bubble over her head: near and yet far away.

Curt looked up at her. He seemed to be smiling. He had pretty eyes.

"I'll tell Kris you're okay," he said. "If I see her."

He drove off, giving her the thumbs-up sign out his window. Bridget felt slightly wobbly in front of the large corrugated aluminum door of the warehouse. It began to rise rattling before her. Then she heard thunder.

She recognized Winston's torso before the door even reached his chin.

Thirteen

1

Kenner knew he was in trouble when he awakened to find Rea in his arms. It was the naturalness that was disturbing. He wasn't stiff or sore; nor was an arm cramped, out of joint. His arms were wrapped around her, one through her arm, cradling her ribs; the other around her, reaching down across her back. It was one of those graceful embraces that are associated with catching, with leaping, arms aloft, ready to hold. The gesture people make to represent rocking a baby. That's the way Kenner's arms were positioned, and encircled within was Rea, asleep.

Passed out, maybe, he thought. Kenner looked around, as well as he could without his glasses, and saw the dim rectangle of light bleeding through the thick tapestried curtains. He heard the hum of the air-conditioning, saw the glints of metallic objects being reflected in the bedroom's mirrored surfaces.

Kenner had learned to be wary of any woman who seemed to fit too well, to slide too comfortably into place, for that meant she would be hard to dislodge—not from Kenner's presence, for that was always too easy—but from his heart. That was what troubled Kenner: Rea fit and he knew what it meant.

Kenner didn't want to abandon the wild life. Not that he lived a wild life. But he always hoped it was still a possibility, ready for him to enter once he pushed open the right door. He had heard and seen indications of its existence all around him. But he had never yet been able to arrive when it was going on. He would either get there too soon and leave before the action heated up, or appear just as the stragglers were breaking camp.

After they returned from fishing, Rea had some business to attend to and she said she would call on him later, which she did. Rea had appeared at the condo's door before midnight, carrying a bag, something you'd bring with you on a plane.

"I'm going to take a bubble bath," she announced, after looking into the bathroom. Kenner had spent part of the evening picking up the condo and it looked—at least, to him—very neat. He was surprised, though, by the matter-of-factness with which Rea took off what she was wearing, the same shorts and red halter she had had on earlier. Kenner had thought that she must have been really busy if she hadn't found time to change.

The halter shrank into a tube, an elastic band, lying on the top of the low chest of drawers; Kenner had a strange thought: it reminded him of Winston's mother, hanging up a similar garment to dry on a line in the backyard of the old neighborhood. She was a thin woman, and the halter had hung next to a brassiere. Kenner thinking himself unobserved had crept up to inspect. He discovered the bra was padded. You could blow it up, was his recollection. Kenner, at the time, wondered if all brassieres were so constructed, till he found himself examining his mother's and finding otherwise. Rea's red tube was some sort of sex-charged Ace bandage.

He returned to watching the six-foot TV, catching up on the latest reports of some sort of struggle between the mullahs and Bani-Sadr, the Iranian president.

Anytime the embassy compound appeared on the screen, as it was now, Kenner was reminded of Cayo Hueso condos. He began to imagine how a helicopter assault would look coming in here. If the hostages had been kept at Cayo Hueso, the nearby airport would have been very handy.

Kenner couldn't bring himself to concentrate on the news. Rea's red tube lying on the bureau, emptied like a waxy shotgun shell found in the woods, distracted him. She called, "Kenner, could you bring me a drink?"

The bathroom door was open. Kenner looked in.

She was up to her chin in bubbles, wearing—she must have

brought it with her—a shower cap, a plastic thing with rubber sunflowers attached to it. It looked ridiculous enough not to be ugly. He asked, "What do you want?"

"Brandy."

Kenner was sure something was going to occur and that gave him patience. A number of women Kenner knew had acted this way: they began somewhere in medias res. A number of preliminary questions then never had to be asked.

He set the snifter down on the edge of the tub.

A pink knee surfaced through the suds, thin skin stretched tight over the patella. An atoll surrounded by low clouds. It sunk back. One set of toes rose from the water. "Care to join me?" Rea asked.

He was puzzled, but he took off what he was wearing. Rea did not watch him; at least, Kenner didn't see her inspecting, only her nose bent into the wide mouth of the snifter. She looked up when he broke water. Kenner was surprised how hot it was. Masking his reaction, he forced himself down. He felt the hair on his legs crinkle; then overall he softened, including the demi-erection he had acquired. How long can an erection be sustained in boiling water? Kenner wondered. It could be a trash sports program on ABC. Displaced water sloshed over the tub's side. Kenner thought of the tenants below. His and Rea's legs were scissored, interlocked.

"What are you, a water sign?" he asked.

Kenner couldn't name all the astrological symbols or associate the commonest interpretation with them, though he knew how to frame a question in a way that made him sound like he knew more than he did know: a most useful trait, he had learned, in his profession.

"Our time together has been in or near water," he went on.

"That's easy," Rea said, "when you live on an island."

The tub wasn't deep. If it were a ship, it would have had a shallow draft. Kenner watched the fog bank of bubbles begin to break up; he saw—and it disconcerted him—the tip of his penis float to the surface, bob there like a channel buoy. Was it lighter than he thought? All those drained vessels, air pockets.

Rea stood up—sounded, but upward, Kenner thought, her movement so sudden. Bright pink legs, white breasts, soapsuds clinging, sliding down.

"Another moment and I would start to prune," she said, grabbing a towel. Patience, Kenner thought, all things come to those who wait and wait and wait.

Rea secured the towel as everyone must, Kenner saw, tucking one end in. Kenner had wondered as a child if everyone—and he always thought of the Chinese when, as a child, he speculated on "everyone"—grabbed the end of their shirt-sleeve with their fingertips, that awkward grip, before putting their arm through the sleeve of a coat. Was it a human gesture that was universal? Wrapping a towel and securing it as Rea did must be.

She then snatched off her shower cap and elaborately fashioned a turban out of another towel. Kenner would have been unable to duplicate it. He liked to consign such things to the mysterious abilities of women. He knew it was his own brand of sexism to believe women had mysterious abilities. The shower cap and her sharing of the tub seemed to tell Kenner that Rea was both uninhibited and practical, two traits not usually linked together. There was something both reassuring and disquieting about that.

"Soak for a while," she said, "you'll enjoy it. It'll be good for you."

Kenner smiled. He felt something the opposite of a fish out of water.

He went into the bedroom a few minutes later and found Rea seated at the long bureau, her legs tucked under its open portion. He noticed then that the bedroom furniture was the sort found in a first-class motel room: the bureau had a flat place where you could lay a suitcase. Rea was dicing some lumpy powder—brown sugar, it looked to him—with a playing card.

Before he could ask—he thought it was heroin—she said, "This isn't South American. This is from the Golden Triangle, hardly processed. The last of a load, the remnant of an age."

Kenner had met up with pleasure drugs only a handful of times: he looked upon cocaine as he had on the sport cars of his youth. The thrill of a teenager riding in a '59 Corvette, a face full of wind. At that age it had been easier for Kenner to see some things as treats: rare occurrences that provided pleasure, and never, never, did he consider they could become quotidian. The daily to him was drudgery, and if he had that sports car now it would be in the shop and he would be waiting for parts.

The TV was still on, but Rea had turned off the sound. Air-conditioning hummed. She had put on a pair of white cotton panties and Kenner wondered what that meant. On the bureau top were four lines of beige powder, and Rea vacuumed up two, her rolled paper tube making a deft U on the glass. She handed the pipette to Kenner, who, without her finesse, inhaled the others. First one nostril, then the other. Air-conditioning for the nose, he thought.

His vision improved, but he realized he hadn't yet put on his glasses. Rea stood up. Her breasts were small and their nipples were the size of a nickel. They had darkened in the cool room after the heat of the bath. She waved her hand over the wall switches and the lights went out, except for the television's. Kenner saw its red, green, and blue beams projected toward the screen.

Rea walked through them and stretched out on the bed. He felt slightly elated, though he didn't ascribe it entirely to the drug.

Taking a woman's panties off for the first time was a sufficient enough thrill for him to justify endless one-night stands, though Kenner hadn't had many of those. That he wasn't kissing Rea on the mouth as yet did not seem to trouble her, since the rest of her body was encouraging his actions. She had small labia, two gill-shaped flaps, and though Kenner was not sure what intoxication—the drug or sex—was causing it, he did feel himself at sea, suspended. She was swollen prettily, the mouth of the vagina tender as a bruised lip, except there would be no pain with any touch. On her coral-colored membrane Rea secreted small beads of liquid. Kenner was reminded of the droplets that rose to the top of a whipped meringue.

He pulled himself up along her body and found her mouth and their lips slid across each other's. She lifted her shoulder and Kenner took that as some sort of body semaphore, and he turned both of them over. She settled on top of him, her head tilted back, looking up toward the top of the wall, at the tapestry, all its stitched wings and beaks. Kenner felt her give way, almost floor by floor, as if the length of her vagina was separated into chambers, and each one had to open doors for admittance: four floors it seemed, each one expanding. When the next fell open, the one below tightened.

He reached up and brought her down on him and took a breast into his mouth. He began sucking and found himself taking more and more of it into his mouth, until he seemed to have it all. It seemed to change shape in the dark, almost to liquefy, till he felt his lips against her breastbone. That shocked him, brought him near orgasm, but he let the breast slip out of his mouth. It resumed a crescent shape, but remained momentarily flushed and wet.

He reached down for her ass, each buttock surprisingly loose, for all the exercising he had seen her do, and lifted her off his erection. He slid her up and himself down the bed, putting his mouth over her open cunt.

Something out in space, Kenner thought, the foyer of Skylab, a coupling device, made only for interlocking. But again he thought of the sea. Something this tenacious would need to shut out the medium it floated in; but space too was a medium, surrounding, and needed to be shut out, not allowed to rush in. Vaults, locks, corresponding pressures.

Now, in the morning, still cradling Rea in his arms, Kenner remembered being pushed on through exhaustion last night, by the powerful closed hydraulics of the cocaine, he assumed.

He and Rea kept at each other like boxers waiting for their legs to crumble. Even after Kenner had climaxed a second time, neither he nor she would stop. Rea on her stomach and Kenner stiff again, but detached from that sensation. Each time Kenner came, it lengthened the time between coming. There was a paradox; his hard-on became less sensitive, but the coming itself was more intense. Earlier it was the reverse. Sensation no longer seemed to be located in his prick, but somewhere in between, a point equidistant between his vision and his consciousness, a place out in front of him.

His last memories before passing out were of his fingers inside of Rea's ass; two, three, reaching up into her, and feeling with shock and some faraway alarm, his own penis through membrane, going back and forth inside of her, below.

2

Winston rested against the concrete on the condo's balcony and looked down at the courtyard. The palm trees were bathed in Christmas colors; red and green spotlights painted the fronds. The swimming pool glowed in the center of the yard. Its lights were kept on until midnight; it reminded Winston of something: the water a thick crystal, tinged with blue-green, shimmering. He finally thought of what it was. A power source of some science fiction movie spaceship, there in the center of the condo complex. Heavy water.

It was a simple thing, he kept reminding himself. Taking the prints. Winston felt that when he stole art, he stole only paint on canvas. The value of art was a fiction, sometimes based on promotion alone, other times scarcity and death. Even when there was beauty, he wondered if genius would be so venal as to set such outlandish prices. He felt as the IRS did regarding deductions: the materials alone should determine the cost.

Scarcity did hold some interest for Winston. It was a sort of mortality dividend. Anything that could survive while others vanished should be valued: there is a thing that has defied death. Art was a talisman, graven objects with occult powers, amulets the owner suspends from his walls of protection. People pay dearly for that hope. They have survived—so may I!

He remembered the first painting he took in Provincetown. There was a public access road to the beach one house from his destination and he walked down it. The tide was out. The sun was beginning to set behind the town. He saw a long row of wharfs that jutted out into the bay; some had structures built atop them. Hanging haphazardly beneath them was a jungle of plumbing, pipes that drained into the bay. Twilight seemed a good time to him; a general lessening of energy pervaded the hour. Activity would be concluding and not quite yet beginning; it was a transitional period, so the unexpected, or the irregular, was not pronounced. Light wavered, people saw differently.

The painting was in his former landlady's duplex. She had once left her key with him when she had to be away and furniture was to be delivered; Winston had had a copy made.

No one had appeared on the street and he saw no one along the stretch of sand his vision commanded. Winston could see only the backs of the houses, those that fronted on the water. On either side of his landlady's duplex were two that were only used in the summer; their windows had already been shuttered with weathered plywood. He would go up the back steps to her apartment unobserved.

The painting he wanted, an early Hopper, jumped out at him from the living room wall. At auction a few months before, a small watercolor of Hopper's had gone for fifty thousand dollars. This oil would do better. He placed the painting on the carpeted floor and removed a plastic case of tools from his jacket pocket. It was a rather crude job of mounting. With a small pliers he pulled the nails that held the painting to the frame. The canvas was attached to the stretchers with tacks; they had stained the bare canvas with spots of rust. Winston had marveled at the neglect. The rusty tacks were rotting the canvas. They should have been replaced long ago. He carefully put the rolled painting into a cardboard tube.

Alone in the apartment, Winston had been beset with the hysteria of unnatural possession; it was a recklessness that, for some men, must be lethal. I've got it and now I have to do something with it. They kill then, Winston thought. A franticness. Vandals must feel it; that is when they destroy. Rapists. It is the hysteria of thinking you're in unwarranted control.

Yes, everything else might be complicated, but the removal of the art was direct and easy. In and out. The Audubon House's alarm simply turned off, the cases opened, the folios transferred. Afterward, it would become more complicated. They should have at least fourteen hours before the folios were discovered missing.

He had wanted to take them off Key West by boat, but the Cubans had made that too risky just now. He was left with the road. One if by land. Up the alimentary canal of U.S. 1. Key West was its stomach and now Winston saw himself putting his finger down its throat, regurgitating. Most everything that came down the oversea highway—produce, beer, appliances, stuff— usually ended up right back in the sea, waste matter, pissed away, deep-sixed.

Things were a bit unstable, he knew, but he always allowed for a little of that. Bridget was falling apart; he had given her a good talking to at the warehouse. Russ and Tony hadn't shown. Kristina and Curt stuck in the crack their absence made. The usual quaking beneath the feet. It reassured him. Done in a day. Bridget would set off her alarm one last time. Impatience would be festering in the local constabulary. If, by some wild chance, they did trigger the Audubon House's alarm, it would most likely be assumed to be another malfunction. It might even be discounted. Regardless, Winston was confident it wouldn't be checked out speedily, or thoroughly. The prints were on the second floor. The house wouldn't look disturbed.

Winston did a bed check in his head. Vern was passed out on the den's foldout couch. Curt and Kristina would be at work. Duane was out. He was looking for Rea, he said. She said she was going out. A night on the town. Bridget was at the trailer with Kristina's kid; Bridget was to drive Curt's car to work and park it in the Front Street lot by the Conch Train station. At first, Winston thought Bridget's float-riding was another Bridget-sized screwup; but then he realized Bridget's sitting alone in the shop during that time would just get her spooked.

Duane was starting to trouble him. After Delmer called, wanting money to rent a car, he told Duane to get the money order and wire it to Delmer. Duane hadn't objected. His apparent lack of paranoia was troubling. It meant that he had other things on his mind.

Bridget still needed to set off the alarm in the shop one more time; she was going to make a fuss and ask that the alarm system be turned off till the company's man could come down from Miami to check it. But she would have an alibi—she would be in the parade.

Winston stared down at the condo's pool. The glowing water, dangerous, radioactive. Red and green lights on the palm trees. Knobs of color. Everything seemed to be the sort of light that came from consoles, control panels, ones with pleasing electronic symmetries.

3

Duane didn't mind that Winston was running the show, since that put Winston out on the point and made him ignorant of a number of things. Winston was good at looking ahead, but not so good at checking his flank. And it was over there that Duane planned to do business. Duane had been impressed by the money that the Audubon prints would bring. Winston was going to sell them as a complete set, for spot cash, a hundred and twenty-five thousand. The buyer was a New York gallery owner. Half the money would be given over when one bound folio was delivered; the other half when the remaining three books arrived. Duane knew they were going to be stored on Delmer's farm. He was going to pick them up and drive them back to his place. And then Duane was to drive them on to Winston's sister's apartment in New York.

If the prints were sold one at a time, Duane knew they would bring more money. He knew why Winston didn't want to do that himself. More transactions would make arrest more likely. Duane was pretty sure the dealer planned to cut up the set.

Winston was different than he was, Duane thought. Rich boys like Winston treated the can like some sort of sorry summer camp. You'll end up in jail, Duane's father had kept yelling. They were almost his last words before he kicked off. But wherever Winston was going to end up, Winston saw jail as just a ditch below the horizon; even though he might stumble into it, it wasn't what he kept his eye on. That boy, Duane knew, was a dreamer.

Duane thought of jail differently. Like gravity. Like the sun. He was always trying to fly, but he couldn't get away from its effects. He had seen the picture and the story in a book. Icarus dripping honey.

He told Rea that: it was the sort of rap that made her run

164

around and get him to apply for his equivalency degree. Made her talk to the admissions board at the university. The rap and the sex. He surprised her. His tears. Hard and soft. Hard and soft. She liked that. Chicks were all alike, except for Rea. They had laughed a lot. She made him laugh. What was different took him a while to figure out. He actually *thought* about what she said. He still couldn't understand how she had gotten inside him. Bothered him. She was around for his old man's funeral. She talked with his mother. No one had ever made an effort to talk with her, but Rea did. And she kept his mother occupied and off his case. She had fronted him some dough for the van. It was as if she were a man and he felt obliged to get even.

They had talked about orbits. Rea went on that what he needed were boosters, rockets that he could fire and use to keep him away from the sun, keep him from falling back toward the earth. College would do it, she said. He laughed. Winston had gone to college, he reminded her. But he did her running around, took tests, got his high school diploma, and even had twenty-eight college credits "waived." Funny word. They let him begin as a sophomore.

The whole notion was the sort of fantasy he couldn't indulge. The orderly life, advancement. He couldn't keep the picture tuned in, the image sharp.

So when Winston had called him, sent him the postcard of the Audubon House—"Here's the sittin' duck"—it seemed like the thing to do. He could feel the heat on his wings though, the wax and honey melting. Key West was hotter than anything he had ever known. He could really melt his wings here. He needed to bring Rea with him. She left a trail. Lots of credentials. It was all that crumb business in kids' stories. A course she took: myths and fairy tales.

What was he, he used to joke with her, the myth, or the fairy tale? He did not like her doling out the money, though he took it. Her old man had cut her off, so even though she had come from bucks, she lived just this side of welfare. It cut two ways: she made being poor not so much of a disgrace and also made being poor seem like her own choice, though a stupid one, Duane thought. She had the money from school and grants, and she lived just like his neighbors, except she didn't want to buy a lot of crap.

Rea had made a big mistake when she hit him back. But, when he pitched a few things at her, she became both subdued and mortified. Because he saw that some part of her had bought into his way of dealing with her. He was not to blame entirely. That's why she came with him, he decided, even though she obviously planned to split. He could feel she had finished with him; she was done with school. They were giving her another degree just for writing poems. What a racket. But he wanted to bring her closer to the sun, down here on the edge of the tropics. Traveling does that—people who would walk out on you, if you were just sittin', will go somewhere with you; because traveling gives them the idea that they can take a turn, step out, go in another direction once they're rolling. Rea made the trip because she intended to take off herself. But it was his momentum, Duane knew, his jet stream. So she had stuck. She had made one more bad mistake.

4

Kenner heard the pounding on the door while standing in the shower. *Pock-pock-pock* was all he had been hearing from the tennis courts below and the rushing of the water. Then he heard the percussion of a fist on the condo's door, followed by loud voices. By the time he wrapped a towel around himself and came into the living room, it was quiet. Rea and whoever were gone. No more voices. He opened the door and looked. No one. He bent over the railing and saw the Sunrise van bounce over the speed bumps and turn onto Roosevelt heading toward Stock Island, not toward town.

Kenner realized things were not quite as he might have wished. Rea was not an unencumbered contract. She was part of Winston's entourage, and he knew they hadn't wanted him in their world. He wasn't even sure how tied she was to Duane. Looking down over the railing he began to hear once again the *pock-pock-pock* from the tennis courts. It reminded him of where he was, made him reach up to his hair, which, he found, had dried. Lathered with shampoo suds that had turned into a sugary scab. Kenner went back to the shower thinking he had been caught unprepared, right in the middle of just what he did not know.

Fourteen

1

Bridget had worked on the shop's float and had agreed to ride on it though the store's owner wasn't going to give her anything extra for doing so. She had gotten him to pay Winston for two weeks' warehouse rent while they worked on it. That was why Bridget said she would ride in the parade. Winston had been mad at her at first, but then he took the money. Candi told her she could take the rest of the day off, right after the parade was finished. That gave her a shock, since she was supposed to be working all day in order to have an alibi. Bridget decided to wait and see how she felt. It had crossed her mind that if Winston really did succeed, he'd probably leave the Keys, leave her.

The float wasn't much. Bridget was to ride on it wearing a bikini. She knew she was as likely to get her picture in the *Citizen* as anyone. Newsprint was kind to her; it softened what was hard and tightened what was soft.

The store owner's car was the float. His old Dodge station wagon had been rigged with a platform and chicken wire; the chicken wire had been stuffed with three cases of blue and pink tissues. They hadn't known what to put up on top at first. The owner wanted a model of Duval Street; Candi suggested an island with a palm tree—or a large lobster; Bridget could sit under the palm tree, or be caught in the lobster's claw. But the owner came up with the idea they used, though Candi didn't like it. He lived in Key West for half the year and showed up at the store only once in a while to throw his weight around; otherwise Candi ran the shop.

Since they sold pottery, he decided to make a fake potter's wheel and have Bridget be the pot they were making. They outfitted the platform with a lazy Susan made from one end of an Anaconda cable spool the owner had found.

He decided they would need water to make it look real; that became their biggest problem. They finally managed to squeeze a fifty-five-gallon drum of water into the back of the station wagon and outfit it with a hand pump. The station wagon's springs sagged and the back bumper almost scraped the road. The owner was pleased with his efforts. He hoped to win first prize. They had put a child's plastic wading pool on top of the revolving wheel; the water for it came from the fifty-five-gallon drum and drained back into it.

Bridget had to wait for Juniper to take Eli to her trailer. Juniper didn't seem happy to be stuck with him for the next two days. Bridget didn't like it either.

"But I like babysitting for him usually," Juniper told her. "He's so quiet. Sometimes it's like he's not even there. Some other kids I sit for are really strange. There's two boys, Richard and Gordon. They always fight. Once the older one, Richard, peed on his little brother. Richard is mean and strange. After I put them to bed, he rocks back and forth, knocking his head against the wall for about an hour. But he's just a kid. Their mother's boyfriend walks me back to my trailer and he's always putting his hand inside my shirt."

Bridget hadn't meant to have a long conversation. She had to leave Curt's car in the Front Street lot, pick up her car, which she had parked there overnight, drive to the warehouse, and meet her boss.

When Bridget arrived, she saw that the owner had made one more change. There was a young girl she had never seen before giggling by the station-wagon float. Bridget and the young girl were to wrestle in the clay-dirtied water for the length of the parade. That's what the girl told her. The boss wasn't there.

Both sides of the station wagon had signs in orange poster paint: COME WATCH US THROW POTS. And then the name of the store. TANKA CRAFTS. The owner had put a few pots around the edge of the platform. "It'll be turning all the while," he had told her the other day, "and everyone will get the connection."

Bridget didn't know what to do. The girl introduced herself, saying that her name was Carolee and that she was a friend of her daughter Kristina. They worked at the same bar. And though that didn't make it all right, it seemed to make it less strange to Bridget. She wondered if she would look foolish, wrestling with a girl young enough to be her daughter. Carolee was skinny and didn't look like she weighed anything at all.

Bridget had once weighed one of her own breasts, after she had read in a newspaper that a Hollywood star had weighed hers on a bathroom scale. Bridget had used the mailing scale in the back room of the shop. A little over five pounds each. She had a dream after that of two infants growing from her chest. She had once asked a doctor about having her breasts made smaller. She had read about that, too, in a magazine. But after the doctor told here there was some chance of her nipple dying, falling off, hardening like an old piece of orange peel, she decided against it. The doctor had also said that, at her age, unless carrying such large breasts was painful to her, caused backaches, he would just as soon leave them be. The benefits, he said, wouldn't be worth the risks.

She had been surprised he had turned down the work. She had given up the idea of becoming smaller. But she had never wrestled anyone before and tiny Carolee just might get flattened. They waited in the damp gloom of the warehouse for the owner to show and it wasn't getting any earlier.

2

Leaving with Duane would solve one immediate problem for Rea: it would get him away from Kenner's door. She thought he just wanted to drive when he started up the Keys. She felt safe, the wind whipping through the open windows. It was familiar; they had done it a lot. Then he turned off the highway on Boca Chica Key. He didn't drive far. You could still see the highway. There was a narrow channel where he parked and a sliver of island on the opposite side of the channel. "Let's swim over. No one will bother us there," he said and Rea had laughed. No one was bothering them where they were, either.

Rea reached the small island before he did. She stood waist-deep in the water and watched Duane pull himself from beneath the water, awkwardly like a chick struggling out of its eggshell, fighting the membrane of water, some five yards from her. She waited as he made his way over to her, walking half submerged through the water, turning his body left and right, using one side, then the other, as a wedge.

His dark hair was plastered down on both sides of his head, making a part right down the middle, white as tile grout. She smiled at the way it looked, reminding her unexpectedly of times they had taken baths together. He looked like photos of old frontier homesteaders when his hair fell that way. She was about to say something sweeter than she wanted to when he reached out and grabbed her around the neck and pushed her off her feet.

The water was chest high and he had her pinned, one hand around her throat, the other restraining her arms, across her rib cage. She kicked, but could not get free, for all the strength she expended. She was strong—he was stronger. He held her under the water till she started to pass out. She dimly saw, through the clouds of coral dust, his implanted feet. A blue crab moved by. The sun illuminated the water, and she twisted her head and looked up into it: a bright spot, as if a light had just been turned on. Her breath had been cut off, but she didn't recognize anything as fear—just deprivation, becoming part of what surrounded her: water, liquid, dissolution, the insubstantial.

Taken under: like the anesthesia when her shoulder was reset. Going under, passing through a membrane, slipping into unconsciousness. No thoughts, just sensations.

Duane let her loose and she broke through the surface, choking and spluttering. She wanted to lash out at him, but he had taken her beyond violence to subjugation. She had once hit him back and it had cost her. She didn't fight, she just attempted to regain her equilibrium. She scrambled out of the water and he did not pursue.

On the tiny island's barren edge, smooth as cuttlebone, she lay down. She could hear the cars on the highway a hundred yards away, but no one could see them.

He didn't come up onto the beach, but turned in the water and swam back to the other shore where the van was parked. Rea sat in the sun and continued to watch him. The van didn't leave. When she realized he wasn't going to drive away, she swam back. Duane stood by the side of the van, smoking a cigarette. He stuck the pack out toward her. That was a signal. He wouldn't hurt her again. Now, that is.

He wouldn't be saying he was sorry. Rea never knew what abject really meant until Duane had apologized the first time, tried to say he was sorry. He hadn't acted impulsively ten minutes ago; he had done what he wanted. It was punishment he was doling out. He was showing her a preview of coming attractions, of what he was capable. It was serious.

Rea supposed somewhere in all of his actions lurked what moved her about Duane. He was prepared to give himself for her. And, somewhere in her state, she appreciated one fact of what Duane had done: he had taken her to an even smaller island, to do what he wanted. If you think things are bad, they can get worse. It was the most deliberate of messages. Island to island.

3

Kenner was out of sorts. He couldn't tell if the dissociation he was experiencing, his sensitivity to light, was due to the residue of the night's drugs, or just the general indulgence. He presumed both. He knew where the soreness of his member had come from. He had been involuntarily celibate for two months, except for occasional onanism. It's odd, Kenner thought, that nature seemed to allow only for total abstinence, or regular use. Infrequent vigorous episodes would just rub you raw. The penis shared a lot of similarities with the palm of the hand.

Kenner realized he was also troubled because his mind kept drifting toward justifications. What had he done? Was Rea in trouble? Was he in trouble?

The gap the van left in the parking spaces below looked ominous, a knocked-out front tooth. The other cars that remained looked equally sinister. Two were shrouded in form-fitting canvas. Things were looking strange to Kenner. What was going on?

He had a lot of questions for Rea, yet he had chosen not to ask any of them. But, he well knew, what you didn't know just might hurt you.

The condo had an electric stove that was a plain surface. Four circular areas became hot. These were designated by a bit of artwork, the faces of a daisy. This was a stove for the middle class, Kenner concluded, setting down the kettle. The upper classes would have no symbols whatsoever. It would just be a smooth white surface; you would know where to put the pots. The lack of precautions would make it chic: danger.

Am I on a blank surface that is about to get hot? he wondered. What was my night of indulgence and pleasure with Rea going to cost? Should it cost something? He made some Taster's Choice for himself and worried that since he actually favored that brand some terrible seed of product identification had taken root in him. Had he caught the American virus? What else was going to break out? It wasn't a good morning. The air was full of vagaries. Kenner decided he'd better get outside. He had been walking around the apartment in sunglasses. There was something very wrong about that.

Smathers Beach was filling up. The health food step-van had arrived, selling everything that Kenner wouldn't eat as a child. The surfboard–beach chair trailer pulled up, all international orange, tangerine, and lemon yellow. Kenner looked at the people who seemed to be keeping house in assorted vehicles parked alongside South Roosevelt, back against the ferny windbreak bushes, under the palm trees. The young women were very tanned, slightly overweight in a way that appealed to Kenner. He was struck once again by the fact that his glances were full of desire. After such a night wouldn't he be sated? He had always felt that way: the better the sex he had enjoyed, the more his appetites were awakened. Bad marriages, he thought, actually worked on males like saltpeter. Kenner hardly ever tested his many crank theories. But he looked longingly at the women crossing the road and received for his efforts a smile or two. That confirmed another dearly held bias of Kenner's. That women responded to sexual success, whenever they saw it. They never smiled at Kenner when he was alone. But let him rise from some redolent couch, raw foreskin and all, and every woman on the street beamed acceptance.

This was the first day in Key West that Kenner felt as if the women in their tiny pennants of cloth—what had Rea said? "The girls on Smathers Beach wear more fingernail polish than clothes"—their swelling warmed flesh, padding barefoot across the fiery asphalt toward the water, were actually waiting for him to walk into their lives.

He shambled along the shore route, heading for a drugstore on Simonton Street where he could have breakfast, though it was now past noon. There was still some undeveloped land along Bertha Street, looking for all the world to Kenner like the scruffy backlots of the Chicago of his boyhood, though it was covered with scattered chunks of white coral, not cinders and bits of glass.

It was hard ground, the hardscrabble feel of it, pieces of trash scuttling over its surfaces that captured the resemblance. Here it was all whites and beiges, not the browns and blacks of South Chicago. There was a billboard offering the land for sale. A king's ransom and a lot of zoning problems to bribe away.

He went by the Monroe County beach and the tin-can space park for kids: barrel rockets, space-station revolving wheels. He went around the municipal tennis courts, by the Casa Marina, now full of well-off Cubans still waiting for relatives.

He neared the drugstore, but activity caught his eye, some unexpected collection of people and equipment—a fire? a fight?

It must be a parade, Kenner thought, looking at what was surely some species of float. He then recalled the store owners' morale-building efforts.

There must be over a dozen floats, Kenner saw, lining both sides of Duval Street, from United to Truman avenues. Every year in New York City, there was a perennial feature story to be had, just for getting up early, or staying up all night. One Thanksgiving even Kenner had succumbed to it.

The spectacle of the inappropriate always seems to lure people—and when it occurs at night it tends to make people giddy. The young woman Kenner had taken along had certainly been affected. They watched the rubber creatures swell up, lift off, tethered with ropes, netted, comic dirigibles, along the Upper West Side streets near the Museum of Natural History. She had been inflated herself by the approaching near-dawn air, and when they reached Kenner's apartment she seemed ready to swell, lift off, be on parade. All her empty chambers were full of inert gases. Above him, in the muted shadows of his bedroom, Kenner had imagined her round fullness to be the bulky limbs of Bullwinkle, the Moose.

The floats parked along Duval Street, though, were of a different order of fantasy.

One was adorned with what looked to Kenner like one of the rocket slides from the Monroe County beach kiddie space park. It was a twenty-five-foot cylinder, set at a forty-five-degree angle. It sported a witch's peaked top hat and a base that was some sort of bin. Kenner couldn't figure out what it was, or had been, except that in its present incarnation, newly painted pink, atop a flatbed truck, it looked just as the float-builders must have intended it to: an Osiris-sized erection, balls and all. Letters painted along its length proclaimed: STAND UP FOR OLD KEY WEST. The base had been turned into some sort of island, covered with co-

conuts, some hairy, some green. A few young people lounged among them.

Good taste and parades were somehow antithetical, Kenner thought. A restaurant provided one float that was, at least, easy to look at. White canvas had been stretched over the bed of a flat truck and a few patrons sat at round ice cream tables, a waiter moving among them. On wires strung above were suspended a dozen spider plants. White latticework masked the cab of the parked truck. It was green and white and easy on Kenner's eyes.

Kenner had seen the waiter on the float before. He did not place him till he saw a more familiar face sitting behind the wheel of the truck. MacNaughton.

"I didn't realize you were also in the float business," Kenner said into MacNaughton's ear.

MacNaughton's head jerked and then slowly turned around. Kenner thought his expression made Kenner seem to be the last of the bad pennies.

"I have a half-interest in a moving company," MacNaughton said. "One of my wiser investments, actually."

MacNaughton slapped the side of the truck's door. Large painted letters read SO HAUL ASS. Kenner looked again and saw some tiny letters in between the larger: SOUTHERN-HAULingASS.

"That's *association*," MacNaughton said.

"I recognized your ward of the state," Kenner said, looking over his shoulder at the waiter. Manuel was wearing an open lime green shirt and tight white pants.

"The owner of this ptomaine factory is a friend of mine, and we had to find Manuel work," MacNaughton said. "Hey, when is that article on me going to run?"

"They've got it," Kenner said. "But I haven't heard yet."

"We'll all be at the Wharf House having a drink after this is over. Come on by. You know, Kenner," he said conspiratorially, "I'm doing this out of a sense of civic duty, to help my adopted home. Papa had the same sort of concern—when Key West went bankrupt in the thirties he bought up the streets, the cobble-stones, for a penny apiece, I think it was, to build that wall around his property. Now that's the kind of civic pride I can appreciate. Leave the burg with muddy streets. That old boy had a sense of the correct gesture. Buy up the streets."

Kenner found himself beginning to like MacNaughton. In any case, he was seeming familiar. Kenner had now run into him at least four times. Old friends.

"Catch you later, kid," MacNaughton said, starting the truck. "Time to line up and be festive. I'll leave you with one bit of advice: *don't alienate the MBAs.*"

MacNaughton maneuvered his truck behind a beer distributor's vehicle. Kenner again felt the need for food, something easily chewed: a shrimp salad sandwich seemed right. A deli down the street made a good one.

"Hey! You! Kenner!" He looked around and saw Curt behind the wheel of what was once a station wagon.

"I got a problem," Curt said. "The guy who was going to drive this didn't show up and I can't stay. Could you drive this thing for them?"

Kenner couldn't make immediate sense of the float's theme. There were a lot of clay pots atop boxes, and a child's wading pool. Next to Curt in the front seat were Bridget and a thin towheaded girl Kenner had never seen before.

"Well, one favor deserves another," he said, recalling Curt's ride home. "Just let me go get a sandwich and I'll do it." Kenner immediately felt invigorated. He was going to be part of the action, do something local, finally be a member of the community.

"Great. Good news," Curt said, getting out. "Bridget will explain what to do. It should only take a couple of hours." The two women remained quiet, both looking to Kenner hot and bored. He turned on his heel and ran to get his sandwich.

4

Winston had been right about the small things, Duane saw. There would have been no chance of finding a parking spot now. Bridget had left the car in the lot by the Conch Train station. By noon every space was taken. This part of Front Street was empty of people, though; everyone by now had wandered over to Duval, to position themselves for the parade. It had already started.

Duane looked at Vern, who didn't seem so out of place in the car, but did seem out of place for Key West. His whole body was industrial: his pitted face, the fat of his jowls. Nothing about him was made for exposure to the sun. He was constructed for the caverns of factories, dark urban streets, brick, soot, and grime. Key West was too clean, too scoured by the sun for someone like Vern. He seemed to sweat continuously from fissures rather than pores; he sucked on a cigarette, looking ill at ease. At least he knew what he was doing. What would they be doing, he wondered, without old Vern? His ring of miniature skate keys, the keys that would fit the Audubon House's alarm, he kept in the shaving kit sitting on his lap.

They were waiting for Curt to show. Duane watched Winston nervously sitting on the park's bench, one leg continually crossing and uncrossing. Curt was to have picked up Bridget's Toyota and driven into town. Duane thought there was something particularly conspicuous about Winston sitting on that bench, with the parade passing by two blocks away. Why would anybody be sitting there when they could be watching the parade?

Well, when Curt showed, it would be his problem. Winston had decided to be in the car. It always did seem safer in a car, Duane thought—something reassuring about the inside of an automobile. Its promise of mobility, its sour-sheet familiarity. It was also the nearness of the police band radio that Winston wanted to have. The comforts of listening in, seeing if anything was amiss.

Duane saw Winston jump up. Curt had arrived. Winston waved his arms in some sort of frustrated speech, and Curt kept his arms tight to his sides, hands jammed into his blue jeans. Winston turned, left Curt slouching by the bench, and came striding over to the parking lot, looking left and right, displaying a fit of furtiveness.

"No one turned up to drive the float. She got Curt, the asshole, to drive it over."

Duane's lips took on a slight curl, the shape of an old-fashioned sleigh rail. Duane couldn't understand Winston's attitude about cars. Winston had some sort of fancy old rust red English car that was always breaking down, in the shop for weeks, waiting for parts. He used Bridget's car. Duane had hated it when he had to use Rea's car, waiting for her to get home so he could take it, before he got his van. It just made Winston seem more a pansy. Duane had wanted to steal a car for the job.

"Vern," Winston said, "you don't look so hot."

Vern's usual sickly skin seemed paler than ever to Duane. Bacon grease congealed in a pan.

Parade noises drifted over from Duval Street. Vern just grunted he was okay.

"You ready?" Winston asked Duane. Duane did not like the look on Winston's face. As if he were going to leap out a window, a face fixed with both panic and glee.

Vern lumbered out of the car. Duane tipped a salute to Winston and followed Vern.

He turned the corner and the shade of Front Street vanished; everything became bright blue. Duane had noticed that

Curt wasn't sitting on the seat of the bench, but on its back. He did not look at Curt as he passed. Duane could feel himself fighting the tunnel vision that seemed to take over whenever he chanced something. Looking dead ahead; it was like driving when he was drunk. He'd focus on something straight out in front of him.

He caught up with Vern once they crossed Greene Street. The cover of palm fronds and tree leaves was restored; it grew cooler again. Surrounding the Audubon House was not just a garden, but a sanctuary. Once they were there they did feel safe. You couldn't see the street clearly and anyone on the street couldn't see you. Vern would, at best, be partially visible when he stood on the porch steps to turn off the alarm. The one difficulty was that the side door they would use to remove the folios was only partially obscured from the Whitehead Street side.

Duane had been surprised that the alarm system was so primitive. Well, it would soon be upgraded, but what would it then guard? Only Vern had not made a tour. He didn't look like a tourist or a lover of Americana and might be recalled too easily. Duane had only one major disappointment when he wandered through the rooms on his tour; he couldn't tell which of the folios had print CCCXXI in it. That had put a crimp in his plans.

Vern had his key ring in his hand; he moved the keys along one by one with his thumb and forefinger, like a nun saying her rosary. The turnoff switch was on the doorjamb, a silver ring the size of a quarter. Vern stared into it for a moment and then began trying keys. Their differences were not great; they were all hexagons, but the tooth that bit into the slot differed. Vern had all the variations.

Duane was cooler in the shade, but Vern was sweating on the steps. For a moment Vern looked to Duane like some Peeping Tom, peering through a keyhole. Vern's fat ass wiggled back and forth. His head rotated as if he was trying to get a better angle of vision. He tried one key, then another. His wrist turned, and, pulling out the key, he stumbled backward; his right leg went out from under him and he tumbled down the porch steps.

The noise of Vern's fall echoed in the quiet air of the garden. Duane felt himself trying to squeeze into a tighter version of himself. Vern was on his back. Had the fucker passed out? Duane wondered. He didn't stir, but Duane saw the large mound of Vern's stomach going up and down.

Duane resisted running over to him. He thought it was lucky

Vern was lying head down; the blood would be going to the right place. Finally Vern rolled over and picked himself up. He limped over to the bushes where Duane crouched in the shade.

"It's off," Vern said hoarsely.

"What happened?"

Vern shrugged, placed his hand on his chest.

Duane followed him back to the house. Vern unrolled a scroll of greasy plastic, took out a long, handmade probe, and the door was quickly opened.

Duane's hands began to sweat inside the surgical gloves Winston had made them wear. They were green-tinged, the inner surface covered with powder, like some condoms. They were the same thickness. He was to use window-shade signals to alert Curt on the bench.

Duane felt, once inside the house, like he was in a submarine fathoms down. Removed from view, but still in jeopardy. He listened for depth charges, explosions, sirens.

Vern stood in a corner, out of sight of the front windows, waiting for Duane to lead him to the cases. Everything seemed light and dark in the house: bright white walls and dark woodwork and antique furniture. Duane walked past Vern and felt him fall into step behind. He came to the hall stairway, more light and dark, all outlines, molding, and walls. He had to wait for more than a minute for Vern to reach him at the top of the stairs. All the folios were in one room, down the hall.

When Vern got there, he stared at the cases with a mixture of anger and dismay.

"They're metal," Vern said. "Winston told me they were wood."

"They are wood," Duane said.

"Not the lids," Vern said, placing his hand, the tips of his green surgical gloves puckering, on top of the slanted glass case.

"This is metal on metal," he said. "I don't have the right tool."

He opened his shaving kit and brought out a crowbar about six inches long. "This is too thick. I need a thin screwdriver."

"You don't have a screwdriver?"

"I didn't bring my tool chest with me," Vern said, wheezing, still catching his breath. "There's things in the car. I'll have to get one." He held the little crowbar in his fist; only the two ends stuck out. It looked to Duane like Vern was crushing a small rodent.

"No, no," Duane said. "I'll get it. You stay here. Don't do anything. Just stay out of sight."

As Duane looked out the side door, he thought, What am I going to do with my hands? What if someone notices my green hands? Did Winston have more gloves in the car? He couldn't remember. Shit. He stepped outside.

Curt went bug-eyed when he saw Duane walking toward him. Duane said nothing, just sauntered past, whistling. He saw Curt signal Winston and knew, by the time he got to the car, Winston would be panicking. The street was still empty; he sprinted toward the parking lot.

"Vern needs a screwdriver," Duane said, sticking his head into the car. "He said there were some here."

Winston handed him the trunk key. Duane could see that he was trying to hold himself together.

Duane found three screwdrivers and, not being sure which one Vern needed, he took them all. He started to stick them down his belt, in front; but then he put them in his back pocket. The longest stuck out and touched the small of his back; he felt as if he were walking with a pin in his hip.

Crossing Greene Street again, he looked toward the clot of people who plugged the Duval Street intersection. A police car was there, but people were sitting on it, trying to get a better look at what was passing. There was applause, the sound of steel drum music. Duane heard it as a shell roaring in his ears as he went through the small front gate and around to the side door. Quiet again.

Upstairs he found Vern lying on the floor. His eyes were shut.

"Vern?"

Vern blinked and lifted his arm and Duane took it, helping him off the floor.

"I was just trying to relax."

Duane held the three screwdrivers fanned out in his hand, like he was doing a card trick.

"Yeah, this'll do," Vern said, selecting the largest.

"This sort of lid bites down tight. Metal against metal makes a good seal. Wood against wood always leaves enough room."

The screwdriver had made a tiny crack and Vern wedged his crowbar's forked tongue into it. Vern leaned his weight against the crowbar and with a metallic crack the lid sprung.

"Nothing to it. You need the right tools."

179

Yeah, asshole, Duane was thinking; you need them. Not me.

Duane reached into the case to shut the big book. Its heavy pages were slightly puffed up at the center. The leather cover was heavy. Duane let it drop; it fell like a sheet of plywood. Air was pushed out and smelled musty. Closed, the book was over three feet across and four feet high. Duane reached down to lift it out of the case.

"Jesus," he said, "this thing weighs . . . fifty pounds?"

He motioned to Vern, and both of them lifted the folio out of the case; they leaned it against the doorjamb.

"Pop the cases and we'll get the others."

Duane went out of the room and to the front of the house. He raised and lowered a window shade twice. That would send for the van.

"You take those two downstairs," Duane said, after he and Vern emptied the cases. "I'll take the rest."

Duane lifted the leather-bound folio with difficulty. He held it out in front of him. It was as heavy as an old mirror the same size and was as awkward to carry. He had to put it down in the hallway.

"Van's here," he heard Vern call.

They had only been at it for fifteen minutes, but each additional minute seemed to Duane to be stolen time. The ice was getting thinner. The passing of time was like the rising of the sun over a desert. Each minute the heat would get more intense. He expected to see Vern turn the corner carrying a folio.

Vern did come around the corner, but empty-handed.

"I can't lift 'em. Too heavy."

Duane felt a surge of anger, but he didn't say anything. He couldn't lift two at a time. He would have to make four trips to the fence, not just two. Should he move them all to the side door, or take one at a time all the way out? He decided to move them all down the stairs first. When he brought down the last one, doing the same awkward dance with the heavy book out in front of him, as if he were leading a stiff old woman in a polka, he froze, seeing, over the top of the folio, the side door standing open. He looked to his right and with relief and rage saw Winston standing there. His hands weren't green.

"Goddamn Vern is in the car having some sort of attack," Winston whined. "We're ten minutes behind schedule."

"Just carry them out to the fence," Duane said. "Don't touch anything else. You don't have gloves on. I'll go up and see we haven't left anything."

Duane looked upstairs for Vern's shaving kit and any tools; but they were gone. Winston had left the door standing open. There was one folio left. Duane looked around, feeling he was forgetting something. He always felt that when he was about to leave, to go away. He hesitantly stuck his head out the doorway. That parade is a big success, he thought.

He closed the door after he leaned the folio against the steps' railing. He reached the fence: it had been sliced open. Kristina was still holding the heavy bolt cutter. The van was parked in the corner of the vacant lot. Duane stood in an alley between a shed and a small building that the museum kept supplies in. A dried string mop and a rake leaned against the shed's wall. Winston had left the three folios there. But he was gone. Kristina put the bolt cutter in the van and ran back to the fence and pulled one side of the chain-link back. The fence opened like a flap of flesh.

At least no one could see him now in between the two buildings. But the van was exposed. One by one he took the folios through the fence, the leather covers an inch away from the prongs of cut wire. After the last, Kristina let the chain-link go. It snapped back. She and Duane lifted the folios into the van, laying them on top of the moving quilts that had been spread out on the floor. Duane thought of his footprints in the dusty ground between the two outbuildings.

He pulled the van's sliding door shut too hard; it slammed loudly as it latched. Kristina had started the van; he opened the passenger's side door. Feeling like he was caught in an explosion, but sensing that all the debris was blowing by him, not at him, he sank into the bucket seat. Kristina backed up the van in an arc, then jerked to a stop; she went forward. Duane looked for the walkie-talkie. At the vacant lot's driveway, he stopped his search and looked left and right, up and down Whitehead Street. No cars. Duane located the walkie-talkie, but decided not to try to raise Winston on it. He put it down and then he remembered that the side door of the Audubon House was shut, but not locked.

Kristina drove out onto and up Whitehead, under the speed limit, away from Old Town.

III

Fifteen

1

Kenner realized that driving the float deprived him of a decent view of the parade. Ah, well, he thought, he was in the thick of things. After hearing what Bridget and the thin girl were going to do, he didn't question their glumness. Mud wrestling, he knew, was unbelievably passé, the staple of B movies, the prole symbol of misogyny. Let the girls get down in the dirt. We should, he thought, draw a lot of stares.

Two parade marshals had come by to check Kenner's position. A young man wearing a long red dress, clutching a clipboard to a sock-induced bosom, was made up elaborately. A young woman accompanied him, outfitted in a tux and top hat.

The businessmen's association must have let this show slip from its grasp, Kenner thought. But, for all he knew, the marshals could be the heads of the Chamber of Commerce.

Kenner was near the end of the parade. He watched a high-school band pass by; they played cutoff steel drums, instead of the old faithful two-sided bass drums. The youngsters wore Hawaiian shirts and molten lava–colored satin running shorts and were playing a passable version of "When the Saints Come Marchin' In."

Kenner was stuck behind the "Square Grouper" float, a pickup truck bedecked with a few nets and cork bobbers and stacked with polyethylene-covered bales hand-lettered FLORIDA TUNA. Two young women aboard wore bright yellow SMOKE FLORIDA SEA-FOOD T-shirts. The pickup truck's captain was puffing on a Rastafarian-sized hand-rolled joint. Behind Kenner was one of the town's lime-colored fire engines; but, instead of normal fire fighters clinging to its sherbet sides, there was an assortment of clown-clad individuals, all of whom wore old-fashioned red fire helmets. Kenner wondered if that was the entire force, or just some happy volunteers.

Key West was attempting to live up to its publicity: smugglers' island. Disneyland for dropouts. But Kenner tried to get into the spirit of things. Bridget and the thin girl must be starting to really mix it up. Kenner's best view was in the Dodge's side mirror; it was the sort that was added if you were going to pull a trailer. The fire engine's driver had a wild look in his eye. The roof of the Dodge had begun to move up and down in an alarming manner, but Kenner kept moving ahead at about three miles an hour.

The parade, Kenner knew, wasn't meant solely for the entertainment of the locals, since they entertained themselves capably every day. The local bigwigs were hoping for thirty seconds on network news. Miami affiliates had come down with cameras.

Kenner gauged Bridget and the thin girl's performance by the reactions of the onlookers. There were hoots and applause, a lot of gyrations from the sidelines, thrusting pelvises, hand-job motions. Cries of "Stick it in my face!" "Jump my bones!" "I'll eat your dirt" were hurled at the station wagon. Across the side of the pink and blue tissue paper that Kenner could see were drips of mud splashings. The wagon was beginning to look as if it had been shat upon by large prehistoric birds.

Kenner thought they had taken about an hour to get from Truman to Fleming. Approaching the La Concha Hotel, the pickup truck's rear end bucked; its bales shifted and the two young women sitting on them were thrown rearward. Kenner hit the Dodge's brakes and heard pots shatter and the sound of bodies, but not the usual *thump-thump* percussion noises that had been accompanying the trip.

"STOP! STOP THE CAR!" Kenner heard. The car was already stopped. Kenner put it in park and got out. The thin girl was sitting outside the wading pool, amid the shards of bisqued pots, holding her knee, rocking back and forth. Bridget was on all fours in the middle of the muddy pool, one breast out of the cup of her bathing suit.

Some of the crowd had breached the sidewalk barriers and had moved up to the car, pushing Kenner closer to its side. Bridget was putting herself back into her suit.

"She should go to a hospital," some unseen samaritan in the crowd yelled. A few other chanted, *"On with the parade!"* The thin girl's gash looked deep; it was behind her knee, a nasty hooked-shaped wound. She straightened out her leg, and Kenner thought he saw the pearly flash of a tendon. Stitches, it will need stitches, he thought. A clown in a fireman's hat pushed through the crowd around the Dodge. A white-gloved hand grabbed Kenner's shoulder.

"You'd better get her to the hospital. We'll clear the intersection and you pull out of the parade."

He signaled and a half-dozen other mummers ran over to the sawhorses that blocked Fleming Street and parted them. The crowd pulled back. The fireman got on top of the wagon with the girl. Bridget climbed down and slid into the front seat. A cop on a motorcycle snaked out from the rear of the parade and led him off of Duval and onto Fleming, siren blaring.

Bridget's mud was starting to dry, and Kenner noticed flakes of gray starting to peel off her shoulders. It looked as if she were covered with dead leaves.

This is the first time I've ever had a police escort, Kenner thought, and then decided to mention it to Bridget. "I've never had a police escort before." Bridget looked at him strangely, as if he were some sort of loon, and then said, "I suppose you won't be able to drop me off before we get to the hospital."

"I guess not," Kenner said. He added, "It must be uncomfortable."

"Oh, it's not so bad," Bridget said, stripping a strand of dried mud from her arm. "I was going to take a shower at the Wharf House after this was over. Winston's got a room there."

"Oh," Kenner said, and before he could continue, Bridget said, "Maybe you could drop me off at the trailer park after. It's closer to the hospital."

"How did it happen?" Kenner asked.

"Carolee and me were just playing around. She had climbed on my back and I was just about to turn her over when you stopped all of a sudden. I must have thrown her into the pots."

"I'll take you back to the Wharf House if you want," Kenner offered.

"We'll see, we'll see," Bridget replied. She sounded coy to Kenner, as if he had asked her for a date.

Kenner was following the motorcycle cop. They both slowed for bumps on South Street and came to a four-way stop. Ahead of them was a van. For a moment Kenner had thought it was a Miami TV station's Action News van, but then he recognized it as Duane's. Rea's image flashed before him. The motorcycle cop swung around the van and Kenner followed.

Kenner saw in his sideview mirror what looked to be Kristina behind the wheel and Duane sitting next to her. They both were staring straight ahead. We must be quite a spectacle, Kenner thought: a clown in a fireman's hat doing Lord knows what to a girl in a bikini atop a speeding pink and blue box of mud-splattered Kleenex. Kenner waved his arm out the window at them. The van turned right and the street was empty behind him. Kenner realized he had hoped to see Rea in the van.

"Wasn't that your daughter?" Kenner asked.

Bridget seemed not to hear. She was absently picking scabs of mud from her body, drawing pieces off like patches of dead sunburned skin.

"It might have been," she said, adding to the pile of mud chips she was making next to her on the seat.

"I didn't know she was a friend of Duane's."

"She's friendly with a lot of people. She's a friendly girl."

"Yeah," Kenner said, "I've seen her at work." For a second he thought that might have sounded like an insult. "She and Curt gave me a ride home one night. She got her looks from you, that's clear." Kenner realized that, too, was likely a tactless remark.

"She was a late bloomer," Bridget said. Having referred to her body, Kenner looked at Bridget again. The flesh of her belly was loose, but tightly pleated, accordioned. Kenner liked Bridget's aging debauchee look.

There wasn't much traffic, which Kenner chalked up to the day's festivities still raging in Old Town. They sped down Flagler and stayed on it till they reached the highway.

The emergency room crew was outside waiting for them. When they lifted Carolee down from the roof of the Dodge, Kenner saw that her knee had already been swathed in white gauze. The fireman had had a first-aid kit with him. Bridget went in with Carolee, the clown fireman, and the attendants. Kenner waited outside, trying to decide if Carolee's injury had been his fault. Would it have been worse if he had hit the pickup truck instead of stopping suddenly?

He looked with some amazement at how low to the ground the Dodge sat; its bottom had scraped a few times on the ride to the hospital. He was surprised its springs hadn't snapped. He lowered the station wagon's back door and pulled down the hose from the wading pool, then turned the drum's spigot. Dingy gray water flowed out over the driveway's asphalt, spilling off onto the crushed coral that lined the roadway. Sunset was beginning to lacquer the horizon. They should be able to get back to the Wharf House before dark.

Bridget came out wearing a green surgical gown over her suit. She was hugging herself, though it wasn't cold.

"Carolee's gonna get stitches. They wanted to check me over, but I said I was all right. It's a deep cut, but none of her big veins got tore up. She was lucky. She was crying though, because there would be a scar. Best drop me at my trailer. It's nearby. I can change. You can just drive this to the Wharf House. It's supposed to be left in the lot across from it anyway. That's where all the floats were to end up."

Kenner waited for the traffic to abate on U.S. 1. As cars drove by, they slowed and the passengers in them would point and wave at Bridget and Kenner. Kenner knew they were laughing at the car. Kenner didn't often make a spectacle of himself and, on this occasion, he didn't care what effect he was having. He was wondering, if Rea was not with Duane, where was she?

2

Winston sat in the car parked in the Front Street lot, trying to calm down. He had heard a call about a hospital run crackling over the police scanner, taking an injured woman off a float identified as the "mud-wrestling float." The name of the woman was unknown. What Winston had been hearing before on the scanner were calls about crowd control. Nothing about alarms, nothing about the Audubon House. All was well, until he realized Bridget might be going to the hospital again, with the police at her side.

Winston decided to let a little time pass. He would find out what he needed by phone. Kristina and Duane were no longer in walkie-talkie range. He told Vern to be cool for a while and to meet him back at the lot when it was dark. They would go back to the condo then. Curt was to go to work as usual. The crowds were heading toward Mallory Square for sunset. People were beginning to spill onto Front Street, and they needed to get out of the car. The parade was coming to an end. Curt was going to hang out, then report for work at the taxi company.

Duane and Kristina would be unloading the books at the warehouse. They would return to the condo. Winston had been planning to pick Bridget up at the Wharf House, be seen, and then return to the condo. Delmer wouldn't be getting to the condo until late; the prints would leave early in the morning. Winston didn't want to think of the options he had if Delmer didn't show up. What car would they use? Not Bridget's. And the van had been seen around town too much already. He didn't want familiarity to prick anyone's interest. Delmer would be driving down a rental.

Curt had wandered over to Mallory Square and Vern went off, heading to a bar near the shrimp-boat docks. Winston walked over to Duval and watched the final float come down the street. KEY WEST THE LAST RESORT a banner stretched across it proclaimed. The crowd would no longer be kept on the sidewalks; they filled in behind the float. The scene looked like New Year's Eve, except the cops Winston saw standing around didn't have their back pockets full of the plastic strips they carried New Year's Eve, used to handcuff revelers, wrap their wrists like you'd tie off garbage bags.

Winston began to feel a bubble of elation well up within him, though thinking again of Bridget made a pin appear, ready to pop it. He had memorized something Audubon had written and now he was ready to say it: "The birds were skinned, the sketch was on paper, and I told my young men to amuse themselves."

He was in the middle of the surging crowd, and he let himself be taken up by the hilarity of the event, allowed himself to shimmy with some of the people who were dancing in the street. He felt two thin hands grab his waist and he stiffened, but seeing that an impromptu conga line was being formed, he grabbed the waist of the crew-cut man ahead of him and went conga-ing down the street.

3

Rea had put down the phone and was reaching for a package of cigarettes when the door opened. Kristina rushed in; she was blabbing before she got all the way through the door. Rea thought Kristina's career in crime would not be a long one.

"We did it, we did it," Kristina was exclaiming. "We almost got caught. A motorcycle cop came after us and I just about went crazy. I almost pissed in my pants."

Rea had already noticed Kristina often didn't wear panties, so if she pissed in her pants there wasn't a lot of pants to piss in. She was a bit damp at the crotch, Rea saw, but that too wasn't unusual for Kristina. She was a hot little girl.

"What happened to you?!" Kristina asked, as if she had just been given back her power of sight. Rea was surprised she noticed. But Kristina did not wait for an answer and went on talking about her mother in the float with Carolee and the clown.

"I ran into a door," Rea said, into the flow of Kristina's speech, but that didn't explain her neck bruises.

"Gee, that's too bad," Kristina said, pausing for breath, interrupting her tale once again. Kristina cast a worried glance back toward Duane, but he was no longer standing in the hallway. "Anyway, we were at a stop sign and I did the right thing. All of a sudden we heard a siren and a motorcycle was coming down the street. Duane wanted me to turn and step on it, but I just sat there. They went around us. They weren't after us. It was my mother. I'm not sure what happened. But it was her float. On top of it was Carolee, who works at the bar with me, and somebody in a clown suit. Inside was my mother. I think the driver was what's his name, the guy who lives next-door. Anyhow, other than that, everything went swell. Except Curt was late, and Vern passed out, and Duane went with me since Curt helped Vern to the car. Hey, where are they? Why isn't everyone back yet?"

Rea heard drawers opening and closing, cabinet doors being slammed in the kitchen. A beer can popped open.

"Winston called. They'll be here in an hour or so. He's going to call back soon if he can't find anything out about Bridget. She hasn't called here yet. My job's done. I'm leaving. I'm going out running."

Rea put on a nylon jacket with a hood. She didn't look into the kitchen, where Duane slouched against a counter drinking beer.

"You'll be back soon?" Kristina asked.

"I'm all done, Kristina," Rea said, going out the door.

It's amazing what you can leave behind by shutting a door, Rea thought. The sun was down, but the sky was still full of color: tangerine and reddish purples filled the western horizon.

She wondered if the purple necklace of bruises Duane had hung around her neck this morning was the last gift he was going to give her. Maybe Krissy would be a help—give him something else to think about. Her connection with Kenner hadn't made him mad. It was the idea of her leaving, period. She really had expected him to hit her. She felt she would have to pay that price. But when he almost drowned her, that was another kind of debit. "I can kill you and would only get five years," he had said, taunting her.

Rea knew she must still be in some sort of shock, or why had she stayed at the condo? Because she had said she would. She had given her word. She was a stand-up guy. It must be something else, she thought: she was stunned.

Rea looked at the sky, the tangerine ripening to a dull orange. The palm trees looked like black pom-poms being shaken in wild celebration. School colors: orange and black, Halloween shades. She had two choices of where to go: inland, to a river town deep in the heartland; that would be a comfort, to get away from the edge of things. Or out of the country. Europe. The latter would be safer; Duane could never handle Europe.

She began to run, feeling her lungs tighten, being rasped, from the cigarettes, from the day's exertions. She passed the high school, which looked to Rea like a set of abandoned buildings— but it was still in session. When she reached the corner of First Street and North Roosevelt, the sky was violet, the lingering purple that would remain and depart much like her bruises. It would be there and suddenly you would notice the sky had gone to pitch. She stopped, ran in place, and saw Kenner behind the wheel of a ridiculous vehicle.

He had turned off North Roosevelt onto Palm. The charter boats had come in with the day's catch. Anglers posed for photographs standing next to their harvest. The fish were hung by their tails, under the signs that advertised the boats for hire. So much gets suspended that way. Rea remembered the photograph of Mussolini and his mistress. It was some sort of inverted prestige. Low esteem got you strung up by the neck; high esteem got you hoisted by your ankles.

Rea's last bit of conversation she had had with Kenner in the morning floated back to her. They had awakened early, and she had told him she had things to do all day. He had suggested she meet him at the Wharf House after sunset and they would go dancing. Kenner seemed to be protected against seeing what he didn't understand. Part of the spectrum denied him. In the past, Rea would have thought that a mark of innocence, those blank spots; but now they were a bit too dangerous to be innocent. He was highly self-absorbed, like most men. Women's only protection, she had thought, was males' self-absorption. They would close off, lose their peripheral vision. Not see. Women could act then.

Rea was not sure what she should do—she would have to interpose something between herself and Duane. Geography would be best. Duane honored his threats since he tended to value them when they were made by others. But Rea had made the mistake Duane made. Rea thought she was immune. You know how someone treats others, but you still never expect them to treat you the same way. Her life might be worth five years to him—parole in three. She had tampered with him, changed his life, given him new zones of discontents, disappointments. It was her fault. He had, at the start, resisted. Rea had taken his giving in as a sign of his promise: she was not the sort of woman he normally would have had anything to do with. She thought she had reached the most valuable part of him. Her background had made her more incautious than his: she, oddly, had less to lose. And agreeing to come to Key West, helping them, she knew, was one of the most dubious enterprises she had ever undertaken. She was trying to erase her influence, return him to his original orbit. She realized that wanting to teach, to change, to affect, was a temptation rather than a virtue. Duane belonged in a world he thought he understood, one that was familiar to him. Rea was concerned that his nature had been altered because of her, and he had lost some natural protection. It had been his instinctual behavior that had drawn her to him and she had tampered with it. And rather than his killing her, he was likely to get himself killed some day, and she would feel that she had a hand in that.

4

Kenner dropped Bridget off at the Pair o' Dice trailer park. A pair of red fuzzy cloth dice, imprinted with the park's address and phone number, dangled from the rearview mirror of the Dodge. Kenner wondered if Bridget's boss lived there or just visited.

The float was now a bit worse for wear. Some of the chicken wire was showing through the pink and blue tissues. The Dodge looked like a cat with a bad skin disease. Kenner hoped to get to the Wharf House before the sky went completely dark, lest Rea arrive and depart.

Most of the perimeter of Key West was fringed with military installations, Kenner was reminded, driving past the navy's officers' quarters on Palm Avenue. Key West, he concluded, was an odd kind of fruit: it rotted from the inside, the middle, while the outer skin was always firm, bright, glowing.

Kenner reached the lot holding the floats at the end of Duval. The attendant informed Kenner that his float had been awarded third prize in the "Most Imaginative" category. A ribbon would be sent to the store. Well, I always like to be associated with prizewinners, Kenner thought, wondering why his spirits immediately picked up.

Kenner walked over to the tables by the beach. A singer with electric piano accompaniment was performing in a thatched-grass-shack kiosk. The beach area was lit up bright as a New York City intersection. MacNaughton was at a table.

"Sit down, man," MacNaughton said. "Been saving you a chair. Heard you departed the parade early. I want to introduce you to a couple of my, ah, associates. You know Manuel." Kenner nodded in the direction of the refugee-boyfriend; he had not changed out of his waiter outfit. "And Freddy and Philip."

Philip was vaguely familiar; Kenner was getting tired of encountering the semi-remembered in Key West.

"Kenner has just done my life story for, what's it called, Daddy Long Legs?"

"Centipede."

"Not a moment too late," Freddy said, raising both his eyebrows and his glass.

"Freddy thinks I'm burning my candle at both ends, and in the middle," MacNaughton said.

"No," Freddy said, "I just don't happen to think that the nostril is an erogenous zone."

"That's the only one Freddy excludes," MacNaughton said, winking at Kenner. "Freddy used to teach music at Iowa, where I taught the mysteries of prose for a year. He's now an antique . . ."

"Now he's calling me names. An antique. Next it'll be my teeth. If I hear another comment about fags and bad teeth I'll throw up."

"Don't," MacNaughton said. "Vomiting's bad for your choppers."

Philip didn't smile, Kenner noticed. Maybe he wasn't gay.

"Freddy runs Southern Hauling for me," MacNaughton said, "that is, between visits to his dentist."

"Are there a lot of antiques in Florida?" Kenner asked, aware of the inanity of the question. He wanted to change the drift of the conversation.

"We bring them down. We don't take them away," Freddy replied. "I have a store in Chatham, on the Cape."

The secret word. The *Cape*. Kenner now recognized Philip. He had once seen him at Rosy's in Provincetown. A fresh supply of cocaine had just hit P'town and a man standing at the bar was pointed out to Kenner as the one who had brought it in. Philip.

"We were talking about music," MacNaughton said. "Freddy is a fan of reggae. At least that's what he calls what the band is playing. We were disagreeing."

"Danny has philistine taste in music."

"It's just that I long ago concluded that reggae music was the product of brain damage, an example of imperialistic abuse. Protein deprivation." MacNaughton paused to let the band be heard for a moment. "That rhythm can only come from brain cells cutting out. Too much ganja. Smokin' too much herb and not eating enough red meat."

"Jesus H. Christ, MacNaughton," Freddy said. "Reggae's wonderful rhythm comes from echoing the heart. It's spiritual. It is the king of kings' music."

"Hey, I bet I know what happened," MacNaughton said. "When they first started to record the songs, the power plant kept going out—brown outs—that's why it sounds that way. What do you think, Kenner? Ain't it brain damage?"

5

Rea was used to running in small towns after dark. She had encountered most of the problems of jogging at night: dogs, men in cars, errant drunks.

In Key West Rea had found the harassment of a different sort. There were a few locked-up houses, absentee owners hanging on for one reason or another. One had a raised front porch, latticework covering its front. Some people had moved in. And moved out. Now there was a solitary male living beneath the porch, behind the latticework. In the early mornings, from behind the crosshatched boards, Rea would be called out to as she ran by. Not the ordinary, *baby baby baby* stuff, *come sit on my face* business, but a weirder sort of entreaty: *Tarry awhile,* once. *Be my consort,* another time. *Relieve me.* It was spooky. *I need your succor.*

Rea had caught a glimpse once of lank hair, skin sunburned almost to a pumpkin color. At night, the lattice was dark, but Rea occasionally saw a glow within, a stirring. No calls, though. Tonight, when she ran by, she heard rustling, guttural sounds, but no language. Never go to an island, a French teacher told her, if you're a fugitive. That's what we learned in the Resistance.

She was now Duane's fugitive, and they were both on an island.

Rea wasn't sure that Kenner would be helpful. He might just be providing her with imaginary fuel: another reality. The life she left behind: the one ahead. She knew she was struggling against what she most wanted: to be alone. She had a large capacity for that, she knew, more than most women, most men.

Her running outfit would not be out of place at the Wharf House; dressing as you wish is a luxury in so far as it implies ownership. The idée fixe of a resort town is that it is one large mansion and you can move through the rooms as you wish. Other sorts of towns do not encourage that illusion.

When Rea reached Greene Street, she turned left and ran in the direction of the Audubon House.

When she got close to the dark pile of wood, surrounded by its camouflaging trees, those with heavy leaves, waxy and shaped like spilled water, she began to react: she had to fight the notion that she appeared suspicious. But there was only the wind, the laziest threshing of the trees.

The Audubon House was pearlescent in the moonlight. It had been a ship captain's house, she recalled, which accounted for its New England styling. Rea now looked at the house as she sometimes looked at a person she noticed at a party, someone whose secrets were known to her, but not to others in the room. The person would appear hollow, excavated; that is how the building looked. It had been emptied. What crude remark had Winston made? We're gonna do a print-ectomy.

Rea didn't know if her thinking had made her not see what she was looking at; nonetheless she jumped, almost gasped, at what she saw: in the dark, at the side of the building, a man was going in the side door. Rea tried to make out who it was. She almost called out, but restrained herself.

Rea watched a flashlight beam play around the downstairs,

a lighthouse beacon madly reeling. Then it went out, and the door opened again, and the man reemerged. He fiddled with the door and then pulled it shut. His wrist turned.

Rea retreated into the darkest shadow and watched the man walk out the front gate and turn down Carolina Street. He was walking slowly, whistling a tune she didn't recognize. He didn't seem at all agitated, or distressed. But Rea felt her skin start to ripple.

Sixteen

Before he returned to the condo, Winston knew that Bridget had not been injured. She had phoned him at the Wharf House from her trailer. Bridget had seen Duane and Kristina in the van. There appeared to be no problems.

The van was where it should be, and Winston pulled into the space next to it. The only thing that had changed was the car on the other side; its canvas shroud had been removed. A black Lincoln Continental reflecting spangles of available light. The owners must be back; they lived in the condo beneath his.

When he had returned to the Front Street lot, both Vern and Curt were waiting by the car for him. "All the taxis were out. They put me down for the graveyard shift."

Curt and Vern were following him up the condo's concrete stairway. They had all been boisterous for a while; but that had been replaced by something akin to a funk. Now they wanted to let off steam.

Passing the second-floor landing, Winston put his finger in front of his mouth to try to stifle their loud talk. When Winston reached his door, he found both locks locked. He only had the bottom key with him, since he never locked the top lock. The condo complex had good security. There had never been a robbery, though one man had been murdered. A retired State Department employee who had been beaten to death by a hustler he had picked up. At least, that's what the story was. Winston felt a rush of rage at having to ring the bell. Its chime infuriated him. He had to listen to it three times.

The door finally opened and Duane's aspect silenced Winston. Duane was only wearing black underwear. His body was wet, but it didn't look as if he had come out of the shower.

Duane left the door open and walked back toward his bedroom. Curt and Vern filed in. "Man, it smells like a Mex cathouse in here," Vern said, and immediately turned into the den where he slept, off the front hall; its air conditioner started up roughly.

Winston saw Kristina pass quickly into the bathroom between the two bedrooms. She wasn't wearing anything. Curt didn't seem to have noticed. Winston was worried about Curt's reactions to the day's events. Instead of settling down, he seemed to be getting more and more wired up. Getting in and out was often the easiest part, though Curt's nervousness wasn't caused by that sort of understanding. Winston looked forward to the day that he could be done with his confederates. He was tiring of shouldering so much responsibility.

2

MacNaughton and his associates had departed, but limbo dancers appeared and captured Kenner's attention while he waited for Rea.

Most of the limboists were guests staying at the hotel; they were led by a Caribbean professional who could manipulate his long lank body downward to slither under a pole held about eight inches above the ground. It reminded Kenner of high-school track practice. Watching the white tourists follow the black man's lead was to see, Kenner thought, the whole shabby history of race relations played out as farce. Whites attempting a useless skill. If that dance stood a chance of increasing the GNP, it would have been mastered at Plymouth colony. Kenner often wondered how much racism he had bubbling down below. He had had only one black girlfriend, and, though her body might have been carved out on some African coast, her mind had been whittled white by Catholic girls' schools.

But he was distracted by watching the women bowing their bodies, attempting to pass under the pole. They had a hard time splaying their legs, using them, as the instructor had, as low-slung buckboard wagon springs.

MacNaughton, Kenner thought, was tied up in some sort of dope distribution. Though full of complaints, MacNaughton had been vague about his present source of income. His indolence could only be supported so long on movie options, though Kenner knew it's hard to give up leisure once it's attained. Mac-Naughton had engaged the entrepreneurial side of his heritage, looking to be some sort of Irish gangster, judging from his friends.

Watching the dancers kept bringing women to Kenner's mind. He had a former girlfriend who had profited from the drug trade. He remembered the day one investment paid off. A fellow had arrived at a party Kenner and the young woman were throwing; he put a rumpled paper bag atop a bookcase, after exchanging a glance with her.

Kenner, knew, though he hadn't been told, what was in the brown bag. The look of acknowledgement his girlfriend and the guy passed had been so subtle, yet so intense, that Kenner knew it must have been sent along the same nerves that carried the most potent sexual messages. That his former girlfriend never mentioned to Kenner the receipt of the money or the tidbit of cocaine that had accompanied the cash (though she did later offer him some of the cocaine) just certified for Kenner the nature of their own relationship and the fact that other worlds existed whereon Kenner did not tread. Other orbits, other gravities. And where, or from whom, did Rea get the cocaine they had recently consumed?

Kenner would vote for all drugs' legalization. There would be a few bad consequences, but not as bad, he thought, as the status quo. Kenner always felt left out of lives, that there was another civilization operating all around him that he couldn't see. Like microbe cities in a drop of water. He resented that.

The dope industry disturbed him. Capitalism at its purest. And the young people he knew who were dope robber barons: risk takers. Ah, yes, all the risk takers: the mob, Madison Avenue, Wall Street. MacNaughton was just taking a few risks.

Kenner took it for granted that you could get away with a lot in this country. But there was a gamble associated with it.

Some few would be sacrificed to the appropriate gods; then the festivals could continue.

Kenner felt uneasy with such thoughts. He knew he was unlikely to be in the company of the Big Score. And, at times, that knowledge did take the wind out of his sails.

Regardless of what he heard or read, Kenner thought the real reason the so-called pleasure drugs weren't legalized was society's appreciation of its own powers of exploitation: the knowledge of what would happen if the cocaine and marijuana accounts were turned over to J. Walter Thompson.

The limbo instructor was slithering beneath the pole one more time and Kenner saw Rea walk into the pool area.

3

Nothing's ever done, Winston thought. You do something and it keeps on doing. The prints were stacked in the warehouse. Duane and Kristina had wrapped them in the giant-size polyethylene bags, double strength. When he checked the warehouse was quiet, but here in the living room jittery energy was being discharged. Curt didn't seem to be able to sit down; Vern hadn't come out of the den, but the volume on Vern's TV kept increasing. Duane was standing on the balcony and Winston could see the back of his head. It looked damp and thick, his hair shiny, like an animal floating in water, seal hide, a cat in a drainage ditch. He watched Duane flick the glowing butt of his cigarette into the courtyard.

Winston thought a little chicken soup might quiet the group, have a paradoxical effect: drain the tension from all of them, just as amphetamines are supposed to calm hyperactive children. He had been given them as a boy; they had slowed him down, made him feel slick, cautious, as if he were walking on watered plastic.

The bathroom door clicked open and Kristina breezed out, wearing shorts and a light blue shirt tied with a bow in front. Now every man in the condo had fucked her, Winston thought, with the exception of Vern. The gang's bang, he thought, and chuckled to himself. He moved his fingers over the glassine bag that held the cocaine. The film had the same slick feeling beneath his fingertips, just how the speed had made him feel.

Winston wondered if Duane had noticed he had been sucking on silicone. Maybe he hadn't taken much interest in that part of Kristina. Duane never looked to Winston as if he sought out females for comfort. Woman as wrestling partner: something to bounce off of, put up some sporting resistance.

Winston had not been surprised when Kristina had showed up again with her chest swollen out into impressive development. Consider the source, he had thought, her mama. But he had noticed, when he slid down her belly, a thin ridge, no thicker than fishing line. And then he realized, because of their symmetry, one under each breast, that he was looking at something man-made. He had laughed out loud. Kristina shrank back into the teenager he had known, when he had pointed at her breasts and said mockingly, Falsies! Falsies! No, they're not, she had spat back, they're not. They're me!

He promised not to tell anyone after she had told him the story. Kristina liked to extract promises from people, though Winston presumed she knew that no one ever kept them. I promise. I love you. Childish vows Kristina always wanted to hear. Until he saw the scars, realized her breasts were fixed, he had been having trouble getting hard. In any case, she wasn't a good lay; she had none of the dark resources of her mother.

Winston shook out some cocaine onto the glass-topped table. Florida furnishings, he thought. Glass-top tables made for serving chicken soup. Delmer had left a strange phone message at the Wharf House. HAD PROBLEMS WILL BE LATE. How late? He'd better get here before dawn, Winston thought. He looked up from the tiny mound of dope and looked into Kristina's belly. She just stood there. Even her belly button looked like a cunt. It was slightly raised, labial; he had stuck his little finger in it and moved it back and forth and was surprised by how that made him feel. Kristina had a pretty upholstery of fine blond hairs on her flat stomach. Would they all turn like her mother's, become pubic hairs when she got older, as if her thatch was growing upward, taking over, like undergrowth in an abandoned city?

"We did okay, didn't we, Winston?" she asked. Winston understood why she came over to him. She wanted to keep something between her and Curt. He was still pacing the room. I'm her protector, Winston thought.

"We did just about die when we saw the motorcycle cop roar beside us. I about peed in my pants!"

"She did pee in her pants," Duane said, sliding back the screen door, stepping into the room. Winston thought Duane's bare feet looked strange outlined against the lime-colored carpet.

"I did not."

"You did right well, Krissy girl," Winston said. "You had a good day."

Kristina turned around, as if she had finally lost patience, and said, "Curt. Why don't you sit down!?"

"I did my part," Curt said. "More than my part."

"Don't worry, Curt," Winston said, "we are just where we want to be. Everything's cool. No problems. Delmer will be here. I got a message. We'll be on the road as planned."

Till the museum opened tomorrow they were outside of time: the world was unlike what people thought, but only they knew the quality of difference.

Winston looked up from stropping a razor blade back and forth across the glass tabletop, fashioning lines of powder. Kristina was now in the center of the room. Duane was at one end. Curt was standing by the opposite wall. The TV spoke for Vern.

Kristina knew all of us, he thought, but it doesn't make her comfortable. Something uneasy was flickering in her eyes.

"Here," he said, in Kristina's direction, "you're first, in honor of your wet pants."

Kristina took the brass tube and knelt down by the cocktail table. Her mouth stayed open a bit; she vacuumed up two lines. She handed the tube back to Winston and he offered it to Duane. Duane shrugged, came closer to the table, lowered his head toward the powder cautiously. For the time it took him to inhale he would be vulnerable. Winston smiled at his caution, since he had seen so many displays of it.

"Curt," Winston called, after Duane backed off, "you're on."

Curt seemed to Winston to be playing the bashful boy, the one who wants to be called, acknowledged, lured into the group. Curt swaggered up, as much swagger as he could muster, getting closer to Kristina than he had been all night. Winston thought she was now the fallen woman in Curt's eyes.

Strange, Winston thought, that Kristina doesn't act as an oasis where we all were able to rest—but as a pit stop, someplace to speed away from, tires smoking. Maybe it's incest taboos. He thought of a course he had dropped at BC. Curt finally erased two lines from the table. He sniffed, pinched his nostrils, made rasping wet noises.

When Winston's own turn arrived, he fought the impulse to shut his eyes and, laying a finger aside his nose, went quickly up one row and down the other. He leaned back, feeling all the light in the room get bright and softer. He felt an ascending stream of beneficence, but then the doorbells chimed. Bridget's voice sounded over the diminishing notes.

"It's me. Let me in."

4

Rea and Kenner ate in one of the Wharf House's restaurants. They sat in wicker chairs large enough to be thrones borne by bearers. The table was set with what Kenner had taken to be the current version of imagined elegance: everything was too large, forks and knives sizable enough for self-defense. Pink cloth napkins were elaborately folded and stuffed into half-liter wine glasses. Unfolded and put on their laps they could, Kenner thought, serve as picnic blankets.

Kenner and Rea had talked about a lot of things, but he hadn't yet asked her about the bruises on her neck. Kenner had always operated on the assumption that anything so obvious would be talked about soon enough. But Rea was keeping her own counsel and hadn't said anything. Kenner realized he could call attention to it without mentioning it. He needed only to touch the swelling, or to put his hand on the side of her neck, let his fingertips rest on the purple islands.

There were some things he didn't like to discuss in public places, so he decided to wait until they were out of the restaurant. Rea had told him she would like to experience a hurricane. Kenner didn't know much about weather, but he thought she looked as if she had had her wish.

"Come on, let's go dance," she said, as soon as they hit the street. Kenner withheld his questions once more, not wanting to dash her excitement. The night air was an odd mixture: waves of heat, full of an electrical smell, and then sudden moments of coolness, like spring-fed ponds.

Duval Street was filling up. They headed for the Monster, which was off Front Street, down an alley. A bouncer guarded the entrance.

"He's just like the security folk at the airports," Kenner said to Rea, "except he only allows in those who fit the hijacker profile."

Kenner could always see the surprise in a woman's eyes that he liked to dance. It meant he didn't look it; even Rea, he could tell after they had danced a while, was pleased. Since they had already slept together he figured she should have been aware of his sporadic capacity for abandon.

When they arrived a ceremony was concluding. The coronation of the king and queen of the day's festivities, Venus and Candida. It was the same duo Kenner had seen in the afternoon with their clipboards. They looked less the worse for wear than he expected. The fellow's red taffeta gown was sweat-stained and his corsage drooped.

Kenner was struck by the atmosphere. It was the same as at a Knights of Columbus fish fry: comradely bonhomie. Kids at a sock hop, the high-school production of *Charlie's Aunt*. But then the pink lights had been turned off and darkness returned: a spinning ball of mirror chips threw binary light around. Strobe flashing, tabloid effects, flash bulbs illuminating accident victims, slain showgirls, black and white violence, open hands outstretched in waxy pools of blood. Kenner noticed, against the wall, a young man passed out, but still upright on a bench, a long line of drool dangling from the corner of his mouth. It caught the light, a silver strand.

Most of the men dancing had crew cuts, and for Kenner it resembled some high-school principal's nightmare locker room of the fifties: all the jocks twisting and shouting together. A lot of narrow torsos. Kenner knew he was overweight, but he saw himself as thick and sturdy, rather than soft and balding.

On the wall, above the dancers' heads, a screen showed clips of old black and white movies. Kenner recognized Tony Curtis and Sidney Poitier chained together.

"Gimme some hot stuff. . . ."

Rea and Kenner danced for twenty minutes straight. Everyone on the floor was thrust together like deportees in boxcars, but it was all sought after, wished for.

The sound system was as much of a physical presence as the dancers themselves. Shock waves; it almost felt as if it could push you around. There were many steamer trunk–sized speakers around the room; most of the music seemed not so much to be played by instruments as manufactured by electronic synthesizers. One thing impressed Kenner: it was the sound of an electronic slapstick. It made the most unnerving thwack. The sound system must be very advanced, he thought. Not only was the music ear-shattering, but it was clear.

It was hard to talk through the din. Rea shook Kenner's arm and pointed to the bartender. He was shoving chunks of lime down the small throats of Perrier bottles.

Kenner understood. Fist-fucking the bottlenecks.

"Freak out freak out."

The dance floor smelled like a hospital, Kenner thought; then he realized it did, since the odor was amyl nitrate.

"Freak out."

The spinning globe cast bright spots over the crowd. First the spots seemed to be coffee-bean shapes; they then began to resemble mouths; then they became a variety of orifices: vaginas, anuses. The images of an old Hollywood musical were projected on the wall: dance routines featuring women's legs opening and closing like the shutters of cameras. Everything swallowing and beckoning at once. Kenner wondered if he was imagining the confluence of images. It couldn't be accidental.

5

Somehow the people in the condo had fallen into an orbit and Kristina was its center, Winston thought to himself. Vern was a dead planet off in the den. Kristina was the sun, at least a hot soft place, full of boiling inner space, and she exerted the pull of gravity, kept all the men who had slept with her at a distance from each other.

But when Bridget had come in, invading the solar system, all the orbits got bent. Another field of force, causing havoc. Bridget, Winston saw, aimed to throw a few things off course. And Kristina's going with Duane, that was unfortunate.

All excitement is the same, Winston figured, no matter how it is generated. Like water filling an ice-cube tray. Once one hollow is filled, it spills on over to the next, and to the next. Bridget was the most excited and her excitement was spilling over onto everything. Winston could see she was wound up, full of sexual charge. It was a phosphorescence pulsing all through her.

He could tell Kristina noticed her mother's state and she, too, meant to deflect it.

"Let's go out," she said to Duane. She looked disturbed by the heat her mother was generating. Bridget looked, to Winston, just shy of a moan. Her body seemed to rotate slowly, effortlessly. Some erotic millstone grinding, some deep shifting of the body's plates, down near the liquid core.

Kristina had to leave in a minute, or else she'd hear her mother come out and ask for it. Fuck me, fuck me.

"I'm leaving," Duane said. "Maybe Curt has some time."

"Not me," Curt said, still circling the dining table. "I'm going to work."

Kristina looked peeved. She announced, "Why did God give men pricks?" recalling a joke Juniper had told her last week.

Everyone just stared at her.

"God gave men pricks so that women would talk to them."

Winston shook his head. Maybe Vern is in luck, after all, he thought.

Kristina stared at her mother. Bridget had sat next to Winston on the couch, her back against one of the sofa's arms, her butt slid low. Then she started to open and close her legs, making some sort of sex bellows, blowing her scent toward Winston. He smiled, wet the tip of his finger, and cleaned up the last of the white powder from the cocktail table.

Winston had slid back down into enjoyment. The cocaine made it possible to turn channels on and off. He would watch Kristina and Bridget on one channel; then Duane and Curt on another. He turned them off and heard Vern and his TV. The eleven o'clock news had come on: some black man being shot in the back at a motel in the company of a white woman. A voice said an adviser to the president would not be indicted for alleged drug use at a New York disco because of insufficient evidence. The phrase made Winston lose his concentration. Things began to run together.

He glanced up. Duane was gone from the living room. He saw Kristina's back heading for a bedroom. Then he heard a slap. Duane came back into the living room dressed, wearing a shirt Kristina had, Winston knew, bought for Curt. Royal blue covered with pink flamingos. Kristina followed, holding her eye, licking her lip.

Her lip was puffy. One small part of it had turned purple, swollen up. Winston, with his vision sharpened and softened, thought it looked like a fat worm, a nightcrawler. You could see the lines. Kristina's tongue was busy licking the spot.

"I'll give you a ride," Duane said to Curt, interrupting Winston's staring.

Winston saw that Duane had usurped all of Curt's duties; first he fucks her, then he punishes her. This whole chain of events, Winston thought, had to be placed in Bridget's soft lap. She was the last straw. She had bent everyone's orbits. Kristina wasn't powerful enough to get the men to collide, or even to get herself hit. Bridget was. She was the cunt who heated up the atmosphere.

If Vern stays put, Winston thought, I just might get my chance. Kristina's eyes were bright with tears, though Winston thought it was mostly rage at her mother. They should, he thought, both be in just the right mood.

Seventeen

When Kenner saw who the taxi's driver was, he was mad he hadn't somehow fetched his Sport Fury. Kenner had only wanted to exit the Monster, get home, and unfasten some of the answers Rea had wrapped so tightly around her. Two cabs were waiting at the disco's front gate. Ah, happy anonymous conveyance, Kenner had thought, as he opened the door to the first cab. Then the sweet anonymity was shattered. We all live on the head of a pin, Kenner kept repeating to himself.

"Hi, there. Take us to Cayo Hueso Condos," Kenner requested, depressed enough by Curt's appearance to forego even the pretense of friendliness.

"Ah," Curt said, "you don't want to go there."

"Oh," Kenner said, "I don't want to go there?"

"No, you don't," he replied, pushing back his yellow cap. "Everyone at the condo is a little strange tonight, if you catch my drift," Curt said to Rea, elaborately winking. "It's early yet. Hey, let me take you out, buy you a drink," he said, turning toward Kenner. "I owe you one for driving the float today."

"That's all right," Kenner said, not wanting to spend any

more time than necessary in Curt's company. Curt made him nervous. "I enjoy float driving. I'm thinking of taking it up professionally," he said to Rea, hoping for a smile. Her face had lost some of its usual animation. She was thinking. All her features were pulled inward, toward some center.

"If you don't want more to drink, I'd check into a motel," Curt suggested. "I know one with water beds and mirrors." Then he looked straight back at Rea. "Duane's looking for you. He gave me a lift to the cab stand. I'm surprised he hasn't run into you already."

Kenner realized that Duane probably was the answer to most of the unanswered questions. Kenner never thought he was stealing someone's girl; in fact, he thought her presence in Winston's menagerie was a sign of freedom rather than confinement. Kenner wasn't in the business of taking women away from other men. But that might be a good business to get into. Maybe MacNaughton would front some capital for it. He seemed to like transportation and transformation.

"Take us to the Esquire Lounge," Rea said. She didn't sound to Kenner like she wanted a drink.

"Right on," Curt said. He took a shoreline route, hurtling the cab down dark streets, bottoming out twice. He kept close to the edge of the island. Kenner stared at Rea, who was still lost in thought, and saw beyond her, out the window, the rigging of shrimp boats, now impounded, tied close together, as if they were hastily collected, pushed together by a storm. Their masts and rigging were spears raised outside a walled city. More than vaguely threatening. Curt turned at the power plant. The building was a substantial one, unlike most of the town's structures: throbbing, factorylike, transmitting, always on. Curt took a left onto Palm Avenue, and they raced by the naval base housing, by the charter boats, all the formerly strange sights that had become familiar.

As Rea and Kenner got out of Curt's cab, a tall, lean man wearing a pilot's iridescent blue flightsuit holding a drink in a plastic glass was waiting to get in. Kenner stuck his head in the front window to pay. "Busy night," he said to Curt, who took the money Kenner held out after protesting that the ride was on him.

"The naval air station on Boca Chica and step on it," Kenner heard Curt's new passenger command. Kenner watched the cab speed away. He always felt people should be paid for their work and this was Curt's work. Kenner followed Rea into the lounge, expecting to see Kristina dancing on the kettle-drum stage, but the round platform was empty. Rea had stopped, but when Kenner pointed to a table, she took his arm and said, "Let's go."

They stood in the parking lot, staring into the black sky above the Blue Lagoon.

"There's a Howard Johnson's down the road. We can talk there," Rea said. Kenner must have raised his eyebrows expressively, because Rea replied, "I didn't want Curt leaving us anywhere we planned to stay."

Kenner remembered with some sense of shame how he devoured egg salad sandwiches in front of the family TV when he was seventeen, watching the news of JFK's assassination. Nothing ever seemed to weaken his appetite. He thought that, looking at the Key Lime pie that languished in front of him, hardly touched, as he listened to the tales Rea told.

Kenner decided it probably wouldn't be best to return to the condo, tonight, after all; across the street from HoJos was a motel. "Wait here. I'll see if there's a room," he said, and pushed the Key Lime pie toward Rea. "Have some of mine."

One wing of the motel sat right on the edge of the Blue Lagoon; a view, at night, which reminded Kenner of the Calumet marshes east of Chicago. There were concrete pylons, tall pillars holding electrical cables, stepping awkwardly across it. Tiny red lights blinking. Power stilts.

Kenner requested a room away from the road. The clerk was happy to oblige. Business had been up for a few weeks; his place had never been so full. But since Carter's embargo bookings had gone slack. Staring out at the water, Kenner realized why he had thought of East Chicago. Things looked different from this side of the island, unfamiliar. And that's how he felt. After he had grown accustomed to the place, he found that Rea's talk had turned him back into a stranger.

Maybe that's why he didn't ask certain questions, Kenner thought. Because he knew he would get the kind of answers Rea had supplied him with. Things had passed Kenner by, once again. He always felt more than humbled when he discovered that. Chastened, slightly embarrassed. Kenner looked through the open door across the lagoon at the flickering lights of Stock Island. He had paid with a credit card, so he didn't use an alias. He laughed that such thoughts should be occurring to him.

Walking back to the restaurant, it also occurred to him that Rea might not be waiting for him. He was filled with mixed emotions when he saw she was, sitting there as he had left her, calmly sipping coffee.

Kenner did not think himself at peril. For all the violence he had seen, or heard of, violence still had the quality of a cartoon about it. There was always something crudely drawn about fistfights: the flaring up, the grappling bodies, the uncommon configurations.

But Rea's story was more troubling to him in ways that had little to do with cuts and bruises. Kenner found himself listening to what was, for him, a story of sexual confession. He was unmistakably jealous, aggrieved. For with every detail of danger and assault Rea related, Kenner felt the weight of her bond to Duane, since, in Kenner's view, only a powerful connection could have kept her that close.

So each degree of malice that Duane advanced was, in some way, a mark in his favor. Rea's plight was not damsel-in-distress stuff, though that was part of what Kenner heard—she just needed to be kept away from him—but, as Kenner was willing to help her, the cause of her distress pierced him in a most uncomfortable way. The need for her to be quit of Duane seemed to be only a testament to his effect on her; and Kenner was already, quite foolishly, worrying about his own effect on Rea.

2

Rea had second thoughts about not telling Kenner the whole truth, and nothing but. She was a lawyer's daughter, after all; and that, along with many other facts, made getting involved with petty criminals something of an indulgence. Not that Winston and his crew weren't hoping to graduate from the petty. But Rea had to laugh: even the cocaine fantasies of Winston were more petty than he would ever know. They reminded Rea of her grandfather's business schemes, her mother's father, who never was able to climb out from under his debts and deals. Cocaine smuggling was to Rea another sort of garment industry. Rag merchants, dream pickers. But *her* father. She hadn't spoken with him for six years; that last conversation had been sufficiently unpleasant to mark, for Rea, the end of their connection. It was after the rape. She wanted his opinion about prosecuting the inept Jethro, the gas-station attendant rapist. The police weren't eager to go to court. She would need to get her own lawyer. She would need money. "Some lawyers extend credit," her father said. But not him. It wasn't so much the disdain in his voice, as the resonance that surrounded it. Rea was sure he believed in her complicity, even more than the local yokels. It had been her fault, her father was telling her.

Well, Rea considered, thus far Kenner was not an accessory. She was going to make him an accessory only to her. All he needed to know was her troubles with Duane.

She was pretty sure she wouldn't be charged in the Audubon theft, even if Winston and the others were caught. She was much too peripheral. She wondered if her father would come to her aid if she was. Perhaps if he saw it as coming to his own aid, he would. Nothing she did would please him; had she gone to law school, he would have noticed the compliment, though. The degrees she did have did not impress him. He had never seen her dressed up; though she recalled every one of his "Why don't you get your hair fixed?" remarks.

She had been dressed up the night of the high school senior prom, but she had gone with a black boy as a protest of sorts, though he was the son of a black judge. Her father took it as a personal affront, but, since he was, in those years, a liberal of sorts, he had to seem to approve. But he certainly did not admire. The judge's son and her appearance at the prom made a stir. And she made a stir in other ways as well at the prom—she ate her corsage. The year before Rea had volunteered for the Kennedy campaign and traveled to his inauguration, standing in the cold, the rain, and, finally, the sun. It struck her, later, how mild her rebellions were; like the times, 1961.

It was touching to Rea to see how such small amounts of truth seemed to satisfy Kenner. He seemed to be clever; or, at least, to have a talent for being in unexpected places, for not standing out, for insinuating himself. Perhaps he could insinuate himself and her off the Keys. Kenner, she saw, would accept some degree of danger, though he didn't know the extent of his own involvement. Rea did fear for his safety. He wasn't weak, but Duane's experience with violence would breach whatever were Kenner's ideas of fair play. Duane might gouge out an eye. She had told Kenner that.

She should just take a cab to the airport. The chances of getting Curt twice were small. Duane wouldn't be sitting at the airport. But there were no flights out till morning. She had jobs waiting for her. She could just arrive early, get settled, lost, insert herself in a haystack. Bright, shiny, hard needle, Rea Kramer.

Why involve Kenner?

When they made love Kenner looked as if he enjoyed what

he was doing. But she would never call Duane a good lover. Goodness didn't enter into it; he was a presence, her own apparition. She had realized that some time ago. In fact, she always knew she had been looking for it: some manifestation of her own desires. That it would turn out to be a thin, dark-haired, working-class car thief did not entirely surprise her. On her stormy nights it was his knuckles that she would hear tapping on the windowpane.

Rea, though she didn't think of herself as overeducated, knew she had some superfluous intelligence, the sort that was dangerous for animals. Curiosity killed the cat. It actually killed wolves, she had read. Hunters buried cheap alarm clocks; their ticking would lure wolves to the spot. Curious. Dead. About a few things Rea had too much superfluous knowledge. About what apparitions and manifestations were, for one. Anything you fashion to master you becomes monstrous sooner or later. Since Duane was made to wear the image of her subjugation, she knew he would also turn monstrous. For all their differences, she didn't feel superior to him. She felt a natural sympathy—the phrase, she knew, was a cliché, but it was apt: it wasn't empathy, that was presumptuous, but sympathy, accord. She understood him biologically, physically, naturally, not intellectually. She realized it was just an understanding all humans have, but only rarely choose to acknowledge.

She had the other sorts of sympathies, too. She had been moved when Duane told her what he feared: that he would turn into one of those chumps you see Sunday mornings walking alone on the deserted downtown streets of a small city. Some bum, someone shuffling along.

That saved Duane from her contempt, which she felt to be the most cauterizing of her emotions. That would close any wound of desire once it was applied. She stayed raw with Duane. No hot poker of contempt to burn the wound. When she realized he could kill her and had demonstrated it, she still could not summon contempt; what emerged was a kind of fear that was mixed with good judgment—a paste, a balm she knew she could put on her open wound, a poultice Rea was sure would let her begin to heal underneath.

3

Highways always made Delmer Grebe angry. Every car that passed him insulted him. Every truck driver who ended up on his tail,

214

all chrome grille, smiling through his back window, was an evil omen. Delmer tried to placate his anger by thinking about black people. But then some coon would drive past him in a big car and his anger was made fresh and hot.

Winston's telegram made Delmer something of a celebrity in his town. Not many telegrams came that way, unless they were from the military. Delmer had been driving produce since he was paroled—at least, till his accident. He might have been driving a bit too erratically, his blood looping with black beauties. He did take the curve a mite spiritedly, though the real problem, he knew, was that his load of watermelons was piled wrong and the truck's center of gravity was much too high. Delmer found himself lying sideways, his truck skidding down the shoulder of the road, sparks and gravel flying, watermelons spewing and bursting out the rear.

Cars dodged the melons as red pulp splattered over the road. He was a bit leery of driving for a while after that. His boss wasn't offering him any more jobs, anyhow. Delmer just stayed close to his mother's farm, did chores. Then Winston's telegram arrived. A red and white and blue post-office jeep pulled up the dirt road and stopped at the porch. Even his parole officer never sent him something so official looking.

It was a short letter for all the fuss it took to deliver it. YOU'RE NEEDED FOR MOVING AND STORAGE. MONEY ORDER WILL FOLLOW. RENT A CAR. ARRIVE KEY WEST 5/30/80. DON'T BE LATE. WINSTON. Now, Delmer thought Winston a strange case. But he did share what little there was in the way of good times in the can. The money order arrived. Four hundred dollars, made out to him, signed by that lifer Jack Dawes's friend, the pretty-boy Duane Rooks. Delmer made plans. It took most of the four hundred to rent a car; they made him leave a hundred-dollar deposit. In the line in front of him at the car rental were three old ladies. The only one who had a valid driver's license wore an artificial leg. But the clerk had rented them a car, anyway. Delmer thought the boy an idiot for renting them a car. They were going to Disney World.

Delmer took the coastal highway, since it made a nicer trip. There were fewer niggers to see on the Gulf side of Florida. Outside of Fort Myers, Delmer decided to pick up a hitchhiker. The one he stopped for looked like a serviceman: a crew cut and brand-new blue jeans. He turned out to be in the coast guard. And going to Key West just suited him fine. He was just filling up his leave time.

They crossed the Everglades on Alligator Alley in the high heat of the day. Delmer's rent-a-car had air-conditioning, but Delmer thought coolant gave you cancer, and he hadn't turned it on. He told the boy it was broken. The boy didn't talk much, which suited Delmer just fine. He had asked him where he was from, what his name was. "Name's Blue, from Missouri," was all the boy said. He was wearing a T-shirt and tennis shoes, and his jeans had white stitching down the leg. Delmer got the car up to seventy, but then it started to shimmy and he had to settle for sixty-five.

The Everglades made Delmer think he and the car were both shrinking. The road was bordered on both sides by high green reeds no thicker than switches, and Delmer did feel that he was some sort of creature crawling along the bottom of sea grass. He and the car had by then shrunk down to bug size. The coast guard boy kept fiddling with the radio; he left it for a while on a revival station. There was a man testifying that sounded to Delmer like his Uncle Ennis, but their stories weren't the same. *"I found Jesus and because of Jesus I don't feel guilty any more about all the money I'm putting in the bank. Jesus wants me to have it, wants me to keep it, and to make more and not feel guilty at all."* Amazing grace, Delmer thought.

It was getting dark by the time they got near Florida City. Delmer knew they'd be late. He was used to Georgia heat, but this was something more. Now that it was dark it felt like a wool blanket was wrapped around him. You could feel its weight; it made him itch. Delmer found it hard to breathe. His mind kept turning over *Blue from Missouri*.

4

Duane took it for granted that people aren't ever as smart as they think they are. Winston knew a lot about Audubon, but, Duane was sure, wouldn't know enough to check the folios once he had them in his possession. He wouldn't think anyone would steal from him. Whichever deal Winston finally made, it didn't matter; Winston wouldn't notice the print missing, and the one print would bring Duane what he needed. Ten thousand dollars worth of cocaine. Duane knew Winston's itinerary: his trip back to New York, waiting for the delivery of the prints Duane was supposed to make from Delmer's farm. Duane didn't know how long they would be in Winston's possession. But Duane had been put in touch with a local art connoisseur who was into barter: Duane would bring the dope back north and get it to Louie. He'd get more than ten grand and also get in solid with Louie. Duane wanted the connection. Duane left Curt off at the taxi stand and continued down Duval Street, on the errand he had spoken of to Curt and those left at the condo: to find Rea. That he would, but first things first. He left Old Town and headed for Stock Island, back to the warehouse. No one was on guard. Winston probably wouldn't even take them out of their plastic bags till they were sold, handed over to the dealer.

Duane drove past the closed-down dog track, along Fifth Street, the back route to the warehouse. Dogs were still kept at the kennel by the track. As he drove by, his crunching tires provoked a few yelps. He parked out of the street light and walked to the warehouse's side door. Under his arm was a cardboard tube, one in which some artist friend of Rea had sent her a painting. Duane smelled a use for it and had packed it in the van. In his pocket was a spool of piano wire.

He would do his cutting by moonlight. Duane walked over to the pile of folios he and Kristina had stacked on a skid. Winston's boat-restoring company had already gone bankrupt, but Winston still had the lease on the building. The franchise of boat bottom–restoring compound he had bought into hadn't proved the bonanza Winston had hoped. He had painted only five boats last year. Not many people believed Winston's claims that his advanced polymers would hold out the sea and keep the hull solid at the same time.

Duane had one problem. The print the man wanted was number CCCXXI. When Kristina and he had covered the folios, he wasn't sure he had marked the right one. He had been able only to glance inside them to see the progression of numbers. He had learned Roman numerals in the Catholic grammar school he went to for a year. He had marked the one he hoped it was in with a diagonal slash of tape.

Duane lifted that folio and moved it under a window, into a trapezoid of blue moonlight on the concrete floor. The warehouse still smelled of fiberglass and chemicals, the stuff of Winston's boat business. He slipped the polyethylene bag down from the leather corners of the book, getting caught on one shoulder. In the semi-dark the bag felt like a cheap slip, some sort of rayon. Duane was holding the book straight up and the bag was snagging at the bottom. He lifted the folio and nudged the bag free with his foot. He then tried to smooth the bag out behind the book, like a blanket, and he lowered the folio slowly down on top of the green plastic. He picked up a piece of two-by-four he could lean the cover on when he opened the book, to keep the cover off the dusty floor. The folio was splayed in front of him. He began to slowly turn the heavy paper. It felt wet, not stiff; the paper was as thick as cloth, as tarpaper, under thumb and fingers; he found himself not looking long at the pages when he turned them. He just wanted to get to plate number CCCXXI.

He felt relieved when he saw it was the right folio. He carefully turned one more page. There it was. The roseate spoonbill. Why would the guy want that one? Duane wondered. In the faint light Duane made out a large pink bird with a green head and a long bill. A spoonbill, he realized. Some things you just can't figure.

He made a loop with his piano wire along the gutter of the volume, then back up its spine. He had both ends of the wire sticking out at the bottom and he could step on them both to hold the wire taut. Duane then began to tear the print free. It began to pull away quite magically, a straight but slightly frayed and thready cut. He did it slowly, worried that the whole print might start to rip. He could see and feel the vector of force, the point at the edge of the wire. He kept slowly adjusting his angle till the entire print came loose in his hand. At that moment it felt both lighter and heavier. It began to luff, bend in the breeze.

Duane stepped away, holding the thick sheet of paper out in front of him, off the ground. He rolled it up and inserted it in the tube. Duane closed the folio. It might have been the ease with which the first print came loose that made him decide to take one more.

He turned back the pages, one by one, till something caught his eye. The print he chose came free without a hitch. He rolled it up, placed it in the tube, inside the other, rewrapped the leather book of prints, and left with his wire back in his pocket, his two prints in the tube under his arm.

Eighteen

1

Kenner didn't usually remember his dreams. He had begun
to see that forgetfulness was part of his character, a clue to understanding himself: a man who made no attempt to recall his
dreams displayed a certain carelessness. But Kenner came out of
the morning's sleep remembering this dream:

He and Rea were at the Wharf House and a storm quickly
took shape. A hurricane of sorts, roiling clouds; tiny tornadoes
hovered above the small island off Mallory Square. But just before the hurricane smashed into shore, the storm and the tornadoes veered off; in the storm's wake—Rea and Kenner were
now part of a crowd that had taken to the street to watch the
wild weather—a bank of clouds rolled in, a sort of sky surf crashing overhead. The clouds fascinated Kenner: their colors came
from a core within, light inside quartz, the same sort of thing
eyewitnesses described viewing early atom bomb explosions. But
after the clouds appeared overhead, they became very black, became textured like brain tissue. The the clouds seemed to begin
to land, as if some sort of craft themselves, to come down over
the assembled crowd; soon they were only twenty feet or so above

219

the heads looking at them. And at that distance Kenner saw the black underbelly of the clouds turn smooth and slick. Black canvas, but with the sheen of oilcloth. Then they tore open. Three cuts appeared and from them tumbled boats, yachts, Chris-Craft-type cruisers, except they were outfitted and painted to resemble what looked to Kenner like fifties Cadillac hearses. The clouds then moved off, leaving the boats behind. They had fallen softly to the ground, drifted down like maple leaves. Kenner went up to the boats and looked in through portholes and cabin windows and saw bodies, drowned pleasure-boaters, but the bodies did not look real.

They looked like mannequins. Kenner in the dream thought that the tornadoes and winds had sucked up the boats from the sea into the clouds, and the clouds were now just redepositing them, dropping them back to earth. Carried off and now returned. He turned from the sight of the mannequins and Rea had disappeared.

What surprised Kenner as he came to consciousness was the dream's vividness and the fact that he recalled it, had let it stay in his consciousness. The boatlift, doubtless, the Cubans who were recently reported drowned.

He turned to tell Rea the dream, but she wasn't there. No noises came from the bathroom. Kenner was a sound sleeper, but Rea must have taken pains to leave undetected. Since they hadn't checked in with any luggage, Kenner searched the room for some sign of whether or not she intended to return. An article of clothing, a comb, a note.

It was hot, but not sunny. The room's air conditioner labored. If he was to have kept Rea from some trouble, he didn't seem to be succeeding. She had eluded her own protection. He moved the window curtains aside; they were woven fiberglass, stiff, unwelcoming to the touch. He felt like the cloth could cut his fingers. He looked at the lagoon, slightly ruffled, reflecting dull sky. Cement pylons marched across it; it must not be deep. He turned around, feeling odd, a washbucket sloshing, about to spill over.

2

Winston was not pleased that Delmer had brought along company. The boy, stuffed into designer jeans and a white T-shirt, couldn't be more than nineteen. His blond hair had been cropped to the skull, and he stood next to Delmer in front of the Perkins Pancake House like some retarded relative who needed to be kept close.

The boy, Delmer explained, was on leave and wanted to see Key West. Winston took Delmer aside, trying not to appear as upset as he felt, and asked, "Delmer, just what the fuck are you doing!?"

Delmer said he never thought he was doing anything uncool. The boy would never think they were up to anything. If they were, why would they let a hitchhiker stand around and observe it? Delmer smiled at Winston, and Winston saw that Delmer thought he had amazed Winston with his reasoning powers. Winston suggested Delmer point the coast-guard lad to town and let him hitchhike. Delmer shrugged, looked around shyly, seemed reluctant to detach himself from the young man just yet. Winston realized that Delmer had resumed some of his prison practices.

"Is that why you were so late?" Winston asked. "You stop somewhere last night?"

"It was real hot," Delmer said and smiled, sliding a calloused finger across his lips.

Delmer would be stubborn abut this, Winston saw; there was no time for blowups. Delmer was to be back on the road again in a couple of hours. The folios were going in Delmer's trunk.

Let the boy hang out.

The prints would be discovered missing by late morning, Winston knew. The caravan was to be a simple one. Duane was supposed to drive in front of Delmer, and if any sort of trouble appeared ahead, or behind, they would be in communication. But Duane hadn't yet showed up. Winston had bought portable CB sets at Radio Shack; perhaps they could make do with just a car ahead. He hoped Duane would show. Kristina was still there. She could drive, if need be; or Curt. Rea hadn't returned, though that hadn't surprised Winston at all.

When Delmer had called, he was still asleep. Kristina had finished off a bottle of Pernod she found and had come into his bedroom to sulk; she was, Winston saw, ready to crash. By the time he convinced Bridget to come with him, Kristina had passed out. Bridget had a feral look in her eyes, horror mixed with anger. When he saw that Kristina was unconscious, Winston found himself wanting her with fresh avidity; but, Bridget, after turning off the lights, went right for him.

He felt like he was slipping down a deep well; it was a physical sensation he had had before in the dark: falling backward, shrinking, while the darkness around him grew immense and rushed past. Even though his penis was at that moment the size of a slug, Bridget didn't mind. Slowly he got hard, but he was out of reach—his member still had no more feeling than his arm. It was just there.

But then Bridget climbed on top of him, and as if to keep it from harm, she sheathed his prick in her cunt, and stayed there, moving her hips methodically, her breasts swaying above his face. Then she started to talk. And it was the sound of her voice, even more than the words she used, that worked. He felt himself begin to thaw. And the picture her prompting induced, dildos of Winston's own imagining being pushed back and forth in her every orifice, brought him near, but when he imagined Kristina's head between her mother's thighs, a circuit finally closed, a switch was thrown and he came: the sensation was balanced on a narrow beam laminated with equal layers of pleasure and pain. As the sperm jetted from the tip of his cock, it felt like something had yanked a long narrow cord of rough hemp out through his urinary tract.

The ringing phone awakened him. During the night Kristina had fastened his hand between her legs. Winston dislodged it and climbed off the bed. Both women stirred and rolled away from the place he left. Back to back: mermaid-shaped bookends, but nothing in between. He heard Vern in the den making industrial sounds, boxcars on a siding, stirring on his fold-out couch.

It was Delmer calling from Sugarloaf Key. He told Delmer he'd meet him at the Perkins Pancake House. It was time to move the goods.

3

Curt was short of cash. Only if he was lucky would a night of hacking put more than twenty dollars in his pocket. Most drunks were cheap. The cab company paid him by check once every other week. Kristina made more in tips than he did, but he was fed up with asking her. He didn't have to pay any rent, but gas and beer and medicines, and Cuban mix sandwiches, and cheeseburgers, and pizza left him with just spare change. There was money down the road, but Winston wasn't doling out any of that now, beyond his version of room and board.

Even to be a proper thief you needed money. Curt wondered where Winston's funds had come from: to start his boat rehab business, to pay expenses for the gang. That condo must be near five hundred a month. The Wharf House room nearly that for a week. His chicken soup they had vacuumed up their noses. Curt had tried to find out where Winston's supply had come from. All he learned from Kristina was that the cocaine came from a man named Sueño—but Curt thought that it was really from a greaseball supplier named Suerte.

You need money to make money, Winston had said. Winston did try to make his operation look successful. Fancy stationery to ward off bill collectors.

But, to Curt, Winston had begun to seem all polish and no spit. Maybe that was just because he was afraid he was becoming all spit and no polish himself.

Men looked up to me in the navy, he thought. Curt was willing to do nervy things; he had leadership qualities. Which is why he saw them in Winston. Winston had a peacetime version of the same thing: big plans, a man with big plans, willing, eager to do things. Curt remembered an ensign telling him, "You don't get responsibility, you take it."

When the kennel owner he had driven around offered fifty bucks for some easy work, Curt had agreed to take it. Curt was to meet the kennel owner at the dog track in the early morning. He had taken the guy to the Casa Marina a number of nights from the track when it was still open; he tipped well. So Curt had started to go by the track at quitting time, and the man had become a regular customer.

All Curt needed to do was take some dead dogs to the dump in the morning. They were dogs either too old to run and not fit for breeding or too young and too slow. There should be a dog meat business; like horse meat. Curt recalled the cages of dogs he had seen on a forty-eight-hour stop in Thailand. He never let himself taste the meat they were cooking, though. Born to run. Lots of greyhounds must get put down every year. The humane society worried abut the rabbits. Curt laughed. They should worry about the dogs. Most were dead in five years.

The area behind the dog track where the kennels were reminded Curt of Mexico. He had never been to Cuba, but this was what all those refugees must be fleeing, he thought, what some little village outside of Havana would look like. Would it do much for a butcher's ordinary business to locate his *carnicería*

223

behind the dog track? Wouldn't it make the customers take a second look at the ground round? But there it was, abutting a sandwich shop, one not frequented by tourists. Good sausage. The dust rose on the unpaved street lined with foliage that was thick and buggy. The scattered trash looked almost pretty to Curt, caught and held as it was in so many flowering shrubs and plants. Curt had a *café con leche* standing up at the sandwich shop's plywood counter. There were a few stools covered with ripped red Naugahyde, slick with grease, polished with the rags of pant seats.

Curt stared at the kennels: they were divided by high chainlink fences; a couple of fences had canvas windbreaks stretched across them. Others had clothes hung out to dry. It looked to him like some families lived at the kennels. Curt supposed the kennels and the track had been constructed on landfill. Mango swamp came right up to the curve of the road; there was only water beyond. Conifers and stunted palms outlined the bend in the road. The chunks of coral looked to Curt like rubble, pieces of something broken apart, remnants.

The kennel owner appeared at the mouth of the driveway and waved at Curt. Curt walked over and followed the man to a white pickup truck, the bed outfitted with a box, a squashed looking camper with louvered slats: part icebox, part screened-in porch. Dogs were transported in them.

"Do you know where the dump is?" the kennel owner asked.

Curt shot him a look of taxi-driver pique; he thought he had been offered this job since it was in the nature of transport. "Has Dolly Parton got tits? Yeah, I take tourists there all the time." The kennel owner didn't laugh. "Yeah, I know. It's over by the community college."

"Good. Just tell the man at the gate you've got dead dogs to bury. Tell him to alert the bulldozer man. He covers them up right away." The kennel owner held back the keys he was about to hand over to Curt. "There's one problem, though. A couple of the dogs aren't dead yet. I was almost out of the drug and I tried to stretch a dose. I didn't put them in bags. You'll have to dispose of them there."

Dispose of them, Curt thought. I am already disposing of them by taking them there.

"You'll have to put them down. Just shoot them in the head. They won't even feel it. You don't want to have them buried still alive," the kennel owner said. A hardy *har-har-har* followed.

"Shoot 'em?" Curt said, nonplussed.

"There's a twenty-two in the glove compartment. Believe me. There's no problem."

"Fifty bucks don't pay for shooting dogs," Curt said, wondering what a vet would charge to kill them.

"Well, I understand that," the kennel owner said, "and that's why I'm gonna give you a hundred." He handed Curt a crisp bill.

This must have come from a stack, Curt thought.

"If I'm not here when you get back," the kennel owner said, "just leave the truck right here, with the key under the mat. No one will bother it."

"No problem, chief," Curt said, climbing in, smelling the inside of the truck, different from the redolent air of the kennels, more intense, compressed, heated: singed hair.

The new hundred-dollar bill in his pocket raised his spirits. A hundred dollars for seven dogs. Fifteen dollars a head. I guess that's cheaper than a vet, or he wouldn't pay me to do it.

The dump reminded Curt of the only record he had had as a little kid: *The Big Rock Candy Mountain*. From the road the mountain of trash had the shape of a volcano. Right at the base, behind the red and white sign CITY OF KEY WEST SOLID WASTE DIVISION, was a cooled lava flow of old tires.

To the left of the entrance was a shack the size of a shopping center photoshed; a large air conditioner stuck out of its one window. There was a cement slab, a large weight scale. The gatekeeper knew the truck.

"A little over four hundred pounds of dead dog," the old man said. "We'll just make four zero zero." He looked to Curt as if he would be retiring soon. Curt wondered if the job was civil service or city patronage. He looked Conch through and through to Curt. The man returned to his shed; Curt noticed that a stream of condensation poured from its air conditioner.

Curt turned and started up the road that encircled the mountain of trash; he drove by mounds of old water heaters, piles of stoves and refrigerators. They didn't take heavy pieces very far up, Curt noticed. The nose of the truck leveled off. He had reached the top, a plateau, one larger than he expected: it looked like the best view in town, the highest point.

Four hundred pounds seemed high for seven dogs. He didn't think those skinny animals could weigh that much. The sky and water looked to Curt like a stretch of tin foil. Clouds' reflections were hot spots on a silver sheet. Waves of heat rose off the plateau, a shaved surface of compressed coral and trash. The truck's smell had registered the increasing heat: it now went to burnt hide, the bad odor of protein incineration.

The last dead things he had picked up were the men on the Enterprise. After they had returned to Pearl, he had thought he and his shipmates would all be reassigned or sent ashore; but the navy reacted with what they called pride and Curt thought shame. He had never worked harder or longer. After they went back out to sea, it seemed like a vacation to be only on patrol, regular duty; his tour after the disaster had been largely uneventful.

On the carrier he felt like a drone. He remembered high-school science-class films: worker bees, protecting the hive; ant colonies, half-exposed tunnels, what the teacher, old four-eyes, called a vermiculated universe. For some reason Curt looked up the word: worm-eaten. The carrier was a hive, a colony, and he kept it clean, working, jaws masticating the wastes, eating the excreta.

Curt slammed on the brakes, awakening from the recollection. The mountain of trash seemed even higher from this side; it slid steeply down to the water. Turkey buzzards perched on garbage along the plateau's rim. Curt was surprised at their size and at the fact that his arrival had not stirred them.

White tanks were near the opposite horizon; Curt could see other white discs, radar, the same lime-white, calcified, flaky. The military was scattered all over, in bits and pieces.

He got out and went to the first hatch door. It opened with a lever, the sort of latch you'd find on a freezer door. There was a plastic bag within, a pink color, vaguely translucent. Curt dragged it out. It weighed fifty pounds, at least; he could see a dog within. Its back made a parabola, outlining the sack. He laid it at the foot of a hill of trash. Curt couldn't tell how the bull-dozer was going to rearrange things. Maybe it would crawl up the other side, push things down from the top. Piles were heaped up, then spread out. The whole land was the bones of things, but Curt thought that someday there would be condos here, right on the water's edge. When they sank the pilings, they'd pull up the delicate bones of greyhounds. There was something weird about the shape of their skeletons. Even with their flesh still on. And these greyhounds didn't have much flesh covering their bones. Curt realized what it was. It looked like a bird's skeleton: bird dog. A flying dog.

Curt thought the owner must have given them one last meal and laced it with poison. He looked through the pink transparency of one bag and saw fresh excrement, greenish; Curt had opened three hatches and put three pink bags on the ground. They looked like their own sort of tropical blooms, blossoms, slick, wet, folded, like the insides of the dogs' ears. Three pink puddles of dog carcasses. He opened a hatch and it was the first without a bag in it, just a dog. The greyhound's tongue hung out; it was barely breathing.

Curt reached in and pulled the dog out and found himself cradling it in his arms. The dog seemed to Curt so hot that for a moment he felt it might explode in his arms. There was no membrane of pink polyethylene between him and the animal; that made a difference. Curt thought how the invention of plastic bags gave people a way to deal with most everything: it made everything neat. Curt had pulled one dead seaman out of the chamber where he had been cooked alive, below deck, below the hardest steel. His arm had pulled out of the socket. They had Jesus bags on the deck. They put the body into one and lined it up side by side with the others. The straight line they made and the thick shiny rubberoid made the horror somehow neat. A few things should be outlawed, Curt had thought a short time after; people would see then. Plastic bags should be outlawed, not guns.

Curt put the dying dog down next to the pink bags and went to get the gun. He stopped. He thought if there was more than one to shoot, he should shoot them all at once.

He opened another hatch and there was a smaller dog within. It seemed dead, even though it was not in a sack.

He opened the next to the last hatch and jumped back: a dog lurched, half sprang from the hole, and fell, its body partway clear of the compartment, sliding down the side of the truck like a snake, some otter slithering off a rotting log.

The dog attempted to stand, managing to get up on one leg, before Curt composed himself and caught hold of the dog's neck, what loose skin he could grab there. Curt dragged him to where the others lay. He decided he couldn't let him go; the dog might run, limp away, and Curt would have to chase him through the piles of garbage. He found himself awkwardly dragging the dog along till he got to the truck's door and reached through the open window to the glove compartment.

It was a twenty-two, not much more than a target pistol. He would have to shoot this dog first. The dog tried to growl, but racing greyhounds are handled by trainers from birth. They are accustomed to people. So, even in the dog's mighty distress, some residual faith made the greyhound respond to Curt's handling.

Curt released the dog and fired. The dog fell back; the shot echoed over the dump, scattering birds. Curt couldn't believe the number of birds around the dump. Gray and white terns noisily sprang up, a large banner whipping over his head. The turkey buzzards flapped their heavy wings, rose awkwardly and circled above him. The chattering birds made more racket than the gun, but nonetheless Curt wondered if the man in the shack would hear; he might not, over the rumble of the air conditioner. The bullet had hit the dog's neck. Blood spurted out, first rapidly, with the pressure of the dog's beating heart; then it dropped, quickly, to the arc that one uses to drink comfortably at a water fountain. Finally it just seeped. Curt shot once again, into the top of the tiny arrowhead-shaped skull; he did the same to the other two dogs, including the one that already seemed dead.

Curt looked up, gun in hand, somehow mysteriously placed there, or grown there, almost forgetting it was still in his hand. The buzzards had landed, but the smaller birds still swooped and dived above him. Their shadows darkened the ground where he stood.

Curt opened the last hatch. There was a pink bag inside. He felt mightily relieved.

Instead of putting the gun back in the glove compartment, Curt left it on the seat beside him as he drove out of the dump, not yet having fully decided what he was going to do with it, or with the rest of the day, now truly begun. Winston wanted him to show up at the warehouse. He had over an hour to kill.

Nineteen

1

Kenner hadn't been in a fistfight since he was sixteen. He never looked weak enough to pick on or big enough to provoke. Oh, well, he thought, Duane was an ex-con—and Rea said he would probably, in jailhouse fashion, gouge out my eyes. The tone of Rea's voice had bothered him more than Duane's fighting style: the mixture of disapproval and respect. It's a violent world, Kenner thought, taking comfort in banality. Violence was always around him, though he'd get there when the corpse was cold, after the glass was shattered. Violence had happened in front of his eyes, but it wasn't usually directed at him. Mayhem flowed around him. Kenner was the sort of onlooker who didn't get hit accidentally. He wasn't an innocent bystander. Kenner paid attention. He was amazed by how much violence he had sidestepped.

Kenner, without a clue to Rea's whereabouts, wandered back to Cayo Hueso condos. He thought he was lucky to live on an island nowhere much more than a mile wide. It was so bright the sky seemed peeled; some thin film had been stripped away and the sun beat down unfiltered. Perhaps the ozone layer was disappearing, Kenner thought. His skin felt probed by the sun, little needles separating the tissue, cell by cell. He considered knocking on Winston's door when he got back to the condo and making inquiries, but that might stir things up. Rea had troubles and some part of them was heading his way: Hurricane Rea. But now she was just tropical storm Rea.

Kenner knew as he walked across the island that *right this minute* something horrible was happening somewhere. Probably many wheres, he appended. The unspeakable amplified. Kenner had made it a habit not to court the worst instincts of his fellow human beings; he avoided prima facie cases of craziness. It wasn't that he could smell trouble; that took little talent these days. But there were certain individuals who gave off the odor of impending mayhem, and Kenner did his best not to put himself in a room alone with that sort.

Rea had abandoned her safe house, or safe motel, and her protector. Had she expected him to wait there? he wondered. He had, till checkout time. Rea hadn't gone around the corner for cigarettes.

Kenner could feel a ganglion of anxiety become sensitive in the balls of his feet; then he realized it was just the hot pavement through his tennis shoes. He moved onto soil, though it wasn't much cooler. The rear entrance of the condo complex was rimmed with cyclone fencing ten feet high. A petition had been circulated a few weeks earlier requesting guard houses at the condo's two entrances. Checkpoints to keep out the riffraff. Berlin gates. Kenner knew what they really wanted was to keep out the unknown riffraff. Know your riffraff was the up-to-date thinking.

Kenner hoped to find a note on the door, or under the door, but he found neither. Winston's place, he saw, was quiet as a tomb. Kenner could, he knew, climb from one balcony to the other and look in. Few people locked their balcony doors. Kenner's apartment was hot and stale, all the petrochemical smells of the carpet and furniture had collected in the undispersed air. He opened the sliding glass doors of the balcony and turned the air-conditioning on high. Its compressor lurched and the phone rang. Kenner snatched the receiver up after one ring. "Where have you been?" he said.

"You mean lately, or this morning?" said a male voice Kenner recognized, but for a moment couldn't place. "I just got back from Omaha where I was interviewing randy teenagers for the sex book. Do you have any idea what fourteen-year-olds are doing in Omaha?"

It was Saperstein, Kenner realized.

"I can't imagine, Sap. Doubtless something else to make us feel bad."

"The biggest problem is that they don't have much of a vocabulary to describe it. I feel like Margaret Mead. I find myself making a lot of obscene gestures. Anyway, I didn't call you long-distance to talk dirty on the phone. Some news, good news, for you, maybe. First, *Centipede* is changing its name."

"Great," Kenner said. "I mean, how long can you live with the name *Centipede?*"

"Oh, I don't know. Ten years, I guess. But they're having identity problems. They want to break away from teenyboppers, do more life-style pieces."

"What are they changing their name to?"

"I don't know. *Pen-Ultimate* is the main contender. By the way, Howie Cohen had lunch with my man and mentioned you and brought up Mariel. I didn't know you knew Cohen."

"Yeah. I saw him down here a couple of weeks ago. He was with sweet Danielle."

"Well, for a variety of reasons, *Centipede*, also to be known as, maybe, *Pen-Ultimate*, is ready to go for a Mariel story. They're talking around a thousand and expenses."

"What do they want, refugee life-style?"

"You're right in the middle of it," Saperstein said. Kenner could hear a little peevishness creep into his voice.

"Sap, you could do it from NYC. It's like the drug trade. All the captains are used to it. The Cubans are just bales that talk."

"Well, it's yours if you want it. And they can make it easy. It seems Howie gave them the name of a Cuban contact. Someone who's planning to make the trip. You call *Centipede-Ultimate* and they'll put you in touch. And the mag is planning to go from bimonthly to monthly. More work for you if this pans out."

"Sap, it's TV, as I told you a month ago."

"You could probably get them to fifteen hundred if you spin an interesting yarn. Anyway, I've got to get back to fetishism in the corn belt. Call them. Send me a card. Let me know."

"Thanks, Sap. Thanks for thinking of me."

"You're at the right place at the right time, kiddo. Adios."

2

It was getting very hot, and the last place Kristina wanted to be was in the rent-a-car with Curt. It had all become, she thought, a big mess. There had actually been a *crowd* around the car when the bird books were loaded in Delmer's trunk. And a complete stranger! Some kid in tight pants with pale skin that already looked burned, turned pink as bubble gum, the color of Eli's gums when he was a baby. Juniper's mother would only let Juniper keep Eli at her trailer one more day.

The books were in their dark green bags, but it certainly seemed strange to Kristina to be so, well, nonchalant about stolen goods. But the books had stopped seeming stolen even to Kristina. Each day was a fresh page, a new start. Since they had them, the books seemed to belong to them.

Luckily, Delmer had rented a big car. "You could put two bodies in that trunk," he said. He and Winston stacked the books one atop another. Kristina had tried to seem natural while the loading was going on, but then she just gave up. It was getting ridiculous, all of them milling around in front of the warehouse that early in the morning. She felt various degrees of lousy anyway.

She remembered drinking half a bottle of Pernod. The chicken soup had made her jittery. She had felt great; then she didn't anymore. She thought she had thrown up. She still had her clothes on when Bridget woke her up. Kristina found a Demerol in Bridget's purse and took it. She felt shitty.

And who cared? Duane was supposed to have been along, but he hadn't shown up. Then Winston decided he couldn't go and why she had to go along with Curt was beyond her, but Winston said she had to and she did. And Curt had been ragging her all morning.

God, it was hot. Men were working on the bridges and the construction made the trip even longer. Kristina watched the half-naked young men carefully. Even though the sun was barely up, the heat was already blistering. How could they work? "How can they work in this heat?" she asked Curt, though she meant not to talk to him.

"Slowly. Very slowly," he said.

He chuckled. That was something else that annoyed Kristina: Curt laughing at his own jokes, no matter how lame they were. She could see why his wife had wanted to get away from him. Kristina thought about Eli—maybe she should take him in and get his hearing checked; he was having a hard time getting used to this heat. His rash hadn't entirely gone away. She wondered if Juniper was taking good care of him today. Juniper was getting spacier than ever, she thought.

Kristina's lip was still tender, and her sunglasses touched the rim of the bruise and were uncomfortable. But the bright light was worse, so she kept the glasses on. Her running shorts felt damp, her crotch itched, and she felt she was going to get the curse any minute, even though it wasn't near time for it. "Curt, can we stop, please?" He just looked at her wildly and didn't say anything. But they would have to stop, she was sure. Curt looked pretty strung out. He usually slept mornings; he'd have to get something to drink, or gas, and every place sold Tampax these days.

Curt had been talking to Delmer on the CB, talking all sorts of coded nonsense. About fishing holes, and other made-up lingo that Winston had worked out. If there was anything like a road-block ahead, or anything suspicious, Curt was to radio back and alert Delmer. The Audubon House wouldn't even open for another three hours. They didn't know they were robbed, so why would anyone be looking for them? All it was was a hot ride up the Keys.

She felt she was going to start bleeding any moment. Her body talking to her, gesturing wildly, like someone who just lost her voice. A loosening; then it would let go.

"Curt, I gotta stop at the next place," she yelled.

Once Curt was moving, he never wanted to stop she well knew; but that didn't matter now.

Curt looked pained, but picked up the CB microphone, one the size of an avocado cut in half, and barked, "Hey, Birds' Nest, Birds' Nest, this is Homing Pigeon. We have to make a quick pit stop. Ten four. We'll be off the road for five-o-min-u-toes. You can spin your wheels or lay back. We just passed mile marker fifty."

Delmer's nasal voice crackled back. "This is Birds' Nest. Where are you going? Give us a hey-ho when you're back on the air. Ten four."

Kristina was pleased she had got her way. Curt turned into a shopping center and parked in front of Eckerd's.

"I need a couple dollars," she said, remembering she had come without her purse, since she hadn't planned to come at all.

Curt looked pained again and said, "All's I got is this hundred-dollar bill."

"A hundred-dollar bill. Where d'you get that? They won't cash a hundred-dollar bill this early for a box of tampons."

"Why don't you buy the super-economy size?"

"Curt, all you are these days is a source of embarrassment."

"Well, you look pretty embarrassing to me," Curt said; Kristina saw his eyes fixed at her crotch, and, sure enough, she had begun to bleed.

"Now, see. You have to go in and buy it. And you have to buy me a new pair of shorts."

"New shorts . . . new shorts . . . what kind of old rag do you want, anyway?"

"Better get Playtex, super absorbent. And get red running shorts, if they got them," she added, in a placating tone. Now they'd have to find a gas station, unless he makes me change in the car. No, she would insist on a gas station. She would need some water to clean up with. She still didn't understand why she had to go along. It was a favor to Winston. He was getting real nervous. He had taken some of Bridget's Demerols and she didn't think she could get any more. Duane hadn't come back; that had made him nervous, too. Kristina tried to suck in her uterus and hold back the bleeding; she tensed her stomach and thighs, waiting for Curt to emerge from the drugstore.

Kristina tried to figure when she had her last period; she wasn't regular, but all she found herself fixing on was when she got her first period. For all her mother's sleeping around, Bridget had never told her a thing about sex. I suppose, Kristina thought, she assumed I'd seen enough to figure out what went on. She had been babysitting for a rich couple who wanted her to stay the whole weekend, even though they would be there, just so they wouldn't have to bother with the kids. She'd feed their dogs, clean up, and watch the two children. She had been wearing a brand-new pair of white jeans, and the couple had come home while Kristina was still watching TV, slouched down in an easy chair, her legs up on the chair's arm. The wife suggested she go to her room right then, and though Kristina thought it strange, she complied. When she got to the bedroom she used, she saw what had happened. A long reddish-brown tongue of blood stain ran along the middle seam of her white jeans.

She still didn't know what was really happening, and, not wanting to ask, she found a newspaper and spread its pages over the bed and slept on top of them, hoping not to soil the sheets. Kristina left early the next morning, leaving a note. She told Bridget what happened. Bridget took her to the closet and said, pointing to blue boxes, "Haven't you seen these before?" Pads. "I thought all they taught you at school these days was sex education. I didn't think you'd be getting the curse until next year, at least. It must be the climate." Kristina heard her mother's voice searching for excuses. Kristina refused to babysit anymore for the couple. The woman could have been more helpful. Even Bridget said that. But to bleed and not to know it: that was what troubled Kristina the most. That night, lying on the newspapers, she thought she might be bleeding to death, dying.

Curt came out of the drugstore, and from the way he was clutching the sack, she knew he wasn't happy.

"You'd think they'd never seen a hundred-dollar bill before. This is goddamn Florida. Ain't nothing but hundred-dollar bills here, and they tried to turn up their nose at goddamn legal tender. Shit, some little girl cashier. Reminded me of you. She had to get the manager before she would break it and me holding up a line with your box of cunt plugs."

Kristina knew Curt hated to be singled out, made to think people were looking too closely at him.

"Where *did* you get that hundred-dollar bill? From Winston? Did he give it to you?"

"Winston hasn't given me shit! I got it from a fare. Soon's I get back, I'm leaving. I can't stand this heat anymore. I sometimes wish I had stayed in Alaska," he said, jerking the car in reverse, about to gun it out of the space. "Boy, that's something I never thought I'd ever say."

Well, maybe you can pay me back some of what you owe me, now, she thought to herself, but she had already written Curt off as a bad debt. Kristina examined the shorts Curt had bought. These are boy's shorts and might be too small, she was thinking when she flew forward and banged her head against the windshield; her sunglasses jammed painfully into the side of her face.

"Goddamn!" Curt yelled. "I can't believe this!"

Kristina looked around, slightly dazed, and saw a beat-up old van. Its side doors were open and three male faces stared out at her. Curt got out of the car and was talking to the van's driver, not one of the three faces she was looking into. Doubtless Curt was trying to convince him that it was his fault Curt hit their van.

Kristina got out of the car, wanting to test her legs, even though it was her head that she had struck. The three men were shirtless, sitting campfire style; the van was filled with what appeared to be a mixture of fishing gear and mechanics' tools. Kristina thought the men looked alike enough to be brothers: curly blond hair hanging down the side of their heads in ringlets. They were drinking from cans of beer, as if nothing had happened. They must be wasted, she thought, to be so calm. Curt's voice kept getting louder than the driver's.

He was acting like the injured party and was asking about the driver's insurance.

"I got insurance," she heard the driver say, "but I don't know if it covers this. Florida Joint Underwriters. Bobby Dikes Coconut Grove Agency."

Kristina couldn't understand why they were all being so easygoing and taking so much of Curt's guff. Maybe they thought he looked crazier than they did. Maybe they had drugs on them and didn't want to call the cops. The van was so beat-up she couldn't tell where it had been hit. Why was Curt worried about the rent-a-car? Its bumper had been messed up just a little. That's all she could see. Maybe I should just get in with them, have a beer, and go wherever they're going, she thought. Would they take me?

Curt suddenly changed. He became the picture of understanding, saying he wasn't going to call the cops, or even report the accident. Maybe, Kristina thought, it had just dawned on him what they were supposed to be doing.

"Listen, man," the van's driver told Curt, "we're just shrimpers looking for work. And we haven't had any for a long time because all the shrimp boats have been impounded by that asshole Carter because of the fuckin' Cubans. I ain't got two nickels to rub together." Kristina figured they at least had the price of a six-pack. Druggies, she supposed.

The three men continued to stare silently at her, sipping beer. She thought she should at least smile at them. "Are you hurt, ma'am?" one of the sitting men asked. Kristina looked down. A thin trickle of blood had run down the inside of her thigh. She hadn't felt it at all. Kristina turned, looking for somewhere to go. Next to the drugstore there was a Chinese restaurant. A delivery man was wheeling a cart through its door. She followed him in. She would fix herself up in the rest room. Curt would just have to wait. His hands were full, anyway.

Walking into the air-conditioned restaurant was like jumping into a swimming pool after the heat of the parking lot. No one in the place had bothered her coming or going. When she walked back out into the sun, Curt was standing by the LeBaron and the van was nowhere in sight.

"Jesus, it took you long enough," he said, not even bothering to look at the lump on her forehead that she had been staring at in the rest room's mirror. She had her stained light blue shorts in one hand and her box of opened tampons in the other. She threw the shorts in the backseat and put the box next to her on the front.

Curt got back on U.S. 1, heading north, and picked up the CB receiver. "Birds' Nest, Birds' Nest, this is Homing Pigeon. Sorry it took so long. We had a few problems. Come back. Ten four."

There was only crackling in return.

Curt put the microphone up close to his mouth like it was something he intended to chew. "Birds' Nest, Birds' Nest, ten four, where are you?"

After a couple of more tries, he threw the black mike down on the seat. Kristina was touching the tip of her bump with her fingertips, feeling the tender swelling. "See, see, now we've lost him and don't know what the fuck is going on!" Curt's face was flaming.

3

Rea had gotten Duane to move out up north; she hadn't thrown him out, but talked him out. Then he had reappeared, first as a presence, someone who had been there while she was away. He had smashed her old Underwood. She never could tell what he had hit it with that had so succinctly crumpled the keys, bent the platen. Just the old generic blunt instrument, she guessed.

Then he set the apartment on fire. *I could kill you and only get five years.* A boast and a threat. Were all threats actually boasts? Second degree; even manslaughter. Out in less than five. And she realized he was getting closer to paying that price. Five years, a life. She could see the sort of defense he would mount, how she would be portrayed. A rich girl—she was amused, since her father had never thrown a dime her way after college and she had always lived on the fringes of poverty—who fucks around, takes drugs, hangs out with ex-cons and ne'er-do-wells, gets herself killed. Asking for it. There would be sympathy for her working-class killer. She had some. Why wouldn't a jury? He wasn't black. A white boy would get five years, unless he cut her up in a dozen pieces.

If he persisted, she might be forced to kill him. Self-defense. What would she get? Away?

She had agreed to come on this trip to release surface tension, to prick the skin of Duane's obsession. He felt too comfortable up north and too claustrophobic. It was his turf, a place

237

where all his fantasies were allowed to syncopate smoothly—even though they had been beaten back, they could never die out in the town where they were first learned. Those roots went too deep. Rea needed to get him out of town. Ex-cons, she understood, were the most provincial sorts of people, the least able to cope with the unfamiliar. If Castro was shipping over criminals from Cuba, real cons, there would be lots of trouble. Cons, she knew, can barely handle their own neighborhoods, much less other countries.

She had managed to blunt the grim momentum, damage the intricate structure of Duane's designs on her life. Put him on a case, a diversion, this scam of Winston's. A lesser crime to forestall a greater one. And when she had heard about it second-hand, that's all she thought it was: a scam. Another of Winston's schemes. She was surprised it had gotten this far; that the folios were out of the museum, in Winston's possession. She ascribed it to Vern, who was the only true professional among them. This bird caper was rehabilitation. The Northeast had become gothic, a setting for a bad outcome. Duane couldn't stay still. Most injuries happen within a mile of home, or in the home. It was madness to think Duane would have stuck it out, finished college—if he had stayed behind bars, perhaps, he could have earned a degree.

Concluding you are capable of killing someone was similar to reaching any sort of conviction: once a decision has been made, some shoring comes magically into place, some sense of leveling, of relaxation, takes over. Rea felt held up. A floor from nowhere was now beneath her feet. She felt steady. She had crossed over into the land beyond questioning. To do, to do.

Dumb as it seemed, she had done the right thing. Come here with Duane; involve him in Winston's scheme. Keep Duane busy. Expand his horizons; it hadn't, it seemed—but he was sufficiently pulled away from his center, toward an edge; and she had gained time. Now all she had to do was leave. If she could avoid him, disappear, there would be no deaths. She had a job, two places to go. Neither of which Duane knew about. Would Kenner be able to understand? What did he see? she wondered. No more than a bad ending to a bad relationship. The cracking and splintering.

But, even though she could now get away, what would prevent her coming home years from now and finding her typewriter hammered, smashed? The next night, the smell of smoke? And the next?

4

"Are you sure the bird paintings are on display?" the short squat woman was asking. The woman already had asked a number of questions that irritated Chester. He had thought he was done with her when she finally went upstairs to look at the folios. It had not been a splendid morning for Chester. His cat had been run over and Francis had walked out. All Chester wanted was peace and quiet. He had only time to turn on the lights before the first Conch Train load of tourists had descended.

"Why, yes, ma'am, but they're not paintings—they are engravings that have been hand-colored. They are lying flat in the glass cases."

"I saw the glass cases," the short woman said, obstinately. Chester found himself annoyed by the sight of the top of her head. It looked as if she wore a wig. "But there aren't any bird pictures in them."

Chester stared at her, incredulously; she, in some important way, had to be mistaken. He had heard everything come out of tourists' mouths. The questions they had asked when he had been a guide at the Hemingway house!

"I'll take you to where they are," he said sweetly, with only the slightest octave of doubt darkening his voice.

Earlier he had only flipped on the light switches on the second floor and then gone back down to replenish the hall stand's supply of brochures, take out the money box for change, and open the front doors. The porch was already creaking with the crowd of people waiting to get in. It was Francis's departure that had made him late, that and the shock of his cat's death.

He wouldn't have to conduct the first tour for fifteen minutes. A handful of people were wandering the rooms. Chester took the squat woman in tow and reached the display room. Other people were looking down into the cases. Everything seemed quite ordinary. Then, a middle-aged man, Chester to his horror saw, lifted up one of the glass case lids.

"Stop that! Don't do that!" he yelled, and the man, shocked by Chester's screech, let the glass lid fall. The crash made everyone in the room jump. The tourists all turned to look at Chester; he noticed they all had expressions of guilt on their faces. They began to back away from him, toward the rear exit. "Everyone stay where you are!" Chester yelled, not quite knowing why. They all stopped. Chester went and looked into the cases.

Chester first called his boss. He didn't know whether to shut all the people in the house or make them leave. He recalled all their hands pressing on the glass. How many fingerprints would be there? When did he last clean the glass?

He decided not to do anything. He let everyone stay, or go, as he or she wished. He called Mrs. Pimento on the off chance that she had had the folios removed for some reason.

"Miss Corinne," he said, using a form of her name that seemed to please her, "this is Chester at the museum. Did you, by any chance, have the folios taken away?"

Chester stared into blank space.

"Why, no, Chester," her voice finally reaching him said.

"Well, they're gone!" he cried, with more emotion than he intended.

"Gone?"

"Gone, yes, gone, gone, gone," he said, feeling that somehow trouble would be coming his way. Everything was leaving him, Francis, his cat, the folios. He would get in trouble for not noticing they were gone before he let people in. They would hold that against him.

He thought he heard Miss Corinne asking if he had called the police. And he realized that was what she must just have asked. "No. No. I haven't," he replied, hoping that had been her question. "But I will."

She would come straight over. Chester hung up and dialed the police. Right on the phone were printed the numbers of the police, firemen, and insurance company. Insurance; oh, Chester thought, they must have plenty of insurance. Had he turned off the alarm before he came inside? Oh, how could this have happened?

While he was talking to the police, before he had even heard a siren in the near distance, Chester was interrupted by the short woman.

"Aren't we going to get a refund, since it was the bird books we paid to see?"

It was then that Chester realized the worst: that he might shortly be out of a job and, once again, looking for work.

Twenty

Delmer had done more than his share. He didn't like to be at anybody's beck and call. All he got for his phone call to Winston, informing him that everything was copacetic, was to be yelled at one more time. It wasn't his fault Curt got lost. Waiting so long in Marathon had made Delmer nervous.

"The fish are in the freezer," Delmer had told Winston over the pay-phone line. "They're on ice."

"Where did you put the chest?" Winston had asked him. Where? What does he mean? Delmer wondered. He was standing in a booth at the Sunoco station close to the interstate exchange.

Eighteen-wheelers kicked up clots of gravel dust. It was about as hot as the damn rent-a-car had been on the trip up the Keys. He had been ready to risk a bit of cancer, but he had kept the air-conditioning turned off. Delmer, once home, had put the bird books in the trunk of his mother's Buick out behind the house. The Buick's engine had frozen up years ago, but the body was still in good shape. Delmer felt odd about bringing the books to his mother's house; that might cause her trouble. Even though

241

the Buick wasn't registered, everyone knew it was his.

"The chest is in my car," Delmer had replied to Winston, "and it's in the backyard."

"Your car!" Winston had shouted into his ear. Damn, that Winston boy is never grateful in the slightest. "The *chest* should be in the house, nice and dry," Winston's voice slithered back, oily and sharp.

"Okay, okay," Delmer had said. Winston then told him some fisher friend would be by for the fish. He would hear.

"Don't let 'em mess up," Winston said, but not even a good-bye, or a thank you.

Delmer would be damned before he would bring the bird books into his mother's house. He couldn't bury them, either.

After he got back home from the Sunoco station, he got his pickup started and, after a good bit of lining up, pushed the Buick backward, till he was able to roll the back half of it into the old tractor shed. He had tried his best not to dent the big grill of the blue and white Buick, but ended up nicking the chrome. It was good chrome, not the cheap sort used nowadays. In some spots, though it was a bit prickly: little points of corrosion sticking up, a day's beard of rust. But, Delmer was pleased to see, the chrome wasn't flaking off.

The trunk didn't leak, anyway; but if Winston asked again, he could tell him straight and true that the catch was under a roof, safe inside. The fish are on ice, the chest is inside, everything's copacetic.

2

"Winston, do you know where Rea is?" Kenner loathed taking the direct approach, but none of his passive sleuthing had turned up anything.

Winston, as usual, didn't seem to be happy to be queried. Winston had been sitting alone on his balcony, reading the paper. Uncharacteristically alone. His menagerie seemed to have vanished.

"No, I haven't seen her, Kenner, old boy," Winston had replied, and added, with a raised eyebrow, "I thought she was with you."

"How about Duane? Do you know where he is?" Kenner asked. There had been no signs of him, either; that, too, seemed a sore point.

"Not at the moment. I expect he'll turn up soon," Winston said. Winston's newspaper began to balloon out, like a spinnaker, in a gust of wind. Winston snatched at it, started to reassemble it; the process was elaborate, like folding sheets.

"I'm going down to the pool," Winston said.

Kenner heard splashing coming from the pool nearer the beach, which had more shade, more foliage about it; but the pool directly below was deserted, surrounded by a fringe of empty chaise longues and chairs, placed at sharp geometric angles to the pool's edge by the condo's gardener. The water's surface looked tight and blister bright.

"I'll come down, too," Kenner said, hoping to learn a bit more. Winston barely stifled a grimace.

Kenner now wondered, putting on swimming trunks, gathering up a towel, radio, and coffee cup, if he had spent more time worrying about Rea than he had actually spent with her. About fifty-fifty, he thought. The old five-o, five-o, as she had put it. Kenner hated to test his understanding of women since so often it had proven faulty. Kenner did know enough about erotic connection to realize that even though Duane was now a figure of fear, he had somehow abducted her heart and mind, and returning to him *one last time* would be tempting. One last time; ah, yes, that had its spice. The last, the very last, the last time. The end. The abyss. Freedom.

When Rea had begun telling Kenner her history, he doubtless looked skeptical. That she tried to provide explanations proved her to be more than superficially attracted to him, he thought. Her reasons were a bit different from those given in the magazine articles Kenner had skimmed, about women who lived with violent men. Rea's explanation seemed reasonable, since it was balanced on a paradox: because the man wouldn't see the error of his ways, the woman had a moral edge; she was right and the man wrong. And think of what people will pay to be right! And through such strange filters fear becomes transmuted into sympathy.

"What would you do," Rea had said, "if one day I hit you with an alarm clock. Pack up and leave? You'd be wary, apprehensive, but since I had never done it before you wouldn't leave. A woman doesn't leave because she gets hit once.

"I like lower-class man, up to the point that they hit you in the nose," she had said.

But the superiority argument was what seemed to make the

most sense to Kenner. She had said that if something horrible happens, it *needs* to be corrected, or your whole world, your way of apprehending, has to change. Kenner realized the difficulty. Rea, confronted with some behavior of Duane's that she knew to be totally wrong, had to be changed. She had to get Duane to change, to stop, to see the error of his ways. Of course, Kenner realized, Duane didn't see it that way at all. He didn't see it as strange conduct, needing alteration. People like Duane could change, he supposed, but only when they *had* to. Rea finally realized, he hoped, that she wasn't quite reason enough.

Kenner remembered things he had done for *the last time,* the enthusiasm that could be compacted there. And about the mysteries of why people do what they do, submit to what they submit to. He was stuck with what seemed crude explanations. At times it seemed so difficult to understand why people did anything that only the smartest could be held accountable for their actions; and, even they, caught in some contradictory behavior, would see it as an intricate problem requiring some elegant solution. So complicated that the teeth of the solution's key could fit only one lock, their own individuality. Rea seemed to know herself, understand what she was doing. But even if most people had little clue to what they did, it always seemed to come to the same thing: the notion of escape, of getting clear, getting out. If you understood it, you could get free from it—always a comforting idea, an intellectual's carrot, or his stick. The truth shall make you free. Hallelujah. But Kenner was beginning to think that that was all wrong. Even if you understood it, you couldn't escape it. The late twentieth century was hard on being right. Kenner knew better than to scorn the jargon of his time. Clichés seemed to bubble up from the collective unconscious of their times: wanting to get clear. That was one he liked. It implied an explosion, a blast, and you wanted to be clear of it, away from the debris, the fallout.

Kenner reviewed some of his conversations with Rea: her analysis intrigued him. The sixties weren't an aberration. They were a mild adjustment to the insanity of the fifties. The fifties were the crazy years. The sixties were just a little acting out.

Maybe he would do a Mariel article, Kenner thought. He would phone.

He tried to understand what it was about Winston he didn't like. Kenner didn't think he was given to the most narrow prejudices, the tics of taste that were rigid and unyielding. But, he thought, there is nothing more repellent than a charismatic man whose charisma leaves you cold. Winston didn't make Kenner laugh. He never seemed to work, though he had some sort of boat-fixing business. Even though Kenner had the same ambition—not to work—he disliked people who had never held steady employment. Perhaps Kenner was like his own father: preferring people to have the same bad experiences that he had.

Winston didn't seem to like him, and that was probably closer to the source of his own distrust, Kenner concluded.

On the way down to the pool, Kenner bought a *Miami Herald* from one of the bear-trap newspaper boxes near the condo manager's office.

Winston hadn't shown yet. Kenner spread his towel over the soft vinyl bands of the chaise longue and turned on the radio to the Cuban classical music station. He began to scan the front page of the paper. Lots of colorful stuff: Cuban refugees riot at Fort Chafee, Arkansas. Lubricious innuendo about the blond woman Vernon Jordan had coffee with in Fort Wayne, Indiana, before he was shot in the back. Abscam had struck again. Bush bows out of the presidential sweepstakes since Reagan has the GOP convention "sewn up." Ramsey Clark and nine others are on their way to Tehran.

The best thing about being a journalist, Kenner thought, was getting to read about people you knew in the papers. It made the world seem, somehow, friendlier.

Kenner turned to the "News of the Keys" section and saw a headline. The Audubon House had been ripped off, its double elephant folio of Audubon prints stolen by person or persons unknown. Kenner smirked. He had meant to tour the house, but hadn't yet gotten around to it. He wondered where the term *double elephant* had come from. Were the Audubon prints as big as elephant ears? Kenner was picturing the leaves of the books, the paper itself, looking like elephant ears, and a shadow fell over him. Winston had arrived.

"Seems there was some excitement in town over the weekend," Kenner said, rattling the paper.

"It's an exciting town," Winston said. "At times, too exciting. I'm a little island feverish. I'll be taking off soon."

"Where to?"

"Up north, the Big Apple."

At any mention of New York, Kenner felt himself wince slightly, a mixture of envy and regret.

"I want to thank you for driving the float the other day."

"Don't mention it," Kenner said, and then wondered why Winston had. It must be because of Bridget. "I enjoyed it. You never know when a little professional float-driving experience is going to come in handy. I might move to Pasadena some day."

"Just what excitement were you talking about?"

"I thought you were catching up on the news earlier?"

"That wasn't today's paper. What excitement?"

"Oh, the Audubon House was robbed," Kenner said, the scratchy strains of some Bulgarians playing Beethoven coming from the radio.

"It says, 'Thieves Hit Key West Museum. Police Suspect Pros.' They're going to put museum employees on lie detectors. Do you believe in those things, Winston? It probably was an inside job. They usually are."

"May I see?" Winston asked. Kenner caught the rare scent of true desire. Winston *wanted* to read the article. A soapy bubble of recollection formed in Kenner's mind, and on its luminescent surface, he saw the bird prints hanging in Winston's childhood bedroom. Kenner held his tongue, bit off the question that almost sprang forth, and, instead, said: "Sure."

Even shielded by Winston's sunglasses, Kenner could feel the heat of Winston's attention as he read the paper. Kenner expected to see a cigarette-sized burn appear in the middle of the page, and then the whole sheet would catch and be consumed by flames.

3

Duane unrolled the print. All three men in the room stared at the roseate spoonbill.

" 'This beautiful and singular bird,' " the older, red-faced man said, slowly, as if reciting, " 'stalked gracefully beneath the mangroves.'

"You know," he continued, resuming a normal voice, nodding his head up and down, scanning the print, "Audubon worked from carcasses. He didn't even take the time to stuff them. The bird rotted in front of him as he drew. He came to love the scent, the odor of putrefaction. Then he'd split open the stinking innards and see what sex the bird really was. He'd rip out organs to find out what the bird ate, so he could draw that accurately."

Duane watched as the man seemed to grow more excited with his own speech.

"A true artist, Audubon. You have to get in there, in the guts. A real doubting Thomas he was. He loved death. Life . . ."

Duane wasn't sure who this man was. The name at the gate was MacNaughton. They hadn't been introduced.

"You gonna hang it here?" Duane asked, looking around the room.

"Oh, no. Back home. This is for the bloodsucking bitch in lieu of alimony. She won't realize just how sentimental a gesture this is. The roseate spoonbill!"

A dark young man stood silently at the buyer's side, smoking. Duane was no one's bunboy, but he certainly recognized one when he saw one. A real punk.

"Have a drink," the older man said. Duane had located a guy named Suerte, someone Winston had carelessly mentioned, at the Marriot. Suerte had set it up. He gave Duane a telephone number and a first name. Danny. "Manuel will get you a drink. Manuel used to be a bartender in old Havana, the jewel of the Antilles."

Manuel, Duane saw, wore gathered white pants and a pink shirt, tight as a bandage around his torso.

Duane realized that Manuel must be more than a bunboy. He was probably a delivery boy, too. Some refugee cocaine. How could he have brought it in? Swallowed condoms? Drug sausage, thick as bratwurst. If I'm getting half a kilo, they must have brought in much more, he thought.

"Danny" was bent over the print, which he held down at the corners with a marble ashtray, paperweights, a silver lighter. The table had been cleared, and the things that had been on it were stacked on the floor beneath: a typewriter, books, papers.

Manuel came back into the room carrying a tray of drinks. He put small napkins under the glasses as he sat them down, like a waiter.

"Manuel has already made use of his skills in his newly adopted country," Danny said, while rooting in the bottom of a small chest. Duane heard bottles clinking. Danny's hand emerged from the chest holding a bag: it was slick and fat. It looked like he had pulled out someone's liver. A zip-lock bag, girded with tape. Duane's due.

"You'll want to test this," Danny said. He put it on a balance scale that he had also taken from the small chest. The weight was right. Then he took a penknife and made a small incision in the plastic, a surgical invasion; he turned the blade and retrieved, extracted, a small amount of white powder. He dumped the tiny pile on the table. He then placed a piece of Scotch tape carefully over the cut he had made. It was like a vasectomy operation. Duane had seen a film of it in the joint; they were hoping for volunteers. It would be done for free.

Duane figured this Danny must be some sort of amateur dealer or he wouldn't have wasted so much cutting open the bag. But, Duane realized, the dude was wasting Duane's, not his own. Duane sipped the drink Manuel had brought him. Bourbon and some kind of soda pop. On the cocktail table where Danny was playing with the cocaine, there was a book with the name MacNaughton on the cover. Duane reached over and picked it up, saw a picture on the back. It didn't look much like him. The face in the photo wasn't swollen. It was younger, winking at the camera.

"Is this what you do?" Duane asked, holding the book out in front of him.

The man, MacNaughton, gave him a peculiar look, part pride, part pique. "Yes, I do that," he said. Duane put the book back down, but MacNaughton continued speaking. "We search out truly disgusting things and then serve them elegantly. Nothing more polite than a book. When the aesthetic sense, the sense of beauty, is touched as much—engaged—as the sense of revulsion, it makes a terrible balance. Horror and appreciation. Disgust and admiration. I used to keep a file. But out of books, not life. Life doesn't serve them up as well. You need an artist's touch. Delectable paradoxes, delicate and evanescent, the raw and the cooked. We cook 'em. The sight of a child being hanged, but the fact that he is too light for the rope to effectively strangle him—that sort of thing. Black epiphanies. Ordinary folk tend to blur horrors together. It takes a man like me to pick the moments out, set them like gems."

MacNaughton paused. His eyes shone in a troubling way. Duane thought of an animal frozen in a car's headlights.

"I have a wife and kids to support," he said, looking at Duane with his frozen gaze. His voice sounded weird to Duane; then Duane saw a strange thing. The man's eyes went out. He stopped staring at Duane. MacNaughton's eyes just went blank. The connection between him and Duane broke off like an icicle cracking off a roof.

248

"I wrote a story once," Duane said. MacNaughton continued to look his way with dead eyes.

"The JayCees started a writing class in the joint. My old lady taught it. She got me to write one later. She's read your stuff, I bet."

MacNaughton only inclined his head in reply. Duane could see there was no more air in his balloon.

Duane did not want to get as close to MacNaughton as he would have to to inhale the cocaine. He just reached for the liver-sized bag. MacNaughton's head bobbed over the table. Three lines had disappeared.

"It looks like good stuff," Duane said, watching Mac-Naughton sink back into the couch.

"Nice doing business with you," Duane said, backing toward the sliding glass doors.

"Manuel," Duane, going down the concrete steps at the side of the house, heard MacNaughton call out, "do it. Do it." MacNaughton's voice was rising to what seemed like a plea, a shrill plea, to Duane's ear almost a whine. For a moment the English became Spanish: "*¿Me das la cobra,* Manuel? *Ahora, ahora . . .*" La Cobra? Duane wondered. Is that what I heard? The Cobra? A whore, a whore? "Please," he heard Mac-Naughton cry, "Please, *mi cochino,* do it."

Twenty-one

1

Detective Alegria sat at his desk waiting for an informer to call. A few of his colleagues thought the Audubon job was professional and presumed all the perpetrators were snowbirds, flown in and out. Airlines had been contacted; lists of passengers secured. They searched for a pattern of names. In and out; here for a weekend.

It was a local job, carried out by locals, was Alegria's intuition, and he had ordered a roadblock. Complaints had already begun. He didn't have the jurisdiction to call for one up in Florida City. It would have been more effective there. The feds could do that, but he didn't want them called in. He was going to have to call off the Cow Key roadblock; the overtime for his men was good and that helped morale. And he thought he might be able to catch and confiscate Lord knows what with this net.

If it was locals, he would hear about it. Small island, big mouths. Something would turn up. There wasn't much at the scene. There were more fingerprints of tourists than leaves on the floor of a forest. What he had was this: a call logged on the day of the burglary. "Watch the bird house." A woman's voice, no location. It had gone unheeded. The caretaker had checked the house after eight that night and found the side door unlocked. He entered and looked around; he thought it had been left open accidentally. He had turned the alarm back on. He was a suspect, but he was Angel's cousin and Angel vouched for him.

The cases had been jimmied open. There were a few footprints outside, sneakers, boots. The chain-link fence had been cut, in between the summer kitchen and the shed. There were too many tire tracks to be useful.

Alegria's first response had been to leave it to the insurance investigators. They would have to pay. Let them work on it. They got better salaries than he did. There would be pressure from above. But he was willing to wait by a phone, in case there was a call.

2

Kenner found a piece of paper stuck by the Sport Fury's shift lever. ATOP THE MARTELLO TOWER AT THREE TODAY. It was written on the stationery of Tanka Crafts. Beneath the script was a drawing of cumulus clouds, with sunlight streaming out: rays. Rea. He wondered who had put it there. Not Rea herself, certainly.

Since the East Martello Tower was located next to the airport, Kenner considered Rea might be departing on a five o'clock flight. Martello was an old Civil War fort, never completed, never fired upon. The military at its most defense-conscious. You needn't be prescient, Kenner realized, when looking at such construction, to see the sort of excess the armed services had in mind for the future. They build for invasions of the imagination. Kenner was of two minds: he would put no stupidity past the military, nor would he put any deviousness past them. Kenner was inclined every once in a while to believe the most rabid conspiracy theorists.

JFK could have been shot by a becrazed loner, or by a long chain of individuals conducting the most delicate intrigue. Except the latter always called for great skill, luck, and bravado; and Kenner tended to discount such displays of excellence.

The East Martello fort faced a sweep of open sea, the same view that the navy base on Boca Chica had. The ocean, the Caribbean, Cuba. The fort, Kenner knew, was a museum of sorts, about as spiffy as the defunct Pirate and Torture Museum, which,

Kenner had been sad to see, had been turned into a health club, a sign of the times. At the fort there were store mannequins wearing rotting old clothes—Kenner's dream came flashing back on. Old rafts and dinghies that freedom-seeking Cubans had been using in the years before Mariel. Furniture and mementoes of Key West's past. The fort was a pentagon in shape, a favorite of the military. There must be some mystical reason, he thought, for them always to come back to that configuration.

The center tower was the place where ammunition was to have been stored. The tower's entrance was also its exit. Why would Rea pick this place to meet him? She could see the person who came up the spiral staircase; but she would have nowhere to go if it was the wrong person.

Duane was not likely to be searching the local tourist attractions. Other spots were more conspicuous. She could see the road from here, see who was driving up. It was cowboys and Indians time.

Kenner never thought of himself as naïve, but he was. And though people thought him cynical, he obviously was not overly suspicious. He had begun to sense a connection between the Audubon theft and Winston's gang; for if anyone had asked him to give a name to the crew that Winston had assembled, Kenner now realized, only *gang* would be the right description.

It wasn't the sort of group you'd invite to a party. It was more like a collection of people who would know each other because they all worked at the same plant. The forced sodality of a company picnic. They probably did work together: on the Audubon job. Kenner had no evidence of this, except for the constellation of events. He found the success—of the burglars, that is—the main thing that argued against its being Winston and his gang. How could *they* have pulled it off?

Kenner felt, once again, left out. But he began to realize, or, as he finally saw the truth of the cliché, it began *to dawn on him:* he saw a light glimmer, begin to define the horizon, the line above, the line below; the shapes come solid in the foreground, and the realization that he might not be as left out of this as he would like.

"That's not the sound of an Indian in the forest," Rea said to Kenner's back, after he had tripped on the last step of the spiral staircase, turning gravel under his sneakered foot, scuffling to regain his lost balance.

"I didn't want to surprise you," he said, turning about. He

realized, gazing at Rea, he was inspecting her for new bruises, some sign of the last day and a half; and he was looking for signs of complicity in the burglary. All there was was some fresh color in her cheeks.

He felt like kissing her, but he realized this was not meant to be a romantic encounter. "Where were you?"

"In another motel. I had some sorting out to do, and I thought you ought to be told a few more things before I let you be my salvation," she said.

"Like Winston being the mastermind behind the Audubon theft," Kenner said.

"Mastermind!" Rea blurted out. "Butlermind is more like it. Does the whole world know, or did you just figure it out?"

"So far, just me. Winston was very interested in the story in the Miami paper. Circumstantial evidence just fell into place. How are you, ah, involved?" The question sounded odd to Kenner as he asked it. Rea smirked, but Kenner found it a charming smirk.

"Hanger-on. The moll. That's not the problem."

"You don't want to turn them in, do you?" Kenner said, a bit too reproachfully.

Rea looked hurt, misjudged. "Of course not. I wouldn't turn them in. Neither would you. I always suspected you had criminal tendencies," she said, and laughed. "But the odds aren't necessarily in their favor, either. No, I was just getting ready to leave. And I wanted to see you before I did."

"I've got another suggestion," Kenner said. "Wouldn't you rather go off with me? Have an adventure?"

"An adventure? I would have thought you had noticed I was already having plenty of adventure."

"It isn't really an adventure," Kenner said, "until they start shooting at you."

3

Business had slacked off and Kristina's hours had been cut back. Her boss was making noises about letting some girls go. On top of everything, Eli had a bad cough. Welfare had been giving her problems, threatening to suspend payments, wanting to investigate. She had told them the New Jersey court had said that Johnny only got visiting privileges if he payed support. He hadn't and she wanted it that way. Welfare wanted more papers from New

Jersey. Juniper met some boy and didn't have the time to babysit much any more. Bridget wouldn't take up the slack.

Winston was getting jumpy, Kristina thought. Rea had disappeared and Duane had supposedly gone looking for her. Winston was upset. Duane was to take the bird books to him in New York. Winston had put off his trip, hoping that Duane would show up. He was threatening to cut Duane's part of the take. The Audubon House had reopened. It seemed that people wanted to see where the robbery had taken place. Their business actually increased. People came and stared into the empty cases. Mom said tourists would pay to see nothing as long as you told them it was something. She still worked at the pottery shop. Everyone was to act *normal,* Winston told them. They had, and Kristina was surprised how quickly the talk about the burglary died down in the bars. For three days they talked about little else: Who did it? How much money was there in it? And then there were other things to talk about.

Kristina had managed to keep quiet. Once, when she almost said something, Curt had flashed her a look and she stuck out her tongue and then held it. It was the first time she had ever held her own tongue; it leapt away from her fingers but she forced it out and held on to it, flapping it, waving it in front of Curt's face. See, I'm holding my tongue! It felt, sort of, like Curt's soft penis.

Everyone else was being cool. They all had something to hope for. Getting away with it. Kristina dreamed about what she was going to do with her ten thousand. One day it would seem like a lot of money—and the next day she'd get upset when she noticed it was the same amount contestants won on "Family Feud."

Curt still cultivated his true weird self, as he was always calling it. And now Winston wanted him to bring the bird books north. For another five, which was to come out of Duane's share. Curt's pills were running out and he needed refills and he didn't want to go to a doctor down here, or even call the VA. But Kristina worried mostly about Eli. She had made an appointment with a doctor. He hadn't been gaining much weight. Being in the sun hadn't made him brown at all. He was just plain pale and Kristina thought it strange.

4

One thing, Winston thought, that he had counted on came true: the cops really didn't care much about the burglary. Key West, the way Winston pictured it, was one of those border towns the outlaws would always head to in fifties cowboy movies. It had been a week and no one was sniffing around his door. There was very little in it for the local fuzz, except for solving the crime—which was not one of their goals. Winston liked towns riddled with corruption, and Key West did not even try for a low profile on that score. He wondered how the city fathers were making money off the boatlift. The shrimpers had had their boats impounded by feds. Winston thought the feds were just taking revenge for all the dope they were never able to catch them with.

Winston was glad the town had its hands full. Shrimpers were demonstrating in front of the post office. Since the papers were sure the prints had left the Keys, it was no longer their problem. Fucking Duane! Bugged out, leaving a note. *Looking for Rea.* Bullshit. It appeared to Winston that Kenner and Rea had both left town together. Vern couldn't drive the prints north; that left Curt.

If Rea and Kenner had gone off together, then Kenner had to know. One loose cannon. Winston remembered the French cannon he had when he lived next-door to Kenner. Should he put an ad in the paper for someone to drive a drive-away car? No. Curt was willing, but was he able?

Winston would have to wire Delmer that Curt was coming. He'd have to send Delmer more money. He'd get Curt to do that. Curt had already fucked up plenty, Winston thought. Getting Kenner to drive the float was stupid. Being late. Then on the trip up the Keys, losing Delmer! He had sweated waiting for Delmer's call. But since Delmer had made it home, even without an escort, he hadn't been too hard on Curt. Curt said he wanted to show Winston he wasn't a fuckup, that he could do the job. Winston sometimes thought of himself as an employer who hired the handicapped. Wouldn't it be cheaper for the government to pay him, Winston thought, to organize these guys and pull off jobs? They could make up some town like Williamsburg for misfits and let us scheme. CETA money could fund it. Winston drifted off for a minute, relishing his crimeland: he'd hire hookers who'd let themselves be raped, tough guys who could be mugged by skinny twirps.

5

"You take good care of yourself now," Kristina said, and Curt heard what sounded like a kiss-off to him; his ex had said the same thing to him the last time he'd laid eyes on her. Curt was to stay in New York while Winston cashed in the chips. He would get his money there. And then? Back to Vail? Kristina was shaking him loose and Bridget was pleased that he was leaving, too. Just when he thought he might be able to get it on with her. But Curt wasn't sorry to leave Key West. The place was giving him the willies. He didn't once get to go deep-sea fishing, which was what he wanted to do. Just cab-driving and shitting around. He would like to stay another week and do the things he had meant to do. But Winston wanted him on the road.

The roadblock on Cow Key had been over for a week. Cars slowed down, passed a crowd of cops with nightsticks, long flashlights, red flares that burned with an electric fizzle that had caught Curt's eye. The cop had shined a torch in his face and he smiled; they had let him through.

So now it was just good-byes, *a-di-os-es, hasta luegos*, see-ya-laters. There was nothing in his car—except for the kennel owner's pistol, which he had kept—nothing until Georgia. Then he just needed to get to New York and a garage on Ninety-fifth off Broadway where Winston had told him to park. Winston had doled out two hundred bucks for the trip's expenses. He had given him three hundred to send in the money order to Delmer. Curt wrote Winston's name on the money order and the wire he had been instructed to send: THE YOUNG MAN WITH THE CURLY HAIR WILL BE ARRIVING TO PICK UP THE FISH.

Delmer didn't have a phone at his place, and Curt hoped the map Winston had drawn would prove accurate. The only other thing he had was a phone number in New York City. Winston hadn't told him where he would be staying. Just to park in the garage at Ninety-fifth and Broadway and call the number. Winston would take it from there. Key West too-de-loo, Curt sang out, pedal to the metal. He drove the airport rent-a-car back toward its home, but, he chuckled to himself, me and the LeBaron are only passing by.

IV

Twenty-two

1

Kenner knew he had a number of faults, and one was an attraction to bargains, sales. He lived in negative luxury: keeping track of a phantom bank account full of how much money he saved on sales. And so when a turn of events presented him with what he thought a steal, he went for it: a way to get Rea out of Key West, out of harm's way, have a vacation, an adventure, and *be paid for it.*

He had called the editor at *Centipede,* now renamed *Pen-Ultimate,* dickered over the price, arranged for a kill fee. He was given the number of a contact, someone who wanted to be the subject of a laudatory article about heroism on the high seas. He was described as a Miami businessman, a self-proclaimed former friend of Batista who had arrived in the States a year after Castro had taken over and had done quite well. He was making his second trip, and, since Carter's embargo, just getting there was to be more difficult than getting back. Kenner did not inquire too deeply into how *Pen-Ultimate* had gotten hold of this fellow: it seemed the usual friend-of-a-friend connection. Kenner had called the Sugar Loaf Key number and had made some loose arrangements. He was to go to the Stock Island marina and look for a sport-fishing boat, a Betram 46—though Kenner didn't know one make from another—out of Cocoa Beach.

"Carter's a cocksucker," the captain said to Kenner. "He should never have given that open-arms-open-hearts bullshit speech. Then he changes his mind. That guy will never learn. What magazine are you from? *U.S. News and World Report?*"

Kenner gathered that it was a relative of the captain's in New Jersey who had contacted the magazine. The captain did not seem abreast of Kenner's plans. He didn't sound like the man Kenner had talked to on the phone. But the *La Compañía* out of Cocoa Beach was the only sport-fishing boat at the marina that showed signs of activity. Kenner wasn't sure if it was a Betram 46.

The captain left them standing on the dock and went to talk in rapid Spanish with another man on the boat, then came back, smiling in a way that made Kenner uneasy, but announced they were welcome to come along. Kenner earlier had told him that Rea was the magazine's photographer. She had produced a small instamatic from her purse and held it in front of the captain like a pass.

Kenner couldn't guess the captain's age, but it had to be somewhere around sixty. He had long hair, white, which hung in ropy strands, the kind of ivory color that has yellow in it, the tint of old piano keys. His face was bright red and had regular features, a pretty mouth and a boyish nose. A pleasant mug, overall. His name was O'Bannion; he did look Irish to Kenner, who was counting on some tribal acceptance, though when the captain began to speak Spanish, which Kenner could make out but not always comprehend, he didn't sound Irish at all. He kept an unlit, but half-smoked, cigar in his mouth and could talk around it with little difficulty.

Kenner had been reassured by the look of the boat: nothing hearselike about it—white with black striping. There was a good bit of fancy electronic gear, antennae; it was outfitted with what looked to Kenner like oil-derrick rigging, some sort of observation post.

The coast guard had been patrolling the straits, the stream, and was turning back any boats that were trying to defy Carter's recent ban. O'Bannion again flashed his troublesome smile when Kenner suggested that with the two of them aboard it would appear to be a typical fishing party. He and Rea did look like tourists. Kenner refrained from mentioning the obvious: that the captain and his one-man crew looked like pirates.

Kenner and Rea had gone directly from the East Martello Tower to a bank—where Kenner transacted a cash advance on his Visa card—then to Sears Town, where they bought what they thought they would need for a week and stuffed it into new canvas bags. Then to the marina.

Kenner had heard "ninety miles to Cuba" so often he realized that they would be there by the next morning, if all went well. He lingered over *if all went well.* Kenner's confidence in O'Bannion was increased by his estimation of how much the boat cost, along with its supply of electronic gadgetry. And the fact that he had already made the trip once. O'Bannion said the other man acting as crew was a relative, though there was little resemblance. A cedar-colored fellow in his twenties. There were more relatives to be brought back on this trip.

The haste of their departure had one effect: they had had so much to do, and so little time to do it, that neither Kenner nor Rea discussed the wisdom of their plans.

"Ah," O'Bannion said, gazing at all they were leaving behind, "the cerulean waters off Key West—that's what the Conchs call them." He rolled his unlit cigar around in his mouth, twisting it between his fingers with a safecracker's delicacy."Except, I never heard a Conch use the word 'cerulean,'" he said slowly, deliberately. "For that matter, I never heard them use the word 'waters' either."

Kenner didn't immediately realize what had overtaken him. Then he admitted the obvious: seasickness. The water had not looked too rough when they set out. He was, in any case, too impressed by the brightness of the wake the boat churned, the bursts of reflection, water and sky. *A Mariel.* Kenner soon began to feel queasy and the only position that seemed tolerable was lying down. He went into the cabin and stretched out, a body in a catacomb, just wanting to be on terra firma. He was depressed by his display of unseaworthiness. Rea searched through her supplies and brought him some Dramamine and went back to the upper deck to converse with O'Bannion. Kenner had heard her questioning him in the way that had always impressed Kenner: questions that seemed to show acute interest in the answers, rather than mere curiosity. With the common laughter he heard, they sounded like they were getting on famously.

Toward the end of sunset, Kenner felt well enough to stand

again. He appeared when the sky was streaked with violet and pink.

The boat was running parallel to the waves, no longer crashing through them. Kenner had the feeling that he was looking at something hugely magnified—a patch of skin, hair follicles the size of redwoods—and he realized he felt that perspective because he saw the boat as a speck, a mite, in the palm of an entity larger than he had ever known. The scale had changed: the mass of water was overwhelming. An inverted sky. Just the fact of it. There was something similar when he had been in the Rockies, high up, but he hadn't felt so vulnerable then; for he now felt as if he were literally walking on water and its magical properties were just that: solid and permeable simultaneously. Accepting and rejecting, withholding and clasping, safe and sinister.

The ocean was at once permanent and impermanent, and that, for Kenner, was usually only an intellectual proposition. It was like the air: it could buoy you up and let you sink, and when Icarus went from one to the other, he was really in the same medium, passing through a spectrum of intensities.

No wonder people became inordinately fond of their boats. The boats preserved them, and Kenner found himself taking an immediate liking to this one.

Rea was in the fighting chair reading, the page clear in the oval of a flashlight.

"The captain provided us with a little background material," she said, holding up the book, shining the light on its title page: *Cuba: Terror and Death. Once Again . . . a Pirate on the Spanish Main.* Kenner turned the page and read the first sentence: "Cuba today is in the throws of communist terror."

He laughed. "What are we in the t-h-r-o-w-s of?"

"You were in the midst of the throws-up," Rea said. "Are you feeling better?"

"Yeah," he said, "a little." He flipped through the book. Kenner realized he shouldn't regale the captain with his tales of lunching with the Cuban representative to the U.N. or of his not so-near brush with death at the hands of Omega 7.

"Well," he said, "who else would be going to Cuba now? To fetch relatives."

He turned around and looked at the backs of the captain and his nephew, up at the boat's controls. O'Bannion was in the helm seat and the nephew stood next to him. They were speaking Spanish, a language that Kenner had studied, but could not speak.

"Did I miss much while I was semiconscious below?"

"Well," Rea said, "there were porpoises and one boat. The captain contacted it on the VHF. He was coming out of Mariel. They weren't encouraging. It looks like Carter has made some deal with the Cubans. They began emptying the harbor after the seas quieted down, and they're not going to let anyone else in. O'Bannion may be too late."

"Well, I've had enough. Let's turn back and go dancing."

Rea just looked at him and didn't seem to catch his humor. Maybe, he thought, his seasickness made him look too serious, too convincing.

"Well, even we found it hard to believe," O'Bannion was saying. "Only a lunatic would accept what we were hearing. All those people crowding onto the Peruvian embassy's grounds. The radio stations in Miami broadcast the story around the clock; they had speakers in the street so the people could listen. Eight thousand Cubans inside the embassy gates! Soldiers taking off their uniforms. Singing in the streets. It was a festival. Freedom! Freedom! *Libertad!* It came from everywhere.

"Castro had no one he could put in jail. No leaders, instigators, since it was spontaneous. It was destabilizing for the Marxists. Our people here put on hunger strikes and there were demonstrations in New Jersey . . . Fifo had to let them go."

Kenner had considered that O'Bannion might be some auxiliary of the U.S. intelligence community. There were plenty of Cubans who made clandestine trips to the island, dropping off various "black teams." The captain's skills were both a comfort and a worry. But Kenner didn't concern himself too much about the political ideas of the pilots of the commercial jets he flew on. Maybe O'Bannion was just what he claimed to be: a concerned relative with enough experience of the sea to go to and fro upon it. Though, Kenner thought he detected the hot breath of the State Department puffing through O'Bannion's monologue.

"They finally took steps to let thirty-five hundred into the country. That was a joke! It was a great stampede. What the U.S. didn't take advantage of is something we all felt in the Cuban nation. *This was the time for Castro to fall!* He was smart enough to open up, to let them go, a release of steam. Ah, the days before the escape began were the best. Everyone in Cuba was talking about the people in the embassy. Business had come to a standstill. It was almost out of control. The U.S. was too timid. It is a scandal how few other countries were willing to take in. We applied pressure. It was the exile community throughout the whole United States that saw to it that the policy was changed. In Cuba it looked like the regime would split its seams. There were demonstrations everywhere. Fights. It was too much even for el Jefe. He finally said, '*Aquí, quien quiera irse, que se vaya.*' Whoever wants to go can go. Thousands rushed to leave.

"Then Castro changed the rules. Then Carter changed his. Some sort of game. Each made a move and the other reacted. But it was the Cuban people who made all the best moves. Carter said all were welcome just after Castro said all were free to go. Then they both clamped down. The press played up Castro's next move of substituting the so-called undesirables for the people who wanted to go. First we had the public behind us, and then, because of the Communist-controlled American media, it went against us. Carter was actually happy with Castro's move, since it allowed him to close his open-arms policy. So they both got what they wanted—but they shafted us Cubans again. That's why I agreed to take you along—so the true story would come out."

Kenner did not feel particularly comfortable with the captain's *true story*. He accepted a good portion of it, though. Poor Carter, Kenner thought. Castro caught him holding another stinking hand.

Kenner's heart was with the Cubans, and, if the truth be known, with Castro. Though Kenner felt the longer you stayed in power the more despotic you became. Eight years did seem the maximum healthy limit. J. Edgar Hoover was in for forty-eight and he showed all the tertiary symptoms. Authoritarian syphilis: blindness, lunacy. Kenner's mind drifted to some senators with too much seniority. Kenner thought all revolutions suspect, but the only thing he actually believed in was the satisfaction the people received when they saw the tyrants driven out. It was purely money changers-driven-from-the-temple satisfaction. Batista, Somoza, leaving town, loading limousines and grand pianos into airplanes, heading for Miami.

It would give the population a taste of pure satisfaction, before the new saviors began to betray them. A day, a week of triumph. But, el Jefe an Iscariot? The fact was that the United States valued Cuba more as a thorn in its side, a foreign-policy catalyst, a switch to whip up xenophobic furor, another agent to increase the defense budgets, than as just another mob-dominated Caribbean tourist island. Kenner thought Castro probably understands Cuba's role and that is another cause of the cynicism he displays.

2

Curt was thinking about animals. He hated the feelings he had when he saw animals twitch, shiver in their sleep. Kristina went on about how they were dreaming. Curt couldn't, didn't want to, imagine that animals could dream. It struck at his understanding of what he thought was different about people and animals. If animals dreamed, then what?

He had been out of downers for three days, and he feared he would have a seizure. The turnoff for Delmer's place, according to the directions he had, should be coming up soon. He was tired of driving.

The car's headlights fell on a pile of pink chunks: exploded flesh, what bodies look like when they have been blown apart. Curt was shocked. He knew what the pile was immediately. What was strange was that such a sight resembled nothing else. It no longer looked like a body, a thing, but just a pile of chunks. Meat was never deliberately cut up that way. Then, in another second, the headlights illuminated another pile, till Curt realized, in the split second he had to observe, that he was seeing something that had been hit by a car, a truck. Something had exploded over the road. Then there was an even larger pile; and since there was a progression in size, in the seconds Curt was seeing this at sixty miles an hour, he thought with alarm that the next pile—for surely there would be one—would be too big to drive over and he would strike it.

But he did not want to slow down; there was a horror in doing that, too. And in a second there it was: what kind of creature it might be Curt had already considered. Big. A horse, a cow, some animal that could carpet so much of the highway with its cubed pink flesh.

A beast had come apart, not in pieces, not extremities—legs, arms, parts—but in its most elemental structures. Bits, chunks, as if a graph, a grid, had been laid over it and it had blown apart geometrically, the force of the explosion dictating the result: and the forces, being equal, blew apart equal size pieces. The military had such charges: they could design the shape the thing exploded would turn into.

A last mound fell into the beams of Curt's headlights: the

head. It was a deer, a stag. The white lattice of the antlers flashed. Milky roots. The car ran over it, and the skull and antlers caught underneath the chassis. Curt could hear them scraping the asphalt. He smelled bone burning. He wanted to slow down, to stop, to end the sound of friction beneath his seat—but then he would have to pry the head and antlers loose—and he wanted to speed up, to go faster, to grind it away to nothing on the highway.

There was a clunk, and the scraping sounds stopped. In the rearview mirror Curt saw the deer's head and antlers kick free, bounce in an arc, land on the antlers' points, and skip into the darkness alongside the road.

Curt found the dirt road that led to Delmer's place. When he turned onto it, he was again regretful that he had agreed to do this, even if it was for more money.

Delmer's house looked haunted. The top-floor windows were blown out and rags of curtains flapped through. Delmer and his mother lived on the first floor only, it seemed. Though Curt had to come a back way to the house, he was surprised when he got there to see that the interstate ran close to it. But there was no exit there, only an overpass above the country road.

Stuck halfway out of a tractor shed was an old car with a wide grille, which, to Curt, seemed a toothy sinister grin. Delmer appeared at the house's side door, flashed a beam lantern at Curt's car. Delmer signaled him. Curt watched Delmer squeeze into the shed with the car. The beam of light lurched around the back of the building, and he saw between flashes and shadows the car's trunk lid go up. Curt had moved up to the front grille of the car and watched Delmer shuffle toward him, carrying one of the bound volumes of birds, its plastic wrapping slipping off.

Curt went back to the LeBaron and opened the trunk. He and Delmer then awkwardly danced together, trying to maneuver the bird book into the space. It wouldn't fit flat and had to lean. It was clear the other three wouldn't go in the trunk. Maybe one more. They could probably get the other two in the backseat. Curt had an idea: "I'll only take the one. That's all Winston needs to make the deal."

For some reason Curt felt relieved; only taking one seemed less trouble than taking all four, less *incriminating*.

It satisfied Curt that he could alter the instructions Winston had given him. The trip now seemed to be under his control. Winston wouldn't like it, but he'd have to live with it.

266

"I don't want to keep them much longer. It's not good for my ma. Can't you take them all, put them in the backseat?"

"Naw, people steal things out of backseats," Curt said, realizing that's what he'd tell Winston.

"We could cover them."

Curt just looked at Delmer. He had made a decision, and he didn't now want Delmer to be changing it.

"I gotta get back on the road." Curt didn't want to go into the half-dead house and meet Delmer's ma. "Got anything that would keep me awake?"

"Yeah, sure," Delmer said, and left Curt standing by his car.

Curt watched the kitchen light come on, illuminate some rusted metal in the yard back of the house. A large metal wheel, some prongs, what looked like a sharp comb, some old farm implement.

Delmer returned, held out his palm. Curt recognized the black beauties.

Curt had thought of staying the night, but had been so spooked by the look of the house it made the road seem preferable, though not much friendlier. Delmer stood in place as Curt turned the car around and went back down the road. He saw Delmer move toward the house, the beam from his lantern going back and forth across the ground like a metal detector looking for coins.

Curt stayed on the road through the night and the next day, but the following night he thought he saw out of the corner of his eye in the rearview mirror the deer's head bouncing on the road behind him. He was tired of being startled that way. He began to see strange bursts of light on the horizon. The horizon would be lit for a second the way a giant flashbulb would light it; but there couldn't be a flashbulb that big. He wanted to stop seeing it, just wanted it to stop, but, after a half hour, the Le-Baron came over a ridge and he saw what had been causing it. The end of a small airfield's runway came right up to the edge of the highway. Some sort of powerful strobe light was operating. The runway itself ran off into the dark at the side of the highway, etched with lines of nightmare blue, some sort of cross shape.

He pulled off the highway at an exit that seemed to bisect some half-mile of what looked like a borehole—a one-inch section of Las Vegas, all neon and bright lights. He pulled into a McDonald's, but then didn't stop to order to take out. Every time he had eaten a Quarter Pounder in the last two days he had been upset by the amount of ketchup on it.

There was only one motel on the strip that had a vacancy sign still lit, an older motor court of separate cottages. Curt got one for twenty dollars and had to pull up on the lawn in front of his door, since there was no real parking place. The room was cold. The front door was partly glass, covered with a venetian blind; its slats at the bottom looked like they had been chewed on. No phone. He felt an impulse to check out, try to get his twenty back, since the room made him feel even more uneasy than he had felt on the road; but he lay down on the bed, which was soft, a doughy softness. It sank into a declivity, and he tried to sleep, shut his eyes with the lights on, looked at the orange circles that swam under his lids. Finally he got up, pushed the dresser in front of the door, shut the lights off, except for the bathroom's. It light fell into the room, made an ironing-board shape across the floor.

Curt fell asleep, but awoke before dawn, feeling disoriented, his mind racing over and over the same simple scene, unable to shut if off. There was nothing horrible about the vision, except for the frantic repetition. He was unable to stop it. He took a piss, stumbled back to bed, but still his mind raced; he felt, lying back down, his whole body begin to swirl about the surface of the bed. He wished he had some aspirin. It began to bother him so much he would have taken anything that would put a stop to it. Anything. He didn't have any more of Delmer's speed. He made plans to stop at a drugstore and buy a variety of over-the-counter preparations, maybe even try to have his scrips refilled, but these thoughts only seemed to slip in around the same frantic scene that was playing over and over in his head. Wisps of smoke. Even though the same thing was being said continuously, over and over in his mind, Curt couldn't hold onto it, or step outside of it, in order to understand. He squeezed his eyes further shut and held onto the bed, clutching the hot soap-smelling sheets in his fists. He finally awoke again and there was gray light outside. His headache had diminished, and he took a shower, unhappy with the thin towels, which wet as quickly as paper when he tried to dry himself. He should be able to reach New York late tonight.

The motel looked normal in the daylight, and he drove out of the courtyard relieved the night was over. There were gas stations and food places on the short strip by the highway exit, but nothing that looked like a drugstore. He finally located a convenience store and bought some aspirin and No Doz. Leaving, he almost backed in to an old Plymouth full of girls.

"Don't you hit my fine ride," the one driving called out. Curt didn't know if he felt angry at her or complimented.

He ate at a pancake house and mixed the yolk of his eggs in the raspberry syrup and started to cut the stack of pancakes up till it began to remind him of the exploded deer meat.

He didn't miss anyone he had left, or Key West. He felt the same way right after his wife had run off with his boy. But he had known where he was when he was on the island. And now, somewhere above the midline of the country, off the interstate, he didn't feel anywhere. He felt as if he didn't have an existence, that he was alone, nowhere. He felt lost, as if he were falling away from the earth, even though he was pointed straight ahead, going crookedly up the edge of the continent like a rocket that was just about to self-destruct.

Twenty-three

1

O'Bannion wanted to appear at Mariel just before daybreak.
Each of them was to stand watch three hours, to awaken the
others if anything occurred, crackled over the VHF, appeared
on the scope. O'Bannion continued his speech-making while
showing Kenner and Rea the equipment.

"Castro used El Mosquito camp near Mariel. It sticks out, is
almost an island, and can be guarded easily. Three groups are
there: the people from the embassy and those whose names were
provided by relatives waiting at Mariel; people from the jails and
mental institutions; and some people Castro just wanted to get
rid of, troublemakers, undesirables. They were all put in big tents,
but kept separated until they were loaded on buses that took
them to the harbor. Some even bought phony criminal records
so they could be put in the last group. Castro put a lot of blacks
in that bunch, telling them stories of how bad they would be
treated in the U.S. All they gave them to eat was boiled eggs and
rice. The camp was guarded by German shepherds."

Kenner listened with little scenes in his mind being illuminated by the flares of O'Bannion's remarks. The last flash ex-

ploded over the watchdogs. Who brought the German shepherds over? Kenner had wondered. The picture he saw was the
Mafia, Batista, and American pet-store owners.

Rea had gone down to sleep in the separate galley state-
room. O'Bannion described what Mariel looked like when he arrived there the first time: hundreds and hundreds of boats, all
colors and sizes linked together, a real daisy chain, the captain
said.

They let him out quickly, but afterward the delays began.
And then friends of his had to wait. The harbor was patrolled
by gunships and they wouldn't even let you get in the water to
swim. It was hot, stinking, the heads were all blocked up and
running over, and if you jumped in the water alongside your
boat they would fire shots at you, making you get back in. Bastards. They were bastards.

O'Bannion practiced an effective economy with the cigar that
was always in his mouth. He only lit it once in a while. He rolled
it now in the flame of a stick match and blew on its tip till the
cigar glowed orange. The captain laughed a lot. Kenner tended
to trust people who laughed. Though he realized it was actually
the reverse: he never trusted people who didn't laugh.

O'Bannion's command of Spanish had already impressed
Kenner, and the captain understood a German expression Rea
had used earlier in the day. He had already quoted Baudelaire
in French. Kenner could use no language other than English,
and he concluded that O'Bannion had been around. Kenner decided he had to ask a few direct questions.

"What did your father do in Cuba?"

"He was an imperialist."

Kenner laughed and the captain laughed too.

"Well, that's better than running a banana plantation."

"Oh, he did that also. He owned a shipping line." O'Bannion rolled his cigar. Kenner was impressed with O'Bannion's
enjoyment of it.

"Let me tell you a few things. You look like an idea might
still penetrate your skull. This is how crazy Castro is.

"First, he wanted to get rid of Christmas. No more religion,
no more nonpagan holidays. Then he saw the peasants missed
it. So, they brought Christmas back. But not in December! On
July twenty-sixth!"

Kenner knew that was a famous date in Cuba, but he would
have to check what it was.

"Well, one reason he brought back Christmas was that the Russians have a lot of Christmas trees they want to get rid of, to help the balance of trade. So they send over shiploads of conifers, which are handed out, along with a bottle of fraternal wine from Bulgaria—there's a lot of toasting to the comrades who made the wine, that's for sure—and the peasants like the wine. Each family is given a pig to eat along with the workers' wine.

"So, on the hottest day of the year, the anniversary of Castro's attack on the Moncada Barracks, they sit by their Russian Christmas trees and drink fraternal wine. You know, they send decorations, too—little crowns, little tin czarist crowns and tinsel! Castro has forgotten that he banished crowns because they were symbols of oppression. They had been forbidden. The peasants don't know or care. July twenty-sixth! How ridiculous! Holy Moses!

"Latin America! What Latin America! No one speaks Latin. That name is some European idiocy. There's no such thing. Democratic socialism! One man-one vote is patently, on its face, demented. And women having the vote!"

O'Bannion flared up like the tip of his cigar. Kenner couldn't tell when the captain's enthusiasms, convictions, had turned to rage. He ranted on about the refugee bureaucracy already set up in the States. Most of the sponsors were looking for maids or gardeners. Kenner looked about for things to remember, but thus far he didn't see how it would make a story. Remarks by the captain, Cuban anecdotes, but it was still just a boat trip, seasickness, and a load of gusano's complaints.

O'Bannion's nephew signaled him, and he cut off his monologue, promising to resume when he had the time. He went forward decorously singing, between puffs of his cigar, *"I'll go to Santiago in a coach of black waves."*

On his watch Kenner continued to think of torture and the history the captain had been relating. What people truly believed: a flame that could be turned up or turned down, left to warm, to simmer ideas. Belief, truly engaged, got hot, and that flame could make anything boil.

Belief, faith, could make you swear to strange imagined truths. Ideologues of any sort bothered Kenner. They would say a few reasonable things, and then you would see their eyes turn into acetylene points, welding arcs. The flame would be turned up and *my God, the things they would say!*

Kenner was sure Carter would lose the election and Reagan would rise. And Reagan and his cronies were lit by that flame:

the former governor had his own bizarre version of history that would sometimes flare and you could see the flame had been turned up. Our future president believed what he said, Kenner was sure, however nonsensical it was.

Whatever O'Bannion believed, it was enough to take them all to Mariel.

Kenner did not like to contemplate too long what humans would do to other humans given the chance. There would always be a few stories every year of independent, rural Mengeles, practicing in the backwoods of the United States. He had always thought it best not to hand himself over to situations where such was a possibility. One reason why he wanted to stay out of any and all prisons.

Rea had never spoken of her troubles as torture, but some of the abuse Kenner had heard about seemed to him to have that potential. Would Duane indulge in a little torture, given the chance?

Kenner now felt like waking Rea up to talk, but he had another hour left on his watch. He should just stay up with her. Much to his surprise, he could already feel himself wanting the trip to be over, to be back in the condo, watching cable.

Perhaps, he thought, listening to the celestial hum of the instruments, observing the sweep of the radar, shaped like a boomerang, looking at the Loran's red digits, watching the waves peeling away from the hull, all the thoughts of torture had to do with his seasickness, the fact of his discomfort, the sloshing back and forth. Water torture, indeed.

Kenner awakened with Rea asleep alongside of him. There was fog everywhere and, reaching for his glasses, Kenner could barely make out O'Bannion standing by the sparkling gold plastic fighting chair, so much mist was settling around him. The engine rumbled, but it did not feel as if they were making progress—just a washing motion and the slapping of the sea.

Kenner had kept Rea company for half of her watch, but found himself starting to fall asleep, in an almost narcoleptic fashion, the sort of thing that could plague him while driving, where sleep seemed the most desirable thing in the world and his body just literally wanted to turn off, to stop. It was difficult to defeat since it didn't seem to spring from exhaustion, but from a sort of hypnosis or lack of function too complex to be mere boredom or tiredness.

What Rea had told him about the Audubon burglary did not

273

put him at ease; but out here in the Gulf Stream it seemed beside the point. Kenner couldn't get over how he now had to readjust his notions of Winston; that bothered Kenner: Winston now rose in his estimation.

Rea didn't know how the prints were to be disposed of. Duane was to play some role in their travels, and, she presumed, he'd be busy with that now. Kenner knew she really had reached someone who plotted revenge; revenge is the blackest sort of flattery. She hoped Duane's fixation had come dislodged, though she realized it could lay dormant and stir itself later.

Kenner eased himself off the cushions and Rea stirred, made noises, but settled back. He got into his clothes and came out of the cabin. The fog was full of the smell of herbs. "Where are we?" he asked O'Bannion.

"In Cuban waters," the captain said. "There's another ship near us and I'm not sure they know we are here. It's a large one. It may be a Cuban coast-guard vessel. But it hasn't changed course, so I don't think it's aware of us."

Kenner was captivated by the fog. It hovered about twenty feet off the water's surface, dripping tentacles down like rain forest vines.

"How long will this last?" Kenner asked, gesturing.

"Not long. It'll burn off."

They both turned their heads at the same moment toward sounds off starboard, a clanky rumbling.

"It doesn't sound like the coast guard," O'Bannion said.

He waved his hand at his nephew by the console; the *La Compañía*'s engine revved, but it didn't compete with the clamor that approached. Kenner thought for a moment they were going to be rammed, but O'Bannion seemed unperturbed, so Kenner suppressed the impulse to ask. The fog had lifted another few feet and the bow of a ship came into view. It was off their starboard side, what looked to Kenner like fifty feet away: its wake wasn't enough to roll them, though the nephew had turned their boat into it, to ride it out. The passing ship looked as if it were made out of boiler plate; the bare metal was the color of rust, reddish-brown as Missouri bottom land, with streaks of light orange. Rivets. Kenner could see rivets. The shape of the bow was the same as an Arabian sword—a scimitar, with an elegant chopping edge. It had been recently painted a milky green. *Red Diamond V* was stenciled there. People were everywhere onboard; it was if the passengers were still at dockside, ready to wave at folk bidding them good-bye. Most of their bodies were lost in the fog; all Kenner could see were different sets of hands clutching the rail of the ship.

They don't see us, Kenner thought. They would have clouds to look through, we were looking up from below them. Blue smoke poured from the ports at the ship's stern and the odor of petrochemicals combusting mixed with the smell of the sea. Kenner was reminded of city buses, a stink that always made him nauseous. The thought raised the taste of bile in his throat; then he realized it was just a heavier version of what he had been smelling all along.

"That's what I hoped it was," O'Bannion said, relieved. "It's only an old Panamanian freighter some people I know leased. They offered a cruise-ship line a hundred thousand dollars to make the trip, but were refused. So they hired that tub. They hoped to bring at least five hundred people out on it. There shouldn't be many boats left in Mariel by now."

"But we're not going to Mariel, are we?" Kenner said, momentarily insightful.

O'Bannion smiled, rolled the unlit cigar purposefully in his mouth, the same safecracker's motion, tumblers turning.

"Well, let's just say it's not our first choice."

La Compañía rose up and down in the wake of the *Red Diamond V*. It struck Kenner as a very silly sort of motion, something you'd feel on an amusement park ride.

2

Curt was nearly out of gas on the New Jersey Turnpike. He would have to stop at the next service area, the Joyce Kilmer. Curt was certain he was being sent messages. He continued to see things that were too strange to be explainable. An hour ago a car had passed him; its headlights were unbelievably askew. One pointed straight up, like a searchlight at a shopping center opening; the other pointed down, straight onto the highway a foot in front of the car. It was crazy. Then, just fifteen minutes ago, another car went by, its lights equally walleyed, one beam crossing in front of the car at a sharp angle; the other pointed like a flashlight up in a tree, looking for a cat. In all of Curt's years of driving, he had never seen headlights aimed in such bizarre directions. It made everything seem senseless. The fact of seeing two within an hour convinced Curt they were an omen of some sort, but he hadn't decided just what its import was, when he noticed his fuel gauge: its red pointer was at E. He felt that if he could reach New York City the spell that had formed around him would break. He should call Winston. The sound of his voice might be a pin, something to pop the bad bubble.

Curt's fancy was that turnpike service areas were actually space stations, or what space stations would look like years from now: rundown way stations for interplanetary travel. Passengers fed, vehicles refueled. It was their island quality, set off, lighted pools in the highways' dark interstellar space. To Curt the service areas seemed to hover and the cars seemed to land; all the people, he imagined, were from different planets. They passed through the cafeteria lines, talking languages incomprehensible to him, unheard in his solar system, looking weird. Curt shivered involuntarily, since he knew he shouldn't entertain such ideas so clearly, since the gas pumps already made him feel creepy. The shining pools of oil splotches on the concrete, shimmering like the bodies of underwater animals, something that could attach itself to his insides, would always be there, feeding.

He grabbed a nozzle from the pump and walked around to the other side of the LeBaron holding the nozzle aloft like a pitcher. He reached for the gas cap when, much to his surprise, and seeming, nonetheless, to be something that he expected— though not knowing why—he found the cap gone. It wasn't there: just a black hole in the side of the car's fender where the cap should have been. He tried to remember the last time he had gotten gas. He had no memory of screwing the cap back on. It was just gone. Now he had a hole were the cap should have been, and that fact began to trouble him inordinately.

Would the gas spill out? Would something fly into it? Would it cause him some sort of catastrophe?

The cap's absence made him shake. And, for a moment, he didn't know if he should put gas in, and he began to walk back to the pump, and then he decided he could fill half the tank and it wouldn't spill out. So, he went back, but he let the gas flow too fast at first and some did splash back out, onto his trouser leg and the side of the car. He continued filling the tank, at a slower rate, till he let in seven gallons.

Curt looked around for something to plug the hole, a rag, paper, something. He opened the car trunk and there was the bird book, its plastic bag slipping off. Curt pulled the plastic covering away from the leather book and began to shape the bag into a plug. He started to put it in the hole when he thought of something new: the gas would melt it and that would make things worse. He looked about the service island for the right thing.

Curt was stuffing the soft, thick blue paper towels in the gas tank's pipe when he felt a stiff finger tap him on the shoulder. "Can I be of assistance?"

Curt felt himself grow cold, but prevented himself from jumping. He turned his head slowly and then looked up. It was a state trooper in full regalia. God, those uniforms were something, Curt thought. Jodhpurs and high boots, leather across his chest, the forest-ranger hat.

"Ah, naw, officer, I just, sort of, lost my gas cap."

"Stuffing it with paper is probably not the best thing," the trooper said. "Where are you headed?"

"New York."

"Well, I suppose you can buy one there," the officer said. Curt pulled out the purple plug of wadded paper. He went around the car to throw the paper in the trash can and the trooper followed him. Curt thought he had made another mistake because the trunk was still open. And now the trooper would be standing right in front of it. Curt didn't even want to turn around, but he did, and he saw what he feared: the trooper was staring down into the trunk.

"I've never seen a book that large," the trooper said. "It is a book, isn't it?"

"Yeah," Curt said, "it's a book. It's a book of birds."

The trooper continued to stare down at the large square of printed fabric and leather, staring so long that Curt felt himself obliged to lift the cover back and reveal the contents.

It was like lifting a trapdoor and that's how Curt felt, as if he were lifting up some sort of door and he would at any moment be looking down stone steps that led into a dark dungeon. It was an engraving of three blue birds on a dead branch. Curt realized that he had never before looked closely at any of the pictures. Egg yolk was running into the open beak of one of the birds. That's what we stole? he thought, shocked at the sight.

"Pretty," the trooper said. "Real pretty."

Curt let the cover fall back and it floated slowly down. There was a little *poof* when it closed.

"Well," the trooper said, as Curt slammed the trunk lid down, "make sure you get a cap in the city." He turned smartly, and

277

Curt watched him walk toward the outer edge of the service area. He could now see the chrome and shiny parts of a parked patrol car. Curt paid for his gas and got back in the LeBaron. His hand shook, and it took him three tries to start the car. He pulled away from the gas pumps slowly and, watching out his rearview mirror, headed back onto the turnpike. The patrol car did not move. Curt watched it glimmer in the shadows.

Twenty-four

1

Duane drove up to Miami, to hang out for a day or two, and find a place to unload some of his coke. If he could lay some of it off and get some cash, then things would be okay. Rea would have to wait.

He had been sleeping in the van, but he had just enough money left to check into a hotel; he was surprised that one with vacancies was hard to find. Construction was going on in the place he found, but it was open and had rooms. Half of it was faded and dilapidated; the other half had been changed into modern decor: metal, burnished, a style that made Duane think of space ships. Everyone, except for some of the guests, seemed to Duane to be some variety of spic. All they talked was Spanish. The clerk at the desk told Duane that the room was forty dollars, in a tone Duane felt meant that forty would be too much money for him. He had some sixty dollars left. One night would have to be it.

A bellboy who reminded Duane of a guy named Paco he had done time with showed Duane to his room, carrying the knapsack Duane had brought with him. After they got out of the elevator, it looked as if nothing had ever been done to the hotel. Soiled hall carpets, flaking paint. The room was damp, musty-smelling, the furniture old and worn, the sort of stuff that never moved at the Goodwill. The windows, though, had been replaced. The hotel must have catered to jumpers, Duane thought, if windows were the first things changed. The spics must have bought it cheap. You couldn't jump out of the windows now; only about a half-foot square section at the bottom would open. Red polyester curtains were half-way closed, one side dripping off the curtain rod; the Miami sun blazed through. Duane felt like he had left the States and landed in some foreign country.

Everyone he talked to so far—the front-desk clerk, the bell-hop, the Spanish kid who had parked his van at the hotel's entrance—most likely knew what Duane needed to know. For a moment, alone in his room, Duane felt something he recognized to be either panic or common sense: he should forget this shit and just get back to where he spoke the same language, back north. He didn't have enough money for the gas now. He had one more Audubon print and a half-kilo of high-quality cocaine. He should have gotten some cash from MacNaughton.

The instinct to flee, the first wave, passed; Duane decided to give this a chance. Get in a cab, have the driver take him to the right neighborhood.

Duane took a shower, disappointed by the trickle of water that came from the old shower head, the type his grandmother had on the end of her watering bucket. He changed clothes, put on a rayon Hawaiian shirt and blue jeans. He still didn't feel like a native.

He went down in the elevator, and when he walked out the front door, there was a flurry of activity. A cab appeared even before he asked for one. A man at the curbside had its door waiting open. Duane got in, feeling as if he had finally gotten some service for his forty bucks.

"Where you want to go?" the driver asked. Duane was happy to see him: an old guy, not Spanish.

"I'm new in town," Duane said, and in the driver's rearview mirror, he could see the driver's tell-me-something-new smirk. "And I want a little action. Take me some place where there's some good times. Bars, women, a little toot, maybe. Sin City."

The driver didn't lose his smirk, but said, "Right away," and punched the cab's meter. He sped out of the circular drive, made a hard right, tires squealing, a hard left and another right. He went two more blocks at high speed. Duane couldn't make out what they were passing. The cab stopped abruptly.

Duane figured they couldn't be more than four or five blocks from where they had begun. The cab was in front of a store, painted yellow, outlined in light bulbs. Black two-foot-high letters read SIN CITY. Underneath, THE MUSEUM OF PLEASURE.

"Are you kidding?"

"This is where you wanted to go, right?" the old man said.

Duane gave him two dollars and thought this might be a place to start. If the driver wanted to cheat him, he would have taken him on a longer ride.

Duane thought all these sex shops must be a franchise operation, like Burger King. They all looked the same, outside and in. There were two walls of magazines wrapped in Saran Wrap. Women with large nipples on the covers, the kind of nipples that reminded Duane of manhole covers, bumpy and embossed. The middle of the store was full of paperback racks; above the clerk's counter and within the case in front of him were rubber goods: inflatable dolls, flesh-colored hardware. The air-conditioning smelled of ink and disinfectant. This could be anywhere, he thought, except the signs were in Spanish and English. A number of the magazines were Spanish. *Fotos*. There were two doorways curtained off, which Duane figured led to peep shows, or booths. LIVE SEX SHOW ESPECTACULO SEXUAL EN VIVO.

Duane walked up to the clerk. He was reading a book: *A New Model of the Universe*.

"Do you have anything for the nose?" Duane asked.

The clerk looked at him for a moment and said, "I thought I had heard people ask for everything here, but that's a first. What do you want to do to your nose, or with your nose, may I ask?"

"I don't want to do anything to it, I just want to use it."

The clerk took off his glasses and peered down at Duane.

"That you can get anywhere: the police station, the public library, the Methodist church around the block. We sell here what you see—or what you can see—for five bucks a minute, whatever you want to see, in the booths."

"Are you into barter? Would you like to trade?" Duane asked. "Something for your nose for a few minutes in the booths?"

The clerk pulled a tissue from a foil-covered box next to the cash register and started to clean his glasses. He didn't say anything, but his silence was invitational. Duane took a Bayer aspirin tin out of his pocket, and, with his other hand, opened his knife, an old switchblade. It looked, Duane thought, like a magic trick. He popped the flat can's lid with one hand and snapped open the switchblade with the other. With the tip of the blade, he lifted out a pyramid of cocaine and dumped it in the middle of the glass countertop.

The clerk looked down at the white pile, and Duane did too. He saw through the glass to the French ticklers below, rubber versions of sea urchins he had almost stepped on when he once went into the water with Rea at Smathers Beach.

"That's about five minutes's worth," the clerk said. "I'll buzz you in. Booth number one." Duane saw a red light snap on above the second door.

He'd let the clerk sample the cocaine and think about it. Five minutes in the booth would be long enough.

The curtained cubicle he stepped into did remind him of a confessional. Bless me father. There was a blue light on, just enough light to see the walls were covered with a Valentine's Day fuzzy paper, slightly raised rough red hearts. They looked purple in the light. A curtain pulled back, and Duane found himself standing in front of a plexiglass door at least a half-inch thick. It could have been a mirror, for beyond it was another cubicle the same size as the one he stood in. He looked at his own reflection.

A bluish hand appeared, separating the other cubicle's curtain. A woman stepped into the dark space, bringing a stool, wearing one of the nighties that had been hanging on the store's walls, thumbtacked above the clerks' head. It, too, looked purple-green.

She was dark, but not black, and, though she could see Duane, she didn't appear to notice. It was a high bar stool she brought with her, one with a soft top, and she sat on it and undid the strings that held part of her outfit on, a little cape, and took it off, one shoulder at a time. Then she unhooked the gauzy vest that was fastened beneath her breasts. That left some sort of bra. It did not seem part of the ensemble, but just a brassiere. It was a chartreuse color in the blue light. She licked her lips as she undid it, looking forward, but she must be staring at my chin, Duane thought. The cloth fell to her lap and her breasts were bared. They were large, larger than he expected, and she stuck her finger in her mouth and then circled each nipple with it.

Her blue light went out and Duane saw some sort of motion and the light came back on. That must be a minute. The light must be on a timer, he thought. Another minute to get out of her panties. The minimum spent here must be at least twenty bucks, he thought. After the light came back on she sat on the stool, opened her legs, and with her fingers made into an inverted V, spread back the lips of her cunt. It took a half a minute for her to insert a finger; then the light went off.

Duane saw that she would do something different in the last few seconds, as bait.

The next minute took her off the stool, and she swayed to recorded music. Duane looked around for its source, but he couldn't find a speaker. Just as the minute was to end, she bent over the stool, her belly on its soft cushion, and with her ass pointed at Duane, she pulled back one cheek, and let a finger rest atop her asshole. The light went out.

The light didn't come back on. Duane saw her make the same push-the-button motion at the wall. She must be like the chicken that performs: she presses the button, but she doesn't really control it. The clerk controls the time.

Light poured into the cubicle.

"Hey, that wasn't five minutes," Duane said to the clerk, who stood in the doorway. He was taller than he had looked sitting behind the counter.

"Well, I decided your barter was only worth four minutes. If you want some more time, maybe we can work something out." The clerk and Duane just looked at each other. "At six minutes another girl joins in."

"How about ten minutes?"

"Didn't you see the hole in the wall?" the clerk said matter-of-factly.

"What I want to get rid of is about four hours' worth. Do you know of anyone who'd be interested?"

The clerk fell silent again, took to staring, but then held back the curtain and motioned for Duane to walk back out into the store.

2

Curt realized that this would be about the appointed time for calling Winston, anyway. But it seemed to be just a coincidence that it had taken an additional three hours to reach this point. He didn't have to dial the number. They did all that for him;

they had also attached a recording device to the phone's receiver, a suction plug attached to a small tape recorder.

"Hello. Who's this?"

Winston's voice seemed scared to Curt, much more scared than he himself felt. Almost as if Winston could see him sitting at this table with five other men. Winston's fear made Curt feel safer, made him want to reassure him.

"Hi, old man. It's your old buddy, Curt. I've had a little trouble."

"Trouble," Winston broke in. "Where are you calling from?!"

"Well, the car broke down. I'm calling from a pay phone, and I just wanted you to know, so you wouldn't get worried, not hearing from me at the right time."

"You mean you just left the car?" Winston sounded alarmed.

"Well, it's got to be towed into a garage. I think it's the fuel pump," Curt said. "I get a lot of spark but no juice. But I've got the book."

"The *fish!*" Winston spit, wanting him to stick to the code.

"*A* fish," Curt said. "I left the rest of them back at the pond."

"What! You were supposed to bring *all* the fish."

"Well, all the fish weren't biting," Curt said, amused with himself. The men's faces around the table looked both bored and concerned.

"I'll call you back after I get there. I just didn't want you to worry. They said it'll probably take a few hours to fix. Maybe overnight, so don't get bothered if you don't hear from me till morning."

"I am bothered," Winston said. "I'm bothered very much."

"Okay. Don't worry, pal. Everything's cool. No sweat."

Winston clicked off. Curt replaced the receiver and looked into the face of the agent in charge.

"Was that long enough?" Curt asked, assuming they were tracing the phone call.

"Long enough? Oh. No. We can get his address from the number. That's no problem. We just wanted to see if your story held up."

Curt felt bad they doubted him. He had had a hard time coming up with an alternate explanation for the book being in his trunk. The same state trooper who had talked to him at the Joyce Kilmer service area had stopped him about ten miles up the turnpike.

Curt found out he had told his partner about the bird book.

His partner remembered something about a burglary of some famous bird pictures. He called in, and about ten minutes later they were on Curt's behind, ghostly lights flashing, filling his car with blue ozone. Curt thought it was all familiar, as if he had dreamed it, the car filling with just that shade of blue light. The runway lights.

The trooper approached and asked to see his driver's license and registration. Then he just said right out: "Do you know you have illegal possession of stolen goods?"

Curt didn't know what to say, so he said, "Yes."

The state troopers brought him back to their barracks. Two FBI men appeared. Curt never learned who called them, but there they were. The state trooper had read him his rights, and he wasn't sure what he should do. Curt thought of various stories he could tell, but none sounded convincing to him. They began to list the things he was charged with, starting with possession of a stolen automobile. The rent-a-car agency had listed it as stolen. That was the story Curt had started with: someone he didn't know loaned him the car in Florida. The man just wanted the car left in New York City. He didn't know what was in the trunk till he opened it up at the gas station.

The trooper said he sounded a lot more familiar with the book than that. Curt said, Ah, no, he had only seen it a few minutes before.

It was just this guy who had him drive the car to New York?

But Curt couldn't give them a name, or much of a description: someone he had met in a bar who wanted a car driven back to the city and left in a particular parking lot. Then he was to send the parking-lot ticket back to Key West general delivery. Curt realized he had made a mistake, since he had now to give them a name. Curt couldn't think of one, or, rather, all the names he could think of had faces attached to them. He finally made one up. Tom Garbo.

He stuck with that story for a while; men kept going in and out of the room and every time one of the FBI men went out, he came back with more paper, till they began to repeat Curt's life history to him, and the more familiar they became, the more intimate the information they had about him, the more stuck Curt began to feel.

They left him alone. And when they returned their mood had changed.

"Do you recognize this?" the agent said. He put a large clear plastic envelope on the table. Inside was the gun Curt had hidden under the LeBaron's backseat. The kennel owner's twenty-two.

Curt stared at it.

"It's been fired recently," the agent said. "The shit creek you're up, Curt ol' boy, has just gotten shittier. A gun just like this has been involved in a few murders we're looking into. You can do, as I see it, one of two things. You can keep with your dizzy story and get tossed in jail, get a lawyer, and spend a few years in the can. Or you can tell us where the rest of them are, where we can find the other books. After that, we will discuss what we might be able to do for you."

They wanted to turn him. And, Curt saw, if he turned, went with them, he would be looked out for. They would be in his debt. It would be like joining up again, he thought. Curt had finally been taken off the road, brought some place away from all the strange sights, weird occurrances, bad vibes. It was clear, looking at their faces, that he could make all these men happy if he just did what they wanted.

3

Duane returned to the hotel wanting a drink. There was no bar open off the new lobby, but the penthouse restaurant served liquor, he was told. He took the elevator to the top floor. Duane had a name, a time, and a location provided by the sex-shop clerk. The penthouse restaurant was the size of a ballroom and smelled oddly to Duane of chlorine. Then he saw that the swimming pool entrance was next to the doors of the restaurant. He wondered about that till he crossed the large empty room, past a bandstand with speakers as big as portable johns, microphone stands, stools, a dance floor in front. All of that sat beneath a murky green window, which was one wall of the swimming pool. No people swam in it. The room looked to be half as large as the entire hotel. Windows ran along two sides of the cavernous room. Cloth-covered tables dotted the floor, floating like lily pads in the murk. Duane sat next to a wall made of glass.

A waiter finally came toward him. Duane watched his long solitary progression from what must be the kitchen, around the many empty tables, set at odd angles to one another, like unconnected pieces of a puzzle. The waiter threaded his way around them smartly. For a moment, Duane thought that this must be what an ocean liner is like, since the waiter bobbed and weaved, as if he had good sea legs. Feeling like he had done a day's work, he ordered a rum and coke. He would bill it to his room, though the clerk at the downstairs desk had made him pay in advance. Let the management spring for his drinks.

The sun was now as high as the top floor of the hotel. It hung outside the far wall's windows. The hotel was on Biscayne Boulevard. He must be looking straight at Miami Beach. There was another row of hotels there on the water. Inland, away from the water's edge, the city shrunk in height. Duane tried to figure where he was. Behind him, behind the dirty green water of the swimming pool, were office buildings, the federal courthouse, downtown.

Closest to him, looking down, was some sort of marina. There were yachts tied up, boats that Duane had seen only in movies and in magazines. Duane thought that he was always staring at a lot of money. He had never seen Boston from this high up. Here everything was white, or yellow, then the water. Haze and the sun just a round hot spot, part of the sight. Everything was some shade of heat: yellow, pink, red, orange. In Boston, even on hot days, everything was brown, gray, green.

The carpet of the big room was old, worn, and red, almost blood red. Incarnadine, Duane thought. One of the words he had learned from Rea. Incarnadine, the color of a blood stain. She used it talking about the prison class. From Shakespeare's time, it was always associated with blood, she said. Thinking about Rea, looking at the stained carpet, he wondered: if she had been here with him and he mentioned it, would that be enough to continue to interest her, enough of a link to her world? She called him an "autodidact," another word he learned from her. Yeah, a street scholar, he had told her. She was going to get me into college.

He had her where he wanted her. Though that was the only way he had her, he realized. Scared. She knew she would be held accountable for fucking him around. But he gave some thought to proving something that would really bother her: that he could kill her—but he would not. She would be stuck with that knowledge. She knew he could.

He finished his drink. The sun continued to drum into the large room. Even with air-conditioning, or because of it, Duane felt the room was a big chunk of ice and the sun was melting it around the edges. Now the coolness was only about four feet high and just in the middle, the center of the room. His drink's ice had long ago melted, and the glass went from being sticky to dry.

Duane looked out at Miami again, all white and yellow under the orange light of the descending sun. This must be what Africa is like, a city near a desert, he thought. Egypt. It was strange. It was like nothing he knew.

Duane parked in one of the Biscayne Dog Track's parking lots. The van would be less conspicuous there. It would be a short walk to the house, a bungalow with a tin roof. When he first drove by it, he saw the front windows were shuttered. You couldn't see in. A cyclone fence circled a scrubby yard.

Approaching on foot, Duane saw that in the back the fence's height rose to eight feet. He heard barking. Dogs. The fence had flowers entwined through its mesh, red flowering hibiscus. Duane knocked on the front door.

A kid about ten years old, maybe eleven, answered his knocking. There were other boys in the room. The air was cold and full of sweet scents. Marijuana. Duane had been listening to the large air conditioner rumble at the side of the house while he waited on the porch.

"Manny's out back," one of the boys said. "It's feeding time."

Manny must be the scoutmaster, Duane thought; he wondered what he fed the boys.

There were about a dozen narrow pens, made out of the same cyclone fencing. They had greyhounds in them. Some old, some young. Duane figured this must be Manny's business. They couldn't be pets. The dogs looked like cooked turkeys to Duane: their back legs shaped like drumsticks, the skin tight and shiny, ligaments and veins swollen and wormlike.

Manny was large. Bent over, his ass looked a meter wide; his thighs were half that each. There was no space between his legs. It didn't look like flab. Duane stared at a pair of calloused heels, with wide cracks rising up at least an inch from the soles of the flipflops the man was wearing.

Manny must have heard him come up; Duane had let the house's screen door slam. Manny righted himself and turned around. Duane blanched. Manny seemed to have tits, or at least that part of his chest, two soft triangular flaps of flesh, hung down, overlapping the rising moon of his belly. He also had a port-wine stain on the left side of his face.

"You're the one I got called about?" he asked in a perfectly ordinary voice. Duane had expected strange sounds to come out of him.

"Yes," Duane said. "The thousand-dollar call."

Duane caught a glimpse of Manny's mouth. Tiny teeth, almost brown.

Duane had not expected to be sent to a house, but, rather, some neutral place. In fact, when he turned off 95 at the specified exit, he thought it would be the dog track he had seen driving by. What are the options, the chances of being ripped off? They cut both ways. He could be a narc, setting them up. He could be set up. Everyone works around the lack of trust and imagined possibilities. A mine field in reverse. Every step blows up except when you step on a bit of buried trust.

"Gordi said your stuff was pretty good," Manny said. He dug a flour scoop into a fifty-pound bag of dog chow; it sounded like a spade being stuck in dirt.

"Yeah, you can cut it a lot. In Key West they cut it with inositol, some health-food shit," Duane said.

"We know what to cut it with," Manny said, sowing the dog feed into a tin trough.

Duane was pretty sure Manny was running some low-rent vice conglomerate: porn, boys, dogs, and drugs.

"Do you race those dogs?" he asked, watching them eat, stabbing their noses at the dry food in the trough.

"No, we just keep 'em here. Most of them get put down, these dogs. You still got to feed them or they make a racket. The neighbors complain."

Manny's neighbors should have lots of complaints, Duane thought. The air was full of the slightly sweet smell of the dogs' feed, a sweetish stink, not unpleasant, the smell of earth giving up some of the day's heat. It wasn't yet dark, but the sun had gone below the horizon.

"Okay," Manny said, picking up the bag of feed with one hand; he hauled it back to a small prefab shed. "Let's do business."

Duane followed him back into the bungalow, through the kitchen. None of the boys played maid, that's for sure, he thought. Off to the left was a bedroom. The air that came out of it smelled slightly mentholated. Manny kept the inside of his house dark.

Duane stopped at the bedroom's doorway when Manny turned into it. Manny went over to a closet with a sliding door, stood there a moment, and then returned.

"Where's your stuff?"

"Where's your money?"

Manny held up some bills. They looked stiff, new.

Duane undid the bandana he wore around his forehead as a sweatband. Folded within was plastic bag of cocaine. It had flattened out, a ribbon of white, the plastic slick with his sweat.

He looked for a clear space on the kitchen's formica table and laid it down. Manny wet his finger, and Duane felt uneasy watching Manny stick the whitened fingertip in his mouth, rub it along the insides of his gums.

"I've got a bad schnozzola," Manny said. "Can't put anything up it anymore. I usually get one of the lads to rub a little on my," and he looked straight at Duane, "asshole. It's not so bad that way. Has its advantages."

Duane's face got hot and tight. Manny was starting to fuck with him. Duane's hands were ready to fly up to the man's throat. But it wasn't a setup, he reminded himself. It looked like he was getting a square deal. He was surprised, though, that Manny hadn't weighed what he had given him. Manny must have a butcher's touch for heft. Maybe, Duane thought, he underestimated the going rate: a hundred dollars a gram. The notion gave him grief. It was over twenty grams.

"Yeah," Manny said, "Gordi was right."

He pushed his other fist toward Duane, the one that held the bills. Ten one hundreds. Duane pulled them out. Stuck up his ass. He still didn't like Manny fucking with him.

Duane walked back toward the front door. Manny picked up the bag and disappeared into the dark bedroom.

The first boy Duane had seen went past him and into Manny's room. Duane opened the front door and went out.

He walked down the street, watching the sky, trying to catch his breath. The sky was purple, about to go black.

Twenty-five

1

Kenner wondered if *La Compañía*'s slipping by the U.S. Coast Guard had been an easier trick than he imagined: if the captain's trip had already been cleared, his route prearranged.

Rea was conversing with the nephew. That they hadn't been introduced seem strange, but Rea was now chatting with him. She seemed to make friends quickly, a talent Kenner lacked. He still couldn't imagine why O'Bannion had agreed to take them along—if this trip was irregular.

Perhaps whatever it was, the captain did want the trip written about; some derring-do ahead. An article that would make O'Bannion and his cohorts look good, and make Castro look bad. Kenner thought anything the captain had in mind wouldn't be much more than a gnat in an elephant's eye, compared—and he realized his image was changing in some fashion—to the egg already on Carter's face.

What would Castro be losing? Fidel, too, doubtless figured Reagan was going to win. He was selling short, dumping what he could before the coming crash.

O'Bannion was right: whatever discontents were heating up

on Havana's streets would be dissipated by the boatlift; some pressure would be released. Kenner wondered if the fellow who drove the bus through the Peruvian embassy's gates was an agent of some sort. Was anybody taking credit?

The boatlift would provide some sort of cover. To put someone on? To take someone off? The nephew? Weren't there other times, other ways, to pluck someone off Cuba?

"Did you learn anything?" he asked Rea as she came back to join him at the stern.

"Like-a-what?"

"Like-a about what the captain and this ride are up to. Mariel is in that direction, I believe." Kenner said, waving his hand toward the blue sky behind them.

"Well, wherever we're going, we're supposed to be there by nightfall. Armando said we should be seeing land in a couple of hours."

"Armando?"

"The nephew. You look sunburned. Aren't you using anything?"

Kenner had a baseball cap on, the kind that had become the uniform of what he thought of as a new sort of class in America: the bush-league class. Every shitkicker with some sort of laboring or semi-laboring job now wore a feed cap, Kenner realized, one firm or another emblazoned on a patch above the bill. It was the team association that bothered him. Whose team were they on, anyway? Farmers began it, the truck drivers were on the other pole, and in between hung every other sort of sorry son of a bitch around. Kenner's cap advertised a sporting goods supply company: SHAKESPEARE. He wore it as a novelty. Rea was wearing a straw hat she had bought at the Woolco during their hasty predeparture shopping spree.

"I did find out one useful thing," Rea said. "The nephew came out on the first trip the captain made. And I'd guess we're going back for something he couldn't bring then. Cargo."

"How illegal do you think it is?"

"Couldn't tell. Drugs would be everyone's first guess. Loot? Religious statues?"

Kenner appeared perplexed.

"I'm beginning to feel less like a journalist," he said, "and more like a witness. You know what they do to witnesses."

"Like-a-what?" she said, still kidding. "We're along for the ride. There's nowhere else to go. It's our adventure. Why would he take us, then get rid of us. Sounds real callous. I think O'Bannion's okay."

"Well," Kenner said, "this trip was just supposed to be against the law—not mysterious."

"Look around," Rea said, indicating the distant horizon, marked by a heap of cumuli. The water was blinding in spots with sun-induced pools of mercury.

"No questions out there."

"No answers, either," Kenner said, inhaling the hot-cinder stink of *La Compañía*'s exhausts.

The captain may have been to Mariel before, Kenner thought, but he surely has been to this spot before, too. He watched O'Bannion and Armando navigate the boat through the narrow tidal creek, staying near the overgrown starboard shoreline. The air was full of birds' startled calls. The nephew would yell out *estribor* or *babor* and O'Bannion would turn the wheel, give it a croupier's spin. Kenner's understanding of Spanish wasn't improving much, but he was beginning to distinguish words.

Rea had had the sense to buy some insect repellent, Muskol, on the shopping trip and she sprayed it on herself and Kenner before the *La Compañía* entered the channel. Mangrove roots barnacled with shells crept out into the water; wide leaves of a variety of trees created a solid green surface. Clouds of insects bounced above the water like huge gray bladder balls.

Kenner had thought he had become accustomed to heat in Key West, but what he encountered here, after the freshened air of the open sea was cut off, was something else: it was dough. It felt as if he were being kneaded, though. The boat, from seeming so tiny on the ocean, now seemed too large. The water was brown and *La Compañía*'s props churned up a fetid, fecund odor. No wind dispersed it.

The opening narrowed till the boat seemed to be sliding between the two banks, close enough to put the waxy mangrove leaves at arm's length. The dense green wall of cypress and mangrove was knotholed with brightly colored birds, enough of them to make Rea ask, "Do you think he's a bird smuggler?" That would be too tame, Kenner thought.

"This is better than the Conch Train," Rea said.

The boat slipped out of the narrow channel. It looked to be a basin, a lagoon, Kenner thought. The temperature had dropped about twenty degrees. The water had cleared up, become silvery, incandescent where the sun struck it. The nephew lowered the anchor, and O'Bannion put the *La Compañía* in reverse till the anchor caught. The engine went off. Caws and buzzings replaced its rumbling, the sounds of flapping, flight.

"We're going to be here a while," the captain said. "You can swim if you like. Some say there is a secret spring here—that this cove is the fountain of youth."

Rea hardly waited for O'Bannion to finish. She dove in, not taking any of her clothes off. She didn't have much on. Kenner wore his bathing suit under his shorts; he undid his tennis shoes, put his glasses inside one, and jumped in. The water was cool, and, though not as translucent as the water off the Keys, he could see through it, though his myopia made everything distant blur.

Kenner sprang to the surface; he found himself floating easily, half his body out of the water. He remembered a sailing term: freeboard. The amount of boat above the water line. There must be a high salt content, though it didn't taste of it. The spring made it cool and forced in who knew what sort of minerals. He began to relax.

Rea was a better swimmer than Kenner, and she had gone as far from the boat as you could before slipping into the gloom under the dark foliage that encircled the basin. There was one other entrance cut Kenner could make out. Rather than swim to her, Kenner decided to get back into the boat and try to get O'Bannion to tell him something other than his history of the Cuban nation.

But when Kenner found him heating up their usual evening fare, Dinty Moore stew laced with hot peppers and whatever scraps of produce O'Bannion found in the provisions locker—neither O'Bannion nor Armando made use of any of the fishing gear—O'Bannion became closedmouthed for the first time.

Kenner jumped back into the water and climbed quickly out again, preferring the diving, the change, to Rea's consistent swimming; it was hard for Kenner to contemplate what would be waiting for them back in Key West. *La Compañía*'s VHF once had been tuned to a news broadcast, but there was no report of crime in Key West. Just the usual: the hostages, Carter, Reagan, Chrysler showing the largest three-month loss of an American auto company.

Going to sea was like dropping into a time crevice, "a fold in the episteme," Rea had said. It now made a little sense to Kenner, as it never had before, what running off to sea really meant: you leapt into space.

Kenner kept thinking about Castro and Cuba. O'Bannion's ranting about el máximo Jefe, Fifo, included genealogy. He said that Batista was actually a real Cuban, a mongrel, a mixture of bloods—Indian, black, Spanish—whereas Castro was pure Spanish—Castilian. Kennedy and Castro were linked in Kenner's mind; he found himself blaming Kennedy for a lot of things: Vietnam, primarily. Not just because he glamorized guerilla war, manufactured the Green Berets, helped fashion the CIA's image of tuxedo-clad terrorists; no, it wasn't that, it was the legacy Kennedy's own assassination left.

It was Kenner's view that the war in Vietnam went on another twelve years as punishment for Kennedy's being murdered. All the young president's men—Sorensen, Schlesinger, MacNamara, Rostow, Bundy—became profoundly sullen. Because Jack had been killed they let proceed, what, in other circumstances, they would have . . . well, they wouldn't have admitted it was wrong, but perhaps ill-advised. For Kennedy's sake they might have stopped it. But, since he was gone, they didn't. They let others dig their own graves. Let them dig Jack's grave. You killed him, they thought, you reap the rewards.

Kenner had been amazed when the widow, Jackie O, had said that Kennedy had a Walter Mitty streak in him. For if the president of the United States had dreams of adventure, who would be safe? He had all the power he could use, but still he dreamed of having more. Kenner realized that might be the case: he had so much power, but he could not always work his will. Kennedy always seemed to be personally affronted by Castro— he seemed to be a larger, darker version of Kennedy's own fantasies.

Kenner did see it as some sort of stag battle, antlers locked. So Kennedy created a lot of monsters, a lot of nightmare people, and finally got himself killed by one of them.

Kenner recalled an old interview he had seen. Castro had been asked if Cuba had anything to do with JFK's assassination; Castro said, no, oh, no. Because world leaders didn't have other world leaders assassinated, for that would make them all equal targets, make them all fair game, and no world leader would be so stupid to let that happen.

Kenner remembered Castro's answer when the Church committee later made all its revelations known. Had Castro actually been confessing to those in the know back then? Been rubbing their faces in their own actions? Or was he being merely ironic, having known of the CIA's attempts? Or, if he never believed the White House was plotting to kill him, was he just being sincere?

O'Bannion had talked about the good ol' days of the early sixties, when there had been one CIA case officer for every five anti-Fidelistas in South Florida. He seemed to miss being so well looked after. What linked all the Cubans involved in Watergate with Nixon was their shared hatred of Kennedy.

And now Carter: a lot more Cubans helping to bring him down. But they had a lot of assistance and confederates. The failed hostage rescue. Carter canceled it and men were killed. He did what Kennedy should have done with the Bay of Pigs. Back out in the eleventh hour. Except Kennedy's popularity went up after the Bay of Pigs. Carter's was going down. Because he did cancel it. Doing the right thing is costly in the popularity sweepstakes. Americans love action. Carter must finally be learning that—and that's what made him appear so sour and bitter, what made his mean streak flare.

Carter was too much at the mercy of events. It bothered the electorate. It made him seem decent, but not very astute. All his predecessors wanted to seem to be manipulators. They acted, others reacted. Even Christ arranged to have himself crucified, an unfortunate public policy precedent.

Carter reminded Kenner of Truman, except that Truman got to balance his simplicity, his everydayness, outright commonness, with the gold weight of dropping the A-bomb. No one could appear tougher than that.

Kenner was dislodged from his sun-induced, drowsy speculations by two simultaneous events: Rea's rattling the aluminum ladder as she clambered back on deck and the sound of a motor coming toward them from the cut on the other side of the basin.

The *La Compañía* took on two new passengers, but its population only rose by one. Armando, the nephew, had departed on the boat that had brought the two new guests: a man and a woman. In addition to some fresh provisions, *La Compañía* now carried cargo. Cargo. There was something about that word that attracted Kenner.

Kenner had known of a few ways to smuggle cocaine—for that is what he presumed it was, since it was slightly smaller than a bail of hay. Marijuana in that quantity would probably be considered, even by the courts of Mississippi or Georgia, just an individual's personal store.

In Kenner's mind, the ways to smuggle drugs were associated with sex and death. Heroin being sent back with the corpses of dead soldiers from Vietnam, secure within their Jesus bags. Cylinders filled with cocaine inserted in vaginas, or condoms swallowed by men and women to be later defecated and recovered in some Queens apartment. *If shit ever has value, the poor will be born without assholes,* Kenner recalled the old Portuguese saying. Well, even some shit has value these days.

Was the capable Captain employed by *our* government, he wondered, or someone else's? The CIA was both laughable and alarming to Kenner. He had run into a few Company men. A common link was the cloth; two of them, at least, were ministers. One taught birth control methods in India with an AID cover, but was somewhat squeamish when it came to instruction. In a rural outpost, he had demonstrated the use of prophylactics by putting one around a stick and jabbing the stick into the earth. He had returned a year later to the village and found that the birth rate had not declined at all. The village leader took him back around a dwelling and showed him an entire garden of rubbers stuck into the earth on sticks.

Kenner had spoken to the man at a wedding of a friend; he was a relative who was not pleased with the match his niece had made. He had become drunk and sour and and told Kenner, "When it comes to India, my advice concerning that benighted country is simple: *Start over.*" Kenner remembered the man's breath: peppermint and scotch.

Kenner never shared his friends' hysteria about the CIA, those who thought the Company controlled everything, even to the point of having its tentacles around the balls of lowly magazine editors, say, the likes of *Pen-Ultimate's*. Not everyone could be on Langley's payroll. No, just because they all thought alike, and wished for the same sort of thing, didn't mean they were suckling at the same cash teat.

The power boat that had brought *La Compañía's* two new faces had no markings. A pea green color, not much bigger than a crab man's skiff. It went off the way it had come. The cargo was covered by burlap, tightly fitted, snug as a new recruit's bunk. The burlap was brightly stenciled and covered with designs, the sort of thing that would sell well as a wall hanging at the Pottery Barn on Greenwich back in his own neighborhood. They stowed it in a forward compartment. Kenner did not get to heft it, but from the way it was dragged across the deck he estimated it must weigh over two hundred pounds. The tight burlap outlined rounded corners, what looked to be a large suitcase.

The captain and his new crew spoke in Spanish. When they did, it appeared that both Kenner and Rea became invisible. Kenner's Spanish was good enough to hear it, but he could only translate a few words and phrases. Rea was fluent in German and French.

"Your languages would be useful if this happened to be World War Two, not nineteen-eighty," he said to Rea, joking.

"Spanish seems to be," she said, "the language of intrigue in the eighties."

2

Bridget was going to bingo tonight and wouldn't look after Eli. And Juniper had run off with a Jehovah's Witness, or Mormon, whoever it was who had been knocking on people's doors at the Pair o' Dice. Kristina thought she should have paid more attention when Juniper had been dreamily describing the man she had met.

Things weren't working out for Kristina lately. When she had a dog, she had given it tranquilizers when she needed to fly to Colorado. If she gave Eli a Valium, he would sleep quietly till she got back. Kristina decided to give him a half a tablet, so she split the apricot-colored pill and ground it up and mixed it with some Tang and put it into the baby bottle for Eli. She was cleaning up, putting the half-tablet back into the bottle when a bang on the trailer's door made her jump.

"Duane," she said, with genuine surprise and relief, happy to see him. "Where have you been? I thought you dropped off the side of the earth." She hugged him, but Duane's arms remained stiff at his sides. Kristina felt as if she'd embraced a telephone pole.

"Have you seen Rea?" Duane asked, without even saying hello.

"No, I haven't, Duane." He stood there.

"Duane, you could do me the biggest favor. Stay here, if you don't have anything else to do. Stay with Eli. He won't be any trouble. He'll just sleep. The cable is still hooked up. And when I get back we can talk."

Kristina hoped that sounded like an appealing invitation, since she meant it to be. She wanted Duane to know she was willing to forgive and forget their last meeting. Though she couldn't keep herself from raising her hand to touch her lip. The swelling had long disappeared.

Duane looked at her strangely, but did not seem to register anything. His thoughts were always his own, Kristina considered, for all he shared them.

"I'll wait here," he said, beginning a command, instead of agreeing to a request. "I've been over to Cayo Hueso, but no one's there. I couldn't get in."

"Oh? Bridget's at bingo," Kristina said, happy that things were becoming normal again.

"There's some beer in the icebox. If there isn't, you can run down to the Tom Thumb. Here's a couple dollars. It'll be all right to leave Eli for a minute," she said, wondering if he would catch on that she had planned to leave Eli alone. Duane gave no indication.

"I'm glad you came back. You'll have to tell me everything later. I'm already a half hour behind. You know how much of a creep my boss is. I've been thinking of quitting, but, well, you know, Winston won't have any money for us for a while yet."

That was the only thing she had said that seemed to scratch Duane's stony face. His upper lip seemed to flutter for a moment, fly off toward a smile or a smirk.

"Winston's back north already?"

"Yeah. But he'll be back in a couple of weeks. I got to go, Duane. We'll talk later. Just enjoy yourself. Stretch out. There'll be something good on the cable. Bye bye. Great seeing you. Eli won't be a problem," she said and closed the door.

Kristina ran to catch the bus. Boy, that was lucky, she thought. She truly looked forward to coming home to Duane, later.

Twenty-six

"I'm not sure we went to Cuba," Rea said. Kenner looked at her sideways. A bird's glance, cocking the head.

"Well, it wasn't much of a visit," he said, "if we did. It wasn't Mariel, we didn't get to meet el Jefe. Close, but no cigar."

Kenner laughed at his joke, but Rea didn't smile.

"The sky didn't look right," she said, producing her star book. Rea's purse had always amazed Kenner because of what she might pull out of it. She had a bird identification book, a sky reference book. Also a pamphlet called "How to Cope with Dangerous Sea Life."

She flipped open to a drawing of a constellation and pointed, "This should have been in front of us. It was behind us. I think we're still north of it." Kenner had thought the drawing alone a bit suspect as a tool of navigation, but he hadn't a clue of where he was. The numbers on the Loran he had seen weren't convertible by him into location. They were now supposedly heading back for Key West.

"Where were we then?" he asked.

"I'm not sure. One of the thousand islands, the Tortugas,

the Marquesas, off Mexico, Honduras, somewhere in that direction."

Since the two new faces had come aboard, with their burlapped cargo, Rea and Kenner had not conferred. Both newcomers continued to speak Spanish, but the girl looked American to Kenner. O'Bannion had only told them they were special patriots who could not leave from Mariel. His nephew had chosen to go back because of his grandmother who couldn't leave.

The man who had come aboard was in his mid to late forties. He seemed to be missing an eye; it was closed and had a poached-egg look. Kenner thought he might have worn a patch. He looked intelligent, had a lined face, a goatee, black hair cut straight, which hung across his forehead, white hairs in his beard. The woman was younger, in her twenties, blonde, hardy; she looked as if she spent a good bit of time outdoors. Both Rea and he, Kenner realized, looked like visitors from outer space: they were the ones out of place on the boat. Rea nicknamed the two newcomers Eros and Thanatos. Kenner then suggested Echo and Narcissus, but Rea's choices stuck.

Kenner wondered what version of his and Rea's history O'Bannion had given to the two new passengers. They had looked at Rea and him with some suspicion. Kenner was sure the captain had told them something, something far closer to reality than Kenner had been told.

Another thing that bothered Kenner was that he didn't have much of a story for *Pen-Ultimate*. He didn't get to see Mariel, no Russian gunboats and commissars. No soldiers beating on the refugees-to-be. No attack dogs attacking. The editor was not going to be happy with a fishing trip in the Florida straits. Maybe *Outdoor Life* would take it. He would have to pump it up. Perhaps there would be some excitement when they docked at Key West and were greeted by the coast guard. Kenner stared out at the sea trying to think of some nature description: all the pastel colors were blending in large squares, like field painting. No, *Outdoor Life* would balk at that.

He set down some notes of things he had seen during the storm last evening: "A fiery light was thrown upon some palm trees so that it made them into enormous crimson feathers. The water was the color of blue steel; the Cuban woods were somber; high shivered the gory feathers." Nope, that wouldn't do, either. Kenner had been surprised by how many fish were just plain visible. A school of minnows had passed under and around the

301

boat in the morning, a dazzling display of darting silver, an undulating platter, a great glittering garment of mail pulled beneath the boat.

Rea had wandered down to where Eros, the young woman, sat. It appeared that they had found a common language. All of a sudden they were animated. Rea gestured, laughed. The other woman, somewhat younger, was quieter, more contained. It sounded to Kenner like Kraut. Eros speaks German, Kenner thought, not pleased with that development. At least Rea would be able to fill him in later, after they were safely ashore. He laughed, thinking that the cliché that had just passed through his mind might be ironic, given what might be waiting for them after they reached the safe shores of Cayo Hueso.

2

There was one beer left in Kristina's refrigerator, and Duane downed that quickly. The movie on the cable was a cut-and-slash flick, but, shrunk down to the size of the television screen, it looked to Duane as if he were only staring into an aquarium of murderous fish.

He decided to take Kristina's two dollars and walk down to the Tom Thumb for a six-pack. He had about ten dollars of his own money left. When he departed Manny's bungalow heading back to his van, Duane had made an expensive detour. He went into the dog track, hoping to double his take. By the eleventh race he had lost nearly eight hundred dollars.

Distracted by his losses, he tried to study the sheet for the last race. He decided to play a dog that looked like a sure winner. He bet fifty dollars on him to win, fifty to place. One race to get it all back. He was left with a couple of twenties and tens. Change.

He stared into space imagining the hundred-dollar bills folded in his pocket as he left Manny's. It took so little to risk it; now it seemed like he had lost so much. He glanced at the tote board and became angry. His dog had become the favorite. Duane's lips compressed, and the corners of his mouth turned down.

Duane's dog led the entire race. But two others had come up along the rail at the finish and passed him. There was a photo for place and show. Duane watched the word blink furiously on the tote board: *photo photo photo*. If his dog held second, he would at least win his bet back, plus a little.

The numbers came up and his dog was third. Duane drew in a quick breath. His dog paid more show money than he would have paid to win. If he had just bet all the money on the dog to show! The parking lot was already noisy with losers like himself: fenders, bumpers, horns, all the clashing swords, looking to joust.

He thought of going into his stash and returning to Manny's, but he decided it would be unwise, especially feeling the way he did.

He ground his teeth heading back to the hotel. He had about forty bucks left. Enough to get back to Key West, but not up to Massachusetts. He would turn something up back on the island. There was a variety of unfinished business. He could still feel the ten hundred-dollar bills, the texture of the crisp paper.

Duane realized he had lost track of the movie on TV. He couldn't tell what was going on. He decided to walk down to the Tom Thumb, but he hesitated at the trailer's door. He wondered why. Then he thought of Kristina's kid. He went to look at him. Duane couldn't remember if he was big enough to walk.

The little room where Kristina and her child stayed was in the front of the trailer. Duane didn't turn on the light; there was enough glow seeping around the edges of the curtains. He looked down into the playpen that was up against the single bed. There wasn't a foot of space left to walk around the room. He could see the child's toes, the soles of his feet. Duane's father once showed him his birth certificate, to prove he wasn't a bastard; he had pointed to the prints of the bottoms of his baby feet: "They'll be getting your fingerprints soon enough." My old man.

Kristina's child's feet were puckered. Duane wasn't sure what he saw looking at the feet that stuck out into a ring of dim light from the room's window, but something made him breathe in, like he did when his dog had come up third, not second.

He walked sideways over to the middle of the playpen and awkwardly stooped over to touch the kid. He wasn't sure what was under his hand, till he felt the child's crinkled neck and the feathery wisps of his damp hair. He had touched dead things before, but, Duane realized, never a dead person.

Duane did one more thing. He called for an ambulance, told them where to look, and left the door of the trailer open. That done, he split. Rea could wait. He had to leave all this behind. He didn't feel cold-blooded, just taken advantage of. Bad news had taken advantage of him.

Back on the highway he realized he did have one other source of barter, in addition to the cocaine. The extra Audubon print, the one he kept for Rea. He would drive right by anyway; he decided to pay MacNaughton a visit. MacNaughton must have some cash, something more legally transmutable into coin of the realm than drugs. He'd sell him the print for whatever he could get.

For a moment he saw himself as a greyhound in a starting box. The rabbit goes by—Winston's bird prints, MacNaughton's cocaine; the exhilaration of pursuit. Then it was over, like now, and he was being put back in a cage, awaiting once more the dark of the box.

The Key West rock station began to fade on the radio before he got to Cudjoe Key. He punched the tabs trying to find some music. All he found were revival programs. JESUS JESUS JESUS.

Duane slowed down just beyond Sugarloaf and turned onto the dirt road. There was something rice paddyish about the road; he had noticed that the first time he had come. They seemed to have been dredged, both the dikes and the roads. He turned left at the dead end. He reached MacNaughton's property; there was a light on in the house. He heard an engine running in the dark carport.

For a moment Duane waited by the gate in his van, expecting car lights to come on, red flares, backup beams, and the car to begin backing out. Nothing moved. Duane shut off his van and walked over to the running car. It was MacNaughton's fancy roadster. So many chrome pipes ran out of the engine that it took him a moment to distinguish that a tube was running into the front seat.

Duane could see a form, a head hovering near the steering wheel. He opened the car's door, feeling this was another thing he should not be reaching for. An acrid odor flowed out. It was MacNaughton. He looked to Duane more bloated than usual. His head was turned, as if someone had twisted it, its side leaning on the top of the steering wheel. He was smiling, grimacing.

Duane slammed the door shut, then the engine coughed, sputtered, and died. It knocked three times, dieseling. Bad gas or it needed tuning.

Duane looked toward the water: the whole area was lit suddenly as clouds passed away from the front of the moon, splashing over the surface of the water. The road had been dark, but now the front of the house was as bright as an illuminated parking lot.

MacNaughton must have come down to gaze at the sea.

Duane walked up the outside stairway of the house. Perhaps if MacNaughton couldn't provide, his house could.

On a table was the largest bottle of Jack Daniel's Duane had even seen. There were a number of copper-colored plastic pill bottles. *That's what he had seen in the corner of the playpen.* He had thought it was a toy.

Duane wondered what he could find to take. He hoped there was some cash somewhere. He started to search but heard a car and froze. Coral crunching under tires: it had turned into the driveway.

A car door slammed; he could make out someone under the house walking in the direction of MacNaughton's car. He then heard: *ayyyy-i-yyyy-i.*

It was Manuel, MacNaughton's boy, who was pulling open the screen door moments later. Duane saw Manuel carried nothing; his hands were empty. It was just family. Duane's apprehension shrank. He was sitting on the couch, draped in shadow.

Manuel said something in Spanish Duane didn't understand. Then he said, "Who's there?"

Duane didn't answer.

"It's you. The man with the bird picture?"

Manuel had recognized his van.

"Yeah, you're right, the bird man," Duane said. He stood up and stepped into a pool of moonlight.

"I got here too late," Manuel said. "Danny had been saying some strange things over the phone. He should have come with me. I shouldn't have left him. Why are you here?" he asked, as if suddenly remembering Duane's presence.

"I had something more to sell him," Duane said.

"A lot of people had that," Manuel said. "What did you want to sell this time?"

"Another bird picture."

"Well, he doesn't want it now," Manuel said. He stared at Duane for a minute. "I got a job for you, though, if you want."

Manuel looked physically different to Duane, now that MacNaughton was dead. Duane wondered why that was.

"How much?" he asked.

"Five hundred dollars," Manuel said. "Danny"—pronouncing the name as if were a question, an exclamation, or exasperation—"was supposed to help."

"You mean MacNaughton was working for you?"

Manuel laughed.

"What? You thought I was his maid? He worked for a lot of people."

"What do you want from me?"

"Just a boat ride. You follow me in your van. We have to clear out anyway. He'll be found sooner or later."

Manuel gestured toward the floor, somewhere below their feet, to the car parked beneath the house. "I shouldn't have left him alone.

"We have to drive over to Sugarloaf, then go out a little ways. We unload a boat. We come back. Five hundred bucks."

Manuel looked less foreign now, less of a grease ball. Did he have the money on him?

"Did you touch anything here?" Manuel asked.

Duane couldn't remember the last few minutes. His mind hadn't seemed to store it.

"Well, it would look worse if things were wiped clean, if there were no prints. They probably won't bother."

Manuel must know the house's inventory, Duane thought, anything that would lead to him.

He followed him down the stairway. Duane tried to walk lightly, not to make tracks. He looked at MacNaughton's car. He could barely make out the shape in the front seat.

Duane saw a dark pickup truck with a shiny roll bar, SO HAUL ASS painted on the driver's door. Hitched behind the pickup was some sort of cigarette boat, but it wasn't glitzy or gaudy. Dark blue with wood trim. The metal exhaust fins were dull black; all the metal on the boat was dull black.

"Follow me," Manuel said. "It's only a couple of miles."

Duane waited for Manuel to pull out; he followed, leaving only MacNaughton's car behind bathed in moonlight.

Manuel stopped after he had gone down the road just far enough for Duane's van to clear the driveway. He went back to shut the wooden gates.

Manuel didn't immediately reappear. But, just at the moment Duane felt itchy enough to go look, he saw him vault to the top of the gate. Manuel jumped down and ran past, into the pickup. It started off. Duane was staring at the blue boat, its name painted in blunt black letters: CARAJO.

Duane was expecting to end up somewhere out of the way, but when Manuel turned off the highway just a few miles from MacNaughton's place he couldn't believe Manuel planned to stop

306

there. It was a public boat launch, below the highway, not in absolutely plain view; but the thought of leaving his van there did not sit well with Duane. What if a cop came by and searched it?

Manuel backed the boat trailer right into the water. Duane then saw why he needed another man along. Launching the black fin was a two-man job. Released from the trailer's restraints, the boat rose in the water; Manuel signaled Duane to pull the pickup forward. Manuel turned on the boat's engine, a powerful burst, brought it quickly down to a low rumble. Duane was going to have to get wet in order to get in. He stood there on the sloping ramp, wondering if this was the time and place to split. He still had no cash.

Manuel waved him aboard. Duane's tennis shoes and pants would dry. Manuel, at the wheel, stood head and chest above the windshield in the wind. He piloted the boat out through a channel. Duane couldn't see what they were headed for, even though the moon, which had so brightly lit the front of MacNaughton's house, also bathed the water here, painted a silver path on it, an arrow tip pointed at the horizon.

Duane finally made out dense mounds in the distance. He looked about and saw the lights on Sugarloaf Key twinkle. After a bit they went out, snuffed by the rising line of water. Duane could see, after a while, that the dark mounds were small clusters of tiny islands. They reached them more quickly than he would have imagined. Manuel cut the motor back, began to idle, churning the water. He told Duane to throw out the anchor, which lay at the back, a dull silver weight in the middle of piled line. He brought it forward, hitched it to a ring, and, standing on the dark prow, let it drop. The splash and the uncoiling stopped. Manuel put the boat in reverse and it moved back slowly. The line tugged. Manuel shut off the motor.

"They'll be here in the morning. I'll wake you," Manuel said.

Duane wondered if he should try to sleep, or if Manuel would then make his unconsciousness last forever. Whatever they were going to pick up couldn't be too large. This boat was built for speed, not freight. A cigarette boat. Cigarettes. Duane found it hard to believe that cigarettes once had to be smuggled.

The boat's motion was lulling. He stared at the changing surface of the water, black and slick, some creature itself. What was he looking at? Duane thought of holding Rea under the water.

He wasn't sure why he stopped. When he pushed her under, it was like other fights: he'd go from here to there with no thought, just movement. But this time he heard himself say, "Let her go," as if one side of him was talking to the other, "Let her go now." And he did.

He had heard of people drowning when they tried to save someone. There was something intricate about that that even Rea might like: she was to drown because she had tried to save him. Well, she finally knows I don't want to be saved. He continued to stare into the black water. He saw strands of Eli's hair floating up toward him and he jumped. Some fish, seaweed. He had started to fall asleep, he realized. He looked up. Manuel was staring at him.

"How about giving me my money now?" Duane asked.

"When we get back. We'll be back before the sun is over the horizon."

Duane needed to hold off his exhaustion with talk. "How long did you know MacNaughton?" he asked.

Manuel stared at Duane for a moment, considering something. Then he said, "Some time. He visited Cuba in the sixties, came with a cultural exchange. We met then. I was a guide, on the streets, a kid. When I came over I gave his name to immigration."

"You mean in this boatlift thing?"

"That's right. They didn't make it easy. I told them I was queer. It wasn't pretty. They wanted to know how queer I was. Did I take it up the ass, or did I stick it? Those machos aren't bothered if you're doing the fucking, only if you're the one getting fucked. You needed to play pansy in order to get through."

Duane remembered: "What's *la cobra*?"

"*¿La cobra?*" Manuel said, a surprised but satisfied smile softening his face.

"MacNaughton said it."

"*¡La cobra!*" Manuel said, suddenly thrusting his arm stiff outstretched in front of him, his fingers knotted into a fist. "This!"

Duane couldn't figure Manuel. "MacNaughton put you on to all this?" Duane indicated the boat.

"No. I put him on to this."

"Why did he knock himself off?"

"What makes you think he killed himself?" Manuel said; then he laughed and shrugged, the peaks of his shoulders rising and falling. Some sort of universal gesture. Manuel's hand went back and forth in the air, as if he were turning a page, one at a time.

"He talked about it all the time. He got pretty crazy. He tried to kill himself a few weeks ago. Took pills, but had his stomach pumped. He said suicide required practice. Run-throughs, was his phrase. He said it was like the Kennedy assassination. He was certain we had killed Kennedy."

" 'We'?"

"Ah, the Cubans. He said the reason no one believed we did it was that it was too lucky, too good a job. But that it was less lucky, less good a job, if you realized that it wasn't the first attempt. He figured out we had tried at least three times before. So, what looked like a wild fluke was really the first success after four tries." Manuel laughed. "I told him it was a good theory, but that it wasn't correct.

"We didn't do it," Manuel said. "You did it."

Duane was feeling queasy. He didn't have much in his stomach, other than the beer he had had at Kristina's. Manuel's voice made him feel bad. Everything made him feel bad. And a new notion began to form, take shape in his mind, just the way the water's ebony surface seemed to take shape and then change. Perish together. The price of Rea's salvation.

"MacNaughton liked to guess. Killing himself was some sort of guess." Manuel paused and looked straight at Duane. "I wonder if he made the right guess?"

3

It was near dawn and Kenner could not return to sleep. Rea seemed to be asleep; she was such a light sleeper it was difficult to tell. She seemed to spring quickly to consciousness. Kenner heard birds, which surprised him, and some wave action that didn't seem connected with the boat. He came out onto the deck and saw that they were between two scruffy land masses, uninhabited apparently. There was a small beach on one. That was the sound of surf he had heard. There were birds, though Kenner didn't know what he was hearing. It wasn't the heron he saw, or the pelicans.

He climbed the ladder to the top of the cabin. O'Bannion was in profile to him, lifting something out of a storage bin beneath bench cushions. It was a weapon, but Kenner had never seen one like it.

"My God," Kenner said, "what is that?"

O'Bannion started, let the bench top drop with a thwack. He smiled when he saw Kenner.

"Deterrence," the captain said, "our deterrence system." He pointed the weapon in Kenner's direction. Kenner saw the ends of rounded projectiles, about the diameter of golf balls.

"An automatic grenade launcher," O'Bannion said. "This is really a prototype. They're not in production yet."

Seeing it clearly, Kenner thought it resembled an old Thompson machine gun, the gangster's favorite model, something Edward G. Robinson would use. But stumpier, squat, and swollen.

"Aren't we meeting friendlies?" Kenner asked.

"Yes," O'Bannion said. "Friendlies. But who knows? Friends betray us, too."

Trust your enemies, Kenner thought. They don't let you down.

"This isn't for killing people," the captain was saying. "It's a property weapon. You sink their boat. They go with it, of course. An accidental side effect."

The inconveniences of the trip now felt more inconvenient, right before they were to be eliminated. Kenner had not shaved for a week, but still did not sport much of a beard. He felt coated over with a glaze of suntan lotion, salt spray, sweat. He began to look forward to simple things: taking a shower, finding what mail had accumulated for him, reading the papers, lying in the condo's air conditioning with Rea, learning what the world had discovered about the Audubon theft.

Rea had told him the few facts she acquired from Eros. Rea wasn't sure what nationality Eros was: she guessed Dutch. She had spoken fondly of Cuba, of Castro, whom she seemed to know. Eros had laughed about the excesses of the boatlift. Her story didn't jibe with the captain's script, at all; Eros had not felt the need to put on any show about her feelings. At least, not when she spoke German. It was a language only she and Rea seemed to share.

Whatever secrets O'Bannion had in common with the new passengers, Kenner felt little curiosity about them. Or he felt that once back to land, to his country-tis-of-thee, he could sort all that out in good time.

They all heard the approaching motor at the same time; everyone peered in the sound's direction. O'Bannion went up the ladder, Kenner supposed, to be near his grenade launcher;

he held binoculars to his eyes. Kenner could see a boat heading toward them. He presumed O'Bannion could make out who it was.

"It's all right," O'Bannion yelled down to the poached-eye man.

Thanatos and the blonde began to unstow the gunnysack-covered cargo. Rea and Kenner had already brought their gear together, what little there was. O'Bannion had told them they would be landing in about a hour.

The motorboat made an arc in their direction, showing itself off. A dark shade of blue, lacquered hardwood. A rooster's tail of spray fanned out from its stern. Light played through the foam, spangling it with bright colors, a peacock's feathery display.

A dark fellow at the wheel began to wave, though not at Kenner, but Kenner felt his arm begin to lift, to wave in return. Kenner realized that his body had recognized the boat's driver before he did. Then, with a doubling shock, he felt another realization fling itself forward, so solidly he felt himself lurch toward the sight. The other man, at the back of the speedboat, was also known to him.

He felt his bicep being squeezed and he knew it was Rea. She had recognized the man in the back of the boat.

Eros had put out rubber bumpers along *La Compañia*'s port side. The speedboat had similar ingot-shaped cushions, colored the same dark indigo of its hull. Two of them were deployed on its starboard side. Thanatos stood ready to catch a forward line, and Eros had retreated to the stern to throw one to the speedboat.

There were some rapid exchanges in Spanish. Both Rea and Kenner stayed where they were. Duane hadn't seemed to notice them. He was throwing the line to the poached-eye man, then inexpertly trying to tie off his end of the rope on a cleat. O'Bannion and the poached-eye man were dragging the cargo to the side of the *La Compañia*, preparing to lift it up and into the hands of the men in the boat. Manuel and Duane both raised their arms for the transfer, waving their hands like enthusiasts at a revival, as the speedboat rose and fell in the water. They were trying to plant their feet firmly to take the imminent weight. O'Bannion and the poached-eye man tilted the case over and, as it touched the outstretched hands in the speedboat, Duane's glance turned to the side. He stared upward and saw.

Duane's arms collapsed, and the burden they were helping

to hold fell. He sprang backward. Manuel tried to break the container's fall, but it landed with a thud on the fiberglass cowling and tumbled toward the water. The two boats were lashed too closely together for it to slip between, into the water. Duane's jumping and the falling cargo made the speedboat and *La Compañiá* jerk up and down. Manuel reached for the container, pulling it back from the boat's rim. Kenner heard the taut burlap rip when Manuel seized it. As Manuel pulled it into the well of the speedboat, Kenner saw on its uncovered aluminum side a strange thing: the three-pronged symbol of radioactivity, the shape of a fat propeller, mustard yellow and black, a radiating scream. The civil defense sign marking underground shelters he had seen so often in the fifties. Below it, print that was just a blur. Kenner thought he made out three large black letters. ADM.

Kenner didn't see Duane climb on board *La Compañia*, his attention fixed as it was on the case that Manuel was now stowing. But he heard Duane's voice yell, "Rea!" and then something Kenner couldn't make out: *I've got something for you?*

Kenner turned his head and saw a gun. Thanatos was pointing it toward Duane.

"Hey," Kenner heard himself crying out. He had, in his imaginative life, wondered what he would do if someone pointed a gun at him. Though it would have mattered who was pointing the gun, Kenner had thought the only action to take, if the gun was pointed by a total stranger, was immediately to try to seize the weapon. He knew law enforcement would find that tactic the most foolish. But Kenner felt the longer you let somebody point a gun at you the greater the likelihood that the person would fire it.

"¿Este tio quién es?" O'Bannion yelled.

Kenner didn't know what was in Duane's mind, but it seemed to be something along the same lines. His left arm shot out to grab the wrist of the poached-eye man. Kenner saw his and Duane's error when the gun went off. Duane's head snapped back and his eyes rolled up. His lunge for the man turned into a pirouette, and he fell backward over the side of the boat, just ahead of where the speedboat was lashed to *La Compañia*'s side, and splashed into the sea.

The shot had stilled all motion on the boat; but after Duane's splash subsided, everyone moved again. Rea stepped to the rail and dove into the water.

"¿Este tio quién es?" O'Bannion repeated angrily.

"*No se quién es. No es mas que un sinvergüenza, nadie,*" Manuel said, "*Es un chulo, es un Don Nadie.*"

"*¡Caramba!*" O'Bannion said. He turned to Kenner and said more slowly in English, "You tell me what that was all about."

Kenner didn't know if he should fall back on the truth. But he did. "He's a friend of Rea's. He was looking for her." The explanation sounded stupid to him, since the evidence of Rea diving in after Duane should have made a connection obvious.

"Why did you shoot him?" Kenner asked the poached-eye man. Thanatos made some dismissive sound and turned away. He spoke to O'Bannion, "*¿Que le vamos a hacer?*"

He replied "*¡Nada de nada!*" and looked toward Manuel. "Let's go, let's finish."

Eros climbed into the speedboat. Manuel put his ear to the side of the aluminum case. Kenner saw Rea splash up through the water's surface ten yards from the boat. He put his glasses in his pocket and jumped in.

He saw immediately what Rea's difficulty had been. The water was clear, but you could only see a foot or two in front of you. The speedboat's engine had stirred up coral dust, and there was a fast current. The water was full of clouds of grit. It was difficult to stay under without weights and fins. Kenner had gone about twenty feet when he dimly made out that the pale bottom began to recede. The water began to turn a cobalt color. He went a few more yards and what he saw froze him.

There was no bottom. It must go down a hundred feet or more, he thought. A drop-off. Kenner immediately pierced the water's surface and tried to see where he was, where Rea was, where the *La Compañía* was.

He felt the current taking him out toward the fall off. He splashed back toward the boat, back to where the bottom became visible beneath him. He reached *La Compañía*'s anchor chain, gasping. He yelled, "REA!"

Eros appeared over the bow. "She's around the side."

Kenner pushed off the taut anchor chain. Rea was being hauled by Thanatos into the speedboat. The captain was lowering equipment to Manuel.

The poached-eye man helped Kenner climb into the speedboat. It started abruptly. As soon as O'Bannion made his way down into the boat, the blonde swung it away from the *La Compañía*. Kenner realized: Eros had spoken English moments before.

"This is fine," O'Bannion said, when they had gone about fifty yards from *La Compañía*.

And much to Kenner's amazement, the captain braced himself, pointed his automatic grenade launcher at the empty, lolling boat, and pulled the trigger. O'Bannion didn't fall down, though he did have to regain his balance.

Heat and a great booming sound, the explosion, bounded over the water to them. Curling, overlapping, artichokes of flame billowed up, became a cloud.

The captain had hit the boat right above the waterline. *La Compañía* began to sink as the fire consumed it. O'Bannion sat down, and the speedboat suddenly lifted its nose out of the water. For a second Kenner thought it was going to shoot right up into the air, take off, and fly. God, we're going fast, he thought. He could see the white line of a Key on the horizon. He looked at Rea, still dripping and catching her breath, appearing stunned. On her face was a most unaccustomed look, one that Kenner had never seen, a vacant expression. She looked unintelligent.

Twenty-seven

1

When the Audubon file was dropped on his desk, Jerry Lynch
quickly saw its difficulties. Criminal investigations conducted on
that island were something of a joke among federal law enforcement personnel. The public laughed, too. The Key West Police
Department's track record of prosecuting drug cases was an embarrassment. City officials and attorneys were routinely switching
sides, indicting and being indicted, defending and needing to be
defended. Lynch was aware it was difficult to tell the cops from
the robbers in a great many jurisdictions, but Key West was a
particular offender. Outside investigators had been sent down
there more times than Lynch wanted to count, with the same old
laundry list: gambling, narcotics, case-fixing.

The Audubon affair was both simple and complex. Simple,
because it was served up on a silver platter. Had it not been a
federal case from the start, if the agents hadn't been at the New
Jersey state police headquarters when the goat had been brought
in, who knew where it would stand today? Seat of Government
wanted to keep this prosecution, so it needed a federal charge:
interstate transportation, conspiracy. The bureau had received

some positive publicity when they recovered the goods. But now they needed convictions. A simply burglary treated like complicated corporate chicanery! Which was the reason they gave the file to someone just transferred from organized crime. There would still be publicity, and the case needed to be handled in the least circuslike fashion possible.

Their goat, the Reliable Informant, had turned quickly enough. He now wanted written reassurances. He had taken to letter-writing. The deal Jerry had struck with him was one of a kind: try him immediately in New Jersey on a lesser charge. A guilty plea. Sentence would be suspended, but only after his testimony in the coming trial. He would be placed in the witness protection plan. Young Curt Wren had been unhappy with the sentencing delay. He wanted to have the suspended sentence pronounced before he was to testify. It would not look good at the other trial, Jerry tried to make clear to him. Curt was writing letters, full of strange stories, other tales of crime he had been privy to, and might, for a price, reveal.

It dismayed Lynch, once again, to see some nonentity like Wren amass such a history, such a file, be on so many people's records. He thought perhaps it would make these nobodies feel less alienated if they could see how many organizations were keeping track of them.

Curt was a costly law-enforcement tool. He was going to receive over a hundred thousand before the trials were over. Jerry grinned: this was kidnapping. The taxpayers were going to ransom back the Audubon prints, pay the same, more, than the perpetrators hoped to see.

No local or state charges were to be filed. According to the 302s, there would be a fistful of possibilities. No breaking and entering, no possession warrants, just interstate and conspiracy.

Some guilty parties were to be left out on the periphery, the gray zone of not-much-of-a-case—at least when conspiracy and interstate transportation were the charges. Jurisdiction problems had been handled quickly; there were no petite-abate difficulties.

With a conspiracy charge, juries would only convict if you could show people corn-holing the goods. They would only be able to get those who orbited closest to the crime: Mercury, Earth, Venus. He didn't think he would even be able to get Mars. They had Curt Wren. That got them Delmer Grebe and Jay Winston Cross, the ringleader. He was the instigator. Put him away and you limit the crime statistics. These other guys needed a boss.

They might get Vernon Crane. Some solid leads there were being followed up. And the man at large. Lynch thought he could rough up the others by indicting them; he might have to do that. To prompt testimony, to acquire information. Then he would drop the charges, amend the indictment.

The one big hole they had to fill, the one thing Lynch was still not certain how to deal with—to keep from the public, the press—was the possibility that the books were no longer intact. No one yet knew. It had been widely reported the books were back. The largest publicity wave had already hit. The bureau looked good. Seat of Government was happy. But, with the trial ahead, they didn't want another round of attention, especially the information that what was recovered wasn't all there was to be recovered. Even the insurance company involved didn't want it out.

No longer intact. Two prints missing. What struck Jerry as curious was that neither Curt nor Winston Cross knew. And since neither of them knew, or had been told, and the backward Delmer seemed to know, as he kept saying, "nuttin' about nuttin'," then the boy at large, Duane Rooks, was the missing piece.

Lynch wondered if one way to turn that key would be to tell a bit of the truth to Winston, to the fellow who thought he had all the answers, who thought he was running the show?

2

Bridget had had so much to think about in the last few hours she found herself not thinking at all. She went from task to task, job to job. She never thought of her feet, never thought she was touching ground. Everything important seemed up in the air, away from the earth. It was as if she were following something above her, caught in a current. It carried her along.

She found herself thinking of Ray Pine, Kristina's father. She kept remembering the look of him on the television set, holding the dead python, trying to make it look alive.

The blows had fallen, one two. Winston in jail; then Kristina's boy in the hospital. First the lightning, then the thunderclap, she thought. Eli was brain dead—that was what the doctors had said; they had hooked the baby up to machines and bottles. The doctors wanted Kristina to donate Eli's organs. They wanted to *harvest* them, she heard a nurse say. Eyes, kidneys, liver—even the tiny heart. Kristina had to decide. The hospital wanted to contact Eli's father, but Kristina refused, wouldn't give them any information. She had been staying by Eli's bed, talking to the baby, holding his hand.

Bridget had heard about Winston's arrest on the radio. And Curt's and Delmer's. "Other arrests are to follow" was the news that really made her sick.

But there hadn't been any more. The FBI had already gone through the condo; but no one had spoken to her. Bridget didn't know why. Somehow it seemed worse that they hadn't. Why hadn't the cops driven by the Audubon House after she warned them that morning? Winston would have called it off then.

She had phoned the shop to tell Candi she couldn't come in. She had heard curiosity in Candi's voice. *Did you hear about . . .* Bridget felt like telling Candi what she knew, but she didn't. She wanted to tell someone. Winston had been trying to arrange bail. He had a New York City attorney. Mr. Topaz. When she talked to Winston, he was sure he'd be out soon. He said he didn't know where Curt was. Delmer had been locked up in Georgia. Possession of stolen goods. The FBI had found some of Vern's stuff in the condo and was looking for him. Winston was caught in New York last week, but was sent straight back to Florida; he didn't know what he was going to be charged with: something about crossing state lines. It sounded like the Mann Act to Bridget, which was one law she knew about.

Visiting Winston scared her; she didn't know what to wear. She wanted to look good, though not too flashy, but all she needed to do was appear at the Federal Building's door and once she asked, it was all done for her, like a funhouse. She stepped on a conveyor belt and didn't have to know anything. She asked to see Winston, and they kept telling her where to go and what to do, and finally there was Winston. He was mad as hell. After his transfer from New York back to Florida, he had found out a few things about Curt.

If it hadn't been for Curt, they never would have known anything. Winston looked around the visiting room suspiciously. He said they were probably taping everything. As she was leaving, he asked her if she was watering the plants. He didn't want his cane plant to die. Bridget looked at him oddly, for Winston never watered any plants, nor took any interest in them whatsoever. Either she or Kristina watered them, or that girl Rea. But, even in Bridget's distressed state, she realized that Winston wanted her to get something, something he had left in the cane plant near the balcony doors.

Bridget got back to the Cayo Hueso condos late. Everything looked like a picture, stopped in time. She parked where she always parked, but it felt like she no longer belonged. The condo's manager let her in; he was angry at the FBI for leaving the place such a mess. It was easy to see the condo had been searched. There was powder on the glass tabletops. She could make out outlines of hands and fingerprints. Drawers were sticking out, clothes hanging from them. Couch cushions were on the floor. They must have taken some things away.

None of the plants appeared disturbed. Bridget went to the cane plant. It was nearly seven feet high.

Winston had once said he was going to make her eat some of the plant's leaves: they would supposedly make you lose your voice. Dumb. That's what its name was: dumb cane. A big-leafed green plant that looked like someone had splattered white paint all over it. There was a little stick in the soil that had the name of the plant printed on it. Would Winston have marked the spot so easily? Bridget thought of going to the kitchen to get a spoon, but since she was standing right in front of it, she decided just to dig in. She felt the dirt wedge under her long fingernails and then one cracked against a small stone. About six inches beneath the top she felt something other than soil, small bits of rock, roots. It was cylindrical, the size of a walnut. It was a film canister. Inside was a small bag of white powder, the last of Winston's chicken soup, and a folded-up sheet of notepaper with names and addresses and phone numbers written on it. A warehouse in Boston. There was also what looked like a little map, with directions.

Now she had what Winston must have wanted. He would tell her later what she should do with it. Would they have thought of digging up the plants eventually?

Now Bridget had to go to the hospital to find out what Kristina had decided to do about poor little Eli.

3

Kristina knew some of the tests for brain death from working at hospitals. A number of them sounded like tortures: no reaction to ice cold water when it was squirted into the ear canal with a small pink rubber syringe. Eyeballs locked in a frozen position.

So much seemed to be mixed with cold, with ice, with all things frozen.

It wasn't the half-pill she had mixed with his Tang that had done this, they assured her. She must not have put the cap back on securely when Duane knocked and startled her. The container was found empty in the playpen. Eli, she was told, must have swallowed around twenty Valiums. Kristina remembered the bottle being about a third full.

His breathing had stopped. The ambulance attendants had restarted it, but the brain had died. They said it must have been at least a half hour without oxygen. Duane must have called the ambulance. No one was there when it arrived. The trailer's door was open and the lights were on. The air conditioner was running on high, a torrent pouring from it. If Duane had only seen him sooner! Of if she hadn't been fooling with the pills at all.

The doctor said she could, might, be charged with child abuse or negligent homicide. She didn't tell anyone about Duane. But she probably wouldn't be prosecuted, especially if they could harvest the organs. The hospital wanted to locate Eli's father, but Kristina told the woman that Johnny had disappeared after the divorce and hadn't been paying any support.

There was a baby who needed a liver, and Eli's was a good match. Kristina was in shock, and they had given her something for it. They wanted her to sign forms. She said she needed to think about it. They might be able to use his heart and kidneys, too, but they weren't sure. She said she wanted to wait till her mother got to the hospital. They were ready to fly the organs by helicopter to a waiting jet in Atlanta. They wanted to do it now and the funeral would be tomorrow. All over in less than twenty-four hours.

While waiting for Bridget, Kristina began to imagine donating Eli's organs. She found herself beginning to favor the idea. She saw it as a lovely explosion. Eli flying apart in slow motion, pieces of him coming to rest in other little girls and boys, seeds that would sprout all over the country. Eli would grow larger in them. His eyes would grow; his liver, kidneys, his heart even—they would all continue to grow. The notion, the picture, became a reverie in Kristina's mind: Eli expanding in children, playing, sleeping, going to school.

Think of all he would be accomplishing, how many different lives he would have! She was ready to sign, but she still wanted to talk to Bridget about it, tell her what she was going to do, how Eli was to multiply. And she thought of telling her what she wasn't going to do. She hadn't had her period during the ride up the Keys. The bleeding had stopped the next day. At first she had thought: *That's the shortest period I've ever had.* Then she realized what it was. That's why she felt like she did. It must have been breakthrough bleeding. When she realized she was pregnant, she was going to have an abortion. But now she wouldn't. She wasn't sure who the father was. Curt, Duane, Winston. The two events began to blend in her mind. The idea of her brain-dead child becoming three different children, in three different parts of the country, three different kinds of laughter constituting the sound of Eli's soul. And the idea that the new child in her body had three possible fathers. Maybe even all three—though she did know that couldn't be. But now she thought the strangest things were possible, even likely.

Sitting in the chilly air-conditioned corridor of the hospital, listening to the bells and chimes from the elevators and the nurses' station down the hall, Kristina began to choose parts of Duane, Curt, and Winston she would like the child to have: whose eyes, whose height, whose manner of walking. And these images blurred with the different children she now pictured as her other children. These filled her mind peacefully, kept her happy and quiet. And when Bridget finally came through the glass doors of the hospital and saw her daughter sitting on the bench, waiting, Kristina looked to be entirely serene.

4

Sitting in a cell, back against the bars, Winston was full of indignation. At Curt. At Duane. At his shyster lawyer, Topaz. Winston knew it had been a mistake not to fight extradition. Conspiracy! His portrayal as the brains behind the burglary was something Winston found hard to disown, but he knew he must. He needed to shift the emphasis, put himself out on the edge. Find another bad guy. That would be Curt, he considered, since Curt now had the most to gain. Winston found himself galvanized, full of plans.

Topaz had cut deeply into his resources. A ten-thousand-dollar retainer. He had to contact his mother. She had read about him in the papers, so she expected the call. Her husband told her to leave him in jail.

Neither Bridget nor Kristina had been picked up. They found Vern watching TV at his sister's home in Dorchester; his last parole officer had that address for him. There appeared to be no interest in Rea or her whereabouts. Duane was a fugitive.

Duane could be his devil, if he played it right. He looks more the bad guy than I do, Winston thought. Rea, he remembered, once said I looked like a British peer. Any jury would believe it. Just one look.

Winston had been left mulling over a disturbing exchange he had had with Topaz.

"You know the set of prints is not intact."

Immediately Winston thought that all along the set hadn't been complete. That the Audubon House had been playing everyone for fools.

"No," Topaz had said, "they have bona fides to prove it was all there. Now the books are missing two prints."

Winston said he knew nothing about it. Topaz said it was in everyone's interest to keep it quiet, for a variety of reasons. Topaz said it had been noticed accidentally. The books had been stacked on top of one another, and a man from the FBI's lab who was interested in binding came to look at them. He noticed that the watermarks were uneven.

"You know," Topaz had said, "the edges of the books have markings on them. When they're shut they make a pattern."

Winston recalled them: water over reefs: brown, purple, blue.

"They're there," Topaz said, "so you can tell instantly whether any page is missing or has been torn out. If that guy hadn't come down to look, I don't know if they would have discovered it."

Who did it? "I don't know," Winston had told him, wanting to think about it before he told Topaz his opinion.

Duane. It explained a number of things. His disappearance. Did Rea know? Bridget said she had delivered a note from Rea to Kenner, and she thought Rea had gone off with him, to parts unknown.

It had to be Duane . . . and now, on top of everything else, he had to find Duane. Who had ripped him off, made him a patsy, and was still outside. Curt couldn't have told them much about Duane; he didn't know much. Perhaps this was the way to deal himself out of this. Let him stand pat on Duane's missing pages.

Twenty-eight

The county would pay for the funeral. Kristina had to fill out forms, but, she was assured, the money would be available. There would be a viewing—that's what they called it, but Eli's coffin would be closed—at Lopez's funeral parlor on Simonton Street. In the vestibule, there was a book for visitors to sign. When Kristina collected it before the ride to the cemetery, there were only four signatures: hers, Bridget's, Winston's, and Candi's, the woman who managed the shop where her mother worked.

Kristina had brought a portable record player with her, and she played a Cat Stevens album, softly, during the hour they had coming to them. "Morning has broken . . ."

Kristina felt she was underwater. The viewing-room walls were blue plastic impressed with a scallop-shell pattern. There were small spotlights at the bottom, making arrowheads, trellises, of light. The large room was full of pews, empty pews. The casket was small, so small they had set it on a pedestal. Kristina, at first, worried about the pedestal tipping over. The casket seemed only to be balanced there.

Bridget and her boss cried, but Kristina didn't. Winston, since he just had been let out of jail, couldn't sit still. He got up, sat down, walked up the aisle to the vestibule to smoke cigarettes, came back in. She thought he was always in motion. The vestibule had half-glass walls, covered with curtains that were drawn back. Kristina watched Winston out there puffing on a cigarette.

Kristina sat on the pew and kept blinking her eyes. It was all blue and blurry around her, just as if she had opened her eyes underwater in a swimming pool.

The casket was white streaked with gold. She wasn't sure they called it a casket, since it was square and held Eli's ashes, not his body. She hadn't seen his body after they removed the organs they wanted. It had all happened one-two-three.

"He was my gift and now he is a gift to others," she told the doctor.

Kristina felt touched by Eli's spirit. She intended to honor it. She had never before known what it was like to feel religious, but she was sure that was the name of what she felt now. She hadn't told anyone of her new pregnancy, not even Bridget. She would, when she made up her mind who the father was. They could do tests, she knew, and find out. Curt, Duane, or Winston.

The casket that contained the ashes was plastic, made to look like marble, white with swirls of gold. It looked like a magic sky to Kristina. It would be put in a niche, one of the cupboards of a small mausoleum at the cemetery.

The hour was nearly up. From the side wall—there was no doorknob on it, but you could tell it was a door—a man stepped out and Kristina knew it was time to go. Winston would drive them in her mother's Toyota. The three women walked up the aisle, after Kristina touched the small casket, surprised at the warmth of the plastic. It was not a veneer, she had been told, but solid, nearly an inch thick, poured, like hot honey, into a mold.

The cemetery was ablaze with flowers. Kristina was surprised by the variety. Maybe she had just never noticed all the bouquets and wreathes and flowers when she passed it before. Bridget said, "No, sweetie, it was because of Memorial Day. You remember?" The cemetery bloomed on Memorial Day, a kind of brilliant moth that lives for a week or so. Most of the fresh color would soon be gone: some of it would fade, some of it would be stolen. Then the graveyard would be normal again.

Winston followed the undertakers' station wagon. As they entered the cemetery's drive, it stopped and a man came back to their car and asked them to stay at the entrance until signaled forward. Kristina thought they didn't want her to see them take Eli's casket out of the station wagon. One man could pick it up easily enough.

Winston was waved on in.

Kristina began to feel faint from the heat, from the tranquilizers she had been taking. When she walked, everything seemed to ripple away from her. She heard a buzzing and thought she was beginning to pass out. The buzzing increased and Kristina saw it wasn't in her mind. It was bees. The cemetery was full of bees.

The funeral home had arranged for a minister to speak at the cemetery. He would have spoken at the parlor for another fifty dollars, but the county wouldn't pay for it. Kristina didn't want to have anyone talk, but Bridget persuaded her.

When the minister began to talk, standing on a patch of bare, polished ground in front of the mausoleum, it surprised Kristina to hear a completely strange voice describe Eli. He said Eli was a holy innocent who now lived with the angels. Eli had flown up to heaven. Was one of the chosen. Both Bridget and Candi were crying again. The minister had an edge to his voice, as if he were skirting something, going around a fact that sat in the middle of his mind. Kristina wondered if he had been told everything there was to tell and was making some effort not to mention it. Something was pushing on him, forcing its way to the surface. He did sound as if he were trying to swallow something.

Kristina heard him say: "And all deaths are in some way accidental, insofar as our lives are themselves accidental, and, so, therefore, are our deaths, which are but a continuation of the blessed accident of life." She wondered: what could he mean? She heard the buzzing again; the bees were back, a small cloud of them, swerving through the air like static made visible.

What Kristina stood before looked like the mailbox array at the condo, but larger. It was three—stories didn't sound right to Kristina—it was three levels high, just like the condo. Each square was the same size. Eli's box would have a lot of empty space around it. She again felt faint, though they were all standing in a bar of shade made by the mausoleum itself. She looked skyward: utterly blue, bluer than the walls of the funeral parlor, bright blue threaded with strands of clouds, wispy like the gold that traced through the plastic marble. She saw the tops of two royal palm trees, far apart, like lighthouses, like beacons.

The minister coughed loudly. Kristina felt someone clasp her elbow, and they all turned to walk back to the Toyota.

Two men stood near it. Both wore dark suits, both had on sunglasses. Instead of going to Perkins Pancake House as they had planned, Kristina and Bridget were handcuffed and put in the backseat of an unmarked car. They were arrested for conspiracy to transport stolen property across state boundaries. "You have the right to remain silent . . ."

Candi began to complain loudly: Kristina could hear her, far off, as if Candi were talking underwater, big bubbles coming from her mouth, saying *How terrible how could they do this to them now.*

2

Kenner and Rea stood to the side, near Duane's van, while the unloading took place. The pickup that towed the trailer held everything that came off the *La Compañía*.

"I'd advise you both to hitchhike into town. The," and O'Bannion paused, rolled his cigar back and forth along his lips, "the . . . authorities . . . will find the van here. This place," and he gestured toward the open water, "will provide an explanation for almost anything. *Adiós, muchachos.*"

Eros said something to Rea in German, and Rea only nodded in response. Bereft of language, Rea seemed another creature entirely to Kenner. It didn't seem to him that she was in shock—just that there wasn't anything to be said.

The poached-eye man, the blonde, and O'Bannion got into the pickup's cab; Manuel climbed into the back with the cargo. When it turned onto the highway, Kenner saw print on the driver's door. SO HAUL ASS. The pickup disappeared from sight, and the trailer behind it carrying the sleek boat then leveled off at the road's surface, and it, too, disappeared, heading north.

He turned around and saw Rea rummaging in her nylon bag. She brought out a blue rabbit's foot from which dangled a single key and walked to the door of the van. The key to Duane's van. Kenner threw in their stuff, and Rea started the engine and drove off toward Key West.

The sun was above the horizon, and the day was already covered by a blue-white crust of heat. Kenner kept trying not to feel good, but it was impossible. He was back on land, in one piece, heading toward the familiar. And Duane was gone. All Kenner's feelings of well-being troubled him.

The vacancy in Rea's expression began to fill in. It was darkening as the day brightened. Kenner knew, in the way anybody knows such things, that anything he said now would be inappropriate. But he couldn't just let the silence stand. He was hoping she would be the one to end it, to break it, furnish it with words.

Kenner looked around at the interior of the van. The floor behind the seats was covered with a sheet of plywood. Sleeping bags, what looked to Kenner like an old Boy Scout camping trunk. Between the seats was a cardboard tube. He picked it up, saw it had a mailing label, and put it between him and the door.

He didn't recognize the address on the label, but it was Rea's name. Kenner kept replaying the last few minutes on the boat. No body. Other than their testimony, Kenner realized, there would be no proof that Duane was dead, unless his body washed up. Kenner pictured the drop-off and the current. Duane's bones would be scattered through the Gulf Stream, brittle and white as coral. Cayo Hueso.

Maybe he hadn't been killed; maybe he swam under the boat, out of sight, made his way to the little scrubby island? Kenner felt queasy briefly, as he always did when he indulged in a fantasy, a distortion of what he knew was real.

He had seen what Rea had seen. She might have wished him that fate, and now that such a black wish had come true, she was absorbing the consequences. And they seemed to be putting Kenner somewhere out of reach. There really was a man between them now, Kenner saw. Duane had interposed his dead self.

"It's addressed to you," Kenner said, lifting the tube a bit.

Rea didn't answer, but began to chew her lower lip. Kenner knew she was someplace he wasn't yet allowed to enter.

"Drop me at my car," he said. "I'll meet you back at the condo."

Rea nodded, which Kenner took as a hopeful sign. He put the condo key on a flat portion of the van's dashboard.

The Sport Fury was where they had left it. Kenner jumped out of the van, his hand still grasping the cardboard tube.

"I'll get some food. See you back at the condo. I'm terribly sorry, you know."

"I know," Rea said. "I know."

Kenner felt odd watching Rea drive off. Behind the van's steering wheel, her profile was an outline of severe concentration. She didn't look back: a small woman with thick hair. She looked to Kenner disturbingly like a stranger, like any person driving.

He opened the Sport Fury's door, found the window's handle that had fallen off and cranked it down. The hot stale air smelled of his past, of the things he had left behind. Before the trip to . . . Mariel? He realized he didn't know where they had gone.

Kenner put the tube in the backseat. He prevented himself from naming what he thought might be in the tube. He drove by the post office and decided to stop and pick up his mail. And, he thought, he would do what it seemed Duane had intended to do. He would mail the tube.

3

Bridget couldn't believe that the young man sitting in front of her was a lawyer, even though he certainly seemed to know some of the lingo.

"There's a bit of a shortage of court-appointable attorneys down here right now, with all the Cuban business. It is a little irregular to appoint the same attorney for both you and your daughter. It could be a conflict of interest, and, if you both don't want it, they will appoint another one for you, Mrs., ah," and he glanced down at his long yellow pad, "Pine."

Bridget continued to stare at him. He looked no more than twenty and was wearing what seemed to her an outlandish outfit. A too-large chartreuse-yellow sportcoat, something a singer in a band might wear, which had imprinted in the fabric some sort of seashell pattern. He wore a lavender-colored shirt with a floppy collar and a pink tie, which was stained in three different places. His pants were bell-bottomed, black and white houndstooth check. Bridget thought he looked like a clown. They had sent a clown to defend her, to get her out of jail.

"We're going to try to get you out on your own recognizance, since you have a job, ties to the community. Your employer will vouch for you. A Miss Candi Swift. It should only take another day or so. It would hold things up if you didn't agree to have me represent you. Though that is your right. Kristina will be a bit more of a problem, but that depends on what judge hears this. We should be able to get her released without bail, too. The charge is pretty thin. I think they just want you to cooperate with the prosecution, which, again, is your right. They might even drop the charges then. I wouldn't promise anything, but I wouldn't slam any doors this soon, either. Do you understand?"

Bridget realized she must be looking at him strangely.

"Where did you go to school?" she asked.

"Why, in New Jersey," he said, somewhat taken aback. "I moved to Florida a few years ago." He didn't look at all embarrassed to Bridget.

"We just have to file a plea and get you out."

"I want to plead not guilty by reason of insanity," Bridget said deliberately.

"Ahh," he said, "well . . . that's not necessary at this point. Just 'not guilty' will do. We can amend the plea later, if that's what is most appropriate. It's an unusual plea in this sort of case. Have you ever been under psychiatric care?" he asked solicitously.

"Yes," Bridget said, remembering the one visit she had had a year ago to the clinic on Truman Avenue. The doctor had let her renew the prescription for Valium over and over.

"Well, after I get you out, we'll have a long talk about all of this. With or without your daughter, whichever you chose. I'll be talking with the U.S. attorneys, and we'll see what they have in mind. Then we'll take it from there. Don't worry. You and your daughter will be out in a day or two."

Pleading insane had just popped into Bridget's head. She had trouble recalling some of what she did. She could feel herself remembering what she wanted to do, rather than what really occurred. She had called the police to warn them, hadn't she? Wouldn't that make a difference? She wouldn't tell the clown anything, yet. She wanted rest. She wanted to sleep. She could say whatever she pleased, and if they believed her, they would all be crazier than she was pretending to be.

Twenty-nine

C[1]urt was to be given a suspended sentence and a fresh identity: a new social security number, license, birth certificate. Curt had wanted his military record left intact: he still wanted to be able to collect benefits. That would be a little tricky, Wayne, his handler, told him, but he said it would be looked into.

Curt had decided what he wanted to do once the trial was over: he could apply again to a police force. He had discovered that the height requirement had been altered in the last couple of years because of an affirmative action suit brought by women against various public security agencies. Certain physical requirements had been changed, and one was the height requirement. Curt was now tall enough to qualify.

Wayne told him all his credentials would not come through till all the pending cases were settled. Curt was given his new name, though, and he wrote to police departments across the country, places where he thought he'd like to be. Small towns, away from the Sunbelt. The heat of the Keys dredged up too many memories. He now looked toward the Northwest. Oregon was his first choice.

He had become friends with Wayne. Wayne had suggested clothes to Curt that would look good, went drinking with him, looked after him in the apartment the government had provided, even double-dated with him. Curt cut his hair differently, and, in the blazer and sport pants he now wore, he looked quite different from the scruffy fellow they had stopped on the New Jersey Turnpike.

He was told he wouldn't have to testify against Kristina or her mother. Charges against them were being dropped. None of the women, he heard, were going to be prosecuted. He didn't even know that girl Rea's last name. He took to calling her "that girl," and they had little interest in her anyway. They wanted Winston, Delmer, Vern—and Duane, if they could turn him up.

Curt and Wayne had gone over grand jury testimony, depositions, and field reports and pieced together a plausible narrative. All of them had participated in the conspiracy to transport the folios across state lines. Curt needed some coaching—he couldn't remember if Vern had been involved in the transporting. Vern never seemed to be around when they talked about it. He tried to place him loading the prints in the car, but he couldn't remember if Vern had been there. Wayne just wanted him somewhere along the chain. Curt found that even when he told just what he knew was true it was hard to put a story together that didn't have holes in it. Wayne played the role of the defense attorney and showed him where his story was weak. But Curt was assured they had a strong case. There was still some chance that Delmer would turn, and, if he did, there shouldn't be any trouble whatsoever. They suggested to Delmer they might indict his mother. That seemed to fill him with terror, Curt was told.

The trial shouldn't last more than a week. His testimony would probably take up half of it. There was still one hitch: if they didn't apprehend Duane soon, they would have to sever him from the case and try him separately later: and, if they had to do that, they might have to sever one of the other defendants, too, in order to have a stronger case then. That might be Winston, they feared. Curt listened intently to the explanations of strategy; it seemed more complicated than he would have ever thought. But, over this last hurdle, he saw in his mind rows of tall, dark conifers, spear-tipped ponderosa, deep woods, rock-faced cliffs, and the cool mists of the Pacific bathing the small coastal town in Oregon that had responded favorably to his let-

ter requesting that he might patrol its streets in the uniform of
a peace officer.

2

Winston's Rover was still in the shop. He didn't have the nine
hundred for the repairs that had been done, and the mechanic
was holding the car. The condo lease had been canceled. But it
hadn't been rented yet. Bridget had retrieved his treasure map.
He had found himself forgetting numbers he never thought he
could possibly forget, so he had taken to writing a few things
down, dangerous as it was. The numbers wouldn't make sense
immediately to anyone else. But they would eventually. Buried
in dirt, he had heard, paper would survive fire.

Winston had the pressing need to dip into his capital: three
paintings he had kept over the years. Getting them out of storage would be difficult, though not impossible. He paid the Cambridge Storage Company five years' rent at a time; he had two
years left. The company was used to storing small amounts, because of all the college students in town. They were a bonded
warehouse, and Winston had packaged the art to appear to be
anything but. The building was all cubbyholes made of corrugated tin, chicken wire, two-by-fours. It was dark, clay-colored,
the shade of southwestern caves. There was no obvious plan, floor
by floor. It was cut up by need, whenever a different-sized room
was called for. A pack rat's planning. Winston had rented a stall,
no wider than its door, a little broom closet. The padlock's combination was one of the numbers on his treasure map.

If he told Topaz about it, as he had considered, because his
lawyer couldn't reveal any of his secrets, Topaz would probably
want the paintings as part of his fee. Winston thought of them
as his Swiss bank account. He still agreed with Topaz that he
would beat the rap. Juries never trusted turncoat witnesses; Curt
would look crazy. Winston's own version, though not yet fully
formed, would be more believable than Curt's. Curt would be
cast as the agent provocateur who had lured his friends into the
crime, had been the true brains behind it all. Curt's own military
background would seem to confirm it. Topaz thought that defense had possibilities. But since it had been his idea, Winston
felt as if Topaz was being paid too much for too little.

The police had impounded Bridget's Toyota at the cemetery, and Winston found an old bicycle between two trailers at

the Pair o' Dice and had pinched it. Bicycling to the Cayo Hueso condos, he viewed his future narrowly. Winston turned into the driveway on the far side of the condo complex. He would take a U-route and come out along the other side, where the apartment was. The tennis courts were empty. He didn't see anyone by the back pool. The one nearest the beach had a few people around it. Maybe he would take a swim. He wondered what would be left behind in the apartment. Duane's stuff? Rea's?

Winston was, and wasn't, amazed when Duane had successfully dropped out of sight. He didn't think much of the prowess of law enforcement agencies. From what Topaz had told him, Curt had done everything but crash into the front door of a police station in order to get caught. Winston's first fervor to get Duane had passed; he had begun to see Duane's absence as useful to whatever story he might finally compose. Duane could be the answer to a lot of things. Bicycling, he turned by the bungalow that housed the washing machines and pedaled up the drive to the end of building number three. When he saw Duane's van parked there, he flushed with more emotions than he could quickly sort out. Of them all, though, it was disappointment that burned his skin.

3

"You're going to Germany?" Kenner said. He stared at Rea. "Has it anything to do with our German co-passenger?"

"Oh, no. I'll be teaching composition to enlisted men and women, officers' wives, and some military brats. I applied over six months ago. It's an extension program run by the University of Maryland. I'm going to Wiesbaden. I'll get PX privileges."

Rea laughed, and Kenner realized she was alluding to O'Bannion's ravings about American soldiers only being able to fight if there was a PX nearby. The troops needed their Coca-Colas, their Post-Toasties. Kenner began to understand that he was both xenophobic and provincial. But Germany was still one of the last places he ever wanted to go. Any time he saw a clip of film on the concentration camps, he wished there had been a Carthaginian peace. Germany did seem to him an emblem for the modern world. All the bureaucrats and directors and owners of companies restored to their positions of power. It made him feel some sympathy for fanatics. Letting that wild deep streak of fierce indignation take over. Herods. Jehovahs.

"I've got another teaching job lined up in the States beginning January. I've made my plane reservations. Miami to Hamburg to Rhein Main Air Force Base."

Kenner thought to ask why she hadn't told him all this two weeks ago; but he could think of a few answers to that question himself, so he didn't. He wanted to say *what about us?* but that sounded too fatuous. Rea was evidently thinking the same question. She said, "Things have to simmer down, anyway. I need to sort out a few things. I don't want to lose you. In fact, I want the opposite. I want to let you into my life. I just want to have the feeling that it is my life."

The door chimes sounded their Mozart air, the melody of the Cuban national anthem. He and Rea exchanged looks, and Kenner went to the door and peered through the tiny viewing eye and saw, slightly misshapen, Winston's face.

"Why, hello, Winston."

"Anyone here," Winston asked, stepping in, "other than you two?"

"Just us chickens," Rea said.

"I saw Duane's van down there. I've been looking for him."

"You have?" Kenner said. He realized that most of his questions would be just restatements of what he had just been told.

"Yeah, I have," Winston continued. "He's got something that belongs to me. Where is he?"

"I don't know," Kenner said. The truth was as large and round as the moon, and Kenner needed only to give Winston a slice of it. He felt the smugness all perjurers must feel, the arrogance they have when they can give a reply that is, in some way, truthful.

"Well, where did his van come from?"

"It's been parked there since we got back," Kenner said, thinking half-truths can just go on and on.

Winston glared at Rea. "He was looking for you."

"I know," she said, quietly.

"A lot of people are looking for him now."

"What has been going on, Winston?" Kenner asked.

"Bullshit has been going on. Duane's going to go down, too."

Kenner saw Rea blanch. The same vision must be going through her mind, he saw.

"How did his van get here?" Winston asked again.

"Your guess is as good as mine," Kenner replied.

334

"The key was in it."

"News to me," Kenner said, surprised.

"The little fucker is going to be on foot from now on, because I've just repossessed it. The first payment on what he owes me."

Winston held up a key: some aluminum alloy, without shine, without glint. The rabbit's foot was the same color blue, Kenner realized, that they use to dye Easter chicks.

"You're lucky *I'm* not cutting a deal with the feds, or you two would find yourself in deep shit."

"Well, Winston, we appreciate that," Kenner said.

"Just for old times sake—in both your cases," Winston said, looking at Rea.

"Tell Duane I'm on his case," he said, and left.

Kenner did feel a bit of nostalgia for Winston. Someone out of his past, out of his present, out now, he hoped, of his and Rea's future.

4

Winston stayed in Bridget's trailer. It had been empty since she couldn't make bail. Bridget had called him there. It wasn't a happy conversation. He told her that he couldn't help her with any money. That she should let her public defender continue to represent her. He couldn't find her a better attorney. That she shouldn't tell him anything. That he'd remember she stood up for him. Ditto Kristina.

Bridget was distraught, almost wild, and he promised to visit her. He said he couldn't do that every day. He had business to attend to.

Winston felt better that both Bridget and Kristina were on ice. Even though, if either flipped, it would go bad for him. But they wouldn't make good witnesses, and he didn't think either of them would turn. Bridget told him that Kristina had begun to pray, spent a good part of each day on her knees.

Winston's bond had travel restrictions, though he didn't think he was being tailed. Manpower cutbacks, he thought, chuckling to himself. He was sure there was no surveillance.

Topaz had left to try another case in New York and instructed him to sit tight. They wouldn't know what the government really had till they received the discovery material on Curt. He had been tried and convicted in New Jersey. Topaz said he

335

would get that transcript and see what was there. Curt had cut a deal. It now seemed that Delmer was trying to cut one too. Delmer couldn't make bond either.

Winston felt himself to be, about town, an object of both curiosity and respect. People either brightened when he appeared or shrank away. He was an indicator of how much people had to fear. He had made inquiries about Duane. He found out that he was around the night Eli went to the hospital and that he had been asking around for some connection. He wanted to buy.

Winston had run into Suerte at the Casa Marina. Suerte gave him a name. Suerte seemed pissed-off at the guy. Somebody who lived up the Keys. The name was vaguely familiar, but Winston couldn't place just why. He must have run into him in town before.

Driving Duane's van for a couple of days had made Duane seem closer to him, just ahead, around the bend. Winston had thought it might contain clues to where he was, or where he would be going. He was sure MacNaughton, on Cudjoe Key, would supply the link he needed. A passage, a tunnel to Duane.

Winston knew Kenner and Rea had information they weren't sharing, but it would just be more dangling threads to unravel. He heard that the FBI, or the CIA, had a lie detector gun, something they could just point in someone's direction and tell if he was telling the truth. Winston wondered how long it would be before some Jap stole the blueprints and he could buy one at Radio Shack.

He had searched Duane's van: crumpled-up bags from Burger King and a Biscayne Dog Track race sheet. Duane had been up in Miami? Is that where the two prints went?

As Winston drove to Cudjoe Key, something told him he was doing something ill-advised. He was going unprepared and he was going because it was a place to go. He had phoned the number Suerte had given him quite a few times, and it only rang and rang.

MacNaughton's name raised a trouble blip in his memory, but he couldn't yet locate where it originated.

MacNaughton's place wasn't hard to find. First right beyond mile marker 21. Entrance was barred by closed wooden gates. Winston parked and got out to look for a bell or an intercom. He saw the gates were not locked; there was an inch of blue air between them. Winston could see a line of white coral and turquoise water and blue sky. He pushed through and walked into a courtyard.

A boat on a trailer had been backed in and haphazardly parked. Just left. That's a drug runner if ever I saw one, Winston thought. Three colors: dark indigo, black metal, and highly polished lacquered wood. CARAJO, out of Key Biscayne.

No human noises. No one had appeared. Winston just stood and looked. The stilt house seemed empty. He walked around the side of the speedboat and saw, parked in a breezeway, a car. It had a canvas top, a small oval rear window.

"Hello!" he called loudly. "Anyone home!"

Nothing stirred, except for the bending cypress trees that provided a windbreak along the edge of the property. Winston had an idea. He backed in Duane's van up to the trailer of the boat. If it was a drug-running boat, there wouldn't be any papers on it, anyway. No police report. He had decided to take it. It might come in handy. Duane—and by extension, MacNaughton, if he did deal with Duane—owed him something.

Winston picked up the trailer's hitch. He banged it against the van's bumper. The sound startled him, and, for a moment, he wasn't sure whether he had made the noise or if it had come from somewhere else. He looked over at the car parked under the house. He decided he better check it out.

After Winston had covered half the distance to the car, his nose stopped him. Sewer gas, sweet and repulsive.

He took another step and suddenly saw in front of him the green spade of lawn in Tucson, the turquoise diamonds of the pool water. He found himself standing at the side of the small car, his hand reaching out as it had reached out to the sauna's door.

Winston stopped himself. It took a moment of mastering. It felt like a visual retreat, film winding rapidly backward. He was now on crushed white coral, the pieces like cinders, except they were bright alabaster, burnt by a clean fire, standing next to a car pointed at the water, at the sun.

He began to gag. Through the tinted side glass he saw a shape: black, swollen, covered with slime, tiny bubbles. He backed off. But that only provided him with a better view. He stared at the carcass: it was in profile and Winston kept tracing its outlines. The body was bent behind the wheel, the legs drawn up unnaturally into a small rectangle. Audubon, Winston found himself thinking, would often contort his birds to fit their bodies onto the page of a double elephant folio.

337

Who was it? The body was purple, the color of eggplant skin. But the hair, wet from absorption, was reddish, not black, as Duane's was.

Winston couldn't guess how long the person had been staring at the beach, the sun and moon rising and setting, one day after the other.

MacNaughton was his guess. And though Winston wanted to flee, he forced himself to back slowly away. He stood outside the circle of smell, or, at least, where the odor had become only a trace.

He continued back-pedaling, stumbling, out of Mac-Naughton's orbit of decay, and fell back against the slick side of the dark blue boat. He stood up and looked down at the trailer's yoke and the back of the van. He remembered what he had been doing. Winston finished connecting the trailer to the van's rusty hitch. Nothing had been towed by it since Duane bought the van. The hitching ball had an even covering of rust on it, which smeared Winston's palm, the earth's blood, the shade of the corpse's hair.

Winston wondered about tire tracks after he shut the gates, but decided the coral wouldn't leave any. And who the fuck cared? It was Duane's van. Nonetheless, he scuffed the dirt between the driveway and the road with his tennis shoes. He would leave the boat on Stock Island, by the warehouse.

As he drove, the memory of his father's corpse and the body in the sports car began to mingle, combine into a critical mass: they shot together, but didn't explode so much as burn within him. He felt himself collapsing inside; every thought he had seemed to be sucked into darkness, not registering, just falling back into itself, iron crumbling in a great blast furnace. In the day's heat, he felt both feverish and vacant. A star, disappearing.

Thirty

1

Shortly after Kristina was released, she took to forms of public penance. In jail she had pledged herself to Jesus and accepted the burden of her sins.

Inmates had been allowed to watch "The PTL Club" on television. Kristina decided she had to become a lesson for others, a vehicle of their salvation, and there was no way to cause her own expiation except mortification in the eyes of others. One night, falling into a fitful sleep, she recalled something she had seen walking out of Lopez's funeral parlor but not, until now, remembered: right across the street from the funeral parlor was the Good Shepherd Bible Study Shop.

She went there straightway from jail and gathered up the shop's free pamphlets. She read about how the new laser scanning machines being put in supermarkets were tools of the Antichrist. They recognized lines across lines—crosses—and one day only those marked with the sign of the devil, a bar on the forehead, would be able to buy food. The other tracts weren't as alarming, but she read them all over and over.

At the Salvation Army store on Flagler, she found what looked to her like proper attire. She was covered from neck to ankle in a rough sort of material, cream color. It looked to her like a fit dress for a daughter of Jesus. It was a nightgown, cut in Empire style. There was elastic in the bodice, which yoked it tight under her breasts. When Kristina had put it on—and had not taken it off for over a week—it revealed her body startlingly well, especially when the sun cut through it. But, even without the sun, her breasts were held and molded by the fabric in a most complimentary way. She didn't know where to display herself, but she alighted finally on the corner of Duval and Eaton. She had first chosen a brick ledge by an insurance company, across from the Bull Bar, but had been shooed away. There was a low white wall around a parking lot where she settled; Kristina put a hand-lettered sign at her feet: MY SON DIED FOR MY SINS.

Because of the sign, those who did not know who she was began to refer to Kristina as the Virgin Mary, or just Mary, or the Virgin. At sundown, since passersby would disappear from the street, she would walk down to Mallory Square and sit facing the descending sun, the sign propped up against her back.

Tourists began to drop coins by the sign. Some people placed food near her: fruit, portions of meals, half-eaten Cuban-mix sandwiches. The police, because she was either not blocking traffic, or, as yet, creating sufficient nuisance, or, most likely, since they did know who she was, had decided to let her be.

Bridget tried to get her to stop. But Kristina just looked through her, focused on some spot no other eye could see. Even when it rained, Kristina sat, legs crossed, hands out, palms up, in an attitude of resignation and amazement.

Kristina had been prescribed sedatives after Eli's death and had taken them till she experienced her conversion. She stopped ingesting drugs, and her body, its chemical furnaces so long banked by various combinations, first began to stall and then to sputter, which, combined with her attempts at meditation, at emptying her mind, put her in something of a trance, made the ordeal she had chosen for herself bearable.

Kristina's presence on the low white wall went through a cycle: first passersby regarded her with curiosity; then, after getting used to seeing her, they treated her with some nonchalance. But, noticing her persistence, nonchalance turned into some kind of respect. Then, after a while, their attitude dipped down into irritation, then moved to a kind of reverence. She became something of an object, an entity anyone could make something of:

340

she had, in some ways, more quickly than she would have ever imagined, become petrified, an institution, a thing people looked at, almost a saint. She was *there*.

Young boys, barely teenagers, openly stared at her body, revealed beneath her weathered gown. She lost weight, but the size of her breasts had not decreased, and, hence, looked even larger. The boys found out where she slept at night. She had only bothered to retain some minimal privacy about that, and it hadn't taken much investigation to uncover. A small gang found her under the porch of a deserted house, marked for rehabilitation, on Telegraph Lane. The boldest boy, though not crawling in himself, egged on another, one far more timid, to do so. He managed to pull her gown up over her waist before she stirred. Kristina howled in a way that made the boy jerk up, his head striking hard against a joist. He, too, yelled, and the others scattered. Kristina's howling turned into a low keening moan. The boys left and she was alone.

Bridget had wanted to put her in a hospital ever since she found Kristina putting tinfoil over the trailer's windows to ward off the powers of the Antichrist, though Bridget hadn't decided that except in her mind: that's what she thought to do, but she wasn't sure how to go about it. Bridget didn't want to get the police to do it. Finally, after Kristina refused to return to the trailer, Bridget called the psychiatrist she had once visited and asked him what to do. When they went to get her, Kristina had disappeared from her perch on the low white wall.

Kristina had taken to wandering. She began to trace the very edge of the island, climbing over whatever obstacles there were. She had gotten as far as the periphery of the town dump. It was as if she had chosen to walk home, since she changed her route along the margins of the island to inland.

Her mind was singing, the infrared heat on her skin as potent as the hot metabolism in her cells. She did feel as if she were cooking. She began to see, or, it seemed to her, her vision was a picture, one frame at a time. Then the frame would sizzle black at the edges, before being replaced by another.

And it was during one of these seizures, these exploding visions, that she saw what made the most sense to her. It was Duane's van. Or, rather, what she saw was a hurtling form of color, the same spectrum that she felt inside her, the hottest yellow, diminishing to a molten purple. It seemed to Kristina to be the tip of a torch, the flaming head of a spear, some bolt of energy being flung her way by one of Jesus's angels, if not Jesus himself. When she saw it, thinking Duane was there, an agent of deliverance, a messenger of impulse, she ran from the dirt access road she had been trodding, over a small hump of earth, and then, before the van's driver could see her and swerve away, Kristina rushed out, arms raised in greeting, into the road and flung herself into the van's flat embrace.

2

To take her mind off things, Bridget played bingo. But it wasn't working. She finally thought she might have to go *some other place.* The bank wouldn't rewrite her trailer loan again, and she didn't know how she was going to meet the payments. She was looking for a buyer. When she had come to Key West, she had at last found a spot where she could just sit down and not move. There weren't many rich people around then, and things were cheaper. It had been nice to get away from them. But now they were all coming to the island, as if they were chasing her.

Bridget was surprised that there were so many rich people. *Some other place* was not where she wanted to go. And now Winston's money, the sum she had hoped to get in order to pay off the bank, had dried up like a mirage over asphalt.

She had let herself fly after Winston, up into his heat, and even as she thought of it in regret, she felt herself tighten, wince with remembered pleasure. Now things were too shattered to mend, and she would have to go to some other place.

Kristina had been too shattered to mend. Nothing flew apart; her thin flesh was still a resilient enough sack to hold her together, but her spleen had burst, her bones had snapped.

"B two."

Bridget daubed her card. In the hospital she had learned things about Kristina she hadn't known. She had had breast implants. One of the bags had burst, and the saline had drained into her body. That breast had sunk, like one of the sinkholes that were showing up all over South Florida these days. Kristina had been two months pregnant.

"I sixteen." Bridget marked her card.

Now Bridget had to go back to Lopez's funeral home. Kristina would be cremated. None of her organs were to be removed. Everything was in some way damaged.

She didn't think anyone would be at the service. Winston had been jailed again. Kristina had evidently thought it was

Duane's van she was running out to, trying to stop, but it wasn't. It was a different one, driven by some eighteen-year-old from Tallahassee. The way Duane's van had been painted seemed to be catching on and this van, much newer than Duane's, had been delivered from the factory, Bridget was told, painted just that gaudy way.

Winston had been taken back to jail from the Winn Dixie parking lot. The police had a warrant out for Duane and a description of his van. They searched the van and found what they called burglar tools. They also found drugs. Winston claimed that he knew nothing about them. That he had just had temporary possession of the van. That it didn't belong to him. But his bail was revoked, and he was put back into jail. Bridget learned that his fancy lawyer had told him that the new charges wouldn't stand up, but he had to wait for his lawyer to get back down to Key West from New York City to be released.

Winston told her he wanted her to be with him, wanted her to stand by him, visit him, look after him. Especially if he should happen to get convicted, he whispered, "in the Audubon matter."

He said they would get married after he got out. His lawyer had assured him that if worse came to worst, he would only get five years. He'd be not yet forty. He had, ah, *resources,* was how he put it. They would be in good shape after he got out.

"G fifty-seven." Another black spot.

But, *some other place.* It took hold in her mind. It was hard to dislodge. She began to think about where to go. She began asking people, even strangers, if they knew of any good places. Sanibel Island; Gatensburg, Tennessee; Atlantic City; Port Aransas, Texas. She didn't want to go north, back to Fall River, New Bedford. Port Aransas sounded closest to what she liked. It was easier to be poor in a hot resort town. There were always people she could work for. She could always clean rooms. As long as you didn't want too much. Port Aransas had the sea, too, the Gulf.

Maybe, she thought, if she got settled there, she could send for Kristina's and Eli's ashes.

Candi had been nice to her. Given her some time off. Robin, Juniper's mother, had told her to come by the Beauty Box for a free permanent and tint. Anyway, she thought, no one would care, or know, about the bird business somewhere else. Unless she told them.

Even the bingo had changed for the worse. It was no longer

343

cards and small wafers of plastic, but just thin paper sheets. Instead of covering the numbers with chips you had to blot them out with a fat pen, which looked like a roll-on deodorant with an ink pad on the end. She realized she had missed the last numbers being called, had heard hardly any of them. Her card only had a few smudges.

Bridget found herself dwelling on Ray Pine, sweet Ray. Had he only lived, all this wouldn't have happened. He would have taken Kristina in tow. She would never have been so messed up. Bridget thought again of the look on Ray's face on the local TV in Orlando when, surrounded by little children, he pulled out that dead snake. And made it look still alive. He could do things like that. That's why she loved him. Ray could make things seem alive. But he died.

3

Kenner had tried to bring himself up-to-date, but events were flashing by. Rea should be landing in Germany about now, he thought. He had discovered that Kristina and her child were both dead. Freak accidents, as they are called. Freak.

Kristina's funeral was set for today and he thought of attending. He had never been to a funeral in Key West. The Audubon theft had been "solved." Another example of G-men at their best, Kenner thought: have the thing fall whole into your lap. Reading the papers, Kenner wondered if the law would eventually have come up with anything. There was no mention of any prints missing from the recovered set, no confirmation of what he suspected. There had been less coverage than Kenner would have guessed. The rest of the world was too redolent with action, too much fat snapping in the pan to get exercised over some bird books. Kenner didn't think the trial would get much attention, since the theft had rated only a small amount.

He had received a half-dozen pieces of personal mail. One was a candidate for the strangest piece of all. Two pages of canary yellow second sheets folded into envelope size and promiscuously stapled together. It was addressed to Reverend Kenner, Cayo Hueso Chapel and Condos. By the time Kenner got the pages apart, it looked as if he had been cutting out paper dolls. The letter was typed. But it read like the sheet of paper you see in the demonstration typewriter at a department store.

Beneath the typed text was writing in ballpoint: "Add this

344

to your interview." Across the top was typed: ADMADMAD-MADM. *Ad majorem Dei gloriam?* Kenner wondered. He tried to recall if BC was a Jesuit college. It had MacNaughton's name at the bottom, though not a legal signature: mac-NAUGHT-on.

After trying none too successfully to make complete sense of the body of the letter, Kenner called MacNaughton's number, but no one answered. Kenner was hesitant about playing detective, since there were, he presumed, enough detectives already at play in those fields. But MacNaughton knew something about Manuel and perhaps would provide a few answers. They would, Kenner thought, be cryptic answers, but no more cryptic than the letter at hand. There was one coherent thought in Mac-Naughton's message. Kenner had the suspicion it was a quotation: "Whoever glorifies order and form as such, must see in the petrified divorce an archetype of the Eternal." Kenner mulled over the phrase "the petrified divorce." It sounded like the title of one of MacNaughton's novels.

Kenner thought of driving out to Cudjoe Key after Kristina's funeral.

Since Kenner was Winston's neighbor, he expected the feds to turn up at his door, for the usual routine interview, if nothing else. They hadn't shown, or, at least, hadn't left a note. One advantage, Kenner realized, of living in a vacation condo was that people didn't expect you to be at home, or even *there*. Kenner still couldn't get over the fact that Winston and the others had been charged with conspiracy and interstate transportation of stolen goods. The feds certainly didn't want it to be a local matter—that was clear.

Kenner wondered, now alone, about his former lack of curiosity, or true suspicion, about what Winston and his crew were up to. Even ordinary gossip only arrived in the porch of his ear after it had visited every other veranda in town.

He still needed to remind himself that Duane was dead, even though he had seen what happened. Saw him disappear into the Gulf. Kristina was dead. Though he hadn't seen that, he believed it. Duane didn't seem dead. Kristina did. He had a hard time remembering just what her kid looked like. And his name. Something vaguely counterculture and biblical, he thought. Ebenezer? Kenner couldn't recall much about Kristina, either, except that she was well-built. Gone gone gone.

All the deaths of the past couple of weeks had not impeded in any way the rest of the world's hurtling mass: particles so small they didn't run into anything, smash anything, deflect anything. Kenner knew some impossibly small matter, neutrinos, was bombarding him now, even through the poured concrete of the condo's walls. It had been described on TV. And Kristina and Duane and Kristina's kid were likewise passing through everybody, but it didn't faze anyone more than the passing of neutrinos. Neutrinos. Some cereal for the eighties.

The doorbell chimed. It took him away from his immediate thoughts, but slowly enough so that he didn't entirely consider who might be standing on the other side of the door. MacNaughton? Come to deliver another crypto-message? The feds with their summons?

"Saperstein," Kenner cried, with a roar of pleasure, "what a sight for sore eyes!"

Saperstein, even Saperstein, whom Kenner knew to be professionally able not to register surprise, seemed baffled at Kenner's joy at seeing him.

Kenner realized one of the things he liked about Saperstein was his look of friendly skepticism. Most people show a look of unfriendly skepticism, which, more accurately, is the look of scorn. But Saperstein's expression was amused, if slightly incredulous. Kenner told him about the Audubon theft, his spectator's seat version, the alleged trip to Mariel; he told it all with the rough edges clipped. No contraband was mentioned, no cargo, no Duane, no arsenal of small arms, no explosion. Just what stories he could think of to explain the last few weeks. Cubans in, Cubans out.

"Well," Saperstein said, "one bit of info you should know is that *Pen-Ultimate* has gone under. They announced with a fanfare that they were going monthly, instead of bimonthly. Then they folded the next week. So, I'm afraid you won't even be getting your kill fee."

"Kaput? Gone under?"

"Yeah," Saperstein went on, "everyone in the water. Both editorial and production staffs are trying to climb aboard one lifeboat rag or another. But other magazines' staffs have oars in hand and they're beating them off, letting them drift back into shark range. Thinking about all that, it's funny what happened to old MacNaughton. Maybe someplace else will be interested in your piece now."

"What *funny* happened to MacNaughton?"

"You haven't heard? Man, it's those satellites. It's easier to get the news a thousand miles away than hear what's going on down the street. He killed himself. I heard it in Boston. It wasn't in the papers, but I know a friend of his ex-wife, or present ex-widow. Or maybe you're always a widow, even if you're divorced. Carbon monoxide, plus pills. He sent his ex some sort of strange letter. She called the police down here. Any idea why he might want to do himself in, beyond the ordinary ones?"

The drive-in-movie screen welded to the back of Kenner's forehead lit up with a lot of old film. He just looked at the memory show for a moment and then turned to Saperstein, who was lounging comfortably on one of the condo's soft couches.

"I don't know, Sap. Probably because he was gay and thought he should be straight. He was a drunk, and he thought he should be sober. He was a has-been, and he thought he should be a flaming success. Who knows? He probably didn't like what he had been doing lately."

"Hey, I didn't know you could talk like Dan Rather. Good luck placing the interview. I don't know how you're going to take the smell of failure out of it."

Kenner looked up and saw his and Saperstein's faces being flung back and forth by the apartment's mirrored walls.

"When are you going to be done with the sex book?"

"I'm off it, man. Taken off. Turned in a hundred pages and they didn't like it. Not enough zip in my style. Anyway, I keep the advance. I don't mind. It was depressing listening to all those kids talk about how much pussy they get. Made me regret my wasted youth. I got pretty bored hearing fifteen-year-old corn-huskers tell me about getting their girls to strangle them so they could come. And vice versa. Some of them beat off, their pricks in one hand, the other hand tugging on the end of a noose around their necks. They are all getting closer to sex *and* death. Anyway, in a few years, there will be manuals for it: *The Joy of Passing Out.*"

"They could call it *Coming and Going.*"

Saperstein looked at Kenner with forbearance. "In any case, I am on to something hotter now, something much better for my rep. Did I really want my name on a book about teen sex? I'm catching the early wave before it hits. Nukes."

"Nukes?" Kenner asked.

"Yeah, that's what's going to be big next, though I've got to get my book out before anyone actually pushes the button. A nuclear war would adversely affect sales. I'm interviewing civil-

347

defense folk in Miami. That's the reason for this surprise visit. South Florida has more military than you'd think. It's a prime target. I'm looking into evacuation plans. You wouldn't believe the cases of stale crackers I've seen."

"Maybe they will spare Miami," Kenner said. "They'll want all those hotels on the water. It's one spot that will remind the Third World of home."

"Well, it's nukes now. Death is in the air—like capital punishment here. Nobody could care during Vietnam. We were killing lots of people. Let the war end for a few years, and all of a sudden our fellow citizens want to start frying people again. War saves lives. At least the lives of those in prison. I'm glad I'm doing something that matters—a bit like old times." He looked to Kenner suddenly younger: the gawky, earnest youth of ten years ago covering a demonstration.

"Sap," Kenner asked, "do the initials A-D-M mean anything in nuke-speak?"

"A-D-M, A-D-M," Saperstein said, and Kenner watched his friend's eyes narrow in concentration. "Yeah. That's right. ADMs. Atomic Demolition Munitions. Those are the real small bombs, ones that can be carried by one or two men. The Davy Crocketts, on the other hand, have smaller atomic shells, but they still need some sort of weapon, a bazooka, to fire them."

"Davy Crocketts?"

"Yeah. In the fifties there was a slogan, 'A Davy Crockett in every pocket.' We have a lot of small devices. ADMs. Now, they're land mines. Land mines."

"Land mines?"

"Yeah," Saperstein said, "land mines. They're about so big."

He held his long arms out in front of him, bending his fingers in at a ninety-degree angle. He made the shape of a large suitcase. An aluminum-colored case, Kenner thought, but couldn't believe.

"Hey," Saperstein said, sitting back down, "where is this hot number you met?"

"Rea," Kenner said, feeling disconnected. "She's taken a teaching job with the military. Temporarily. In Germany. She'll be back. She may be Ms. Right."

Saperstein looked at him with an expression Kenner couldn't interpret.

"Hey, since all this *Pen-Ultimate* crap fell though, I've got another lead for you. I was offered a job I don't want, but I

348

pimped you for it. All your projects seem, oh, moribund. If you don't want to do-do-do for a while, you can always teach. Your rep as a freelancer ain't good. You only need to send a résumé and a letter expressing interest. I talked you up quite a bit. It's a small private college in Vermont. Chutney. Some place. I've got the address and the guy's name. It's teaching journalism to a lot of Persians. A lot of places these days have been meeting their budgets with foreign exchange students. Anyway, the college should be solvent for a couple more years. The pump is primed. If you want a year in the woods, out of the fray, apply."

"Thanks, Sap. I'm considering all offers these days."

"You know, all us baby-boomers will be going back to college when we're old. We'll all be living in the dorms after they've been converted to old folks' homes. The campus forever. The good ol' days."

"Sap, we really have atomic land mines?"

"Oh, yes. 'A Davy Crockett . . .' "

"You mean, World War Three could start because some-body *steps* on one?"

"That's right, my boy. Watch where you tread."

4

Winston wasn't wholly disconcerted by his second arrest. He had left the boat and trailer behind the warehouse on Stock Island. Then he realized he had few places to go anymore. Before his first arrest, Key West had been full of little oases, the Wharf House, the condo, Bridget's. Each its own sort of watering hole. He could go back to Bridget's trailer at the Pair o'Dice, but she would likely be there. The rest of the town was being slowly repossessed. He felt strange and was thinking strangely. He knew he had to get control of himself and that was when he pulled into the Winn Dixie lot, just to relax, settle down, stop.

He didn't notice the police cruiser pulling up. They had recognized him from the Audubon publicity. At first they weren't going to hold him, but then they asked to see the registration for the van. Winston couldn't produce it.

"Just who did you say owns this van?" one cop kept asking.

Radio calls buzzed back and forth; they took him in and impounded the van. Before the van left the Winn Dixie lot, one officer lifted the metal trapdoor over the spare tire, unscrewed the large wing nut, and pulled up the spare. Sitting there, amid

349

paper trash, was a large baby-blue cardboard Q-tip box. He slid it open. Duane's attempt at concealment almost worked: the officer began to slow down when he saw old Q-tips. But what would a Q-tip box be doing under a tire? And a box of Q-tips doesn't weigh a pound. He kept pulling and saw, past a few cotton-tipped swabs, a plastic bag of white powder.

Topaz had assured Winston that without a warrant it was an illegal search and seizure. They would drop possession charges against him. Nonetheless, Winston had been cooling his heels for nearly a week until Topaz filed the right papers.

Winston hadn't minded the time. He had been able to put in perspective the sight of MacNaughton and the memory of his father. He knew he acted strangely because of what he saw. He didn't tell Topaz about MacNaughton.

Topaz had believed him when he said he had been unaware of the cocaine in the van. Winston had been surprised in the past that people often didn't believe him when he told the truth, but they would when he lied. Winston hadn't been overly confounded when the cocaine was discovered; that made it seem that he had always known it was there. The lack of surprise on his part made him seem guilty. Would that fool a lie detector? Winston, during his first stretch, had read Ferguson and Miller's *Polygraph for the Defense,* hoping to learn a few tricks.

Being picked up solved the problem of where he was going to go. Bridget had been in sorry shape since Kristina died. Living in her trailer would have been a drag. Since he was going to be let out, the problem arose again. An outline of a place had come to him in his sleep. He would go to Mexico in MacNaughton's boat, to Cozumel. From there, after an appropriate interval, after all pertinent arrangements, the old paintings from storage disposed of, he would assume a new identity, return to the States and begin anew once more.

The plan had comforted him the last few days. In the dark he had pictured its parts. He did not sketch the most obvious specifics: that he would need a stake in Mexico and that he had very little cash. Maybe he could get Bridget to sell her Toyota. He let the larger outline of his plan envelope him. He found it soothing.

He figured Duane had traded MacNaughton the missing prints for the chicken soup. Since it was in Duane's van, Duane might be in the same shape as MacNaughton. Or he was covering his tracks. Two people were connected to Duane's van, at least, by proximity. Rea and Kenner. But they more than likely didn't know anything about the cocaine either.

It was still a puzzle. But Winston didn't feel obliged to work it out yet. He thought of Audubon, how he would let others paint in the busy backgrounds. He let himself imagine Cozumel, life in Mexico, the rate of exchange, the absence of jeopardy. During the nights in jail, his images of flight became very real and filled the black hours with startlingly clear pictures, full of color and sun, all kept aloft on the bright wings of flight, escape.

Thirty-one

1

Kenner was gratified to see notice of MacNaughton's death finally appear. One newsweekly reported it as a suicide, another as a heart attack. One literal, the other figurative. Kenner thought. The euphemism that was used in the obituaries he most enjoyed was the one the newspaper of record favored: "died after a long illness." He liked that one. He first took note of its use after a woman he knew had thrown herself out of her ninth-floor apartment window. The paper reported it as a death after a long illness. The same for MacNaughton. Yes, Kenner thought, a long illness, life.

Kenner was beginning to get his bearings. He was still trying to put two and two together. The boat trip now appeared to be some nautical version of three-card monte, a shell game of now you see it, now you don't. Even though he stood a good chance of still being wrong, he had figured the chain of events this way: first, they had most likely found the wrong boat. Kenner had talked with the editor who assigned the piece. He was brusque, though he did say he got the information from a contact in Union, New Jersey. The day after he talked to Kenner, he heard that the trip had been canceled. He couldn't reach Kenner, Kenner was told.

Yes, *Pen-Ultimate* was folding. There would be no kill fee. The editor, through a former college roommate, had been offered a position as a White House speech writer. He said that he was too busy to talk to Kenner or to find out anything further for a dead letter like Kenner's article.

A rat climbing aboard a sinking ship, Kenner thought, but did not say. Try a magazine like *Mother Jones,* the editor suggested.

The Editor had now metamorphosed into the Speechwriter—Kenner imagined the china dog, the motto, "his master's voice." The editor's new job seemed to smack of something more pertinent. Yet Kenner could believe it was just the new old-boy network humming smoothly. Kenner didn't think he would be writing anything about the *La Compañía*'s adventures. His interest in investigating the nontip part of the iceberg had dwindled—it would take a lot of time and he couldn't finance it.

No one wanted Kenner's revised interview-obituary-tribute of MacNaughton, either. He had made a couple of calls. One editor demurred, telling Kenner the review must get at least one a month, these "dead-author articles," and the editor didn't want to run any of them. Kenner pictured authors around the country dropping like flies. MacNaughton's death had not made his literary stock rise. Just the opposite, Kenner discovered. In MacNaughton's case, it seemed to be the ordained conclusion of his swift decline. It confirmed the style police's judgments. Kenner knew if he wanted to see the piece in print it would have to be in one of the most obscure of nonpaying publications.

In any case, he and Rea had been on the wrong boat to Mariel. Now, if that hadn't been prearranged, somehow, by the once and future speechwriter, and it was purely accidental, why had O'Bannion taken them?

They looked harmless? Cover? The captain was to pick something up, but not refugees. From the glimpse of the gadget that Kenner got—if it was a gadget, an ADM, slipcased in the burlap sugarcane bag—it was being brought home, along with two friendlies, who, most likely, were government people. The captain brought out two people, left one, and extracted a low kiloton nuclear device from the Cuban swamps?

But was it Cuba? Kenner consulted his atlas: Belize, Honduras, Nicaragua, Mexico. If it was Cuba, when had the gadget—

and could there be only one?—been salted away there? The Bay of Pigs? Was it an old CIA operation, only now being deactivated? Is that what MacNaughton had been trying to tell him in his mad letter? *Never Again* for real?

But what if it was just an aluminum case containing millions of dollars worth of cocaine? And that emblem Kenner saw, or thought he saw, that fat propeller, the black and yellow radiating scream, was just . . . something else? Kenner once owned a pickup truck that had tires stenciled PROPERTY OF THE ATOMIC ENERGY COMMISSION. The tires had been bought in New Mexico, used.

It had to be ours, Kenner reasoned. It couldn't be someone else bringing it into the country. That grenade launcher was American. They weren't harassed on the trip, which, to Kenner, was the best evidence that the trip had been sanctioned. What Kenner saw of the ADM made it look old, rather than new. Late fifties technology. Had it been someone else's, it would have looked newer. But, he realized, everything the Russians made looked like fifties' technology, anyway. Their space suits used buttons, for Christ's sake.

What Kenner finally settled on was this: the CIA smuggled small atomic weapons into Cuba. In connection with the Russian missiles, or the Bay of Pigs, whichever. It or they were left there. A mistake. And, finally—and this is where Kenner speculated entirely—Carter was told. And, with the suspicion that he was going to lose the election, and not bearing to think it or they would still be there when Reagan became president, he decided to take it/them out. Great confusion was required. It couldn't be a military operation.

The question Kenner entertained was: did Carter and Castro work up the whole Mariel thing together? Or did Carter just take advantage of it when it began?

Make the Florida straits resemble Dunkirk. Churn up the scene with waves of distraction. Plenty of cover for one boat, a few odd people, and one small gadget.

2

Winston saw himself as an executive handling venture capital. He wanted to behave as CEOs did. Bridget's money was going to be his golden parachute. Not that golden, he realized, only rainy-day paper money.

Bridget had a role to play yet. She would likely be the go-

354

between for the paintings in storage. He went to her trailer directly from jail. The air conditioners were running, but her place, the old fuck hut, was still hot.

Bridget had netted two hundred and seventy dollars from her garage sale; she couldn't, couldn't, she said, sell the Toyota. She had already borrowed against it. She told him she was thinking of leaving town for a while. And, though he didn't want to tell her what he was planning, he said that might be a good thing to do. She wanted to talk about Kristina. Bridget had decided not to inter her next to Eli after all. She kept Kristina's ashes. The canister had been shipped to her UPS. It was about eight inches high, tin metal with an overlapping seam. The top fit snuggly. Winston thought it looked as if it held expensive cigars. Bridget said she wanted to scatter Kristina's ashes in the next place she went, so it would seem like a place that wasn't strange to her. She would never testify against him. She would plead the fifth, she told him.

Winston got out of her bed and went into the trailer's bathroom. Bridget had given him the money; he wondered if she had already dipped into it.

The sight of the can containing Kristina's ashes made Winston feel strange. He began to have an erection. Before then he hadn't felt like fucking Bridget. But, for the first time, she didn't seem interested. She just lay there. He told Bridget he was going to Miami on legal business, but that he would be in touch. It was very important, he told her, that he should be able to get hold of her. As he was talking to her, he stroked the side of her breast and found his fingers were playing with something within: pebbles, smooth, each the size of a lima bean. He stood up then. Bridget did not get out of bed. Both of her large breasts had fallen to her sides. It was as if there had been an earth slide, parts of hills tumbling down, blocking a road.

Two hundred and seventy dollars. Winston left, not thinking of what was behind, but ahead. The Yucatán was only slightly more than twice as far as Cuba from Key West. The cigarette boat could go over sixty-five miles per hour. Even with the current, it should only take a day.

He found a kid hanging around the docks to help put the black fin in the water. He filled extra plastic water jugs with fuel. That would be more than enough. There was good weather forecast for the next three days. Calm seas. He had purchased the right charts. The boat had a depth finder and a short-wave radio. It had a tape deck, but no tapes. Winston bought three at Woolco, along with other supplies.

He had given some thought to motoring by the Wharf House, to going around Mallory Square, one last sweep of Old Town before he bid the old burg too-da-loo. But he forewent the gesture, since it would take him the wrong way and have him cruise by too many military installations.

Winston had thought to wait for the liner that stopped at Key West on its route to Yucatán and follow it discreetly. But it would be hard not to be conspicuous doing that. He had instruments. All he had to do was stay on course.

Winston had an ice chest packed with provisions: beer, cold cuts, coleslaw, cheese, and a bag of bread and potato chips.

He was truly impressed when he started the engine. It sounded more powerful than any hot rod he had dreamed of as a youth. He rumbled out of Safe Harbor's channel and along the south side of Key West. For a while he had Smathers Beach in sight. He could make out, behind a line of swaying palm trees, the bone white color of the Cayo Hueso condos. Soon the buildings hardly made a rib on the horizon.

He sighted a freighter and then, even with the salt spray in his face and the feeling of the preternatural power of the boat under his hands, something he knew was alarm came over him when he reached the main ship channel. He glanced around, and, in every direction, he saw only watery horizon, lines of blue pulling toward one another, with seams so fine stitching the sea and sky together it was impossible to tell where they joined.

3

The first thing Kenner received from Rea was a plain penny postcard sent airmail. But the post office's chaste, bland face had been appliqued with cutouts, color illustrations from what source unclear. There was what looked like a fifties homemaker rising from bed in the morning, but with the covers still tucked about her knees. She, red hair, but redder lips and nails, was hugging, not tightly, her own knees, looking, well, starry-eyed at the ceiling. Advertising folk occasionally knew their business, even in the fifties, Kenner thought, to get just that look of ambiguous satisfaction. She was pleased, in some sexual context, but also looking forward to the day of, one would presume, household chores.

Above her red head, Rea had drawn little balloons of thought containing printed lines taken from yet another source: *Men walk on fiery rocks and women sing to turtles.*

Kenner didn't recognize the quotation—he wasn't very well read. Rea's note began: "It's so nice to have you at the end of the air traceries of the international mail from here to there that I'm encouraged to utter any sort of nonsense at all just to make the connection."

The next day he received a small package, its label also embroidered. There was a picture of a cliff and on it very tiny people walking along the precipice. Blue sky above. Then a large white cloud on which Kenner's name and address were printed. Inside the puffy envelope was a small red velvet sack, which, a note explained, contained all the little things Rea had kept with her in the past few years: a cheap metal pin of a Japanese Zero airplane; a stamp with Richard Nixon's face on it; a small red pin of Lenin; a packet of sugar with what looked to Kenner like Russian script; a military service ribbon, blue with five white stars; and a fortune cookie fortune, badly printed: *You are contemplative and analytical by nature.* It was clear that Rea was sifting some history for him, the parts of her that had nothing to do with Duane. She was attending his wake solo, and Kenner realized she was not going to enlist him among the mourners.

Kenner received what he considered a real letter, instead of signs and portents, a few days later. It contained some description of the flight to Germany, but then went on to other matters: "To want to love someone completely may not sound very remarkable, but for me it constitutes a major change of heart. The point of playmates and potential men . . ." Kenner knew the reference. Potential men. Rea had explained the theory one night aboard the *La Compañía.* Discussing Duane. She had talked about potential men. The point was she expected nothing from them. All you get then, he remembered her saying, is bonus. At the same time, she had said, they may be deeply charming and pardonable in their shortcomings. *Shortcomings,* Kenner had thought at the time, was a bit mild for the potential homicide Duane had in mind. But Kenner certainly would be the first to allow for the generosity of memory. He returned to her letter: ". . . is that there is no danger of completing the arc. But attachment does set in, and with me connection through time is inevitably followed by catasterism . . ."

Kenner went looking for the dictionary at that point, to dis-

357

cover what *catasterism* meant: a. a treatise attributed to Eratosthenes giving the legends of the different constellations. b. a constellation.

He would have guessed it had something to do with catastrophe, and, he concluded, maybe it does.

". . . that is, good guys and bad guys alike all fly up and become starpoints in my constellation. I refer to these polestar configurations of the past far too much. I knew in every case from the outset that these were impossible matches for me and perhaps that is why I was able to indulge in them . . ."

Kenner thought: Duane was something of an impossible match. Though, an impossible match it still a match.

"The trouble was that I had taken so long and, I feared, wreaked so much havoc in figuring out what I wanted that it was impossible to believe the avenging angels of Jehovah were not alerted and standing ready to prevent me from ever stumbling across it or even seeing what it was if it hit me in the face . . ."

Kenner couldn't help seeing Duane's face flinch when the gun went off. Kenner still couldn't recall seeing any blood. Just Duane completing his own arc into the water.

". . . I was waiting for a man who was complete (instead of potential) and who would exceed my expectations . . ."

"Whoa-ho," Kenner said aloud.

"This man had to be more than I could conceive in order for me to believe in him . . ."

Whether Rea knows it or not, Kenner thought, I'm in big trouble. "I've told you that I don't like most couples (there are a few notable exceptions). It depresses me that people should be content to hammer out a little platform to descend to meet upon, out of the most unappealing parts of their personalities: their weariness, indifference, irritability, their fear of being alone. If I was overtaken by a fear, finally, it was a fear of not being loving enough, a fear of not delivering up my own capacity for feeling—a failure of the heart."

Some of this meditation was in response to Kenner's—well, it was more a suggestion than a request—earlier suggestion that Rea forego Germany and live with him. Kenner had hesitated for a number of reasons: not least of them was that putting Rea in the protective arms of the U.S. military seemed like a good idea. But now he saw the more considered nature of her hesitations. The letter concluded: "So you're right that you came into my vision when I was most likely to see you, though I wasn't actively looking. But I hope you can see that I look on you as a very great adventure indeed, introducing me to parts of myself I had only the faintest notion were there."

Kenner realized he never thought of much on airplanes. Just getting there. But such were Rea's thoughts on her flight—it was obvious that Rea existed on two planes, at least. Her mind and what went on in the world. Recent events, he saw, were somehow not as rigorously connected to what she believed. Ideas had more power for her, carried more conviction, than the mere playing out of events.

But he also saw she was not unhappy over the hiatus in their relationship. Some pause where she could be alone, make her own elaborate constructions and then decide if she wanted to be with him.

More mysteries. It did seem to Kenner that Rea was in his orbit, though they would be in contact only when she came around from the shadow of other planets and signals could be reestablished. Catasterism. He doubted, though, he would ever have used that word in a sentence, no matter how long he lived.

Kenner had never met anyone quite like Rea. Such a claim, he knew, was on the lips of practically anyone who has fallen in love. It was everybody's boast for uniqueness. But it seemed to be true in Rea's case. He had known a lot of intelligent women, though she had an intelligence of a more complicated sort. He had known people with a sort of crazy brilliance, but Rea wasn't crazy.

But he worried that an intelligence so circumspect, so particular, so inclined to perfectionism, would, after discovering a model as intricate as the roots of a ginkgo tree for the way her love had secured itself and convicted her—he knew such an intelligence could later and with the same conviction find him guilty, or, worse, not in love. In other words, the huge mechanism of her intellect could recoil and, as quickly as it could be turned lovingly in his direction, could also be turned against him: and her reasons for finding him insufficient would be just as elegant, just as filigreed with reason.

He had had a glimpse of that side when he had taken Rea to the airport. Though he well knew she was still affected by the shock of the events they had witnessed a few days earlier, she did let loose what seemed to be an entirely unedited sentence.

Kenner was sure that if you could just hear what was going on in someone's head for about a minute, you would then know whatever needed to be known. Kenner heard Rea say, speaking slowly—and seemingly not even to him: "I am concerned that you seem to be—at times—a parasite on other people's emotions."

Kenner knew exactly what she meant. He had begun to realize that his whole professional life, if he could call such a ragtag output as he had managed a professional life, had been at the expense of others. All journalists might be professional parasites, but Rea's phrase seemed to be more exact, pointed, particular. Kenner pictured one of those more symbiotic than parasitic creatures, a tick bird on the back of a rhino, sucker fish attached to sharks: there, ready.

He knew he wasn't, in an erotic way, a voyeur. Or, at least, not actively, first and foremost. When it came to sex, he would rather do than watch, though the idea of watching was not out of the question. But an emotional voyeur. He saw some truth to that. He liked being on the sidelines, observing, taking notes. He had watched people he knew go to jail, heard tales of humiliating defeats or excesses, and stood, not removed, but in a parasitic role, the beneficiary of someone else's suffering. The unafflicted guest occupying the ravaged host.

Kenner wasn't much of a mystery to Kenner these days; but, just as the puzzling elements of his recent past didn't seem all that mysterious, so, too, Kenner felt about himself: I know what has happened, but why has it happened just that way? He had, as he had for the trip of the *La Compañía*, two or three plausible explanations. Did it matter which was correct?

If he knew himself well enough to make what he did plausible, wasn't that sufficient? Do we ever know ourselves well enough to have an answer, he wondered, which still isn't something of a Zeno's paradox, forever divisible?

And it seemed to Kenner that, unless he got run over by the Conch Train, he was going to be able to get out of Key West none the worse for wear. True, he hadn't stolen the Audubon prints, but he had been, in some ways, an occupant in the Winston boarding house. Winston would take the rap. Duane had already taken the rap. And, Kenner judged, thanks to institutionalized sexism, all the women involved looked to go free, except for poor dead Kristina.

Drink a dozen bumpers to a dozen beauties, and the lass that floats to the top of your memory when you've finished is the one that has bewitched you; or something like that, he remem-

bered from some Restoration drama. His mind, Kenner saw, was
wandering. Saperstein was traveling the country interviewing
public officials, custodians of atomic weapons. It was weird, all
the genius that went into destruction. Kenner tried to think of
some folksy analogy, but he couldn't. What did it do to us all,
that the absolute pinnacle of human intelligence, the very tip,
was constantly bathed in blood? Such beautiful science. It was
the esthetics that pleased people like Oppenheimer, Kenner knew.

He thought he would apply for the teaching job in Vermont. And he had to decide what he should do with his New
York apartment. He considered emotional parasites again: Do
they all die when the host dies, or do they have enough sense to
detach themselves, have some kind of DNA that tells them when
their free ride is about to buy the farm? And, then, do they, too,
pack their bags and apply for a teaching job in quiet, peaceful
Vermont?

4

What makes the water white? What makes the water white? What
makes the water white? The question repeated over and over in
Winston's mind. It was a child's question, one he had posed to
his father, Max, any number of times. Winston and he had made
a trip out of Arizona, and Winston had looked at the Pacific,
seen an ocean, for the first time. What made the water white? he
asked. Winston was thinking of the waves. His father looked at
him distractedly and never answered. Winston, later, thought of
trying to find out. He came to believe it had to do with light
reflection. He had never found the exact answer. Now the question kept coming back to him. It kept repeating, and he was unable to turn it off.

Earlier the water didn't appear white, but crystalline, melted
diamonds. Winston thought of himself and his boat as an imperfection, a flaw that would lower the diamond's value as soon as
some jeweler looked through his eyepiece at the speck he and
the boat made, bobbing, barely embedded, near the water's surface.

Winston had then thought himself in a truly precarious position: the surface was only a bright film, filled with rainbow
spectrums, on which he sat, and the breeze would blow too firmly
and the thin membrane of attracted molecules would break and

he would tumble into its crevice, down down down, never to be found.

But no breeze blew then, and Winston settled into the lulling cadences of the boat's rocking; it was just a disc of a pendulum, the earth swinging him at the end of its cycles. He tried to shield as much of himself as he could from the sun.

What had seemed so simple had proven not to be so: he had had little more distance to traverse than that from Miami to Key West, and, he had thought, could have no better vehicle in which to do it, but after five hours of exhilarating speed, it had come to an end.

There had been two terrible occurrences. The ocean had looked as empty as a Nebraska plain, but he had hit something. He slowed to an idle and looked for damage. The hull had sustained a gash high on its port side; you could see the threads, the webbing of fiberglass. He made out the corner of a crate or trunk bobbing in the water behind him: something tossed or thrown overboard. By a Marielito, no doubt, he thought. Winston couldn't tell if the hull's wound was taking in much water. He started up again at half the speed he had been traveling. Then the plastic gallon jugs of extra fuel turned soft and split open, flooding the boat. When he started to mop up, more split open. He threw them overboard and felt the ones that remained. Their skin was in some manner decomposing, becoming malleable under the corrosive effects of both the sun and the fuel itself. Two were still intact. As he was picking the last one up, it crumpled in his hands; some fuel splashed the engine and there was a flash fire.

He shut off the motor and managed to snuff out the flames, but the engine had been fouled. He was unable to restart it, try as he did.

Winston decided not to use his VHF and call for help, but to wait on two things: one, the possibility of the boat engine restoring itself to health, with the help of whatever minimal aid he could provide; and the chance that some vessel might pass by. The boat didn't seem to be sinking. Winston tried to put things on board in the best order he could, ladling out spilled gas, throwing out the sopping shirts he had used to soak it up. By nightfall, as sunset burned before him, the boat still stank of petrochemicals and made him dizzy.

The nights were welcome but uncomfortable. He kept waking, chilled, even wearing the remaining clothes he had packed.

362

He looked at his ice chest of provisions with alarm. There was food, if he didn't eat much, for a couple of days, but he had not brought enough water. He had started a six-pack and a gallon jug of water, which had not burst. But after three days, he was down to one beer and a swig of water.

He finally used the VHF to send out a Mayday. He didn't know his position, but he wasn't sure anyone was listening. He couldn't raise anyone and only heard snatches of Spanish, static, and symphonic music.

Winston longed for the day's end, so the sun would be gone. He had gotten used to the fish striking the bottom of the boat. The first time one had hit he was thrown into a panic, but the fiberglass hull seemed to be holding. He decided to fire the flare gun. He had three flares. He thought all day whether he should fire all three at once, or during the night at different intervals, or just one a night, three nights in a row.

He picked the second choice, finally sending one flare up as soon as the last bit of afterglow disappeared from the sky. He waited an hour and shot off another. And then, near dawn, just before the first crack in the black sky, he fired the last.

He shot each flare in a different direction: three arcs, three hooks barbed into the night sky, hoping to snare someone's attention.

Winston awoke in the morning with *What makes the water white?* throbbing in his head. He was half-pleased with his delirium; drifting in and out seemed slightly pleasurable, one state away from a state of no consciousness at all. He thought of the eucalyptus smell of his father's sauna, the rendered fat scent stirred in. Now he smelled the chemical odor of the gas mixed with the mulchy scent of the sea. Winston found it satisfying. They were both to expire in great heat. *What makes the water white?*

Winston, lying between the bucket seats, his head crooked in what shade he could find under the wheel, did not see, or hear, the approach of the storm-gray wooden gunboat that had spotted him.

It was the Cuban cruiser *Galgo,* which, in her disconsolate search after her country's missing children, only found another fugitive, a fleeing American felon.

EPILOGUE

What Kenner would come to think of as "The Tragedy of the Eighties" had befallen him: the tenement building he had moved out of in September on Charles Street in the Village had gone coop. His old slum apartment had been touched by a real estate Midas and, had he kept it, he could have purchased it for the "insider's" price. Never an insider, he thought, dejectedly. A mere ten thousand dollars—he felt he could have raised it somewhere. Kenner realized that would have been his one and only change to become a capitalist, a landlord, an owner of a nibble out of the Big Apple, his own wormhole. The apartments were selling to outsiders for a hundred grand. Better odds than he had ever won at the dog track. Now he was an outsider again. Economic ironies, he realized, were harder to absorb than any other sort.

He had given up his apartment when he took the teaching job in Putney, Vermont. He had lingered for another month in Key West before returning to the city, watching some of the pieces fall into place. Before Kenner left the island, Winston had provided another bit of excitement. The U.S. Coast Guard had received a Mayday, which keepers at the Dry Tortugas light station reported receiving from a boat called *Carajo*. It had not given a location or the nature of its distress.

A shrimp-boat captain, one of the few whose boat was not impounded at the time by customs, coincidentally reported that he had seen a flare south of Loggerhead Key in the Tortugas. U.S. Coast Guard planes searched a ninety-mile area around the Tortugas for some trace of a boat. One coast guard official concluded that a total of some thirty-two thousand square miles of ocean had been searched. When Kenner read this information in the local paper, he was again impressed by how government agencies plastered over their lack of success with stupefying statistics.

Winston, eventually, was picked up by some branch of the Cubans off Camagüey, Cuba. The U.S. State Department arranged for his return. Kenner thought they might just have left him there; one U.S. thief should be worth at least ten Cuban thieves, or at least that's how he used to hear the ratio expressed for U.S. soldiers versus the Cong.

Winston's bail, upon his return, was summarily revoked, though Winston claimed, it was reported, that he was just on a pleasure cruise and had had motor trouble. Winston was returned; the Cubans kept the boat.

Kenner wondered if there had been any Winston-Mac-Naughton-CIA-State Department overlapping, and he concluded he'd never know. Unless MacNaughton left behind a manuscript titled *Never Again*. His last novel, *Fond Enemies*, had come out in the late fall, but so silently even Kenner was unaware of the event. He finally had to order it, because the novel never made its way into any store he visited. Kenner expected MacNaughton's death to prompt some reviews, but even the novel's publication did not resurrect any mention of his demise—it was old news. Oh, they're a coldhearted bunch, Kenner thought.

He read MacNaughton's posthumous novel in his rented faculty apartment, part of a large house that the college owned. It had been cut up into warrens for junior faculty.

Kenner read the book hoping for clues to the past summer's events. The CIA figured in the novel, but those parts seemed implausible. Kenner had one warm moment of recognition. The protagonist had attended Boston College, from which he had been recruited into the Company, and, while a student, he had published a story in the student lit magazine of a trip to London by a boy who wanted to be a jazz musician. The story then followed, intact, down to the redcap's salute.

Through an interlibrary loan, Kenner located the issues of the BC student literary magazine from the years MacNaughton attended, and, sure enough, there it was. Winston must have read the story when he attended BC for a semester—or perhaps he heard MacNaughton give a reading of it?—and then appropriated the story as his own.

Fond Enemies was chiefly about suicide and Kenner realized it wasn't, in that regard, fictional anymore.

Before Kenner left Key West, he had walked to the store where Bridget worked, to see what he could find out. Bridget had disappeared from town. All he discovered from Candi was that Bridget had gone to a Miami hospital to have some sort of surgery. Cancer surgery. She didn't want to be specific, chose to be discreet, to protect Bridget's privacy. Kenner did not inquire too deeply. Candi did say, as Kenner left the shop, "She even lost her trailer because of that bum!"

Kenner went north, taught three journalism courses, and received many letters from Rea. He wrote in return, but only a fraction of what she wrote him. But there was one story he heard that he felt compelled to tell her and so he wrote:

"I had an odd conversation with a guy in the music department here. It seems he knew MacNaughton, the writer I mentioned to you, during both their college days. They took a trip to the Keys together back then, MacNaughton's first time there. They were both amateur birdwatchers, of all things. The music professor is a Quaker and still wears sandals. I haven't heard any of his music, but it's all supposedly influenced by the language of water creatures: whales, dolphins and the like. He and MacNaughton were hoping to see a roseate spoonbill. On the Keys they came across an Audubon preserve that was offering tours—with the promise, the certainty, that they would see a spoonbill.

"The tour was seven bucks, which in the late fifties was a lot of dough for a tour—but they paid. So, the music teacher told me, they went along with the expected group of little old ladies in tennis shoes. Midway through, they saw a pink smudge on the horizon. That was the roseate spoonbill they had been promised.

"They didn't care much for the tour and went off angry and depressed. They continued down to Key West, and along the highway, off the water, they saw something pink. They stopped and the music teacher said they could see it was a spoonbill tied up in some mangrove roots.

"Much to the music teacher's surprise, MacNaughton dives in and swims out to it with a knife in his teeth. 'No telling what alligators or dangers he escaped,' the music teacher said, still genuinely alarmed after all these years. MacNaughton comes back to the shore dripping and hugging this big pink bird covered with mud and blood. Its wing was injured. While MacNaughton had been doing the rescuing, the music teacher had spread a blanket over the rear seat of their car, and they put the bird there and drove back to the Audubon preserve.

" 'Look what we have!' the music teacher exclaims. But those people aren't happy to see them. They don't want anything to do with the injured bird. But they do tell them where to take it, to a man who can help.

"They end up at a ranger station and, much to their delight, find a compound full of roseate spoonbills recovering from various injuries. They watch while the ranger amputates their spoonbill's broken wing by garroting it with a string."

As Kenner wrote that line to Rea, he remembered his paternal grandmother had removed a large black mole from her forehead by encircling it with thread and each day pulling the ends of the thread a little bit tighter. He left that recollection out of the letter.

"Years later the music teacher says he discovered that that very ranger was *the* expert on roseate spoonbills and had published a 'big fat book' about them. He says he and MacNaughton lost touch with one another after college, but he had read MacNaughton's novels as they came out. He looked to see if that episode ever turned up in any of them, but so far it hadn't. He mentioned that the population of spoonbills in the Keys had gone down dramatically over the years. He said it was a shame—but that he never would forget what MacNaughton looked like coming out of the water, dripping, hugging that great big pink bird.

"I told him there wasn't anything about the bird in his new novel, which I had just finished—the music teacher hadn't known it had come out, either. I said, though I had no proof of it, that MacNaughton had continued an interest in Audubon, in birds, but that I didn't know if it had involved the roseate spoonbill."

It was the longest letter he had written to Rea. Kenner was surprised at the emotions the music professor's story had generated in him.

And then, right before Christmas, Kenner had received a package. *The False Mare,* a book of poems, by Rea Kramer. Kenner thought, at first glance, that *mare* had something to do with the sea, with the trip they had taken, *mar*—the sea; but he quickly saw he was wrong. They were poems about animals. He was amazed at how good they were. The book had already won a prize. He expected Rea's writing to be good—he had her letters—but he was surprised by how good.

Ronald Reagan had been elected president. Even Massachusetts voted against Carter. Kenner faulted the peanut farmer for a number of things, but had cast his useless vote. Carter's toadying to the shah had upset Kenner quite a bit, all that toasting and praise; so it did seem fitting that the Iranians played a starring role in his defeat. But the cast list was long: his idiotic draft registration, lowering thermostats to freezing, and so on. Kenner was not surprised, but in a way mortified, that a majority of the so-called youth vote was cast for Reagan. It was as if they all chose to elect their senile grandfather, the affable dunce who never yelled at them as their fathers had.

Reagan did fit Reagan's own cartoon view of history, being a Disneyland creature himself. His countrymen, it seemed to Kenner, would tolerate any sort of ignorance, even bigotry, as long as it appeared to be coming from a benign source: as long as it didn't appear mean. That's what Americans don't like. Meanness. And the notion that you might know more than they do.

Had JFK lived, he now would be nearly the same age as Reagan, Kenner realized; they were the same generation. We have come, he thought, a full, dark circle, completed an eclipse of history. Kennedy had been the last president wreathed with so many symbols, until Reagan—but Reagan symbolized all things opposite Kennedy, except for wealth and eternal youth.

Kenner was flying to Rea. His belongings would be following him. He had contracted some Ali Baba moving company, the cheapest he could find. They had taken his small cache of worldly possessions, but they would not be coming west until their eighteen-wheeler finally filled up. The military had been much more congenial for Rea. They had shipped everything before she even arrived in the Midwest. The chairman of her department had overseen its delivery and placement.

During early January, Kenner had kept expecting to see Rea

on television. They had spoken transatlantic, but whenever a news report appeared on the tube about the return of the hostages, Kenner would search the screen for her, thinking she'd pop up and wave. The hostages were to be flown to Rhein Main Air Base and taken to a hospital at Wiesbaden, near where Rea taught.

The Iranians showed the same flare of showmanship as the new prez, timing the departure to coincide with his swearing in. Reagan took his oath and Carter squirmed on the platform.

Winston was found guilty the same day. The jury had retired the night before, but hadn't reached an agreement; they had to reconvene the day of the inauguration. Kenner had subscribed to the local Key West paper in order to follow the trial.

It had gone without too many surprises: Curt, wearing a suit similar to the prosecutor's—he had even adopted the fellow's hairstyle—testified to good enough effect to get Winston convicted. Delmer also testified against Winston, after pleading guilty to a lesser charge; but, unlike Curt, Delmer was going to have to serve a year. The professional burglar, Vernon Crane, was found not guilty. The jury wasn't convinced that the prosecution had linked him to the charge of conspiracy or interstate transportation. Kenner scoffed. That's the problem with those fancy charges. They're big-fish charges; all the little fish swim away. All the government had been able to jail at the taxpayer's lavish expense were Winston and Delmer. Kenner couldn't follow Curt's travels. He disappeared after the trial into the federal government's witness protection program.

Delmer and Winston had been sent to different cans. Winston got five years and would be out in three. Inside for not yet two months, he was already working with the JayCees, taking self-help programs, business management courses. Winston had always been a model prisoner. In his sentencing plea, he announced to the judge that he intended, upon his release, to work in the "new burgeoning industry of solar energy."

Kenner's job only lasted one semester. The Vermont college did go under. Top-heavy with Iranians, when their families' checks stopped coming, the administration had a cash-flow crisis. Kenner received his last check at the end of January and managed to cash it. Rea visited him for a week on her way to Missouri.

There had been a change in their lovemaking: a carefulness had entered in, as if she had had some injury, something broken, and both she and Kenner were wary of snapping it again.

They decided to live together, see what happened. Kenner stood a good chance of getting a part-time appointment at the journalism school in the same small university town.

Kenner thought that since they had made it through the high heat of Key West they could put up with the flash fires of domesticity. But when he changed planes in Saint Louis and flew on to the college town in a small commuter airline, seeing the midwestern landscape below a frozen ocean of snow, he began to wonder.

It had been odd to go from the tropics of summer in the Keys to the cold Vermont climate. And now, in February, white caps of snow as far as the eye could see. He and Rea had lived through fire, but would they be able to endure this ice?

She would be in class teaching when his plane arrived, so he had been instructed to take a cab to her house. The door would be open.

In the small plane, he looked down at the cold, encrusted earth, and his mind wandered again to all that was buried beneath and behind him. Kenner hadn't yet had his hunch proven: nothing about the folio no longer being a complete set had come up at the trial, at least as reported. She hadn't mentioned receiving anything strange to Kenner—though she might not realize that he had played a hand in sending it. A gift from Duane.

Rea had stayed clear of all the legal shrapnel. The FBI wasn't after her, wasn't even sure who she was. The military had clothed her in its wings, and the two government agencies didn't seem to overlap. Only the truly paranoid, Kenner knew, saw all government agencies as paragons of efficiency. He was always astounded, though, to have it made clear just what a hit-or-miss operation they were.

The cab made its way through slushy streets and deposited Kenner in front of Rea's address, which turned out to be a typical midwestern bungalow directly across the street from the campus where she taught. Bony spirea shrubs sticking out of mounds of snow. Kenner found himself besieged with a variety of intense feelings. Maybe Duane wasn't dead? Maybe he was just a *desaparecido*. No. No. He had disappeared into the mist.

As Kenner walked up the steps of the front porch, he found himself uncontrollably smiling. Crime pays, he kept thinking. At least it pays for some.

Rea had left the lights on, blazing, and through the translucent, flowery curtains she had hung over the living room windows, Kenner could see, quite prettily framed and under glass, a large rendering of two tiny songbirds. He couldn't name the birds, but he certainly could name the artist who, long ago, drew them painstakingly from nature.